THE FURTHER CHRONICLES
OF
SHERLOCK HOLMES

By the same author:
The Lost Chronicles of Sherlock Holmes
The Lost Chronicles of Sherlock Holmes, Volume Two
The Riddle of Foxwood Grange

THE FURTHER CHRONICLES OF SHERLOCK HOLMES

DENIS O. SMITH

First edition published in 2018

Hardcover ISBN 978-1-78705-319-9

Published in the UK by MX Publishing
335 Princess Park Manor, Royal Drive,
London, N11 3GX
www.mxpublishing.co.uk

For Penny, Dorothy and, especially, Harriet, who have all, at various times, read and commented on previous collections of stories, in the hope that they will find something to enjoy in the present collection.

CONTENTS

1. The Five Keys 1
2. The Tregorran Heir 36
3. The Victoria Street Mystery 64
4. The Inn on the Marsh 93
5. The Green Umbrella 115
6. The Jet Brooch 153
7. The Man in the Green Tweed Suit 178
8. An Unusual Interview 220
9. The Zodiac Plate 243
10. The Watcher in the Woods 289
11. The Yellow Glove 327
12. The Thirteenth Step 376

THE FIVE KEYS

"BUT, MY DEAR FELLOW," said Sherlock Holmes, as we sat on either side of the hearth one morning after breakfast, "it is a question we have surely settled already!" It was a pleasant, sunny day in August, and we had been discussing the fascinating and unpredictable nature of the world. I had ventured the opinion that in the future the strangest and most surprising things were likely to be found in the unexplored jungles of Africa or South America, but at this suggestion my friend shook his head.

"The strangest and most surprising things are to be found right here in London, here and now in 1882," said he in a vehement tone. "It may be that you are less likely to be attacked by a crocodile in London, or to discover a previously unseen pink and blue parrot; but London is, *par excellence*, the haunt of mankind, the domain he has built for himself, and man is, as you can scarcely deny, the most complex and surprising creature on this earth. It is here that man weaves his webs of unpredictable action and reaction, here that he creates his puzzling riddles of behaviour. I am quite content to let others travel to the jungles you speak of, and chance, if they are lucky, upon their new parrots: for myself, seeking as I do all that is *outré*, all that is *recherché*, there is no field of enquiry so stimulating as present-day London.

"Just consider what is practically an everyday occurrence," he continued after a moment: "In one street a man is devising some scheme which he intends to shortly put into operation. It may be legal, it may be illegal; that is immaterial. Ten doors away, another man is devising a scheme of his own. These two men have passed in the street, but do not otherwise know each other, and neither knows that his own plans and schemes will be affected by those of the other. Three streets away lives a woman who has her own wishes and hopes, and who does not know either of the two men, but whose chance presence at a crucial moment will affect the plans of both of them. Each of these three bears a unique strand of life, and each strand is itself made up of an uncountable number of threads. When they meet, the strands become entangled and entwined, the threads merge in ways which are quite unexpected and could never have been predicted. It is then that I am consulted, to attempt to tease out the threads and make comprehensible what appears at first an utter confusion."

As he spoke, there came a sharp ring at the door-bell. I laughed. "Perhaps this is someone come to consult you about such a state of confusion," I remarked. "I think I shall withdraw and leave you to it."

"No, don't go, I pray you," returned my friend. "If it is indeed a client, I should like you to hear the description of the matter, and, if it isn't, we can continue our discussion."

I had risen from my chair, but paused at his entreaty, and a moment later a well-dressed, middle-aged man and woman were shown into the room and announced as Mr. and Mrs. Arthur Whitfield.

"What can we do for you?" asked Holmes as he ushered the visitors to the chairs by the hearth.

"I wish to retain your services for two days, Mr. Holmes, to act on my behalf," the woman responded in a business-like tone of voice.

"You see," said the man after clearing his throat, "my wife's uncle – that's my wife's father's brother – Ephraim Hardcastle – you might have heard of him – has recently died, and it is well-known that he was a man of some substance. He himself never married, and thus has no immediate heir. Under the circumstances–"

"Never mind all that, Arthur," his wife interrupted. "The simple fact is, Mr. Holmes, that Ephraim Hardcastle had five nieces and nephews, the sons and daughters of his brother and sister. These are his only heirs, of whom I am one. He died last week, and his will is to be read tomorrow. I wish you to be there."

"Are you unable to be present at the reading?" enquired Holmes.

"No, not at all," returned Mrs. Whitfield with emphasis. "I shall certainly be there."

"Then I don't understand what you wish me to do."

"I simply wish you to keep your eyes and ears open for anything underhand which may occur, and ensure that I am not cheated out of my rightful inheritance."

"I hesitate to disappoint you," said Holmes with a chuckle, "and I don't know what you have heard about me, but I have no formal legal training. It seems to me that if you wish someone to watch over your interests, you might do better to instruct a lawyer to act for you."

Mrs. Whitfield shook her head. "Not at all," said she. "I don't trust lawyers. They always have half an eye on lining their own pockets. In any case, it is not so much the possible legal issues which concern me as other things. I need someone I can trust to keep his eyes open and his wits about him, and I have heard that you are such a man."

"What, precisely, do you expect to happen?"

"I don't know. That is the trouble. If I knew what might happen, I should know what to do about it, but I don't. However, I strongly suspect that someone will attempt some chicanery, if they have not already done so."

"Whom do you suspect?" queried Holmes.

"Babbage," interposed Mrs. Whitfield's husband.

"It is not just Terence Babbage," said his wife quickly. "I dislike having to say it, but my own sister, Fulvia, is capable of acting in the strangest and most dishonest ways. She is very unworldly, you understand, and is the most unreliable person I have ever known."

"With the possible exception of Babbage," said Mr. Whitfield.

"One moment," interposed Holmes, taking a note-book and pencil from his pocket. "I cannot yet say if I will take your commission, but if I am to do so, I must have a clearer understanding of who is involved. Tell me, as briefly as possible, the names of all relevant people. Begin with Ephraim Hardcastle's generation."

"Very well," said Mrs. Whitfield. "There were three of them in the Hardcastle family: my father, Jacob, who was the oldest; his brother, Ephraim; and a daughter, my Aunt Miriam, who married a man called Gilbert Babbage. Is that clear?"

"Perfectly so. And the next generation?"

"My mother and father had three children, of whom I, Rosalind, am the oldest. I may be a Whitfield by marriage, but I am a Hardcastle by birth, and proud of it. Next is my younger sister, Fulvia, who has never married and devotes her time, in a half-hearted sort of way, to various charitable causes. Third is my younger brother, Anthony, who busies himself at the Commodities Exchange in the City. Don't ask me what he does there. I have asked him before, and I always find his explanations incomprehensible, but he makes a very good living out of it, anyway."

"Is he married?"

Mrs. Whitfield hesitated. "We thought he was. We had heard that he had married quietly somewhere, without telling anyone. We even met the girl – Gladys – a few times in Anthony's company at different functions. But now he never mentions her and it seems he was never married at all. Quite frankly, I was not sorry to hear that, as I had thought her quite unsuitable for him."

"So these three, Rosalind, Fulvia and Anthony are the three children of Jacob?"

"That is so. Jacob's brother, Ephraim, who has recently passed away, was the only one in the family who was really wealthy. He has no children – he never married – and was always known as something of an eccentric. He was certainly a miser, anyway. He amassed an enormous fortune in financial speculations, but never shared any of it with anyone else, spending his recent years cooped up alone with his money in a large house on the southern fringes of Brixton. His only interest, other than money, so far as I am aware, was in odd scientific experiments, concerning magnetism, electricity and the like, and he had a large room in the house converted into a laboratory so that he might indulge his interest whenever he wished."

"Did you ever pay him visits there?"

"Yes, occasionally. I would have gone there more often, but he always made it clear that he did not encourage visitors. On the odd occasions we did go to see him, he was never very welcoming. He would provide us with a cup of tea and a single biscuit and keep glancing at the clock as we spoke, as if waiting impatiently for us to leave."

"I see," said Holmes. "Now, did the third member of the Hardcastle family, your aunt, Miriam Babbage, have any children?"

"Yes, two: a daughter, Philomena, who is married to a publisher named George Gilpin, and a son, Terence, who is unmarried and is something of a dilettante in the world of art."

"So, let me see if I have got it clear: the five heirs to your late uncle's estate are yourself, Rosalind Whitfield; your sister and brother, Fulvia and Anthony Hardcastle; and, from the other branch of the family, Philomena Gilpin and Terence Babbage."

"That is correct."

"Have you any knowledge of the provisions your uncle's will might contain?"

"Not precisely, but it seems to be common knowledge that he has left everything he possessed to the five of us equally. How I know that, I can't remember, but I suppose it is from odd remarks made by my uncle himself, to me or to one of the others. Of course, there may be some specific bequests of which I am unaware, but I don't believe there will be anything significant of that nature."

Holmes nodded. "Can you give me the name of Ephraim Hardcastle's solicitor?" he asked after a moment.

"Certainly. It is Mr. Augustus Farjohn, of Welbeck, Lidgett and Farjohn, of Old Oak Chambers, in Fleet Street. As far as I am aware, my uncle had had the same solicitors for the last thirty-odd years. I have heard him speak very disparagingly of Mr. Farjohn, but I don't think he ever seriously contemplated moving his business elsewhere. Besides, my uncle was inclined to speak disparagingly of almost everyone who was not present. I don't doubt that he spoke that way about me when I was not there. He was an odd man in many ways, with a hard, sneering sort of manner and a distinctly unpleasant sense of humour. I don't think he had any friends – none, at least, that I was ever aware of."

"Is the will to be read at the house, or at Mr. Farjohn's chambers?"

"The latter, tomorrow morning at ten o'clock. Will you be there?"

Holmes nodded. "And my colleague here, Dr Watson. Have no fear, madam," he added quickly with a chuckle, as an expression of doubt crossed Mrs. Whitfield's features: "one fee will serve us both."

When our visitors had left us, I turned to Holmes in puzzlement.

"Of course, I don't mind at all accompanying you," I said, "but I am surprised at your accepting the commission, Holmes. It sounds to me a perfect example of the sort of thing you generally go to great pains to avoid: a case with no features of interest whatever!"

"That can scarcely be denied," returned my friend with a wry smile, "but you can never tell how things will turn out. It will at least be a novel experience, to learn how a miser leaves his money! Besides, I have nothing better to do tomorrow morning, and it should not occupy us for more than an hour or so, after which we can enjoy a stroll around Fleet Street and the Temple and perhaps, in celebration of gaining a professional fee for doing nothing, take lunch down there."

The remainder of that day passed uneventfully. About four o'clock in the afternoon, however, there came another ring at the bell, and a moment later a young woman was shown into our chambers and announced as Mrs. George Gilpin.

"I chanced to run across my cousin, Mrs. Whitfield, in Regent Street earlier today," she began when she had seated herself in a chair by the hearth. "Is it true that you have agreed to act for her at the reading of my late uncle's will tomorrow? You have?" she continued as Holmes nodded his head. "I might have known! Rosalind is always seeking to gain some financial advantage for herself, by any means she can."

Holmes shook his head. "I have no particular expertise in either financial or legal matters, so if your cousin somehow gains a pecuniary advantage over you or anyone else, it will certainly not be on my account. My brief, as I understand it, is simply to watch and see that everything is straightforward and above board. If any benefit results from my presence, which I rather doubt, it is just as likely to be for you as for Mrs. Whitfield."

Mrs. Gilpin rose to her feet, then hesitated.

"I wish I could believe you," said she.

"That is a judgment for you to make," returned Holmes. "I can only describe things as I see them."

"Very well," said our visitor, then, with a nod of the head and a rustle of her skirts, she left the room as hurriedly as she had entered.

"These cousins don't seem to trust each other very much," I remarked with a chuckle.

"Indeed," said my friend. "It will be interesting to see them all gathered together tomorrow. Perhaps they will come to blows and make what promised to be a singularly dull business a little more entertaining!"

At a few minutes before ten the following morning we reached the solicitor's chambers in Fleet Street, where a page showed us into an oak-panelled waiting-room. Mrs. Whitfield and her husband were already there, and she introduced us to her sister, Fulvia Hardcastle, a somewhat untidy-looking woman who at once engaged me, in an indignant, heated manner, in a discussion of some government policy of which I knew nothing whatever. As we were speaking, our other visitor of the previous day, Mrs. Gilpin, was shown in, accompanied by a smartly dressed man whom I took to be her husband. A moment later, a formally attired elderly gentleman – evidently the solicitor – entered the room, rubbing his hands together and smiling at everyone in turn.

"Is everyone here who is coming?" he asked.

"Not yet, Mr. Farjohn," responded Mrs. Whitfield. "My brother, Anthony, has not yet arrived – I know he has been tremendously busy lately – and there has been no sign of Terence Babbage either, although that is not so surprising."

"And who are these gentlemen?" he enquired, turning to us. "Are they standing in for the absent relatives?"

Mrs. Whitfield shook her head. "This is Mr. Sherlock Holmes and Dr. Watson, who are here at my request, to act on my behalf if necessary."

"To act?" the solicitor queried in a tone of puzzlement. "In what sort of way?"

"In any way that seems appropriate."

Farjohn's eyebrows went up in surprise. "Their presence seems somewhat irregular," he murmured, "not to say superfluous, but I don't suppose–"

His reflections on the point were interrupted by the abrupt opening of the door, as a young man, somewhat dishevelled in appearance and breathing deeply, burst into the room.

"Sorry I'm late," he said in a breathless voice. "My train was held up for ages at Loughborough Junction."

"No matter, Mr. Babbage," said Farjohn. "Your cousin, Mr. Hardcastle, has still not arrived. Would anyone care for a cup of coffee while we are waiting?" he added, turning and addressing the others.

"Rather!" said Terence Babbage in an enthusiastic tone. "I haven't had a drop of nourishment since I got up this morning!"

"Perhaps you should have got out of bed a little earlier, then," said Mrs. Whitfield in an acid tone. "Really, Mr. Farjohn, I would much rather we got on with reading the will now. Perhaps the coffee could be brought into the reading-room. I'm sure that Anthony will be here any minute, and we can soon explain to him anything he has missed."

"Very well," said Farjohn. "If you will all follow me, I shall get everything ready."

The solicitor led the way along a narrow corridor and into another oak-panelled room. In the centre was a large, highly polished square table, around which were set a dozen or more chairs. Farjohn left the room, but returned in a few minutes with a large deed-box which he placed on the table before him. Opening the lid, he took out a folded and sealed document and five small, flat wooden boxes, each about six inches by two, by an inch deep. On one of the long, narrow sides of each box, I could see the outside edges of two little brass hinges, and, on the opposite side, a simple metal catch. By the catch, preventing the box-lid from being opened, was a large gout of red sealing-wax, impressed with some sort of design.

"Your uncle, Ephraim Hardcastle, has included a message for you all in his will," Farjohn began, as he broke the seal and unfolded the papers, "which I shall come to in a moment." He glanced round the table, cleared his throat and started to read. The last will and testament of Ephraim Joseph Hardcastle began in the usual, conventional way with a declaration by the testator that he was in sound mind and so on, then, after two legacies to domestic servants, which struck me as surprisingly generous for a supposed miser, he decreed that the remainder of his possessions, in whatever form they were, were to be divided equally between his five heirs, the sons and daughters of his brother, Jacob, and his sister, Miriam. At this news, there was a general murmur of satisfaction, and I heard someone remark that the will seemed unusually straightforward for something of Uncle Ephraim's devising. Farjohn held his hand up, to request silence.

"However," he said after a moment, "this division of your late uncle's worldly possessions is subject to the following provisions:

"'First,'" he continued, reading from the sheet in his hand, "'I have observed' – so says your uncle – 'that none of you appears able to get along harmoniously with any of the others. I have therefore arranged it so that unless you co-operate with each other, none of you will get anything at all, and you will regret it.

"'Second, I have sold all my stocks, shares, bonds and other securities, and have used the proceeds to buy precious stones, mainly diamonds. You will learn where these are if you follow the instructions I have given to Mr. Farjohn. These precious stones must be divided up into five equal shares. If any odd stones are left over after this division, they will be sold to a dealer by Mr. Farjohn, the proceeds of this sale being divided up five ways after Mr. Farjohn has taken five per cent, as his commission for handling the transaction.

"'Third, several doors must be unlocked before you come to the precious stones, as you will see. For this purpose, you will each be issued with a key by Mr. Farjohn. Which key fits which lock you will not know until you try them. All the keys will be needed to gain your inheritance, and there is no advantage in possessing one key rather than another, so do try not to quarrel or come to blows over the issue. Be aware that there are no duplicate keys, so you must look after your key very carefully, or you will be unable to get past the doors. The builders who did the work for me provided me with two keys for each lock, but I took one set of these keys up to town with me some time ago and flung them into the Thames from the middle of Waterloo Bridge.'

"That is it," continued Farjohn after a moment, looking up and placing the sheet he had been reading from on the table, "saving only a note to state that if one of the five legatees is unable to be present at the reading of the will, then, with the approval of the other four, I am to act as agent for that person, hold in trust his or her share of the precious stones, and report back to him or her in due course. If, however, two or more legatees are absent, then we may not proceed at all – so it is fortunate that you arrived when you did, Mr. Babbage."

"What an absurd rigmarole!" cried Mrs. Whitfield.

"It does seem a trifle convoluted," murmured her husband to no one in particular.

"Oh, I don't know," said Terence Babbage. "For old Uncle Ephraim, with his odd way of thinking and odd way of doing things, it seems remarkably clear!"

"May I have a look at those little boxes?" asked Holmes, who had followed the proceedings without comment.

"Certainly, if you wish," returned Farjohn. "Ah! Here is the coffee! If anyone has any questions, please feel free to ask them!"

"These boxes, I take it, contain the keys," Holmes continued. "I note that they are not all the same weight."

"Indeed," responded Farjohn. "That is because the keys themselves are not all the same size."

"You were present when the keys were placed in the boxes and the boxes sealed?"

The solicitor nodded. "I then brought the boxes to my chambers here, where they were to be stored until required, in accordance with Mr. Hardcastle's wishes."

Their discussion was abruptly interrupted by a sharp female voice. "What is that man doing with those boxes? And what are they, anyway?"

I turned to see that Fulvia Hardcastle had risen to her feet and was gesticulating in Holmes's direction.

"These boxes contain the keys your late uncle referred to," said Holmes. "I am simply examining them. They are not marked distinctively in any way," he continued, turning to

Farjohn, "so I take it they are to be distributed to the five named parties at random."

"That is correct," replied the solicitor. "It doesn't matter which box each person gets. Would you care to distribute them for me?"

"Certainly," said Holmes. He stood up, picked up the five little boxes, and was about to walk round the table with them when he was stopped by a sharp interjection from Philomena Gilpin.

"This doesn't seem right or proper," said she with a frown. "Mr. Holmes is acting as agent for Rosalind. Everyone knows that. So why should he be in charge of allocating the boxes to anyone? It should be done by someone with no interest in the matter."

"It really doesn't make any difference which key anyone has," said the solicitor. "However, if you insist upon the point, I shall find someone else to do it. Thelwell," he called to the youth who had brought in the tray of cups and saucers and had been busily pouring out the coffee, "leave that for the moment, will you, and hand out these boxes in random order, to Mrs. Whitfield, Miss Hardcastle, Mrs. Gilpin and Mr. Babbage. You'll have to give one to me, too, for the moment, as Anthony Hardcastle has not yet arrived."

"Very nicely made little boxes," remarked Babbage with a chuckle, as he turned his box over in his hands, "almost artistic in their own way. Are we supposed to open them now, or wait until Christmas?"

"You may open them whenever you please," said Farjohn. "When you have finished your coffee, we shall all go down to your late uncle's house to complete his instructions."

The seals were duly broken, the catches unfastened and the little boxes opened. Inside each of the boxes was a lining of green felt, upon which lay an old-fashioned iron key

"Why is my key smaller than all the others?" demanded Mrs. Whitfield of Farjohn, as she glanced round the table.

"It doesn't seem quite right," murmured her husband.

"I assure you it makes no difference to the outcome," said Farjohn in a tone which suggested he had just about had enough of the whole business.

"You should feel flattered, my dear Rosalind," remarked Babbage. "Your key is so much more delicate and lady-like than the others!"

Mrs. Whitfield appeared about to respond to this facetious comment, but in the end turned away, a look of distaste on her features, and drank her coffee in silence. At length, everyone had finished, and turned to the solicitor to see what was to happen next.

"We must now proceed to Mountsorrel House, your late uncle's residence, for the next stage of the matter," said he. "Mr. Hardcastle's old servants, Mr. and Mrs. Wilkinson, are still there, looking after things. Mr. Hardcastle gave them written permission to remain there until it has been decided what is to be done with the house. It is not far, so I think the easiest thing is if I get the commissionaire to call us, say, three cabs, and we make our way there that way."

As we filed from the room a few minutes later, Farjohn and I were the last to leave. He was picking up his papers and the key-boxes from the table when he abruptly paused.

"That is odd," said he.

"What is?" I asked.

"There were five little boxes here before, and now there are only four."

"Perhaps someone took one as a memento of the occasion," I suggested.

"Perhaps so," said he, nodding his head. "Well, well. It doesn't matter. They have served their purpose now."

Outside the solicitor's chambers, three cabs stood waiting for us in the street. Mrs. Whitfield, her husband and her sister, Fulvia, travelled in the first one, Mrs. Gilpin travelled in the second one with her husband and her brother, Terence, and Farjohn, Holmes and I took the third. We spoke but little as we made our way slowly through the crowded, dusty streets of south

London. Holmes appeared to be turning something over in his mind, but what that might be, I could not begin to guess. It was certainly a singular expedition we were engaged upon, I reflected, and the terms of old Mr. Hardcastle's will were highly unusual. I found myself wondering, with heightened interest, what the legatees would be required to do with their keys when we reached Mountsorrel House, and I asked Farjohn if he had ever executed such an odd will before. He shook his head and declared that, in his long experience of such things, it was unique. I would have asked him other questions about unusual wills, but I could see that he was not inclined to discuss the matter further, so I was left to my own conjectures. There must, I thought, be some kind of safe or strong-room at Mountsorrel House, although why five keys should be required to open it, I could not imagine.

At length we pulled up at the gate of a large, gloomy-looking house, near the top of a steep hill. Within the gate was a very large garden, overgrown and unkempt, which surrounded the house on all sides. Away to the right, all along the far edge of the garden, stood a stone structure consisting of a row of pillars supporting a low, tiled roof, with a stone wall at the back of it and a long stone bench beneath, resembling nothing so much as the cloisters of a mediaeval monastery.

Farjohn led the way up the path to the front door of the house, where his brisk bang on the door-knocker was answered by an elderly, somewhat morose-looking man.

"Good morning, Wilkinson," said Farjohn. "We have come to fulfil the terms of Mr. Hardcastle's will."

"Yes, sir. I have been expecting you," responded Wilkinson, standing aside to let us enter. Within the house, all was silent and still, and there was a musty smell in the air.

"Now," said Farjohn. "Most of you are probably familiar with Ephraim Hardcastle's eccentric arrangements here, but I will just explain for those who are not. The structure you no doubt observed in the corner of the garden, with a row of pillars in front, was Mr. Hardcastle's summer-house, or part of it, at least. There is also an enclosed room there, at the left-hand end of the structure, where he sometimes took his meals, but when he was out there he spent most of his time just sitting on the stone seat which you probably saw behind the pillars. He liked to sit there and take the air whether the day was a sunny one or a rainy one. In fact, he particularly like sitting there when the weather was atrocious – he said the worse the weather, the more interesting he found it. He did not, however, like being out in such weather unprotected, and he had a positive mania about being watched or spied upon by what he termed over-curious neighbours or passers-by as he crossed from the house to the cloisters. He therefore had a long tunnel constructed under the lawn, so that he could pass from the one to the other without exposing himself to the elements or being observed by anyone. That may strike you as an expensive way to solve a slight problem, but that was his whim, and I suppose he had as much right as anyone else to spend his money as he saw fit."

Farjohn glanced round. "I don't know if any of you ever saw the inside of Mr., Hardcastle's tunnel, but he showed it to me shortly after it was built, when I visited him here about eight years ago, and I can tell you that it was very solidly constructed."

"He conducted me along it once in the middle of a thunderstorm, about five or six years ago," said Fulvia Hardcastle. "It was certainly a strange experience, to be so deep under the ground, and not one I particularly cared for."

Farjohn nodded. "I can understand that. More recently, when Mr. Hardcastle knew he did not have long to live, it occurred to him that his underground tunnel would be a secure place to store valuables, and, in particular, the precious stones he intended to leave to his heirs. He therefore had the far end of the tunnel, by the cloisters, blocked off completely, leaving a chamber under the middle of the lawn which is only accessible from this end. He also had a series of sturdy doors installed between the house and the underground chamber. It is these doors to which you have the keys."

"Where is the entrance to the tunnel?" asked Terence Babbage.

"I will show you," said Farjohn. "Follow me." He led the way along the hall, to a door beneath the staircase. "This is the cellar door, which is the way we must go. Be careful on the stone steps, which are a little uneven. Don't worry, Mrs. Whitfield," he added quickly, as she began to protest. "It is much lighter down there than most cellars are."

As we reached the foot of the cellar steps, the truth of the solicitor's observation became apparent. Large gratings, high in the side walls, admitted so much daylight that no artificial lights were required to see where we were going. I glanced at Holmes. He had been uncharacteristically taciturn throughout the morning's proceedings, and I wondered what he was making of it all. His features gave no clue to his thoughts, however, and, for all that I could tell, he might have been simply looking forward, as I was, to getting away from this odd assortment of people, returning to town, and finding somewhere to take lunch.

"This is the entrance to Mr. Hardcastle's tunnel," said Farjohn, indicating a stout wooden door a little to our left. As I looked closer, I saw that by the keyhole of the door, across the narrow gap between the door and the frame, a large gout of red wax was smeared, impressed with a seal of some kind. "I have been down here twice since the occasion I mentioned," Farjohn continued. "The first time was when he was having the underground chamber constructed, although the work was not quite finished then. The second time, more recently, was after Mr. Hardcastle had sealed these doors. That was the second-last occasion I ever saw him. He brought me here specifically to show me the seal on the door, and as he had already done it, this is as far as we went, so I don't know precisely what lies beyond this point, although I understand there are more doors."

"You say that that was the second-last time you saw him," said Holmes. "What, then was the last time?"

"When I came to collect the keys. I believe he had intended to give me the keys in their boxes on the occasion he showed me this door, but there had been some delay in the manufacture of the boxes and they were not ready. He therefore summoned me later to witness his sealing the keys in the boxes, after which I took the key-boxes away with me. That was the last time I saw him."

"Where had he been keeping the keys before he sealed them in the boxes?" asked Holmes.

"He had had them for some time on a cord round his neck."

"How dreadfully uncomfortable and inconvenient for him," remarked Fulvia Hardcastle.

"Never mind that," interrupted Mrs. Whitfield in an impatient tone. "How are we supposed to know which of our keys fits the lock?"

"I imagine," said Holmes, "that the idea is that you try each of them in turn until you find the right one."

"What an absurd waste of time it all is!"

"Look on the bright side, Rosalind," Mrs. Whitfield's husband interjected in a calm tone. "At least, with all these keys and seals involved, you can be absolutely certain that no one has forced his way in and stolen your inheritance."

"I should think not," replied Mrs. Whitfield shortly. "Try your key, Fulvia!"

Fulvia Hardcastle did as her sister had bidden her, but the key would not turn. Mrs. Gilpin then tried her key, but that, too, proved ineffective.

"Perhaps it is Anthony's key," said Mrs. Whitfield. "Have you brought that, Mr. Farjohn?"

"Yes," replied the solicitor. "It is here." But when he tried it in the lock, it would not turn even one degree.

Holmes chuckled. "The key you yourself are holding, Mrs. Whitfield, appears too small for that lock, so, by an admirable process of logical elimination, we have arrived at the truth: the correct key must be the one held by Mr. Babbage."

"What are you waiting for, Terence?" asked Mrs. Whitfield of her cousin. "For goodness's sake, don't keep us all hanging about!" she added in a sharp tone.

"I was just trying to remember," returned Babbage, "when it was that you were appointed senior overseer of this little enterprise."

"Now, now," murmured Mrs. Whitfield's husband.

"Someone has to take charge," retorted Mrs. Whitfield, "to prevent everything from descending into chaos. I'm sure that if Anthony were here, he would say the same. In fact, I'm sure if Anthony were here, he would naturally assume a position of authority. Some people have within them a natural sense of leadership and responsibility, which others can only envy."

"He certainly likes ordering other people about, as I have observed," remarked Babbage. "It's just a pity he's not quite responsible enough to show up at the reading of his uncle's will."

"At least he's made more of himself than certain other members of the family have," said Mrs. Whitfield in an angry voice. "I'm sure there is some very good reason for his absence today."

"Can we please just get on with it, and stop all this bickering," said Mrs. Gilpin. "It's giving me a headache."

Babbage put his key in the lock and turned it. There came the dull sound of the lock moving smoothly, and, when he pushed at the door, it opened easily. A hush fell on the cellar as we all craned forward to see what lay beyond the door, but it was very dark there, and I could make nothing out.

Holmes stepped forward, struck a match and lit a lantern which hung from a hook just inside the doorway. By this light we could see that beyond the doorway was a short flight of half a dozen steps leading down to a lower level. This was evidently the beginning of Ephraim Hardcastle's tunnel. It was about seven feet high and three feet wide, the walls and arched ceiling all lined neatly with bricks. Little of the tunnel was revealed, however, for less than ten feet further on was a second door, exactly like the one we had just opened.

"Let us see which key will open the second door," said Holmes, leading the way down the steps.

Fulvia Hardcastle pushed her way past him and tried her key in the lock. This time it turned easily, and she pushed open the door, to reveal more of the dark corridor. Another lantern hung on the wall there, which Holmes lit. As he did so, I saw that there was yet another door in the corridor, about a dozen feet further ahead. This third door, however, was somewhat different from the other two, and appeared even more impregnable. The whole front of the door was covered with what looked like a sheet of metal, in which there were not one but two keyholes, the one eighteen inches above the other.

"These keyholes look too large for your key, Mrs. Whitfield," said Holmes, "but you may as well try it. It's hard to tell sometimes from the outside how big a lock is."

"She did as he suggested, but failed to get anywhere with it. "I think, as you say, this key is too small." said she.

"This should be straightforward enough, then," said Mrs. Gilpin's husband. "There are two keyholes in the door, and only two keys left unused, my wife's and the one that Mr. Farjohn is holding for Anthony."

Farjohn tried his key in the upper keyhole, but reported that it would not turn at all. He then tried it in the lower keyhole, but with precisely the same result. "That's odd," he said. "Mrs. Gilpin's key must open both of these locks."

"It does seem a trifle pointless having two locks if the same key will open both of them," remarked Holmes, "but let us see."

Mrs. Gilpin tried her key in the lower lock, but could not turn it. Her husband then lent his strength to the task, but without effect. She then tried her key in the upper lock, and with a smooth click, it at once turned easily. "Now what do we do?" she said. "None of the keys will turn the lower lock, so we're stuck."

"*Nil desperandum*," said Holmes with a chuckle. "Try your own key again in the lower lock, Mrs. Gilpin. It may be that turning the upper lock not only moves its own door-bolt, but also releases some impediment on the lower lock. Such interlocking devices are not unknown on strong-room doors."

She did as he suggested, but without success.

"If you would like to try your key again in the lower lock, Mr. Farjohn," said Holmes, "you might find that it now works."

"I follow your reasoning, Mr. Holmes; but if it does not work, then we are, as Mrs. Gilpin said, 'stuck'."

"Not necessarily," returned Holmes. "One of the keys left in the two previous doors might also fit this lock. But I think it most likely that the one you are holding will do the job."

Farjohn inserted his key in the lower lock, gave it a twist, and, with a satisfying, dull click, the lock moved.

Terence Babbage clapped his hands together. "There we are!" said he. "Undeniable progress!"

"I suppose," remarked Fulvia Hardcastle, "that this illustrates Uncle Ephraim's remark about co-operation being necessary in order to gain access to our inheritance."

"Indeed," said Holmes. "And as there is now only Mrs. Whitfield's key remaining, which is a different size from all the others and may open a chest or cupboard, I think your quest is almost over."

Mrs. Whitfield stepped forward and pushed at the door, which opened silently and smoothly. Beyond the doorway, as before, there was a hook on the wall, but this time no lantern was hanging there. By the dim light of the lantern behind us, however, I could see at once that beyond the double-locked door was not simply a continuation of the underground passage, but a much larger chamber altogether, about ten feet square. The walls of this chamber were completely covered with dark, glossy tiles which reflected the flickering light of the corridor lantern, and it was evident that this chamber marked the end of both the tunnel and the legatee's quest.

"I think there is another lamp hanging on the far wall," said Whitfield. "I'll light it. Yes, there is," he continued as he disappeared into the darkness of the room, but his voice broke off abruptly and there came a sudden shriek and a cry of pain.

"What is it, Arthur?" cried his wife. "What have you done?"

"I've fallen over something," Whitfield replied after a moment, a note of pain in his voice. "There's something like a heavy sack on the floor." There came a sudden point of light, as he struck a match, followed by a blood-chilling cry of horror. "It's not a sack," he cried. "It's a body!"

"A body?" returned his wife. "What sort of body?"

"A man's body. I think he's dead."

We all pressed forward to see. Holmes lit two further lanterns which Whitfield's match had revealed on the side-walls, and their flickering light revealed a ghastly scene. There, immediately beside a central table, lay the body of a man, stretched out face down on the stone floor. I quickly bent down to examine him, turning the head slightly and feeling the neck, which was as cold as ice. As I did so, there came a sudden ear-splitting cry of horror from behind me, which made my hair stand on end. "It's Anthony!" came Mrs. Whitfield's voice, then she burst into violent sobbing.

"Keep back!" said Holmes, who had been examining the table in the middle of the room. "Don't touch anything!" he added in a tone of authority. "There's something very strange here."

I rose to my feet and took a look at the table. On the top of it was a curious little tunnel-shaped structure, somewhat like a food cover, except that it was made of gilded wire mesh. On one side of it there appeared to be a lock with a small key-hole in it, and, at one end, a small handle such as that of a music-box or hurdy-gurdy. Beneath the wire mesh was a shallow white bowl, containing what looked like a large heap of precious stones. From the table-top, dark curtains hung down to the floor, completely concealing the space beneath. I bent to the body once more, as there came a babble of voices from behind me.

"How in God's name did Anthony get in here when all the doors were still locked and sealed?" cried Gilpin "It is impossible!"

"And what was he doing here?" cried his wife.

"More to the point," said Whitfield, "why is he dead?"

"If I didn't know it was impossible, ten feet below the ground," I responded as I examined the body further, "I should say he had been struck by lightning!"

There were cries of astonishment and ridicule all about me.

"But that is absurd!" cried Fulvia Hardcastle.

"How can you possibly suggest such a ridiculous thing?" demanded Babbage.

"There are no obvious wounds or marks of injury on the body," I began.

"Perhaps he was poisoned, then," interrupted Babbage, "or had a heart seizure."

"Perhaps," I returned, "but that would not account for this." I indicated the tips of the index finger and thumb of the dead man's right hand, which showed slight marks of burning. "Nor would it account for what appears to be damage to the inner ear," I continued, pointing to the small dried trickle of blood which was evident on the edge of his ear. "It also appears that he has broken or dislocated some vertebrae in his neck. All these symptoms are characteristic of having been struck by lightning."

"Are you an expert on the subject?" asked Babbage in surprise.

"I don't need to be. The symptoms of a lightning-strike are generally remembered by every junior medical student, as they are such an unusual and distinctive group." I unfastened the cuff on the right shirt-sleeve of the body and pushed the sleeve up a little way. "There," I said. "That settles the matter. That faint tree-like pattern of red lines you see there, beginning at the wrist and spreading out as it ascends the arm can be caused by nothing else but a massive charge of electricity passing through the body."

At this, there were further cries of astonishment, and, after the beginning of a scream, Mrs. Whitfield staggered backwards, almost insensible, and was only saved from slumping to the floor by Sherlock Holmes, who caught her as she fell. He handed over his limp charge to her husband, then turned to me.

"A very precise analysis, Watson, and exactly correct, of course, except for the small detail of the lightning strike, which did not exist."

"What, then?"

"A massive discharge of static electricity, every bit as deadly as a lightning strike. How long would you say he has been dead?"

"It is difficult to be precise. It is very cold down here, which would tend to slow down some of the post-mortem bodily changes, but taking all things into consideration, I should say he has been dead about two days, perhaps three."

Holmes nodded. "I agree."

"But," persisted Mrs. Gilpin in a tone of utter bafflement, "where did this supposed electricity come from?"

"From this," replied Holmes, drawing back fully the curtains beneath the table. On a lower shelf stood eight strange-looking large glass bottles, the outsides of which appeared to be coated with some kind of silvery substance. From the top of each of them, poking through the large cork which sealed the neck of each bottle, was a metal spike, and these metal spikes were all joined together by thick metal cross-pieces.

"What the devil are those things?" demanded Whitfield.

"They are Leyden Jars," said Holmes, "a device for accumulating and storing a large electrostatic charge. The shock from just one of those jars would probably be sufficient to fling you across the room. Linked together as they are by those copper rods, the charge would have been increased tremendously, and would certainly have been sufficient to give a fatal electric shock. If that were not deadly enough, there is also this little handle at the side of the cover over the gemstones, which presumably lifts the cover by means of the little gear wheels you can see; but it is also attached, by way of this band which passes through a slot in the table-top, to discs beneath the table. They are also geared, so that turning the handle even slowly will make the discs revolve at high speed."

"What would that achieve?" asked Babbage.

"It is, I believe, a miniature Holtz machine, another device for generating a huge electrostatic charge. This, as far as I can make out from the connections under the table, would feed into the Leyden Jars, which would store the charge."

"What!" cried Babbage. "You mean that that evil old devil, Hardcastle, lured us here with a promise of inheritance, only to try to murder us all?"

"I think that unlikely," returned Holmes with a shake of the head. "I imagine that his intention, however barbarously and maliciously conceived, was simply to protect that dish of gems from being stolen by an intruder. If his instructions had been strictly followed, and only those who were entitled to be here had entered, using the keys he provided, there would have been no danger. If you look at the bottom of the last door which we unlocked, you will see a flexible metal contact there which has rubbed along some metal strips on the floor, which are in turn connected by wires to this central table. I cannot pretend to understand all the complexity of what Ephraim Hardcastle has constructed here, but it is clear that the opening of the door has broken one contact and completed another, which has probably had the effect of conducting the electrostatic charge to earth and rendering this device safe."

"But what in Heaven's name are you saying?" demanded Fulvia Hardcastle. "You are implying that Anthony somehow got in here without unlocking and opening that door. That is utterly and completely impossible!"

Again Holmes shook his head. "That, I believe, is precisely what happened. Anthony Hardcastle did not come through the tunnel from the house as we did, but from the other direction, from the cloisters in the garden."

"But that, too, is impossible," protested Mrs. Gilpin, looking round the room. "There is no other door into this chamber but the one by which we entered. Apart from that one door, the walls are all completely solid and impenetrable. Besides, Mr. Farjohn has already told us that the far end of the tunnel has been blocked off."

"It's not true, though, is it, Mr. Farjohn?" said Holmes, turning to the solicitor. "No doubt there are doors built into the tunnel on that side – there must have always been at least one locked door – but I don't think the tunnel is entirely blocked off."

Farjohn stood in silence for a moment, a frown on his face, as if considering his reply. "I understood from Mr. Hardcastle that that was the case," he responded at length.

"I'm afraid I don't believe you," said Holmes. "On the contrary, I believe you reached a private agreement with Anthony Hardcastle to get in here before anyone else had a chance to do so and help yourself to some of the diamonds."

"How dare you!" cried Farjohn in an angry voice. "How dare you make such an outrageous accusation! And in the presence of such tragedy, too! I shall sue you for slander, sir, make no mistake! These people are my witnesses!"

"What's the idea, Mr. Holmes?" queried Babbage in a tone of puzzlement, a question which elicited murmurs of agreement from the others. "How can you possibly justify accusing Mr. Farjohn of having anything to do with this horrible business?"

"I make the accusation," replied Holmes, "because it is true. Mr. Farjohn is quite welcome to sue me for slander; I have no fear of that. The law holds that if the facts are true, no slander has occurred."

"But wait," interrupted Gilpin. "Perhaps Mr. Hardcastle's manservant, Wilkinson, let Anthony into the house, and so into the tunnel, and then, when Anthony was killed, returned the way he had come, sealing the doors as he went."

"No," said Holmes, with an emphatic shake of the head. "That really is impossible. I see no reason to doubt Mr. Farjohn's statement that Ephraim Hardcastle had kept the keys on a cord round his neck before they were sealed in their boxes, nor Hardcastle's own statement that he had thrown the duplicate keys into the river, in which case neither Wilkinson nor Anthony Hardcastle could ever have had access to any of the keys. Besides, all the doors we have passed through were sealed, and not recently, either. The surface appearance of sealing-wax alters slightly over time. I examined the seals, and it was clear to me from their dull and slightly dusty appearance that they had been placed on the doors some time ago. Anthony Hardcastle died about two or three days ago, whereas the seals have clearly been on the doors at least two weeks. It is therefore impossible that he could have come through the tunnel from the house as we have done. If we then dismiss entry from the house as impossible, what does that leave? It is an axiom of mine that when you have eliminated the impossible, whatever remains, however improbable, must be the truth. Anthony Hardcastle could not have come through the tunnel from the house; therefore he came through the tunnel from the cloisters. Coming that way, of course, especially if it were dark, he would avoid being seen by Wilkinson, and would only need one of the five keys, the small one now being held by Mrs. Whitfield. That, I take it, is the key to unlock that cover on the table. It was, I believe, when Anthony Hardcastle touched that key to the lock of the cover that he received the electric shock that killed him."

Mrs. Whitfield, who appeared to have recovered from her faint but was still leaning on her husband, looked down at the key in her hand, an expression of horror on her face.

"If what you say is true, Mr. Holmes," remarked her husband, "then how did Anthony manage to get hold of that key, which was being securely kept in Mr. Farjohn's chambers?"

"And how on earth," interrupted Gilpin, "do you suppose he passed through that solid, tiled wall behind you?"

"I take it there is a concealed door in that wall, directly opposite to the doorway through which we entered," said Holmes. "There must be – anything else is impossible – and I shall find it in a moment. As to how Anthony got hold of the one key he required to get at the gems: he could only have got it from Mr. Farjohn, who was his partner in this enterprise."

"It's a lie!" cried Farjohn.

"I have mentioned," Holmes continued, ignoring the solicitor's outburst, "that I examined the wax seals on the doors and satisfied myself that they were several weeks old. I also noted that they were all marked with Ephraim Hardcastle's own personal seal, bearing the initials 'EJH'.

"What of it?" demanded Farjohn in an aggressive tone.

"Nothing. It was as one would expect. But the boxes containing the keys, although also sealed, were not stamped with the same seal, but with one which bore the image of a bird in a circle, with some smudged, indecipherable initials. What drew my attention to this when we were in your chambers, was that I also observed there the seal which had made that impression in the wax. It was hanging from your watch-chain, where I see it still. It is your seal, Farjohn, and you sealed those boxes yourself."

"Yes, of course, I do not deny it," returned Farjohn in a tone of annoyance; "but there is a perfectly simple explanation for that fact. I have mentioned that I had called here to see Mr. Hardcastle, when he showed me the first of the sealed doors to this tunnel, and I have also mentioned that the key-boxes were not then ready. He knew then that his end was not far off, and the unfinished business with the key-boxes was causing him great anxiety. He had been carrying the keys about with him for some time, as I mentioned. His fear, I believe, was that his manservant, Wilkinson, might enter the tunnel and steal the gems."

At this, Mrs. Gilpin interrupted in a sharp tone. "That does not seem either likely or fair," said she. "Wilkinson is one of the most loyal servants one could imagine, and in the face of continual provocation from his master, too."

"Quite so," said Farjohn, "but your uncle was of a most suspicious and untrusting nature. Anyway, he sent a message for me to come and see him again a couple of weeks later, just a few days before he died. He was bed-ridden by then, and I attended him in his bed-chamber. Wilkinson brought in everything we needed on a tray, including the key-boxes and some sealing-wax, then left us. Hardcastle produced the keys themselves from under his pillow, where he had been hiding them. I put the five keys into the boxes at random, as he instructed me, and we sealed them up. However, he had misplaced his own seal, which could not be found anywhere, so he instructed me to impress the wax with my seal. That done, I carried the boxes back to my professional chambers, where they have remained ever since, until today. That is why the seal on the boxes is not the same as the seal on the doors."

"I congratulate you," said Holmes in a dry tone.

"What do you mean?"

"Your story is a very plausible one – although you have, of course, had some time to prepare it. Unfortunately, plausible or not, it is completely untrue."

There was an incoherent cry of rage from the solicitor, but Holmes ignored it. The others all fell silent as he continued:

"There are two points against your account. One is a matter of logic, the other a matter of observation. In the first place, regarding Hardcastle's supposed instruction to you to use your own seal to seal the boxes: that would be utterly pointless, and I don't believe for a moment that Hardcastle would have agreed to it. Once the boxes had been sealed, you were to keep them locked away in your chambers, and there would be thus no way that the legatees or anyone else outside of your chambers could get at them. The seals on the boxes were therefore not to prevent outsiders opening the boxes illicitly, but to prevent you or your colleagues at Old Oak Chambers from opening them."

"Preposterous!"

"There is no point your putting on a show of indignation at the suggestion, Mr. Farjohn. Such a precaution would not necessarily reflect personally upon you or your colleagues, but would be standard practice, as you are perfectly aware. In this particular case, however, there is a further reason why Hardcastle would take such a precaution. He was, as everyone agrees, and as you yourself remarked just a moment ago, a secretive and suspicious-minded man. If he could not even bring himself to trust his own loyal manservant, Wilkinson, then I very much doubt he would trust you. The suggestion that he would permit the boxes to be sealed by one of the very people he wished to prevent from opening them is ridiculous. As you possessed the seal, there would be nothing to prevent your breaking the wax seal on one of the boxes and opening it, then re-sealing it again later, which is precisely what I believe you did."

Farjohn's face had turned a white, sickly colour, but he said nothing.

"This brings me to my second point," continued Holmes. "I inspected the key-boxes when we were in your chambers, Farjohn, and I have brought one with me as evidence." He drew from his pocket one of the flat wooden boxes I had seen earlier. "This is the box which contained Mrs. Whitfield's key. It is clear from the most cursory inspection that this box has been sealed twice. The first lot of sealing-wax has been scraped off with a pen-knife, and later a second lot has been dripped onto the box and impressed with your seal. But this kind of red sealing-wax always seeps into wood a little and stains it. Scraping the wax off with a knife does not remove this stain, which is perfectly visible on this box where the second lot of wax has not quite covered the mark left by the first lot."

Holmes paused, but Farjohn made no reply, and there was a moment of utter silence in that strange underground chamber.

"You can't prove any of this," said the solicitor abruptly.

"We can perhaps settle the question of whether Hardcastle's seal really was lost by asking Wilkinson, who, as you stated, brought in the boxes and sealing-wax on a tray, the last time you saw his master."

Farjohn made a sudden movement, and in an instant he was holding a revolver in his hand, pointing it steadily at Holmes.

"You interfering busybody," he snarled, his voice full of hatred. "You clever devil! I knew you would be trouble the moment I saw you! What has any of this to do with you? Why don't you mind your own damned business?"

There was a slight movement from Terence Babbage, no more than a slight shuffling of his feet, but in an instant Farjohn had turned the revolver in his direction.

"Get back!" he cried, in a voice full of desperation. "All of you, get back! I'll use this pistol if I have to! Don't think I won't! Yes, I came in here with Anthony Hardcastle. I didn't want to. He forced me into it against my will. And I knew nothing of Ephraim Hardcastle's devilish man-trap there. If Anthony had not been such a stupid fool, he would still be alive now! He used to crow about how much money he could make from speculating on commodities; he didn't consider how much he could also lose."

"Is that what happened?" asked Mrs. Gilpin.

"Yes, and not just his own money, either, but many thousands of his clients' money."

"I always thought he was reckless," murmured Whitfield.

"When you say," queried Holmes, "that Anthony Hardcastle forced you into joining him in his attempted theft of those diamonds, do you mean he blackmailed you?"

"If you want to use that word, then yes. He claimed to have evidence that I had helped myself to old Mr. Hardcastle's money. Any defalcations of mine were utterly trivial and petty, I can tell you, compared to what Anthony had done with his clients' money, but he swore he would expose me if I did not do as he said and help him get at the diamonds. Anthony Hardcastle was a swine, a black-hearted swine! However, it makes no difference now," he continued after a moment. "I was intending to retire in a few weeks' time, anyway. I'll just bring my retirement forward a little. All my preparations have already been made. I am going where no one will find me." He backed away, towards the door, his pistol still pointing towards us. "By the time you raise the alarm, I shall be far away."

"Don't be a fool, Farjohn," cried Holmes. "Don't make matters worse. It's obvious what has happened here. No one will accuse you of causing Anthony Hardcastle's death."

"Perhaps not, but I have enough experience of legal proceedings to know that once they begin, things will get dragged out into the open which I would rather remained hidden."

As he spoke these last words, he stepped quickly through the doorway and pulled the door shut behind him. An instant later we heard a key turn in the lock. Babbage flung himself at the door, seized the handle and tried to pull it open, but to no avail.

"Careful of those metal strips on the floor," Holmes called to Babbage. "The whole thing may be deadly again now the door is closed. Everyone else keep away from the table."

Mrs. Whitfield let out a wail of despair. "What ever can we do?" she cried.

"We shall all be suffocated!" cried her sister, Fulvia.

"I think not," said Holmes, indicating a grating in the centre of the ceiling. "There appears to be a ventilator there, no doubt concealed above ground by the urn in the middle of the lawn. I shouldn't waste your energy on that door," he called to Terence Babbage, who was still pulling at the door-handle. Our best hope of getting out of here quickly is almost certainly to find the door hidden behind these tiles and make our way along to the cloisters."

"Why are you so sure that there is such a door?" demanded Babbage.

"I have explained my reasoning. There must be another door. My theory of the crime demands it. Nothing else makes sense." As he was speaking he had taken a pen-knife from his pocket and opened it. Now, with a glance at the door in the opposite wall, presumably to estimate the likely position of the concealed door, he began to stab the blade of the knife into the narrow spaces between the tiles. After a minute of this probing, he stepped back with a cry of triumph, as one of the tiles swung abruptly open.

"It is hinged," said Holmes, "and was evidently held in place by some sort of sprung catch. And here, behind it, is a simple latch!"

He lifted the latch and pulled at it, and, with a creak, a whole section of the tiled wall swung open. Taking one of the lanterns from the chamber wall, he led the way along the dark corridor which was now revealed. About five-and-twenty feet along this tunnel, we came to a flight of stone steps, at the top of which was a stout wooden door. Holmes ran up the steps and seized hold of the door-handle.

"There is no lock on this door," said he over his shoulder, "but there are two large bolts, which appear to be pushed soundly home. Then how the deuce did Farjohn get out this way on the night he was here with Anthony Hardcastle? Ah, I see! The metal sockets into which the bolts are pushed have themselves been forcibly wrenched from the wooden door-frame. Entry was obviously gained to this tunnel by forcing open the door with a large metal lever of some kind. Of course, I should have expected it! They could not have had a key to this door. And the advantage of forcing the door open in this way is that it would at once suggest to the police that the robbery was the work of strangers, and no suspicion would attach to any member of the family. I admit that I had thought before that Farjohn and Hardcastle had intended to take just a few diamonds each, so that none of you would know that anyone had been here before you. But the way this door has been forced suggests to me now that they may have intended to take the lot, and leave the rest of you with nothing."

All the time he had been speaking, he had been trying to pull the door open, but it appeared to be jammed very tight. All at once, as he strained every sinew at the task, the door flew open, and as it did so a thin little piece of wood fell to the floor.

"Farjohn must have jammed that sliver of wood in there as he slammed the door, to hold it tight," said Holmes. "Let us now see where we have got to!" The others all seemed to be talking at once, evidently horrified at how close they had come to losing their inheritance entirely, but Holmes held up his hand. "There will be time for recriminations later," said he. "We must report what has happened to the proper authorities so they can get on Farjohn's trail without delay." So saying, he led the way through the doorway and into a light, airy room, where a table and several chairs were set out. Directly ahead of us was another door with a large glass panel in it, through which we could see the garden, bathed in sunlight. We passed through this second door, which was not locked, and found ourselves in the cloisters.

"What a blessed relief, to get out of that horrible, dark tunnel!" said Mrs. Whitfield.

"What do we do now?" asked Terence Babbage.

Holmes sat down on the stone bench and took out his pipe. "As I have been retained to keep an eye on everything pertaining to Ephraim Hardcastle's will, which, it seems to me, now includes both those diamonds down there and also the body of the unfortunate Anthony Hardcastle, I think I should remain on duty here. However, someone must notify the authorities at Brixton Police Station as soon as possible, so that they can put out an alert for Farjohn. Would you mind fulfilling that duty, Watson?"

"Not at all," I replied. "I know where the police station is, and it's not far from here."

"I'll come with you, to help explain it all," said Gilpin

"I was also going to suggest," said Holmes, as he began to fill his pipe, "that someone should tell Wilkinson what has happened, but here he comes across the lawn now, with a determined-looking step. It may be that he saw Farjohn coming up from the cellar and leaving the house in an almighty hurry, and is wondering what has been going on. Perhaps in return for a little enlightenment he will make us a pot of tea."

There is little more to tell of this strange affair of Ephraim Hardcastle's will and the five keys. Although Farjohn managed to elude the police for twenty-four hours, he was arrested the following day as he was attempting to board the continental boat train at Victoria station, and charged with conspiracy to commit theft. As he himself had predicted, numerous other facts emerged at the subsequent trial, concerning his dishonest handling of Ephraim Hardcastle's investments, which meant that Farjohn began his retirement with a spell at Portland Prison.

Three days after the events I have described above, we had another visit from Mr. Whitfield.

"I have a cheque for you, Mr. Holmes," said he, as he took a seat by the hearth. "I could, of course, have put it in the post, but I wanted to thank you in person for all that you and your colleague did for us the other day. Without your presence, your perceptive observations and your decisive actions, I dread to think what might have happened. Words alone cannot express the gratitude I feel, and the cheque is therefore for a significantly larger amount than your standard professional fee, but I hope you will accept it as a small token of my appreciation. I might add that my wife – though her pride may inhibit her from expressing such sentiments openly – feels exactly as I do, and specifically asked me to convey to you her immense gratitude."

"If you insist upon it," said Holmes with a smile, taking the offered cheque and glancing at it, "then I should certainly not be so rude as to refuse such a generous gesture."

We chatted for some time in a friendly fashion, reflecting on the strange and surprising events which had taken place at old Mr. Hardcastle's house, and after Whitfield had left us Holmes looked again at the cheque before passing it to me. It was at that time, I think, the largest fee he had ever received for his professional services. And yet, I could see from the look in his eyes that, notable though it was, the fee meant far less to him than the sincere expression of appreciation he had received from his client.

THE TREGORRAN HEIR

SHERLOCK HOLMES rarely showed much inclination to travel beyond the bounds of London. His preference, both professional and private, was to dwell in the midst of four million souls, and the countryside beyond the capital held little interest for him.

Nevertheless, it happened not infrequently, as his name became more widely known, that he was consulted by those whose lives were lived far from the bustle of the capital city, and cases took him, on occasion, to the most remote parts of the country. Among these cases were some of the most memorable I can recall, including the singular mystery concerning William Penney and the Knightsfleet Tower, and the strange and inexplicable disappearance of the Duke of Honingham, who was seen to enter the maze at Pomfrey Park in Hampshire one summer's evening, and was never seen again in this world. Perhaps the most remarkable such case, however, was that associated with the Tregorran family of Cornwall, and the mysterious and terrible events at Gipsies' Croft. It is this last case I shall now recount.

It was a wild and tempestuous day in the early spring, and we had taken breakfast to the beat of wind and rain against the windows. Afterwards, I had filled my pipe, and drawn my chair up to the fire, for the raw weather had caused my old wound to throb with a dull persistence. There, I had attempted to absorb myself in the morning papers, but they contained little of interest, and after a while my attention wandered and I found myself staring into the blazing fire and lamenting the dullness of my life.

"Perhaps you will find this a little more stimulating," said Sherlock Holmes, responding, as was his wont, to my unspoken thoughts. He passed me the letter he had been studying, which he had received by the first post that morning. It was addressed from Whitstock Farm in Cornwall, dated the previous day, and ran as follows:

DEAR MR. HOLMES, – I should greatly value your opinion on a proposal that has been put to me. You have, I know, succeeded in bringing light into the most perplexing of matters, and I hope that you may do so in my case also.

My home is at Fowey, on the south coast of Cornwall, where my father's family has for many generations been prominent among the fishing community. Recently, however, I have been approached by Mr. Michael Tregorran of Whitstock Farm, near Bude, who is one of the largest landed proprietors in the north of the county. He has no children, and proposes to name me as his heir if I agree to take his name. In accordance with his wishes, I have of late been residing with him, while I consider my decision.

It might appear that this proposed change in my circumstances is a very fortunate one; and it might be thought singularly ungrateful of me to have any reservations in the matter; but there are certain considerations which would, I imagine, make any man pause before agreeing to the proposal. It is commonly accepted in these parts that the Tregorran family has been dogged by ill-fortune for generations, and there are circumstances surrounding the family and their estate which cause me unease, and make me wonder whether it would perhaps be foolhardy of me to accept Tregorran's offer. Events this last week have only served to increase my concern. My benefactor wishes me to make a decision by the end of the month, so I have but a few days left in which to consider the matter. I therefore propose to call upon you tomorrow, when I can give you the details.

Yours sincerely, JOHN PENRYAN

"What a very strange communication!" I remarked, as I finished reading the letter. "I am surprised at your finding it of such interest, Holmes. The notion that a family might be 'dogged by ill-fortune for generations' surely belongs only in the pages of an eighteenth-century gothic romance!"

"And yet, there are possibilities," returned my companion in a thoughtful tone.

"Possibilities for people to let their imaginations run away with them, no doubt," I remarked.

"You do not recall the Tregorran murder case of three or four years ago?" queried Holmes. "No? Yet it occurred before you sailed for India, Watson. No doubt you were too immersed in your medical studies to notice such matters, but the case was certainly something of a sensation, and attracted considerable attention at the time. The most striking feature of the matter, as I recall it, was that the victim appeared to have been murdered twice."

"Whatever do you mean?"

"She had been throttled with great force, as evinced by the broken bones in her neck; but she had also been stabbed through the heart with some sharp implement."

"Good God!" I cried.

"I can give you the details if you wish."

My companion drew his own chair nearer to the fire as I nodded my head, and, after a moment, he continued:

"The Tregorrans were by all accounts a contented couple. They had no children, and lived a life of quiet rural seclusion, at Whitstock Farm. There appeared to be no particular anxiety in their lives. The husband occasionally hunted during the season, but had few other interests beyond the boundary of his farm, and, save an occasional visit to Bodmin, rarely travelled further than the few miles to Holsworthy, the nearest market town, to buy and sell stock. The wife was well known locally for the interest she took in the poor and the sick of the parish, and for the charitable work she engaged in with the wife of the local vicar.

"One foggy evening in the early spring she left Whitstock on foot, with the declared intention of walking the two miles to a neighbouring farm, where the farmer's wife was ill. The farm in question was on land owned by the Polcathro family. Now, the Tregorrans and the Polcathros, the two largest landowners in the district, had been engaged in a bitter legal dispute for many years, and, because of this, the woman's husband was against her going. According to the servants, the couple had words on the matter before she left. That was the last time she was seen alive. She never reached her intended destination, and her body was found the following morning in a remote part of the Tregorran estate near the coast, known as Gipsies' Croft. The question at once arose as to what had taken her to that part of the estate; for the natural route from Whitstock Farm to the homestead she had intended to visit was some miles inland of the spot where her body was found. No one could suggest any explanation for this. When the district medical officer came to examine the body, he found, as I mentioned, that she appeared to have been murdered twice.

"At the inquest, the coroner queried whether the strangulation might not have simply rendered the woman unconscious, in which case the stabbing would have been the cause of death. The district medical officer, however, gave it as his opinion that the strangulation was so severe that it alone would have caused the woman's death, which, in his opinion, was what had happened."

"How did he explain the stabbing, then?"

"He couldn't."

"What a brutal and horrible affair!"

Holmes nodded. "As you will imagine, the case aroused enormous public interest. Extensive enquiries were made, both locally and further afield, but no facts were discovered which could shed any light on the matter. The husband himself was questioned at great length, but no charges were ever laid against him, nor against anyone else, and the case remains as puzzling now as it did then. You will perhaps appreciate, therefore,"

Holmes continued after a moment, "why my interest was aroused by Mr. Penryan's letter. Whether his account will add anything to our knowledge of the matter, we cannot tell, but I think we should hear what he has to say, however fancifully he might express himself."

John Penryan arrived that afternoon. He was a stockily built young man of about five-and-twenty, clean shaven and with thick black hair. He had the dark colouring of the Cornishman, with ruddy cheeks which bespoke a life lived in the fresh air of the countryside.

"It is not clear to me," said Holmes, when Penryan had recapitulated the contents of his letter, "why Michael Tregorran should have chosen you to be his heir."

"My mother is the younger sister of Tregorran's late wife," returned our visitor.

"The woman who was murdered?"

"Precisely. We were all greatly shocked by her death, which seemed so utterly inexplicable. Of course, in the district in which she lived, the tragedy was taken to be simply the latest manifestation of the Tregorran family's ill-fortune."

"Perhaps you could give us some details of the family and this supposed ill-fortune," said Holmes, leaning back in his chair and placing his finger-tips together.

"Certainly. Our families – the Penryans and the Tregorrans – have been linked for over thirty years, since the day that the two sisters, Hannah and Rebecca Tressillick from Lostwithiel, attended the county fair at Bodmin with their parents. There they happened to meet the two Tregorran brothers, Ulick and Michael. It was the older brother, Ulick, so I understand, who first caught Hannah's eye, with his loud, energetic manner, but as she came to know them better, she found Ulick's manner too wild and boisterous for her tastes, and her affections soon shifted to his quieter and more reserved younger brother, Michael, whom she married the following year. My own mother, Rebecca Tressillick, soon afterwards married Job Penryan of Fowey, who is my father.

"At the time of Michael Tregorran's marriage to Hannah, the young men's parents were still alive, and the whole family lived together in the great rambling farmhouse at Whitstock. It was in those days that Hannah first heard the old tale of the Tregorran Curse, which she subsequently related to my mother during a visit to Fowey. The story is soon told. It is said that two hundred years ago a family of tenant farmers on the Tregorran estate were cruelly and mercilessly evicted when illness had reduced them to poverty and they were unable to pay the rent. The tenant's wife, who claimed to be of Gipsy stock, pronounced a curse upon the Tregorran family and their estate as she was being driven from the land. There is a barren, rocky field on the extreme western edge of the estate which is popularly supposed to be the site of this event and is known as Gipsies' Croft. In a corner of this field is a ruined building which is said to have been where the evicted family had lived.

"The Tregorrans themselves utterly deny this story and say that not one word of it is true. They say it is a falsehood maliciously fabricated by the neighbouring Polcathro family, to blacken the Tregorran name. The Polcathro estate adjoins that of the Tregorrans, and the two families have been disputing the position of the boundary for a century or more. This quarrel is known throughout the whole of north Cornwall, for it has been pursued in the courts for generations, and is now, I understand, the longest-running case in Cornish legal history."

"Has Michael Tregorran ever spoken to you of this supposed curse?" asked Holmes.

Penryan shook his head. "He flatly refuses to do so, and became quite angry one evening when I raised the matter. My knowledge of it comes partly from my mother, and partly from a local source. Tregorran's own distaste for the subject is perhaps understandable, for there has been much tragedy in the family during his lifetime. Events occurred soon after his marriage to my aunt which destroyed the happiness with which they had begun their married life. His older brother, who was, as I remarked, of a wild, unrestrained temper, took to drink and quarrelled with everyone. Wilful and headstrong, he would never do anything which was asked of him, and was constantly in trouble. Eventually, when his dissolute life led to a period of confinement in Bodmin gaol, his father, Ezekiah, made a will leaving the estate to the younger son, Michael. Within six months of this will being made, Michael Tregorran and his wife were the only members of the family remaining alive.

"Old Ezekiah was found dead one evening in Gipsies' Croft, his skull fractured. His horse was wandering nearby, lame in the foreleg, and it was conjectured that the horse had stumbled over a rock and thrown his rider to the ground. Not long after this tragedy, the older son, Ulick, was journeying to Australia with a considerable sum of money, the intention being that he should study the novel methods of the sheep-farmers there, when the ship he was on was lost with all on board, off the west coast of Africa. These tragedies, coming so close together, affected old Mrs. Tregorran – Ezekiah's widow – very grievously. She fell ill, declined rapidly, and was dead within a month. Michael Tregorran and his wife, Hannah, were thus left alone to administer the cursed estate. Since that time there have been numerous minor misfortunes, which the local peasants were always ready to ascribe to the workings of the curse, but no serious incident until three years ago. Then, as you know, Tregorran's wife was murdered, in the most terrible and mysterious circumstances. That," said our visitor after a pause, "is the recent history of the Tregorran family and their curse."

"You said you had a local source for some of this information," observed Holmes. "Is that local source one of the neighbouring farmers?"

"No," replied Penryan with a shake of the head. "I have seen little of Tregorran's immediate neighbours during my time at Whitstock. Besides, although I have little doubt that they talk about these things among themselves, I doubt they would mention them in front of me. I have recently, however, made the acquaintance of two gentlemen who have a keen interest in these matters, although with widely differing interpretations. I will tell you how it came about. Several weeks ago, in early February, there was a local fair and ball at Bude. It is, I understand, an annual event at that time of the year, when the worst of winter is drawing to a close. Tregorran never attends, and although he did not positively prohibit me from going, it was clear that he would rather I did not. The last thing he said to me, as I left the house, was 'Remember, John, do not have anything to do with those bearing the Polcathro name. Avoid those devils as you would avoid the plague!'

"At the ball in the evening, which was held in the local church hall, my presence aroused a certain amount of curiosity. This was scarcely surprising, considering that I was a stranger to everyone there. Presently, as I ambled about, sipping from a glass of punch and listening to the very lively music, I was approached by a winsome and pretty young lady with very dark eyes, and dark curly hair which hung in ringlets about her temples.

"'Do excuse my boldness,' said she with a disarming little smile, 'but I don't believe we have been introduced.'

"'My name is John Penryan,' said I with a little bow.

"'Ah!' said she in a tone of recognition, 'the young man who is to inherit the Tregorran estate.'

"'Possibly,' said I. 'But how do you know about that?'

"'Oh, everyone knows about that,' she replied dismissively, with another arch little smile. 'Word gets around.'

"'And might I know whom I have the pleasure of addressing?'

"'They call me Catherine,' said she. 'How do you like the music, Mr. Penryan?'

"'I like the music very much,' I returned. 'Would you care to join in this next dance?'

"The young lady assented to this suggestion and we took our places in the long lines of men and women in the middle of the floor. As the band struck up a new melody and we whirled about, I was conscious that my partner scarcely ever took her eyes from my face, as if endeavouring to read the most secret depths of my character. It is an odd and disturbing feeling, to be the subject of such close scrutiny. I was conscious, too, that she had avoided – deliberately, so I judged – giving me her surname, and I wondered if the name she had failed to give me was in fact Polcathro.

"As the dance came to an end, we stood a moment recovering our breath, and then she began to ply me with questions, about myself and my situation. I had hoped that in the interval between the dances I should be able to learn something of her, but so rapidly did she question me, and so pressing was her manner, that by the time the music began for the next dance, she had learnt much about me and I had learnt nothing whatever about her.

"When our second dance ended, we were both out of breath, and I escorted her to the wooden chairs that lined the walls of the hall, where we sat down. As we did so, a young man approached. His appearance was so similar to that of my partner that I could only assume he was her brother. This assumption was confirmed by the familiar way in which he addressed her, as he asked her to introduce us.

"'This,' she answered him, 'is Mr. John Penryan of Whitstock, and this,' she continued, addressing me, 'is my brother, David Polcathro.'

"I nodded to him in what I thought was an agreeable way, but his only response was to stare blankly at me, in a way I found both rude and unpleasant. Then, without another word, he took his sister's hand, drew her to her feet and led her away. This, as you will imagine, I found a very unsettling experience, and it left me sitting all alone at the side of the room, feeling extremely self-conscious. Fortunately, my isolation did not last long. A few moments after Catherine Polcathro and her brother had left me, an elderly, white-haired gentleman approached and introduced himself as Edward Calvert.

"'Do you mind if I sit down here?' he asked.

"'Not at all,' I replied. I had heard that Calvert lived in the district, and knew him to be a retired professor from Oxford University, but I had never met him before.

"'You and I are perhaps the outsiders at this little festival,' he remarked, when I had explained who I was. 'As a matter of fact, I guessed who you were when I saw that young Polcathro boy acting so rudely towards you,' he continued, 'although I think his very charming sister may in fact be the more dangerous from your point of view, Mr. Penryan. Such young ladies have a way of using their charms for their own ends.'

"I nodded my understanding. Despite her prettiness, I had not been blind to a certain slyness and cunning in her manner.

"'But surely you are not still an outsider, Professor?' I said. 'I understood that you had lived in Bude for many years.'

"'That is true. I retired earlier than I might have done because of ill-health, and came to live in Cornwall because my doctor recommended the moist, mild climate. His advice was sound: within six months I was as healthy as I have ever been in my life, and have remained so ever since. But I have no roots here, no Cornish ancestors I can refer to in conversation, so, in the eyes of many – including the Polcathro family – I am still an outsider and will no doubt always remain so.'

"I asked him how he filled his days, for it was clear that, although advanced in years, he was still alert and lively in his thoughts.

"'As I had been professor of English and other literature in my Oxford days,' he replied, 'it seemed natural that in my retirement here, with time on my hands, I should turn my attention to the contribution of Cornwall to the body of English literature. I thought I should have my survey completed in three years or so, but three times three years have passed, and I am still working on it. In the last two or three years, I have moved on to Cornish folk-tales, the sort of things that are often not written down, but passed on orally from one generation to the next.'

"'Does that include the story of the Tregorran Curse?' I asked, at which he nodded his head.

"'Indeed,' said he. 'That is a fairly typical example of the sort of tale I am collecting. It is slow work, for it obliges me to travel all over the county. Not all the tales are as dark as the Tregorran story, but they often are, for, of course, the more dramatic a tale, the more likely it is to be remembered and passed on, sometimes with considerable embellishments!'

"I expressed my interest in the subject, and Professor Calvert invited me to call round and take supper with him one evening, when, he said, he would show me some of his research and we could discuss the matter further. His house stands on a headland just to the north of Bude and is very solidly built, to withstand the Atlantic gales which batter the coast there from time to time. I accepted his invitation with pleasure, and have dined with him there on three occasions. It has, I must say, been a great relief for me to get away from Whitstock Farm, even if only for a little while, and Professor Calvert's company is always both stimulating and entertaining, for he is a very learned man. His view of the 'Tregorran Curse' is that the tale was made up by some particularly imaginative story-teller, about a hundred and fifty years ago – he can find no earlier reference to it than that – to account for the poor and rocky terrain in the field now known as Gipsies' Croft. He informs me that such stories and legends, providing a dramatic explanation, of sorts, for perfectly natural – if unusual – features of the landscape are as old as civilization itself.

"On the last occasion I was at the professor's house, about two weeks ago, he had another guest to dinner, an elderly gentleman from Brazil. This was, therefore, yet another stranger to the district, and one who is, like the professor and myself, fascinated by the old traditions and legends which abound in Cornwall, which he has studied in some depth. He is certainly an odd, exotic character to find in such an out-of-the-way place. He is very large and exceedingly corpulent, and there is something quite imposing in his manner. He has a very large black moustache and swarthy skin, which is heavily lined from exposure to the sun. His yellowed, bloodshot eyes suggested chronic suffering from some tropical disease which is sapping his life away, and I noticed when he left us, to walk down the hill to his hotel, that he walked slowly and with some difficulty, leaning his weight upon a stout walking-stick.

"His name is Carlos Perreira, and he is a man of some wealth, being the owner of extensive coffee plantations in Brazil. I asked him what had brought him to such a remote spot, and he explained that several years ago, when he had been accompanying a cargo of coffee beans from Rio de Janeiro to London, a fierce storm in the English Channel had forced his ship to seek shelter in the Carrick Roads, off Falmouth. Laid up there for a couple of days, he had been attracted by the picturesque scenery, and had decided to explore the area, wandering on, as the whim took him, until he had eventually reached Bude. Enchanted by this charming little watering-place, he had vowed to return and spend a few weeks there each year, during the Brazilian summer. The tropical illnesses from which he has suffered have left him weak, he says, and he finds Rio unbearable during the hot months.

"When Professor Calvert was introducing us, Perreira smiled as he shook my hand. 'Your name is already known to me, Mr. Penryan,' said he, 'for you have been pointed out to me in the town as the man who is to inherit the Tregorran estate. You are aware, I take it, that it is said to be accursed?'

"I nodded. 'Professor Calvert and I have discussed the matter at length,' I replied. 'My view of it is much the same as his, that, interesting story though it is, there is no truth in it. Besides, I do not really believe in superstitious tales in general.'

"'Perhaps you are right not to do so,' said Perreira, 'but they are an interesting subject of study, nonetheless. There are many such traditions in my own country, and I have seen the effect they can have on the people there, and the countryside in which they live. Of course, the power of superstition is very much greater in Brazil than here in England. There, magic of all kinds is accepted without question by many peasants as an everyday fact of life, and such stories are believed implicitly. Who is to say if either view is entirely right or entirely wrong?

"'You and Professor Calvert are rationalists: you strive always to reduce the unknown to the known, the incomprehensible to the comprehensible. All well and good; that is your inclination. But what if there are some things which cannot be so reduced? After all, as your greatest poet says, through the mouth of Prince Hamlet, "There are more things in Heaven and Earth than are dreamt of" in the philosophy of a rationalist. There are many things we do not know, many questions to which no conclusive answer can be given. It is for this reason that I have taken an interest in the curse of the Tregorran family, and have made myself familiar with its history.'

"He discoursed at some length on the subject, comparing it with some very similar stories from his own country, and as it was apparent that he spoke with authority, I ventured to ask his opinion.

"'What do they say in your country about such curses?' I asked. 'Once pronounced, do they endure for ever, or is it possible that with time they may at last fade and pass away?'

"'Such things begin always with an evil deed,' replied Perreira after a moment, 'and until justice is restored the curse endures, like an open wound that will not heal. Then, one day, without warning, a fatal blow falls, and all is over – so!' As he spoke, he raised his hands above his head, then, with a sudden movement, brought them together with a loud clap. 'That,' said he, 'is my experience of such things.' And that, Mr. Holmes," said Penryan, "is the extent of my knowledge of the subject."

Sherlock Holmes sat in silent thought for some time, with his eyes closed. "And now," said he at length, opening his eyes, "the events of this week, if you please, Mr. Penryan. You remarked in your letter that something had occurred to cause you concern."

"That is so. I cannot pretend that my residence at Whitstock Farm has been an entirely enjoyable one, for an atmosphere of gloom pervades the place. Tregorran is a stern, reserved man, and is often uncommunicative for days on end. There have, however, been no incidents worth reporting, until Monday of this week. We were seated at the breakfast table, and I was reading a letter which I had received that morning from my mother. I was paying little attention to my host, who was glancing through his own post, when a slight cry, as of fear, made me look up sharply.

"At the other end of the table, Tregorran's eyes were wide with terror. His mouth hung open limply, and his face was as white as a sheet, as if every drop of blood had been drained from it. 'What is it?' I cried in alarm. His lips moved slightly, but no sound emerged. I dropped the letter I was reading, and sprang from my seat. In front of him upon the table lay a small brown-paper package he had opened. It contained nothing but a small quantity of children's bricks in a little cardboard box, of the sort which are decorated with letters of the alphabet and simple pictures of farm animals. It is no unusual thing for unsolicited articles to arrive in the post at Whitstock Farm – Tregorran frequently receives samples and testimonials from seed merchants and other such tradesmen – and I took it that this was something similar, incongruous though it seemed. But such thoughts were dashed from my mind as another inarticulate cry came from his lips, and he struggled to rise to his feet.

"He pushed back his chair, which fell over with a crash, and for a second swayed unsteadily on his feet, his fingers clutching at his throat. Then, before I could catch hold of him, he fell in a senseless heap to the floor. I rang for Lydford, his manservant, and between us we carried him to a couch and loosened his collar, for he seemed scarcely able to breathe. It was several minutes before he regained his senses, and then we helped him to his bed, where he stayed all that day. The following day he rose as usual, and made no allusion to what had happened. When I tried to raise the matter, he quickly changed the subject. It was then I resolved to seek your advice."

"You are quite certain it was the packet of bricks that disturbed him?" queried Holmes, a note of keen interest in his voice.

"Without a doubt. He had just opened it."

"There was no note in the package?"

"No."

"Did the letters on the bricks spell out any message?"

"Absolutely not. I looked to see. They were in a perfectly random order."

"Did you observe where the parcel had been posted?"

"At Bodmin Post Office."

"Has anything remotely similar occurred before?"

Penryan shook his head. "I questioned Lydford and the other servants on the matter, and they said they had never seen such a thing in all the years they had been there."

"Where is the parcel now?"

"I have no idea. Tregorran evidently instructed Lydford to dispose of it somewhere, for I have not seen it since the morning it arrived."

Again Holmes sat for some time in silence, his eyes closed and his brow furrowed with thought. At length he opened his eyes, an expression of decision upon his features, and addressed his visitor.

"These are deep waters," said he. "When do you propose to return to Cornwall?"

"By the nine o'clock train from Paddington, tomorrow morning."

"Then I shall accompany you. There is great danger at Whitstock Farm."

` "Danger? For whom?"

"For whoever holds the Tregorran estate. Will you come with us, Watson?"

"Most certainly," said I, "if I can be of any assistance."

"My dear fellow!" cried Holmes, smiling. "You know how highly I value your presence! Until tomorrow morning, then, Mr. Penryan!"

We met at Paddington the following morning as we had arranged, and began our long journey to the West Country. At Exeter, we took a branch line which meandered across the moors, and shortly before four o'clock reached the little market town of Holsworthy. Penryan had wired ahead, and the farm trap was waiting for us. By it stood a ruddy-faced countryman in leather jacket and leggings, a downcast expression upon his face.

"What is it, Polford?" asked Penryan. "You appear troubled!"

"Mr. Tregorran has taken his own life," returned the other in a sombre tone.

"What!" cried Penryan in disbelief.

"He shot himself this morning," the man continued.

"Have the authorities been informed?" asked Holmes.

"The police are at the house now," returned the groom.

"Then we must get there without delay," cried Holmes, springing aboard the trap.

In a moment we were rattling off at a great pace down winding country lanes. Above us the clouds were low and dark, and a stiff wind was blowing. Holmes, I could see, was consumed with intense excitement and impatience, drumming his fingers upon his knee, biting his nails and consulting his watch every few minutes throughout the journey. But Whitstock Farm lay several miles distant from the town, and it was almost forty minutes before we turned in between the lichen-blotched stone gate-posts and saw before us the ancient grey-stone farmhouse, flanked by barns and other outbuildings.

As we alighted from the trap, the front door of the house opened, and a tall man dressed in a frogged jacket and braided cap emerged. He introduced himself as Inspector Culliemore, from the police station at Holsworthy, and upon learning Penryan's name, led us back into the house and along a dark, wood-panelled corridor to the study. In the centre of the room stood a large desk, covered with documents and slips of paper.

Sherlock Holmes handed his card to the policeman, who glanced at it for a moment. “I don’t think we’ll be needing any detectives here, consulting or otherwise,” he remarked in a dismissive tone. “The facts appear very straightforward. Tregorran left home this morning at ten-thirty, carrying his shotgun. His housekeeper observed the gun, and assumed he intended to shoot crows. At about one o’clock, his body was found by a shepherd, in a remote part of the estate known as Gipsies’ Croft. The police-station at Holsworthy was notified soon afterwards.”

“Where is the body now?” Penryan enquired.

“It has been taken to Bodmin for further examination by the medical officer; although I doubt if he will have much to add to the opinion he has already expressed, that Tregorran died by his own hand, with his own shotgun. He took the full blast in the chest and neck, and must have died instantly.”

“What makes you so sure it was suicide?” queried Holmes.

Inspector Culliemore looked round in surprise. “It is clear,” said he, counting off the points upon his fingers. “He went out by himself with his gun. He did not tell anyone where he was going. He died by his own gun. There is no indication that anyone else was involved in any way. The servants all state that he had been in a grim, dark humour all this week. And, he left a note.”

“May I see the note?” said Holmes.

“Certainly,” replied the policeman. He picked up a sheet of note-paper from the desk and passed it to us. It was a plain white sheet, upon which was written: “Gipsies’ Croft. Thursday. Eleven o’clock.”

“A singular note,” remarked Holmes.

“It appears,” observed the policeman, “that he had already determined when and where he was going to end his life. That is not so strange as you might suppose. You may not be aware of it, but the place he chose was where his wife died, three years ago."

"I am aware of the significance of the place," returned Holmes. "This sheet has been folded in four at some time," he continued, as he examined the note carefully with the aid of his pocket lens. Where was it found?"

"On the desk," said Culliemore. "I observed the folding, and wondered at first if it had come in the post, although it did appear to be in Tregorran's own hand. But there is no envelope about anywhere, so I think it most likely that Tregorran made the note himself, to stiffen his resolve to go through with what he had planned, and folded it so that he could carry it about with him in his breast pocket. I have known suicides do such things before."

"No doubt," remarked Holmes. "Yet, in this case, he did not carry it with him in his breast pocket, or any other pocket, but left it here on the desk. If this note did come in the post," he continued, as he took the note to the window, with a couple of similar sheets of paper that he had picked up from the desk, "the envelope it came in may have been destroyed."

"His housekeeper says he received no post this morning," returned the policeman.

"And yesterday?"

"He received two letters. The envelopes were quite plain, and she does not know what was in them."

"Where are those envelopes?"

"Thrown away."

"Then one of them may have contained this sheet. Indeed, as the note specifies a day by name, it is more than likely that it did not arrive today but yesterday, or even the day before."

"Ah, Mr. London Detective!" returned the inspector in a tone of annoyance; "but you do not yet know all the facts! When I was questioning Tregorran's housekeeper about his recent mail, I showed her this note, and she instantly identified the hand as her master's. She says she is confident she could pick it out from a hundred such sheets!"

"Hum!" said Holmes, frowning as he replaced the papers on the desk. "That rather settles the matter, then. Would you mind showing us where the tragedy occurred?"

"I must return to the station, to write my report," replied Inspector Culliemore, shaking his head. "The groom will show you. He accompanied me when I first attended the scene of the death."

So it was that we climbed aboard the trap once more, and set off, by narrow lanes and cart-tracks, to the northern edge of the estate. The wind was very fierce now, blowing from the west, off the Atlantic, and whistling through the leafless wintry trees beside the road. At length the groom reined in the horse by an open gateway in a stunted hedge of thorn. "This is Gipsies' Croft," said he.

Through the gateway was a dismal, steeply sloping and barren-looking field. The lower end, to our left, appeared to be little more than bog and reeds, while the higher part, to which the groom led us, consisted of coarse grass and outcropping grey rocks, their surfaces blotched with moss and lichen. Ahead of us at the top of the field was a small ruined building. The two gable-ends were still standing, but the building between them had partly collapsed, so that, as we climbed the hill towards it, it appeared as a grim, horned silhouette against the leaden grey sky beyond. Before this gloomy structure, its fallen stones almost smothered by a tangled mass of brambles, our guide paused and indicated a spot on the ground where the bare mud had been churned up by the passage of many feet. On the nearest stones were dark splashes which were undoubtedly blood.

For a few moments, Holmes surveyed the ground, then he shook his head.

"A herd of buffalo could scarcely have done a better job of obliterating all significant traces," said he with a bitter sigh. "Still, that is as I expected. Let us take a look round the side of the building."

We followed him round the right-hand wall of the ruin, and watched as he examined the ground there carefully and then slowly made his way behind what remained of the rear wall.

"Ah! The cunning villain!" cried he all at once, pointing to a flat patch of bare mud, close beside the wall of the building. "See how he has sought to conceal the evidence of his presence!"

I looked closer, and saw that the surface of the mud, which I had taken at first to be perfectly featureless, was in fact marked by many shallow parallel lines. I was puzzled as to what might be the significance of this, until Holmes drew our attention to a clump of twigs which lay a few feet from the mud, and which had evidently been broken from a nearby tree.

"He has dragged this bunch of twigs back and forth across the mud to obliterate his footprints," said Holmes. "We must show that we are equal to his devilry! Is there any other way of reaching this field," he continued, addressing the groom, "other than the lane we took?"

"Yes, sir," returned the man, pointing to a gap in the hedge at the far side of the field: "through yonder gateway."

"Keep behind me," instructed Holmes, as he set off across the field, examining closely every patch of bare ground. "Ah!" said he at last, pausing before a broad swathe of mud which lay between two low clumps of grass. We leaned forward to see. In the centre of the flat mud was a small, perfectly circular hole, perhaps an inch across, and two inches deep. "Note that well," said Holmes, "for that marks the passage of this devil! He has stepped across the mud, from one side to the other, to avoid leaving a footprint, but it was a little wide for him."

"I do not understand!" cried Penryan in a tone of bewilderment. "I thought that you agreed with the inspector in the end, that Tregorran's death was suicide."

"Not at all," returned Holmes. "You evidently misunderstood. It is not suicide. It is cold-blooded murder!"

We hurried on, and passed through the gap in the hedge and down a short, steep track to a narrow lane. For several minutes, as the cold wind swirled about us, Holmes walked back and forth, examining the road surface and the grass verges at the side. Once he stooped, picked up a small object from the grass, and placed it carefully in an envelope which he took from his pocket.

"A pony and trap were drawn up here this morning for an hour and a quarter," said he at length. "The pony was tethered to a spike in the ground, on a rope six yards long. The extent of its grazing is quite clear," he added, by way of explanation, "and half-way between the two extreme points there is a small hole, indicating where the spike was pushed into the ground. Where does this lane lead to, Polford?"

"Up the hill will bring you to the Polcathro estate," replied the groom. "Down the other way, to the coast."

"Do you think you could manage to bring the trap across the field, to here?"

"I reckon so, sir," returned the man, and hurried off. Holmes took out his note-book, tore out a sheet, and scribbled a long note upon it. A minute or two later, the groom returned, leading the horse and trap, and Holmes handed him the note he had written.

"Make certain this message reaches Inspector Culliemore without delay," said he. "You will have to return to Whitstock on foot, I am afraid, Polford, for we must take the trap. We have no time to lose. Come!" he cried, springing up to the seat and taking the reins. Penryan and I clambered up beside him, he flicked the reins, and we set off at a brisk canter down the lane.

"Where are we going, Mr. Holmes?" asked Penryan.

"To Bude," returned Holmes. "We have failed to prevent the murder of Michael Tregorran. We must ensure at least that we bring his murderer to justice!"

"But who, then, is his murderer?"

"A man of very deep hatred and vindictiveness: your exotic friend, Senor Carlos Perreira."

"What!" cried Penryan in disbelief. "That cannot be true! Why on earth should Perreira murder Michael Tregorran?"

"Because Carlos Perreira is Ulick Tregorran."

Again Penryan cried loud in protest, and I, too, was stunned at this claim.

"But Ulick Tregorran has been dead for thirty years!" I protested. "The ship he was travelling on was lost off the coast of Africa!"

"He was only presumed dead," returned Holmes. "I rather fancy he had left the ship at Lisbon, and was thus not on board when it went down. We have heard that he was reluctant to ever do anything that was recommended to him. Perhaps he did not much care for the thought of Australia, and preferred to strike out in a direction of his own choosing. He had a considerable sum of money with him at the time, you will recall, no doubt sufficient to set himself up in whatever enterprise he wished. Probably he heard in Lisbon of the great financial potential of the coffee plantations, and took ship from Portugal to Brazil, where he appears to have prospered."

"But if he is still alive, why has he never made this fact known?" I protested.

"Why should he? There was nothing for him here. His younger brother, Michael, was in possession of all that might have been his: the Tregorran estate, and the woman, Hannah Tressillick. We heard how she had at first been attracted to the older brother, Ulick, but had subsequently switched her affections to the younger. This may have been of greater significance to Ulick than was generally appreciated. His opinion on the matter, after all, is not on record. I believe that for the last thirty years he has harboured the most intense hatred of both his brother and the woman who turned away from him, and has planned his vengeance carefully."

"You think he also murdered Tregorran's wife?" I queried, aghast at the horror of Holmes's theory.

"I am certain of it. No doubt he had made himself familiar with her movements, and waited for her in the lane near the farm on the night of her death. Perhaps he then identified himself to her, and persuaded her to take a stroll with him, until they were far from any homestead, and he had her at his mercy."

"Why murder her twice, as all the newspaper accounts reported?" asked Penryan, a look of horror upon his features.

"Who can say? Perhaps he simply wished to ensure that she was really dead. More likely, though, I believe, is that his stabbing her through the heart had a symbolic meaning for him, and represented his final triumph over her. You recoil with horror and disbelief at this suggestion, but if I am right, we are dealing with a quite exceptionally evil and determined man, who has spent thirty years in planning his terrible vengeance."

Holmes whipped the horse up, and we sped along the narrow lanes. We were close to the sea now, and off to our right we could hear the boom of the waves breaking upon the rocky coast, and see the sea-birds wheeling high in the sky above.

"It seems too fantastic to be true," remarked Penryan after a moment.

"It is the only hypothesis which will fit all the facts," Holmes responded. "I already considered it a possibility before we left London, and events since have only served to confirm it. You described to us how horror-stricken Michael Tregorran had been when he received the packet of children's bricks in the post. But why should that be? What could his reaction mean? It was clear from what you told us that Tregorran regarded the Polcathro family as his mortal enemies, but any communication from them would surely have been more likely to rouse anger in his breast than the dreadful shock and horror which so overcame him at the breakfast table on Monday. Clearly, for him, some great significance attached to this little toy. But what could that significance be? He and his wife had had no children of their own, and the domestic staff who had been at Whitstock for many years could shed no light on the matter.

"In the absence of any other explanation, I conjectured that the significance of this strange package might lie in some incident from Tregorran's own childhood. But why should this reminder of his childhood cause him such a terrible shock? Evidently the bricks conveyed to him some fact which was so utterly unforeseen and incredible that he was driven quite out of his senses. The likeliest answer, I considered, was that the bricks brought to his mind some incident – perhaps a childhood squabble he had had with his older brother – which only he and Ulick would know of. If that were so, then the bricks would at once convey to him that Ulick was still alive. This, I conjectured, might well have been sufficient to bring about his collapse. And if my hypothesis were correct, it also cast a little light on the mind of Ulick Tregorran, for it suggested that he remembered clearly some childish dispute of forty-odd years ago. Perhaps Ulick's hatred of his brother had its origins in those distant days.

"When we arrived at Whitstock, and Inspector Culliemore showed us the supposed suicide note, it at once struck me that it might, rather, be a summons from Ulick Tregorran to his brother. The housekeeper had confidently identified the handwriting as her master's, so Culliemore concluded that Michael Tregorran had folded the paper himself, so that he might carry the note in his pocket. But it was evident to me, from a close examination of the paper, that it had never been in any pocket. The folded edges were not at all rubbed, and the rest of it was very smooth and uncreased. Furthermore, a comparison with the other sheets of white paper on the study desk showed that the folded sheet, although very similar, was in fact of different manufacture. I was therefore convinced that I was right, and that the message had arrived in the post, in an envelope which had subsequently been destroyed. But if that were the case, then the hand which had written it was not that of Michael Tregorran, and the housekeeper's identification of it as such could mean only one thing: that the note was written by Michael's brother, Ulick. As far as I was concerned, the housekeeper's testimony settled the matter beyond question. The study of handwriting is a fascinating one, which has not yet received the attention it deserves, although I have myself contributed one or two brief monographs to the literature. It is a singular fact that the handwriting of close relatives, even those whose lives have taken very different courses, is frequently so similar as to be practically indistinguishable.

"What I suggest happened this morning at Gipsies' Croft is that Ulick Tregorran arrived some time before the appointed hour, tethered his horse out of sight in the lane, and finished the cigar he was smoking, the end of which I found upon the grass there. Then he no doubt hid behind the ruined building until he heard his brother approach, when he emerged and took him by surprise. That Michael Tregorran had some notion of what was afoot, and expected trouble, is evident from the fact that he took his shotgun with him. How the older brother got this from him, we can only conjecture, but it is probable that Ulick himself was armed with a pistol. Perhaps there was some discussion between them, then Ulick discharged the shotgun at point-blank range, killing his brother instantly, and afterwards returned this way to Bude. During his passage across the field, careful though he was to leave no footprints, he inadvertently left the unmistakeable imprint of his walking-stick, as you saw. But, we approach Bude, where we must hope we can lay our hands on this cunning devil!"

We sped past a scattering of outlying houses, the clatter of our horse's hooves echoing back to us from their thick stone walls, then, as we rounded a bend, there on our right, spread out below us, was the vast expanse of the sea, leaden-coloured and rough, the rollers crashing and foaming on the beach far below. High above us, seagulls wheeled and soared, their blood-chilling shrieks seeming to echo the tenor of my own thoughts as Holmes finished his summary.

Penryan directed us to the Atlantic Hotel, high on a hill overlooking the sea, but there we met with a check. Senor Perreira, we were informed, had hired a carriage and left within the last hour for Holsworthy, intending to catch the seven o'clock train there, and make his way down to Plymouth, from where he sailed for Brazil in the morning.

Sherlock Holmes clapped his hand to his head. "Fool that I am!" cried he. "I should have foreseen this, for it was clear that his plans were reaching their climax!"

There was nothing to be done but follow our quarry to Holsworthy. We quickly secured a fresh horse, therefore, and set off in pursuit. Along the high road we flew at a tremendous pace, sending up clouds of dust in our wake, all the while straining our eyes to catch a glimpse of the carriage ahead of us. It was not until we were within a mile or two of Holsworthy, however, and the daylight was fading, that we hurtled round a bend in the road, our trap swaying wildly from side to side, and saw ahead of us two vehicles stationary in the middle of the road, with a number of men standing beside them. As we drew closer, I saw that the larger of the two vehicles was a police van.

"It is Culliemore!" cried Holmes. "Thank Heavens my message reached him! He and his men must have been coming from Holsworthy when they encountered Perreira's carriage."

We drew to a halt and sprang down. Inspector Culliemore was standing in the middle of the road, speaking to a very stout man in a large grey overcoat and wide-brimmed felt hat, who had his back to us.

"Ah! Mr. Holmes!" called out the policeman. "I got your note. But Mr. Perreira is very indignant at being delayed like this. Unless you can give me good cause to do otherwise, I shall have to let him go to catch his train."

Holmes did not reply to the policeman, but instead addressed the man in the grey overcoat. "Tregorran!" he called sharply as we approached, "Ulick Tregorran!"

The other turned his head abruptly, then, as if realising he had made an error, remained perfectly rigid, and glared at us. In that moment, his eyes met mine, and for an instant I had the awful, chilling sensation of gazing into the very soul of evil. Those hooded, bile-shot eyes seemed to blaze with malevolent fire from that dark, sallow face. Involuntarily, I stopped, as did Penryan. But Holmes stepped forward, and spoke again.

"Why did you murder her twice?" said he, in a matter-of-fact tone.

The other man's mouth opened slightly, his eyes flickered from side to side, then, with a sudden hoarse roar, he raised his stick and made to bring it down upon my friend's head.

It was the last thing he was ever to do in this world. Even as Holmes raised his arm to fend off the blow, and two police constables sprang forward to seize the assailant, he abruptly stopped. His fingers seemed to lose their grip upon the stick, which slipped from his grasp and clattered to the ground. For a moment, he clutched at his chest, his face contorted with pain, then, with a faint gasp, he collapsed heavily upon the dusty road.

I stepped forward, hastily loosened his collar, and examined him. It was evident he had suffered a massive heart seizure, and though I did all I could, it was to no avail. The man was dead.

Inspector Culliemore was not clear what part this Senor Perreira had played in the tragic events at Whitstock Farm, for Holmes's message to him had been of necessity very brief, but my friend soon apprised the policeman of his view of the matter. Then a discovery was made in the dead man's travelling trunk which cast a clear light on the case. Among numerous papers and documents was a thick diary, bound in red leather, in which Ulick Tregorran had recorded his thoughts over many years. Late into the evening we studied this dreadful volume, and read there of the evil pleasure he had taken in selecting the field known as Gipsies' Croft to be the scene of his terrible crimes. Of the murder of Hannah Tregorran, he had written as follows, in words which still make my blood run cold as I recall them: "Once this woman promised her heart to me. Then she gave it to another. So, now I destroy her heart. No one denies me with impunity!"

It also became clear from the account in the diary that Ulick Tregorran had murdered his own father when he learned that his father had willed the estate to his younger brother, afterwards beating his father's horse with a stick until he had lamed it, in order to conceal his terrible crime. It appeared, too, that his mother had suspected his involvement in the matter, which was the main reason she had sent him abroad. Holmes's conjecture that he had left the ship at Lisbon also proved an accurate one. From there he had travelled to Brazil, as Holmes had surmised, where he had remained for many years, until thoughts of further vengeance had brought him once more to these shores.

"I rather fancy," said Sherlock Holmes to me, as we returned to London the following morning on the Cornish Express, "that the death of Ulick Tregorran will mark the final act of the Tregorran Curse, which has cast such a blight upon the family and all those connected with it. Let us hope so, anyway, for it has certainly been a grim business. Now, Watson, I seem to recall that there is a concert of airs by Rossini at the Lyceum Theatre this evening. On the whole, my own taste is more for German music than Italian; but Rossini is light and cheerful, and an hour or two in his pleasant company may perhaps serve us as a suitable restorative!"

THE VICTORIA STREET MYSTERY

MY FRIEND, SHERLOCK HOLMES, the foremost criminal investigator in London, would sometimes expound upon the nature of his art. Although he would, at different times, address the matter in different ways, the general drift of his analysis was always largely the same.

"There are three principal factors in any successful criminal investigation," he would say. "The first is the training which the investigator has undergone, with regard to observation and deduction. This constitutes the foundation stones of the whole business, the *sine qua non* of the matter, without which the investigator must perforce rely simply on good fortune or the word of unreliable witnesses. The second is the experience he has gained from his previous investigations. This modifies and improves the accuracy of his observations and deductions. The third, which tends to be the least appreciated by the Scotland Yarders and the more sensational sections of the press, is the scientific outlook, which in practice means the keeping of an open mind. It is no use having had all the experience in the world if this very experience serves only to stifle and prejudice your logical faculties. Yes, we can say, the explanation which has proved correct a thousand times in the past may prove correct in the present instance, too, but it also may not. This cautionary principle must be borne in mind at all times, if you are to avoid falling into serious error."

This series of sketches in which I have attempted, however inadequately, to depict the varied career of Mr. Sherlock Holmes, has been designed to illustrate the points of theory which lay behind many of his cases. The third factor he listed in the remarks I have recorded above, concerning the importance of keeping an open mind when faced with apparently familiar facts, has never been better illustrated than in the case recorded in my notebook under the heading of "The Victoria Street Mystery," and it is this case I shall now recount.

One of Holmes's most frequent visitors, in the first year or two I shared chambers with him in Baker Street, was Inspector Lestrade, one of the senior detective officers of Scotland Yard, who would often consult my friend over difficulties he had encountered in his investigations. It came as no surprise, then, when, one foggy evening towards the end of November, 1882, a peal at our front doorbell was followed a few moments later by the appearance in our sitting-room of the keen-faced detective.

I rose from where I had been sitting beside the blazing fire.

"No doubt you would rather conduct your discussion in private," I began, but Lestrade waved me to my chair again.

"Not at all, Doctor," said he. "There is nothing especially confidential about the matter. Indeed, I would rather you remained. Your observations may prove invaluable, as they have on occasion in the past."

"I quite agree," said Holmes, ushering the policeman to his own chair by the fireside and drawing up the old basket-chair for himself. "A view from a different perspective is always interesting and sometimes enlightening. Now," he continued, turning to Lestrade, "what problem brings you to see us on such a cold and damp evening? I can see from your expression that there is something which puzzles you, but, unlike on some other occasions, it appears there is no great urgency attached to the matter. I surmise that your visit is not an official one, but undertaken purely on your own initiative."

"You are correct in every respect," returned the policeman in surprise, "but how do you know?"

"Had the matter been urgent, you would have taken a cab. Had your enquiry been an official one, you would also have taken a cab, and charged the fare to your employers. But I heard no cab before you rang at our bell and you have therefore come at least part of the way on foot. Your visit is therefore neither particularly urgent nor an official one. But I am sure that, for all that, it is an interesting one. You have our full attention!"

The policeman nodded his head. "It is a fairly straightforward business in most respects," he began, "but there are one or two points about it which are decidedly puzzling. In brief, the matter is this: there was a burglary at a warehouse down Shadwell way a few days ago, during which one of the thieves – a man who has already served time for burglary – was killed. It seems he must have had a confederate, but we can find no trace of this other man. It also seems that he had some connection with a very respectable address in the West End, but I cannot for the life of me think what that connection could possibly be. I have therefore come to you, Mr. Holmes, in the hope that you might be able to see some light in the matter where I cannot."

"Pray give us the details."

"It is soon told," responded Lestrade, taking out his note-book and turning the pages over. "Three nights ago – that is, on Monday evening – a constable – PC Dobbs of 'H' Division – was on his beat down Shadwell way when, as he passed along Dartmouth Street, about twenty past ten, he happened to notice a door ajar round the side of a warehouse, which he knew should have been locked up for the night. He therefore entered the building with his lantern in his hand. The place was in complete darkness and, as he cast his light about, he saw nothing to indicate that there was anything amiss. When he called out, however, there came an answering cry from the darkness, some distance away on the ground floor. He called again and got another answering cry, rather fainter than the first. Following the direction of these cries, he came at length upon a man – not anyone he knew – lying on his back on the hard floor.

"As he bent over him, Dobbs could see at once that the man was very seriously hurt. There was blood on the floor all around his head, and he seemed unable to move. Dobbs asked him what had happened, and, in answer, the man's eyes looked beyond Dobbs and upwards. Glancing up, Dobbs saw that some twenty feet above them was a metal walkway which connected with stairs from the ground floor to the upper floors, and it seemed clear that the injured man had fallen from there.

"Seeing that there was nothing he could do for him, Dobbs said he would go and bring a medical man, but before he left he asked the man what he was doing in the warehouse. To his surprise, the man abruptly raised his arm and, seizing the constable by the shoulder, pulled him closer and spoke in his ear.

"'Victoria Street,' he said in a weak, feeble voice. 'One-forty-one.'

"'One hundred and forty-one?' the constable queried.

"'Yes,' returned the man. 'Victoria Street.' Then he released his grip on the constable and put his hand up to his own throat where he seemed to be pulling at the scarf he was wearing. Dobbs carefully unfastened this and saw that behind it was a cord, tied loosely round the man's neck. The man put his hand on this cord and pulled at it, as he had done with the scarf, so Dobbs asked him if he wanted him to unfasten it.

"'Yes,' whispered the man. 'You take it.'

Dobbs unfastened the cord and pulled on it, drawing up from within the man's shirt a small soft leather pouch which was attached to the cord. He could feel there was some weight in the pouch, so he loosened the top and tipped the contents into his hand. To his surprise, he saw that there were ten gold sovereigns there.

Dobbs asked the man if the money was his, and, receiving a whispered assent, asked him what he wanted him to do with it.

"'Take it.'

"'Take it where?'

"'I've told you. One-forty-one.'

"'Victoria Street?'

"'Yes.'

"'I'll look after it for the moment, anyhow,' said Dobbs. He put the pouch of coins in his pocket and hurried off to get help. He says he was gone only about twenty minutes, but when he returned in a police-van, accompanied by the police-surgeon and two other men, the man in the warehouse had passed beyond all human help. The surgeon, who examined him more thoroughly later, says that he had undoubtedly fallen from a considerable height, as Dobbs had supposed, and in doing so had fractured his skull and several other bones. In his opinion, no one could have survived such a fall, and it was little short of a miracle that he had lasted long enough to speak to Dobbs as he had done."

"Is this constable, Dobbs, reliable?" asked Holmes.

"Absolutely," returned Lestrade. "He's very highly regarded. I would stake my life that his account is accurate."

"Has he been long in that district?"

"About three years, and on that particular beat for just over a year."

"But he did not recognize the man?"

"He said he thought he had seen him in the street a few times, late in the evening, probably returning home from some ale-house or other, but he did not know his name. As there was nothing on or about the dead man's person to indicate who he was, the authorities down there were stumped for a while. They called in Scotland Yard, and I went down there, but by the time I got there they had managed to identify him."

"Very well," said Holmes. "Pray continue."

"As you will no doubt be aware," said Lestrade, "establishing the identity of all the dead bodies that turn up in London is one of the most frequent and time-consuming tasks that fall to the lot of the police, and the men of 'H' Division soon applied their experience to the problem. One of the detective inspectors there, a smart officer by the name of Stanley, is a man after your own heart, Mr. Holmes. He examined the dead man's clothing and footwear, and observed that the little wedge of mud in the instep of his boot contained a considerable amount of sawdust. He speculated from this that the man had been employed in one of the timber-yards close by the river."

"Excellent!" cried Holmes.

"Yes, I thought you would appreciate the deduction, Mr. Holmes. Anyway, Inspector Stanley's surmise proved correct. After a few hours spent enquiring at every wood-yard in the district, it was established beyond doubt that the dead man was Alf Barnes, who had been employed at Chas Benson's timber-yard at Wapping. He had been in their employment for nearly two years, and had, they said, been a good reliable worker, never once failing to turn up for work until this week.

"Of course, once we knew the dead man's name, we were able to dig up a little more information about him. We discovered that about seven years ago, Barnes was arrested and charged with burglary from a warehouse near where he was found the other night. He was convicted and sentenced to five years' imprisonment, which he spent first in Pentonville and then in Wormwood Scrubs. At the time it was strongly suspected that he had been in league with two other men, Daniel Wolfe and Dick Cross, but nothing could be proved against either of them, so they were never charged. In fact, one of them, Wolfe, gave evidence against Barnes, stating that Barnes had tried unsuccessfully to persuade him to join him in his criminal activities. Barnes was therefore the only one who was convicted and sentenced. He was released from prison just over two years ago, and, after some time working as a casual labourer in the docks, got the job at Benson's wood-yard."

"What was it he stole seven years ago?" asked Holmes.

"Nothing very valuable," returned Lestrade. "He and whoever was in it with him were very much petty criminals. When caught he was attempting to make off with a cartload of stolen crockery – china plates and so on."

"Crockery?" I cried in surprise. "What a strange thing to steal. You wouldn't think it would be worth his while!"

"So you might think, Dr. Watson," remarked Lestrade with a chuckle, "but you would be surprised at the variety of goods that go missing all the time in the vicinity of the docks. The rule of thumb among some of the police officers down there is that if something can be stolen, then sooner or later it will be.

From the point of view of these petty criminals, it's often not the stealing that's the difficult part, but the disposing of the stolen goods afterwards."

"Yes, I can see that that might prove difficult," I said. "How, for instance, would one go about disposing of a cart-load of stolen crockery?"

"That's something else you would be surprised about," replied Lestrade. "The truth is, there are always some shopkeepers, market-stall-holders and others who would think nothing of selling stolen goods if they thought they could get away with it and turn a penny by doing so. We know from experience that some of these crooked people even 'commission' the burglars to steal specific goods for them – things they know they will be able to sell. As it happens, I suspect that that is the case in the present instance."

"What was stolen on Monday night, then?" asked Holmes.

"Furs, Mr. Holmes, very valuable furs. The warehouse in question is one of those owned by a property company, Bailey Brothers. They have nothing of their own to store there, but let out parts of the building to other businesses by the week, month or longer. Most of the building is actually empty at present, but half of one of the upper floors is let out to a fur-importing business, J R. Rosenstiel, whose offices are on Cheapside. Their part of the warehouse is walled off from the rest of the building, and the door to it secured with padlocks. When my colleagues in 'H' Division inspected that door, however, on the night Barnes was found there, they discovered that it had been forced open and the padlock mountings wrenched from the wall. They summoned someone from Rosenstiel's who confirmed what they had suspected, that a considerable number of the furs had been stolen."

"That certainly suggests that Barnes had a confederate," said Holmes. "The missing furs were, I take it, nowhere to be found; Barnes did not have them; therefore someone else had already gone off with them."

"Quite right, Mr. Holmes. My own train of thought precisely. As to why Barnes's confederate had gone off and left him there, we can only guess. Perhaps the other man took the furs and Barnes was supposed to lock the place up and follow him, but fell from the metal walkway as he was coming downstairs. Perhaps Barnes had his accident while the other man was still there, and the other thought he was dead, or close to it, and decided to abandon him. Or perhaps it wasn't an accident at all: perhaps Barnes and his confederate quarrelled about something and had a fight on the walkway, during which Barnes fell – or was pushed – off it. We've no way of knowing what happened. Besides, there's little point in thinking about it at the moment, as we have no idea who Barnes was working with. He seems to have lived a very solitary life since he came out of prison, and doesn't appear to have had any friends at all. The only acquaintance of his that we've managed to find is a neighbour in Beckman Street, which is where he lived, a man by the name of John Gilbert. He's a respectable man with a wife and family, who has a senior job in the docks which he's had for nearly twenty years. He's just the sort of man whose testimony you feel you can rely on, and he says that Barnes lived alone, always kept himself to himself and never had any visitors. As far as Gilbert is aware, Barnes never spoke to anybody other than Gilbert himself and the man at the corner shop."

"What about those men who were suspected of having been involved with Barnes in the earlier robbery?" asked Holmes.

"What, Wolfe and Cross? There's nothing there, as far as I can see, Mr. Holmes. Barnes fell out with them completely when he went to prison – not surprising, really, considering they'd given evidence against him – and, so far as I've been able to discover, he's never spoken a word to them since. I can't find a single person who has ever seen them together since Barnes came out of the Scrubs, two years ago."

"Did you question PC Dobbs as to whether he had seen anyone in the nearby streets before he found Barnes?" asked Holmes.

"I certainly did," replied Lestrade. "He said the only people he saw were two men and a lad on a builder's cart, a few minutes before he turned into Dartmouth Street. He says they didn't seem to be in any particular hurry. He spoke to them and they told him they had been working late to finish a special job. He had a look in the back of the cart as they passed him, but says that all he could see there were a couple of planks of wood, a lot of timber off-cuts, a pile of house-bricks and some sacks of sand and cement."

"Did he recognize the men?"

"No."

"Was there any name displayed on the cart?"

Lestrade shook his head. "I specifically asked him that, but he said not. It would therefore be the very devil to find that cart now – and, of course, it's probably got nothing whatever to do with the crime, anyway. It is for that reason that I have been trying to approach the problem from the other end, as it were, that is, by investigating the Victoria Street connection. Unfortunately, I've not yet had any success there, which is what brings me here tonight."

"What do you mean?" I asked.

"I mentioned to you that just as important for these petty criminals as the theft itself is to find a way of disposing profitably of their plunder. I also mentioned that sometimes such thefts were 'commissioned' by those who were hoping to sell the stolen goods. With this in mind, I wondered if Barnes's repeated references to the address in Victoria Street might not provide us with a clue in that direction. I know, of course, that this sounds absurd: Victoria Street is one of the finest modern streets in the whole of London. It lies in the very heart of Westminster, with the Houses of Parliament and Westminster Abbey at one end and Victoria station at the other, and with fine new shops and offices in between. You simply cannot find anywhere more solid and respectable, and I am sure that most of the businesses in a street like that are of the very highest probity. But, as I know from my twenty years on the force, you can never tell for certain: sometimes you come across a cunning, plausible villain mingling with the most decent and honest folk you could imagine.

"I have therefore been making discreet enquiries about the address Barnes gave to PC Dobbs, one hundred and forty-one Victoria Street. It is one of those solid but somewhat anonymous buildings which have sprung up in that street in recent years. The owners are a firm called Westminster Commercial Properties Ltd, of which the chairman and largest shareholder is Lord Westfield. I can't think that there is anything suspicious there. The building itself is let out in six separate lots, one of which is vacant at the moment. I'll tell you who the five present tenants are."

Lestrade turned another page in his note-book, and read out a list he had made there: "First," he began, "there is the St Thomas Missionary Society, which, as the name suggests, is a charitable organization, which collects donations and pays for missionaries in parts of Africa and India. Second, W. P. Walker & Son, civil engineers. Third, the London and Moscow Importing Company – they specialize in Russian pictures, jewellery and other trinkets. Fourth, Snelgrove and Company, house and estate agents. Fifth, Nelson and Newsome, timber importers – they deal largely with the Scandinavian countries, so I understand." The policeman paused, a wry expression on his face. "And that, I'm afraid, is that," said he. "Not very promising, is it! Have you ever had any reason to come across any of these people, Mr. Holmes?"

"I don't believe so," replied my friend with a frown. He stood up and selected a couple of volumes from the long shelf of commonplace books in which he pasted newspaper cuttings on any subject which struck him as interesting. "No, there's no reference here to any of those people," he remarked as he turned the pages over rapidly.

"Is it possible," I asked Lestrade, "that there is another Victoria Street somewhere in London to which Barnes might have been referring?"

The policeman shook his head. "I've looked into that possibility already, Dr. Watson, and it's no use. Save only a short street in Greenwich, there is no other."

"As civil engineers sell only their expertise and mathematical calculations," I remarked, "and can have no use for furs, W. P. Walker & Son can surely be ruled out."

"Indeed," said Lestrade, "and, for similar reasons, the housing agents, Snelgrove & Co, can certainly be dismissed from consideration. The missionary society, too, has obviously nothing to do with any criminal enterprise, which leaves us with only the two importing companies, the one of Scandinavian timber and the other of Russian art and trinkets. Neither seems to have anything to do with furs, but it is an odd chance that the northern territories of both places – Russia and Scandinavia – are known for hunting and trapping, and I imagine a lot of furs do come from there."

"That is true," I remarked. "But I have been wondering about the missionary society, Lestrade. Not that there might be anything criminal about it, of course, but I wonder if Barnes might have been telling PC Dobbs that he wished to donate the money in his purse to it. He certainly made a point of drawing Dobbs's notice to the purse he was carrying."

"I suppose that what you suggest might be possible in theory, Dr. Watson, and there is, as they say, 'always a first time' for everything, but I can't really see a criminal like Alf Barnes thinking of contributing to a missionary society – and with such a large sum as ten pounds, too. If you'd brushed up against these villains as much as I have over the years, I think you'd agree with me."

"Perhaps you're right," I conceded. "But there is another possibility: perhaps one of the businesses at that address in Victoria Street was robbed by Barnes on some previous occasion, and in a fit of remorse he wished to make restitution to them for it."

"I should say the same applies to that suggestion as to your other one," responded Lestrade in a dismissive tone. "I just can't see one of these petty criminals thinking that way. In any case, it would be a deuced funny thing to have remorse for an old crime while busily engaged in a new one! What do you think, Mr. Holmes?"

Sherlock Holmes frowned. He had taken a street-map of London from the shelf as we had been speaking, and was studying it intently in silence. "Did you say that Barnes's home address was in Beckman Street?" he asked the policeman at length.

Lestrade consulted his notebook. "Yes, number thirteen," he replied. "Beckman Street is near the south end of Montgomery Road."

"I see it," said Holmes, eyeing the map closely. "And the address of Benson's timber-yard?"

"Upton Street, close by the river, in Wapping."

"Hum!" said Holmes, who appeared to be deep in thought. "I can't help feeling that there is something suggestive about all this! I think, Lestrade," he continued after a long moment of silence, "that, if you wish it, I shall look into the matter for you tomorrow."

"I should be very pleased if you would," returned the policeman.

"In that case," said Holmes, "I should be obliged if you could let me have a signed authority, so that there will be no difficulty about my viewing the body, borrowing Barnes's house-key for a little while and so on."

"Certainly," said Lestrade, taking a folded slip of paper from his inside pocket. "I have a suitable form here which I shall just fill in and sign. But, if I may say so, I don't think you will discover anything fresh in the East End, Mr. Holmes. I think that, between the two of us, Inspector Stanley and I have examined every possible aspect of the case in those parts without turning up anything of value. It is for that very reason, as I have explained, that I have been concentrating my efforts today on the possible West End connections of the matter, which I shall continue tomorrow."

Holmes nodded, a smile on his face. "I understand," said he. "I am sure that you and Stanley have done as thorough a job as you can, Lestrade. But you know my methods: I like to start afresh at the beginning of a case and see everything for myself, even if it is exactly the same as a hundred other people have already seen!"

The following morning Holmes had risen early and left the house before I descended for breakfast. Leaning up against the marmalade-pot, however, was a note he had left me, which ran as follows:

> I know you take an interest in my cases, Watson, so here is something for you to consider concerning the present business. On the chemical bench you will see the street-map of London, folded to show the East End. I have marked three places with little pieces of a broken matchstick. See what you make of it. When I return we can compare our conclusions on the matter. – S. H.

I crossed to Holmes's chemical bench and examined the map. One piece of the matchstick was placed on Upton Street, in Wapping, close to the river. That, I remembered, was the address of the timber-yard at which Barnes had been employed. The next piece of the matchstick lay on Dartmouth Street, which ran approximately south to north, towards the Commercial Road, and was, of course, the location of the warehouse in which Barnes had been found by PC Dobbs. The third piece lay on Beckman Street, a short cul-de-sac running due west from near the south end of Montgomery Road, the long road which runs north from Commercial Road up towards Stepney. I remembered from our discussion the previous evening that Beckman Street was Barnes's home address. I was still contemplating these matchsticks on the map and wondering what was in Holmes's mind when my thoughts were interrupted by the arrival of the maid with my breakfast tray.

As I ate, I pondered the matter further, my thoughts so abstracted that I scarcely noticed what I was eating. Then, all at once, a fresh thought struck me. I put down my tea cup and crossed to the chemical bench once more. For a minute or two I studied again the streets which lay between Wapping, where Barnes had worked, and the southern part of Stepney, where he had lived. Yes, I was right: although there were a number of different routes Barnes could have taken on his way home from work, the shortest, most direct way would almost certainly have included Dartmouth Street, in which Bailey Brothers' warehouse stood. Thus, unless he had made a specific *detour* to call somewhere on his way home, he would probably have passed the warehouse every day of the week. But what, if anything, did this suggest?

As I considered the matter further in the light of this observation, I thought for a moment that it suggested that the warehouse in question would be one of the likeliest places for Barnes to burgle. Passing the warehouse every day, he would probably have gotten to know what was stored there and whether it was worth stealing or not. He would quite possibly, also, have become familiar with the regular routines at the warehouse – when the men who worked there locked up and went home for the day, whether a night-watchman was employed there and so on.

I had no sooner reached this conclusion, however, than I saw that one could just as well argue the exact opposite, that this particular warehouse was probably the very last place that Barnes would choose to burgle. For if he had passed it every day, it was quite likely that he had been seen to do so by others, including the local police-constable on his beat. Indeed, PC Dobbs, who had found Barnes, had mentioned that he had several times seen him in the street in the late evening. In that case, if the burglary had gone off as planned and Barnes had got away without mishap, he would almost certainly have been one of the first people the police would have questioned about the matter, not necessarily to accuse him of being involved in the crime, but simply to find out if he had observed anything suspicious as he passed by the warehouse. But such questioning by the police was, I imagined, one of the last things that petty criminals would welcome. For however much he might try to conceal it, a guilty man is always anxious lest he give himself away, and that anxiety can quickly be recognized by an experienced detective officer.

Having thus argued myself to a stalemate on the question, I could make no further progress, and remained unsure as to what had been in Holmes's mind when he placed his matchsticks on the map. On another aspect of the case, however, it did later occur to me that we had perhaps been a trifle too quick to dismiss from consideration some of the tenants of the office building at 141, Victoria Street. After all, although it was certainly unlikely that the house-agents, the importers of Russian *objets-d'art* and the rest of them had any connection with petty criminals in the East End, it was always possible that one of these respectable firms unknowingly employed some individual who did have such a connection. That aspect of the case was certainly a profound mystery, and I wondered if Holmes, or Lestrade himself, would discover anything which might cast light on the matter.

It was late in the afternoon when Sherlock Holmes returned. He greeted me cheerily enough as he rang for a pot of tea, but he appeared a little weary. He threw off his hat and coat, dropped into a chair and took up his old clay pipe. Then, for several minutes, we sat in silence as he filled his pipe, lit it and sat puffing away contentedly. At length I could contain my curiosity no longer.

"Have you had any success with the case?" I asked.

"Yes, I have had some success," replied my friend, although there was something in his tone which seemed to suggest that he was not entirely satisfied.

"But not complete success?" I queried.

"Well, well," said he after a moment. "Lestrade consulted me on the matter, I have given him my opinion, and it is now up to Lestrade himself to complete the practical details – if he can."

"I should be most interested to hear about it."

"And I to recount it, when – Ah! Here is the tea! Let us refresh ourselves, and then I shall give you a full account of the matter. There are one or two instructive points in it, which I think you will find of interest."

A few minutes later, suitably refreshed, he continued:

"Before I begin," said he, "I should like to know if the markers I left on the map suggested anything to you."

"Indeed," I replied and described to him my reflections on the matter and the unsatisfactory conclusions I had reached. "So you see," I said, "although it seems likely that Barnes might have passed Bailey Brothers' warehouse every day of the week, I could not see that that really proved anything, one way or the other, about the robbery itself."

"You are quite right," returned my friend. "It is always a mistake to try to read too much into simple facts, which can very often be interpreted in diametrically opposite directions. But you correctly perceived the meaning of the matchsticks, Watson, by which I simply wished to indicate that, as you say, Dartmouth Street was the natural way for Barnes to go to and from his work. Of course, this does not in itself 'prove' anything, but it allows for the possibility – which Lestrade did not seem to appreciate – that Barnes's presence there on the evening PC Dobbs found him might not have been at all indicative of criminal intent on his part: on the contrary, we have every right, logically speaking, to expect him to have been there, on that evening as on every other, and it is thus possible that he may have had no involvement with the robbery whatsoever."

“But he was found inside the warehouse.”

“Yes, that is true. But he may have gone in there simply because he saw something as he passed which caught his attention and led him to think that something was amiss, in which case he would be a perfectly innocent party. So I reasoned, anyhow. I could not, of course, say for certain that that was so, but it was at least a possibility, and I therefore kept an open mind on the question.

“Bearing this in mind, I had decided before I set off this morning that I should like to know a little more about the character and habits of Alf Barnes, so I made Benson’s timber-yard, where he had been employed, my first port of call. There I saw Mr. George Benson, one of the owners of the business, who acts as general manager. He told me that he had been very sorry to hear about Barnes’s death, for he had liked the man, which, as he informed me, was not always the case with his employees.

“‘Did you know when you took him on that he had served a spell in prison?’ I asked.

“‘Yes,’ said he. ‘He was quite open about that. But there was something I liked about him when I interviewed him for the job, so I thought I’d take a chance with him. I must say I never regretted doing so. Although he had little education, he was interesting to talk to, and got on well with everybody who worked here. His work was not particularly demanding, but he attended to it very diligently. The chief part of it was to keep the place neat and tidy, to clear up after the men who were cutting the wood and so on, which makes a lot of mess. For that reason, he generally started work later in the day than everybody else and stayed later after the others had gone home. After he had been here a few weeks and had got used to the work, the whole place began to look more spick and span than it ever had before, in all the time I had been here.’

“‘He sounds a model employee,’ I remarked.

“‘He was,’ said Benson in an emphatic tone. ‘I only wish everyone else was as good. He was also very trustworthy. For the first year he was here, I was always here in the evening, too, working on the accounts, sorting the sales documents and that sort of thing, and Barnes left when I did. But a year ago I gave him his own key and told him to lock up when he left. I don't think I have ever seen anyone look so pleased about anything. I gave him a small increase in his wages at the same time, for which he thanked me, but I don't think he was half so pleased about that as he was about being trusted with the key.'

"'What were his usual hours of work?' I asked.

"'He generally worked in the evenings, from two in the afternoon until about ten at night.'

"You can imagine how interesting this information was to me, Watson. It meant that Barnes would have been making his way home every night between ten and half-past. Thus the assumption that PC Dobbs had made when he had seen Barnes at that time of day, that he was returning from an evening spent in an ale-house, was almost certainly mistaken. On the contrary, Barnes had simply been walking home from his employment. The picture of Barnes which Lestrade had painted for us, then, of a criminally inclined drunk, was thus quite expunged, and another picture, that of a sober, industrious and trusted worker took its place.

"After leaving Benson's wood-yard, I made my way to the police-station, where Barnes's body was lying. There I was able to confirm for myself the man's injuries as they had been described to us, but did not learn very much more. One thing I did observe, however, was that Barnes had been using some kind of hair-dye. This was a surprising and puzzling discovery. I might have dismissed it as a trivial matter, an excusable vanity, if his hair had been turning grey, but that did not appear to be the case. While I was at the police station, a message was received from Lestrade, saying that he had completed his enquiries in the West End and would be coming to join me later, so I left a message of my own, informing him that I had taken the key and was going to Barnes's house, in Beckman Street.

"Beckman Street is a short, drab little cul-de-sac, Watson, with a dingy-looking row of smoke-begrimed terraced houses on either side. The inside of number thirteen, where Barnes had lived, was as drab and plain as the exterior, but was at least neat and tidy. A few items of frayed and worn furniture were placed in an orderly way about the place, but there was nothing of any interest there. A couple of books and magazines lying on the kitchen table offered the only suggestion in the whole house of any recreation or pleasure in life."

"It does not sound a very cheering place to come home to," I remarked.

Holmes nodded. "That is certainly how it struck me," said he. "I think that Barnes's long period of incarceration in Wormwood Scrubs had perhaps driven much of the *joie-de-vivre* from his life. I wandered from room to room, upstairs and downstairs, seeing all that was to be seen, but there wasn't very much. Two things only are worthy of mention. In the kitchen, beside the sink, was a bottle of hair-dye and a little brush for applying it, which confirmed the observation I had made at the police station. I confess I stood and gazed at this for some time. There seemed something so very incongruous about it. Why would someone who appeared to take little pleasure in life have gone to the trouble of using hair-dye? I felt there must be some special significance in it, but I could not think what that significance might be.

"The second interesting thing was a picture – an old photograph – which was hanging on the parlour wall. I had glanced at it earlier, but now I returned to it and examined it more closely. It was a formally posed photograph of a middle-aged man and woman – presumably man and wife – sitting down, with a small child – a boy of about eight – standing in front of them. The clothes they were wearing appeared to be those of thirty or more years ago. The photograph was obviously of some significance to Alf Barnes, as it was the only such picture in the whole house, and as I studied it, I wondered if the adults might not perhaps be his mother and father, and the child Barnes himself.

"One feature of the picture which caught my eye was the woman's hair. It was arranged in a very formal way – no doubt she had had it specially dressed for the occasion – but at the front, a clump of the hair – what one might, I suppose, call a forelock – was a distinctly lighter shade than the rest. I was unsure at first whether this was a natural, if unusual feature, or was the result of art, but then I noticed that the little boy's hair displayed exactly the same feature. I had not observed this at first because the boy's hair was fairly short, and the photograph was not a very clear one. As I gazed at this, comparing in my mind the boy's hair and features with those of Alf Barnes, I became convinced of two things: first, that the two – the boy and Alf Barnes – were indeed one and the same person, and, second, that Barnes had used the hair-dye specifically to darken his lighter-coloured forelock. But what, I asked myself, could this mean?"

"It sounds from your description a very unusual feature which anyone would recognize," I remarked. "Perhaps Barnes was ashamed of his criminal past or of his time in prison, and did not wish to draw attention to himself."

Holmes nodded his head. "And yet," he said, "I couldn't believe the effect would be sufficient to achieve that end."

"What do you mean?" I asked.

"For those who did not know Barnes from before his time in prison, what he did with his hair would be immaterial. On the other hand, those who did know him would, I think, have recognized him whatever he did to his hair. And yet, as I considered the question, I was inclined to agree with your suggestion, Watson, and thought it must be something to do with his crime or his prison sentence. As it happens, one of the seven hypotheses I had devised to explain the whole business could readily accommodate this new feature, and I decided to waste no more time in putting that particular hypothesis to the test.

"I locked up Barnes's house and made my way to the corner of Beckman Street, where it joins Montgomery Road. Most of the streets in that district are quite short, but

Montgomery Road is the exception, being very long. It runs roughly southwest to northeast, towards Stepney. I proceeded northwards up this long road, looking at the door-numbers as I passed them. I dare say you can perceive what I was looking for, and what I expected to find there."

"On the contrary," I replied, "I haven't the faintest idea."

Holmes chuckled at this honest expression of mystification. "No doubt you will see it in a moment, then," said he, "as my account progresses. After some time I reached the house I was seeking and knocked briskly on the door. It was opened a moment later by a little girl, about nine or ten years old. I am sure people would say she was a charming child, but I didn't really notice. What seized my whole attention was the forelock of her hair, which was several shades lighter than the rest of it. Here, in an instant, was a ringing confirmation of my hypothesis."

"Barnes's child!" I cried in surprise.

"So I surmised," said Holmes. "'Is your mother in?' I asked her. She turned from the door, vanished from my sight and I heard her calling her mother. After a few moments a woman appeared in the doorway, drying her hands on a small towel.

"'Yes, sir?' said she. 'What is it?'

"'I imagine you have heard about Alf Barnes,' I said.

"She nodded her head and made to speak, but her feelings overcame her and she bit her lip.

"'I regret the necessity of raising the matter with you,' I said as she dabbed her eyes with the towel, 'but I am trying to get to the bottom of the case, which has, I believe, been misunderstood.'

"'Are you from the police?' she asked.

"'No,' I replied, 'but they were puzzled about the matter and asked me to look into it for them. May I come in for a moment?'

"She nodded her head without speaking, and I followed her into the small parlour.

"'You are, I take it, Alf Barnes's wife?' I said as we sat down.

"'Yes, sir.'

"'But have been living under the name of Mrs. Street?'

"'Yes, sir. 'Street' was my maiden name. Alf told me to go back to it after he got locked up. He said he didn't want me to be associated with a convict.

"'Particularly for the sake of your daughter, I imagine.'

"'Yes, sir, exactly.'

"'Whose name is Victoria.'

"'That's right, sir. You seem to know all about us.'

"'Well, well. I have had to work it all out for myself. The police don't know about you or Victoria, and are on a wild-goose-chase for non-existent clues at the moment. They believe that Alf died while attempting to rob the warehouse, but I believe the opposite: that he died while trying to prevent a robbery.'

"'Can this really be true, sir?' she asked.

"'So I believe. But in order to prove his innocence, I need some more information. Do you know either Daniel Wolfe or Dick Cross?'

"At the mention of these names, Mrs. Street pulled a face. 'They're villains, both of them,' she said. 'Neither of them's ever done an honest day's work in their lives. It was them as got Alf into trouble in the first place. And when they'd got him into trouble, they left him there and lied about him. They both said he'd organized the robbery himself, which wasn't true, and said they'd had nothing to do with it – and that wasn't true, neither.'

"'Do you know where either of these men are living now?'

"'Not exactly. I see them about sometimes. I think Wolfe lives in Peterborough Street – that's the third turning on the left down the road – and Cross lives in Swansea Street – that's a bit further down on the other side.'

"'Does either of them own a horse and cart?'

"'Wolfe has a cart. I've seen him on it. I think he hires a horse from somebody when he needs it. He goes out collecting old rubbish, but I think that's just an excuse to look into people's backyards to see if there's anything there worth stealing.'

"'Did Alf see much of either of them after he was released from prison?' I asked.

"'No, he didn't. He avoided them. To be honest, he hated them for what they'd done to him and what they'd done to other people.'

"'Do you know if there is any other man associated with them?'

"'I don't think so,' she replied with a frown. 'Except,' she added, 'a young lad, David Webster, who I've seen about with them a few times. He's only about seventeen or eighteen. I remember Alf mentioning him to me one day and saying what a fool he was. 'Wolfe and Cross will only get him into trouble,' he said, 'and then abandon him, like they did with me.' Alf was really angry about it, I remember. I've hardly ever seen him so upset about anything.'

"I thanked her and made a note of this information, all of which strengthened my own hypothesis of what had happened on Monday evening. My view, you see, Watson, was that something quite out of the ordinary must have occurred to lead Barnes to enter that warehouse. If you will put yourself in Barnes's shoes for a moment, you will see what I mean. Here is a man with a criminal record, who has served time in prison. Should he see a crime in progress, his natural inclination will be to keep well clear of it and pretend he has seen nothing, for he will fear that should the authorities make any connection between him and the crime, however mistaken and unfair, they will not believe him, but will pursue him and hound him until he is back in prison again. And yet, despite this perfectly understandable inclination to prudence, Barnes, as I believe, saw something which caused him to enter the warehouse and thus put his own freedom in jeopardy. What could this have been? It must, I believe, have been something more compelling than simply a door that was ajar."

"What, then?"

"I believe he saw Cross and Wolfe with the young lad, Webster. We know from Mrs. Street's testimony how angry Barnes was at the way the older men were corrupting Webster and leading him astray; perhaps he entered the warehouse to give them a piece of his mind on the subject, and to try to get Webster to leave."

"From what we have heard, that certainly sounds possible," I agreed. "And then, no doubt, in the ensuing quarrel, one of them – Cross or Wolfe – pushed him off the walkway."

Holmes nodded. "That is what I believe happened," said he. "Having reached this conclusion, I made to leave, but Mrs. Street was keen to talk, so I stayed a little longer. 'It must have been difficult for you when Alf was locked up,' I said to her.

"She nodded. 'It weren't easy. But I do washing and ironing for other folk, and just about scrape by.'

"'Have you seen much of Alf since he got out?'

"'Every week, on his day off, he'd come round here, regular as clockwork. We used to chat, and he'd often slip me a bit of money if he could afford it. I told him he was welcome to move back in here any time, and it would be cheaper for all of us if he did, but he wouldn't hear of it. He loved to see Vicky, but he was terrified she would find out that he was her father and he'd been in prison.'

"'I understand. You probably haven't heard, but Alf had some money with him when he died, in a pouch he kept with him all the time. I believe, from what he said just before he died, that he wanted your daughter to have it.'

"'That'd be just like Alf,' said she, biting her lip and dabbing her eyes again.

"'At the moment, though,' I said, 'the police are looking after the money, and we can't do anything about it. But I should think that when I've got the whole matter sorted out we'll be able to convince the authorities that you and Victoria are the rightful recipients of it.'

"'Thank you, sir,' said she.

"'Don't mention it,' said I. 'It is I who should thank you. Your information has been very helpful to me. I'm going back to the police station now, and, with a little luck, should be able to get the police off the wrong track and onto the right track before the day is out.'

"I left her then, Watson, and made my way through the drab, foggy streets to the police station, considering that my day so far had been well spent. I had made several bold conjectures, and all of them had proved correct. As I mentioned before, my opinion was that Barnes's use of hair-dye would not have been sufficient to prevent those who knew him from recognizing him. It might be, however, I conjectured, for a child who was too young to remember him from before his time in prison. But I doubted that he would have been too concerned about what a child thought of him unless that child were his own. If that were the case, the child might well have the same unusual hair as he had, and if Barnes wished to conceal the relationship between the two of them, his use of the hair-dye to alter the appearance of his own hair would be perfectly explained. Furthermore, if this child I had hypothesised really did exist, then it would surely be the most natural recipient for the money Barnes had asked PC Dobbs to take. Perhaps, then, I conjectured further, his repeated references to 'Victoria Street' were not to the thoroughfare in the West End, nor any other thoroughfare, but to a person, namely the child herself, a daughter by the name of Victoria. This was certainly possible, I judged, for 'Street' is a not uncommon surname.

"But what, then, I wondered could be the meaning of the 'one hundred and forty-one' which he also repeated several times? Most likely, I thought, it was indeed a house-number, in some other street which Barnes had failed to specify, either because in his distraction he forgot or because it seemed to him too obvious to need mentioning. Now, his daughter must live in the same district as Barnes himself, I reasoned – there would be no point in his attempting to disguise his hair otherwise – and the only residential street in those parts long enough to contain a house-number as large as 141 is Montgomery Road. That, then, was the house I was seeking when I left Beckman Street and set off up that long road. Now, encouraged by my success in finding the correct 'Victoria Street', and by the information her mother had given me, I was confident that my theory as to what had occurred on Monday evening was the correct one, that Barnes had been innocently walking home from work at his usual time and by his usual route when he had chanced to see something which had caused him to believe that Wolfe, Cross and the young lad, Webster, were engaged in robbing the warehouse. This, I believe, was the reason he entered the warehouse, where he probably quarrelled with them over their corruption of young Webster, and ended up by being pushed from the walkway to his death, as you suggested, Watson. The other three had then, I conjectured, made their escape on their builder's cart, with the stolen furs stuffed into those empty sand and cement sacks which PC Dobbs saw but did not examine. As far as I could see, this theory was the only one which not only solved the crime, but explained all the puzzling details.

"When I reached the police station, I found that Inspector Lestrade was already there, in confabulation with Inspector Stanley. Lestrade informed me that he had ascertained that none of the tenants of 141 Victoria Street in Westminster had ever had occasion to use Bailey Brother's warehouse in Dartmouth Street, nor any other in that vicinity. This, as you will appreciate, came as little surprise to me, but I waited patiently until he had finished his account, before beginning my own. At first, he and Inspector Stanley were disinclined to believe my theory, chiefly, so it seemed to me, because they had not thought of it themselves, but as I explained my reasoning – the details of which I have described to you – they were at length forced to agree that my account of the matter was almost certainly the correct one.

“Having reached agreement, we then discussed what was to be done. I argued that they should waste no time in getting search warrants for the premises occupied by the three men I believed had been involved in the robbery. My view was that they would have heard that Barnes had died and, realising that any arrest might therefore involve a capital charge, would probably have been too afraid to try to dispose of the stolen furs, and would very likely, therefore, still have them. And that, Watson, is that. Whether Lestrade and Stanley have yet been able to organize a search party, and, if so, whether they have met with any success, I have no idea.”

It was after eight o’clock that evening when there came a ring at our doorbell. A moment later, Inspector Lestrade bustled into our sitting room.

“You look pleased with yourself, Lestrade,” remarked Holmes with a chuckle.

“So I should be,” returned the policeman with a broad smile, seating himself on the chair I had pulled up for him in front of the fire. “I thought that as you had taken part in our discussion earlier, Mr. Holmes, I would let you know how we got on. You recall the plan Inspector Stanley and I decided upon, to make a thorough search of the houses of those villains, Wolfe, Cross and Webster?”

“Indeed I do,” replied Holmes with another chuckle.

“We managed to get the necessary warrants a couple of hours after you had gone, and set off with four of the biggest constables in the division, just in case there should be any trouble. Our search didn’t get off to a very good start, though: We turned Cross’s house and outbuildings upside-down without finding anything, and then had no more luck at Wolfe’s place. We didn’t have young Webster’s address, so I asked Wolfe what it was.

“‘Who?’ says he. ‘Webster? Never heard of him.’

“‘Yes, you have, Dan,’ said his wife, who was there and who, I could see, just wanted to be rid of us as quickly as possible. She started to tell us the address, and her husband started shouting at her and then launched as vicious an attack on her as I have ever seen. I had to use the truncheon on him to quiet him down, and I can't say it troubled me to do so. Besides, it gave me an excuse to arrest him there and then and not wait any longer. He's a nasty piece of work, Mr. Holmes, and it will be good for everybody if he's taken out of circulation for a while.

"We made our way to the address we'd been given. Of course, Webster denied knowing anything about the business, just as the other two had done, but it didn't take us long to find the evidence that proved him a liar. In a coal-shed, in the yard behind the house, we found half a dozen cement sacks stuffed full of the stolen furs, which proved, of course, that our theory was exactly right in every detail."

"Congratulations!" cried Holmes. "It sounds as if you have brought the case to a successful conclusion!"

"I certainly have," returned the policeman, whose chest seemed to swell with pride at Holmes's praise. "All these villains are now safely locked up at the station. They are being questioned separately, and I don't think it will be long before they're singing like canaries, each of them blaming the others in order to save his own skin. There is no honour among thieves, you know!"

When Lestrade had left us, I turned to my friend. "Why," I cried indignantly, "the cheek of the man! He refers to 'their' plan and 'their' theory, when it was you who had suggested it all to them in the first place! I am surprised you did not say something to correct him!"

Holmes threw his head back and roared with laughter for several minutes, until he was almost limp with the effort. "My dear fellow!" said he at last. "You have been good enough to take an interest in my work in the last year or two. You should therefore have learnt by now that there is no necessary connection between he who does all the work and he who receives all the praise. It is for this reason that in such cases –

and there are many of them – the work itself must be its own reward, and I must be satisfied with that!"

Lestrade's prediction, that the villains would inform against each other in an attempt to avoid conviction, proved accurate. In particular, the young lad, encouraged to do so by his family, turned Queen's evidence against the two men who had sought to take advantage of his youthful gullibility and inexperience. As a result, both Wolfe and Cross received lengthy prison sentences. On the capital charge concerning the death of Alf Barnes, they were acquitted, the jury finding the evidence insufficient to prove that either of them had had the intention of causing his death. Barnes himself was completely exonerated of any involvement in the crime, and, in due course, the money he had been saving for his wife and daughter was handed over to them, as we learnt from a touching letter which was received at Baker Street some months later from Barnes's widow, Mrs. Street.

THE INN ON THE MARSH

IN GLANCING OVER THE RECORDS I kept during the time I shared chambers with my eminent friend, the renowned detective, Mr. Sherlock Holmes, I am struck by the many occasions on which what appeared at the outset to be but a trivial affair became, in the end, a deadly serious investigation. Not infrequently, too, a case which began in London would oblige us to travel far beyond the capital and deep into the countryside in search of a solution. The case associated with The Wild Goose of Welborne, which I shall now recount, provides a good illustration of both of these points.

It was a pleasant, breezy day during the first week of September, 1883, the sort of weather that seems to freshen the air after the heat of the summer, and freshen, too, one's own energies and aspirations. Holmes and I had both spent the morning endeavouring to tidy and bring order to the sheaves of papers and documents which had built up on every surface during the previous months. We were about to take lunch, satisfied with our morning's work, when a ring at the doorbell announced a visitor. A moment later, our landlady ushered a young couple into our sitting-room, announced as Mr. and Mrs. Philip Whittle.

"I am sorry to intrude if you are eating," the young man said in an apologetic tone, "but this was the only time I could get away from work to see you."

"Not at all," returned Holmes affably, putting down his knife and fork and standing up from the table. "One can eat at any time. I had much rather hear what it is that has brought you here to see us."

"We have had a very odd experience," said the young man, as he and his wife seated themselves on the chairs I brought forward. "We cannot think what to make of it."

"The details, if you please," said Holmes.

"It is soon enough told. We stayed recently for a few days at an old inn, The Wild Goose, which lies in the marshland near the north Norfolk coast. It is the second time we have stayed there. The first time was at the beginning of June, when we stayed there for a week."

"Upon the occasion of your honeymoon, no doubt."

The young man looked surprised. "Yes, it was, as a matter of fact," said he, "but how did *you* know?"

Sherlock Holmes chuckled in that odd, noiseless fashion which was peculiar to him. "Since your wife removed her gloves, she has been displaying two very fine rings upon the third finger of her left hand. One is undoubtedly a wedding ring, and the other, with a sparkling stone in it, is no doubt an engagement ring. They both appear relatively new and shiny, and, moreover, the wedding ring is still a little loose, as is apparent when your wife touches it with the fingers of her other hand, which she has done several times already. It demands no great leap of logic to surmise that your wedding took place not very long ago, and that your week's holiday in Norfolk constituted your honeymoon."

The young lady flushed to the roots of her hair.

"I apologize for alluding to your personal circumstances," said Holmes quickly in an urbane tone. "It is a little hobby of mine – trifling and no doubt silly – to deduce facts about people from their personal appearance."

"That is perfectly all right," said Mrs. Whittle with a little smile.

"Such a hobby may prove useful in this case, if it helps you get to the bottom of the matter," remarked Whittle. "We were married at the very end of May, and immediately took a week's holiday in Norfolk, as you surmised. One or two of my married friends had spent their honeymoons at the seaside, at Margate, Brighton and places like that, but my fancy was for somewhere a little quieter, and Prudence agreed. When we heard from a cousin of mine of The Wild Goose, on the Welborne Marsh in Norfolk, it sounded ideal. It is a wild and beautiful spot, very popular with bird-watchers, I understand, as it is a haven for birds of all kinds. We spent most of the week there, in walks over the countryside or by the sea, and when we moved to Cromer, for the last two days of our holiday – even though Cromer itself is a quiet, charming and select sort of seaside town – it seemed to us very noisy and bustling compared with where we had been staying.

"We had enjoyed our stay at The Wild Goose so much that when the opportunity arose recently to take another brief holiday, both Prudence and I at once thought of returning there. We therefore travelled down to Norfolk last Friday, and stayed until Monday morning. However, the pleasure of being there, which we had been looking forward to so much, was marred by one odd little circumstance. As I was entering our details in the register, I turned the pages back to see the entries for the beginning of June, with Prudence looking over my shoulder. You will appreciate, no doubt, that the occasion of our honeymoon meant a lot to us both, and the urge to see 'Mr. and Mrs. Whittle' written somewhere for the first time was irresistible. Imagine our astonishment and dismay, then, to see that on the week in question there was no trace of our names whatsoever! Of course, I looked on the page before and the page after, but we were not there. Our names had simply vanished from the book completely, as if our visit to The Wild Goose had never taken place!"

Holmes rubbed his hands together in delight, a look of interest on his face.

"Did it appear to you that a page had been removed from the book?" he asked.

Whittle shook his head. "Perhaps it had, but if so, it must have been done very neatly, for I didn't notice anything of the sort. Besides, there were other names written in on the dates we had stayed there. It was not that everyone's name had disappeared from that week, just ours."

"Did you recognize any of these other names?"

"No, but I scarcely knew the name of anyone else that was staying there. We rather kept ourselves to ourselves, if you know what I mean, when we were there in June. As a matter of fact, it was very quiet then, anyway; there were very few other people staying there. I understand it gets much busier during the wild-fowling season. But the register now shows that a Miss Stebbing, a Mr. and Mrs. Williams and a Mr. and Mrs. Myers were staying there at the same time as we were, and I don't remember any of those people."

"Did you mention the matter to anyone at the inn?"

"I certainly did. I mentioned it to the girl who was attending us as we signed in. But she said she had only worked there for a month and didn't know anything about it. 'If you've got any questions,' she said, 'you'll have to ask Mr. Trunch.'"

"He being the landlord?"

"Exactly. I raised the matter with him that evening. He said he couldn't remember as far back as June. 'I have lots of visitors coming and going all the time,' he said. 'You can't expect me to remember everyone.' I pointed out to him that his memory was not the issue. Rather, it was the disappearance of our names from his register. He then suggested that we must be mistaken. 'I don't think you were ever here at all,' he said, and suggested that we had, rather, stayed at The Old Duck, which lies about three miles distant, across the marsh. Of course, it is ridiculous to suppose that a man could forget in three months where he had spent the very first holiday with his wife, but when I pointed that out to him, he became very irritable and almost abusive, and I had to let the matter drop. I must say his manner quite spoiled our memory of our previous visit there."

"It is certainly an odd experience," remarked Sherlock Holmes after a moment, "but there may be some rational explanation for it. Perhaps, for instance, a jug of water was accidentally spilled onto the register, rendering some of the pages illegible, including the one on which your names were written. Then, perhaps in attempting to rewrite the page from memory, someone has simply failed to recall your name. It may be that the 'Mr. and Mrs. Williams' which is now written in the book was someone's attempt to remember your name. Of course, that would not explain the landlord's unpleasant manner towards you. One would imagine that if such an explanation were the case, he would simply have informed you of the fact. But perhaps he has an unusually poor memory, and is embarrassed about it. Perhaps he drinks heavily. If so, he wouldn't be the first landlord of a remote country pub to consume all the profits in liquid measures, and I understand that excessive drinking has a very detrimental effect on the memory. Or is there something else?" he enquired, eyeing the young man closely.

Whittle nodded. "There has been a further development, which we have both found very upsetting, and for which such simple explanations cannot account."

"Very well. Pray proceed."

"We returned to London on Monday, having enjoyed our few days away despite the inauspicious beginning. Yesterday morning, however, this letter arrived by the first post." As he spoke, the young man took an envelope from his inside pocket and passed it to Holmes, who took from it a single sheet of paper which he unfolded upon his knee and studied intently for a few moments.

"What do you make of it, Watson?" said he, as he passed the letter to me and turned his attention to the envelope. The note, which was not signed, was a brief one, written in black ink in the centre of an oddly square-shaped sheet of paper, and ran as follows:

> Asking many questions can be a dangerous course. Keep out of matters that do not concern you, and mind your business. This is a warning to you.

"What a very unpleasant and menacing letter!" I remarked to Whittle. "I am not surprised it has upset you both."

"It was posted in central London," said Holmes, "so it is unlikely to have come directly from the landlord of The Wild

Goose himself. But the information that you have been 'asking questions' must surely have come from him, so he is evidently in communication with someone in London. The paper is unusually thick and heavy, and is an odd size. I wonder–"

He took his lens from the shelf and examined the letter closely through it. "Something has been cut off the top of the sheet," he said, "probably a printed heading which included an address. It has been carelessly done, though: there are a couple of tiny black marks at the top edge, where the scissors have clipped the bottom of a row of printed letters. There seems something familiar about it. Let me see–"

He sprang from his chair and began rummaging through the piles of old letters on his desk, which he had spent the morning putting in order. Presently he selected one and held it up beside the letter Whittle had received. "This is a letter of thanks I received from a client to whom I had been of service a few months ago," he said. "I think it is the same. Yes, undoubtedly it is the same. See," he continued, passing the sheets to our visitors. "The type of paper is a precise match, and the little traces of a line of printing that the scissors have left correspond exactly to this line on the other sheet."

"But that letter is from the German embassy!" I cried in astonishment, as I leaned over to verify his observations. "I cannot believe the German embassy would send such a crude threatening letter to Mr. and Mrs. Whittle! And why should they, anyway?"

Holmes nodded. "The Germans may be a forceful people, but – in my experience, at least – they like things to be done in a legal and proper manner. There is evidently nothing official about this letter. I imagine that someone employed at the embassy, acting on his own initiative, and without official sanction, has simply used a sheet of official notepaper as it was to hand, having cut the top couple of inches off to preserve, as he hoped, his anonymity."

"Then it is of no help to us in solving the problem."

"I should not say that, Watson. It confirms, after all, our suspicions that the writer of the note is probably a foreigner, as suggested by his incorrect rendering of the common idiom, 'mind your own business.' Can you recall, Mr. Whittle, if there were any foreigners staying at The Wild Goose at the time of your first visit there?"

"Yes," replied Whittle. "Now you mention it, I do recollect that there were two men there who I thought were probably foreign. One was middle-aged, with close-cropped sandy hair and a very large moustache, the other was a young fellow, about my own age, a little on the plump side. They kept very much to themselves and never spoke to us, but I overheard them talking once or twice. Sometimes they spoke in English, but with very strong accents, and sometimes in a foreign language. It may have been German for all I know – I am not familiar with that language, so I can't say."

"We thought they were probably keen bird-watchers," added Mrs. Whittle. "The landlord had told us that people come from all over Europe to study the birds on the Welborne Marsh."

"One evening when we were eating," Whittle continued, "a third man arrived and joined them at their table, a tall man with a bald head, and they all talked together very quietly. Later that evening, when we were in bed, I heard what sounded like a quarrel developing downstairs – raised voices and so on – and I remember wondering if it were those foreigners, but I fell asleep and heard no more."

"Nor me," added Mrs. Whittle. "Later in the night, though, I was abruptly awakened by a strange loud cry, as of pain or fear, and thought at first that it had come from downstairs. But when I mentioned it to the landlord in the morning, he said it was probably an owl, or one of the marshland birds, some of which have very strange cries that can sound almost human, he said."

"Anyway," continued Whittle, "the two foreign gentlemen left the next day, soon after breakfast. We didn't see the third man at all, so we presumed he'd left earlier, before we got up."

Holmes nodded his head and sat in silent thought for some time.

"I shall look into the matter for you," said he at length, addressing his visitors, "and let you know what I discover. As for the unpleasant letter you have received, I should not worry too much about it. It is a warning, after all, and not a direct threat, probably designed simply to deter you from asking any further questions. If you go about your daily business in your usual way, I don't think you will be troubled. However, it cannot hurt to observe due caution. Keep your eyes and ears open at all times, and avoid lonely places and dark alleyways."

When Mr. and Mrs. Whittle had left, Holmes hurried through his lunch and went out immediately afterwards. He returned two hours later, but there was a look of disappointment on his features.

"I have been scouring the back issues of the daily papers," he explained to me as he threw himself into an armchair by the hearth and took his old clay pipe from the rack. "My reasoning was that as the menacing letter had been posted in London and written on a sheet of paper from the German embassy, then the mystery was as much connected with London as it was with Norfolk, and the solution might as well be found here as there. However, all my efforts have uncovered precisely nothing, which is a somewhat frustrating result, although not so uncommon as you may suppose when you are compiling those records you keep of my successes."

"I don't imagine it helped that you didn't really know what you were looking for."

"A perceptive remark," said my friend, nodding his head. "I have looked closely at all the newspapers that appeared in the last week of May and the first week of June without finding anything there which refers in any relevant way to the German Empire, the Norfolk coast, German visitors to this country – whether to Norfolk or elsewhere – or anything else which might possibly have a bearing on the problem. However, I have learned one thing this afternoon."

"What is that?"

"That the Whittles were followed here earlier."

"How do you know?"

"Because I myself am now being followed. I observed the same man in three different places. I have no idea who he is, but he was clearly watching my every move."

"What will you do?"

"I think I shall run down to Norfolk and look into matters there. There are local papers there which may contain reports which did not reach the London Press. Perhaps I shall find some suggestive fact there. Unfortunately," he continued, with a glance at the clock, "although I could get down to Norwich this evening, it would be too late to do anything by the time I got there. I am thus obliged to sit here doing nothing until tomorrow, and I hate wasting time in this way."

I laughed, and my friend turned to me with a raised eyebrow. "I know what you are thinking, Watson," said he, "that you have never known a man to waste time in as thorough-going a fashion as I do on occasion. It is true. I do not deny it. If a national championship in time-wasting were to be held, I should probably set a new all-comers record. But that is when I have no case to engage my brain. When I am on a case, it is a different matter, and it is infuriating not to be able to get on as quickly as I would wish."

"You could go down to Norwich this evening, anyway," I suggested after a moment. "You could lodge for the night somewhere in the city centre, and make an early start in the morning."

"Of course, you are quite right, old man. That is the sensible course of action. It is only tiredness and irritation that prevented my seeing it. I will take your advice, Watson, on one condition."

"What is that?"

"That you accompany me."

"I should be delighted to do so. I was thinking only the other day that it would be pleasant to get away from London for a day or two before the nights start closing in."

"Then it is settled," said he, putting his pipe down and springing from his chair with a renewed vigour, "although I can't promise that you will find our expedition the holiday you have been looking forward to, Watson." He pulled open the top drawer of his desk, and, taking out his revolver, began to examine the chambers, then he glanced my way. "Pack a bag, then, old fellow, and let us be off!"

We caught the early evening train, reached Norwich just before nine o'clock, and put up at a small hotel near the station. In the morning we rose early, took breakfast at the hotel, and were in the office of the local newspaper, the Eastern Daily Press, soon after it opened. There we learned that as well as the daily newspaper, several weekly papers were also published, containing news specific to particular parts of the county. Holmes selected the daily papers of late May and early June, while I looked through the weeklies. Most of the news was trivial, or of purely local interest, and I was beginning to doubt we should find anything even remotely relevant, when my companion abruptly stopped his rapid page-turning.

"Hello!" said he. "Here is something, Watson!"

I leaned over to see what had caught his eye, and read the following:

CROWN PRINCE VISITS SHOE FACTORY

> Prince Otto von Stamm, crown prince of Waldenstein, has this week visited a shoe factory in Norwich, where he was conducted round the premises in the company of the Lord Mayor, and was said to be greatly impressed by the modernity and efficiency he saw displayed there. Waldenstein has long been a notable producer of hides, but most are simply exported, and Prince Otto is keen to establish a leather-working industry within the principality to help alleviate the problem of unemployment.

"That sounds harmless and banal enough," I remarked.

"Yes, Watson, but it gives us, if not a German, then a German-speaker at least, in the county of Norfolk at the relevant time. Do you know anything of Prince Otto von Stamm?"

"He appears in the Society pages of the Morning Post fairly regularly," I replied. "I have frequently read such references as 'Prince Otto seems to prefer London to his homeland,' and 'We hear that Prince Otto has got himself into trouble again.' It is the usual sort of thing: a young foreign nobleman with more in his pockets than in his head. For some reason, London seems to act like a magnet to such people. I think he leads a fairly harum-scarum existence: visiting a shoe factory is the first sensible thing I've ever heard that he's done."

"Anything else?"

"Not really. I know he's fairly young – perhaps eight-and-twenty – but I know nothing else about him – and I know nothing whatever about Waldenstein, wherever that is."

"Waldenstein is one of those curiosities of European history," said Holmes. "It is one of the very few central European principalities which has not been swept up into the German Empire. It is very small – the population is probably not much greater than that of the town we are now in – and of no significance in itself. But its geographical position is a strategic one, lying adjacent as it does to both Germany and Austria. Its very existence creates a rivalry between the two great powers, both of which attempt to exercise an influence over it, and both of which would probably like to subsume it into their respective empires. Let us see if we can find anything else in these papers about Prince Otto's visit to Norfolk."

Our search for further reports on the young nobleman proved fruitless, but just as we were about to put the papers back in order, something caught my eye in one of the weeklies from the second week of June.

"This is a remarkable coincidence," I said.

"More on Prince Otto?"

"No, but a fellow-countryman of his, surprisingly enough." I folded the page over and read aloud the following report:

FOREIGN VISITOR PRESUMED LOST AT SEA

Franz Krankl, a visitor to Norfolk from the principality of Waldenstein, is missing, feared drowned, after a boat in which he had rowed out to sea on an angling expedition was found washed up on a beach near Sheringham. The owner of the boat, inn-keeper and part-time fisherman, Albert Trunch of Welborne, says he had warned Krankl of the dangerous currents off the north coast of Norfolk, but Krankl had insisted he was very experienced in small boats. Herr Krankl holds a senior position in the government of Waldenstein, but was apparently here alone on a private holiday, and had been out of touch with his relatives for some time. A statement issued by the coast guard makes the point that all visitors must be made aware that there is a very great difference between conditions on inland waters and those encountered at sea.

"That is it!" cried Holmes. "It must be! Whittle informed us that the landlord of The Wild Goose was called Trunch, and now here is Trunch again, connected to a mysterious disappearance."

"It is certainly a striking coincidence."

Holmes shook his head. "It cannot simply be coincidence, Watson. The odds against it are enormous. Rather, these separate events are all links in a long chain of cause and effect, which will lead us to the truth. Trunch is clearly a link, so is this man Krankl, and so, I believe, is Prince Otto von Stamm, for I feel certain that he was the younger of the two men that the Whittles saw at the inn. It is to conceal his presence there, I believe, that the register has been altered."

"But if you are right," I said as we left the newspaper offices, "and it is Prince Otto's presence at The Wild Goose that someone is trying to conceal, why should the warning note to the Whittles have come from the German embassy?"

"As I understand it," Holmes replied, "Waldenstein does not have its own diplomatic representation in London. I believe that the German embassy acts on Waldenstein's behalf when necessary, in an informal sort of way. But someone at the German embassy may also, of course, have his own reasons for keeping the truth concealed. Don't look now, old fellow, but I think we are being followed."

"Is it the same man you saw in London?"

"I believe so. Anyhow, I observed this one – a man with a large moustache – outside our hotel this morning, and now he is outside the newspaper office. Evidently he – or a confederate – followed us to the railway station in London yesterday evening."

"What shall we do?"

"Nothing – or, at least, nothing other than what we were going to do anyway, which is to catch a train to Cromer, and make our way along the coast to the Welborne Marsh. It will be interesting to see if he comes with us."

The short branch train was already standing at the platform when we entered the station. We took seats in the compartment nearest to the front of the train, and Holmes positioned himself by the window, so that he could see anyone that came onto the platform. For almost ten minutes, he had nothing to report, then, just as the guard walked past our carriage after a consultation with the engine driver, and it was evident he was returning to his position at the rear of the train to give the signal to start, Holmes gave the "view-halloa."

"There he is!" cried he. "He has just broken cover, run onto the platform carrying a large leather bag, and climbed into the last compartment! He is following us to the coast!"

We reached Cromer in a little over fifty minutes, and hurried from the train to make sure we secured the station fly. Of the man apparently following us, there was no sign.

"He is lying low in his compartment," said Holmes under his breath, as we rattled off along the road by the station. "I saw the crown of his hat through the window. He evidently has no idea we have seen him."

Our journey took us at first through undulating countryside, but presently descended to low-lying, marshy terrain, where the narrow road meandered like a snake past rivulets and creeks, never far from the mud-flats and the sea. From time to time we heard the sound of distant gunshots, and saw the little puffs of smoke rising up from the hollows where the wild-fowlers crouched, waiting for the birds to fly their way. At length, after about half an hour, we reached a small, isolated village, which I saw from a sign was Welborne. The wind was blowing sharply off the sea now, the clouds overhead were dark grey, and there were a few spots of rain in the air. Our driver did not pause, but passed right through the village and on towards the sea. Half a mile farther on, we at last reached The Wild Goose. It was a low, spreading building, with grimy lime-washed walls and a weathered-looking thatched roof, and appeared as ancient as the ground upon which it stood.

"We don't yet have all the threads in our hands," said Holmes to me, when we had paid off our driver and stood before the weather-beaten front door of the inn, above which a painted sign depicting a flying goose swung and creaked in the wind. "We shall therefore have to approach the matter in an oblique way. If in doubt, just follow my lead."

He pushed open the door, and I followed him into the dark interior. After a moment, a young woman in an apron appeared through a doorway, but when Holmes asked if we might speak to the landlord, she informed us that he was out, and would not be back for another hour. We decided then to leave our bags at the inn and take a walk across the marsh towards the sea.

It was a wild, tempestuous day now, and the nearer we approached the sea, the stronger the wind became, and the more the gusts seemed to veer and shift about us. At length we surmounted a steep shingle bank, and there before us lay the broad, heaving expanse of ocean, the breakers pounding the shore with a boom and a crash, sending mountains of spray into the air which the sharp wind whipped into our faces. I opened my mouth to speak, but abandoned the attempt almost at once: the thunderous noise of the sea blotted out all other sounds. After we had stood shivering for a few minutes by this deafening maelstrom, Holmes plucked my sleeve and indicated that we should retire behind the shelter of the shingle bank.

"The sea is very rough today," said he as we crouched down in the lee of the bank. "I suppose you were reflecting on the conditions the unfortunate Herr Krankl may have encountered."

"Among other things, yes."

"I should not trouble yourself with that thought, Watson. As I read the matter, Krankl was never in a boat at all. I strongly suspect he lost his life at The Wild Goose, on the evening the Whittles heard a quarrel there."

"You believe he was the third man, the tall man who arrived one evening, but was nowhere to be seen the following morning?"

"That does seem to me the likeliest explanation. But, come, let us get back to the inn, and see if Trunch has returned yet."

At The Wild Goose, in answer to our query, Trunch himself appeared after a moment from some back room. He was an absolute giant of a man, a good six-foot-four if he was an inch, with a chest like an ox. For a moment he stood looking down upon us with an expression of disdain.

"Well?" said he at length.

"A friend of mine stayed here not long ago," Holmes began.

"What of it?"

"When he came again more recently, he found that his name had been removed from the register."

"Oh, *him!* A snivelling trouble-maker from London! If you're on the same errand, you can sling your hook!"

He made to turn away, but Holmes persisted:

"It is, of course, a criminal offence to fraudulently alter books used for accounting purposes. The authorities take a dim view of that sort of thing."

"Oh, *do* they? What is that to you, Mr. Know-all? Are you one of those blood-sucking tax-collectors yourself? No? Then listen, friend, and I'll tell you what my father told me when I was a young man. 'Mark my words, son,' he said to me: 'there's always some swine wanting money, and the best way of dealing with them is to tell them to go to Hell.'"

Sherlock Holmes remained unmoved. "Something else you may not be aware of is that to attempt to conceal something criminal is itself a crime. In attempting such concealment you also lay yourself open to being charged as an accessory to the original crime, even if you had nothing directly to do with it."

"Just what are you saying?" demanded Trunch. His voice was still loud and scornful, but there was a note in it now, too, of apprehension, and it was clear that Holmes's remarks had had an effect. Holmes himself evidently perceived this, for he quickly pressed home his advantage.

"We know that Prince Otto von Stamm was here, and the other men."

"What if they were?" said Trunch defiantly, but the tone of bluster in his voice was rapidly ebbing away, and it was clear he was on the defensive.

"Whatever occurred here, you, as landlord, will be held responsible–"

"What humbug!"

"–especially as you helped conceal the truth by fraudulently altering the register."

"Someone else pulled out the page. I had to re-write it from memory. There's no crime in that. What else could I do?"

"But you didn't put all the names in again, did you? You deliberately omitted some."

Trunch's bullying manner had quite disappeared now. It is difficult to say what might have happened next, but we were interrupted by the re-appearance of the young serving-woman.

She whispered something to the landlord and he nodded his head. “Come this way,” he said to us, “and I’ll tell you what happened.”

We followed him through the doorway, along a corridor and into a back room. As we entered, I saw a large leather bag lying open on a side-table. Holmes evidently saw it, too, for I saw him glance that way and stop. But it was too late, the door slammed shut behind us. We turned, to see a man with a large, straggling moustache, who had been concealed behind the open door. In his hands was a large double-barrelled shotgun, which he pointed at us.

“Leave them to me, Trunch,” he said in a strong, guttural accent. “I’ll deal with them.” He yanked open a back door and indicated we should go out that way.

“Now,” said he, when we were outside in a small backyard, the cold wind whistling about our ears, “start walking.” All about us as we left the yard, the Welborne Marsh stretched away as far as the eye could see.

“Don’t be a fool,” said Holmes over his shoulder, as we followed a muddy, winding track. “If it’s your intention to murder us here on the marsh, you’ll never get away with it.”

“You forget, Mr. Busybody, that the wild-fowling season has now begun,” returned our captor from behind me. Even as he spoke there came the sound of gunshots – one, two, three – from all about us on the marsh. “Your deaths will be ascribed to an unfortunate sporting accident. Sadly, such things do happen.”

“You murdering swine,” I cried. “Don’t think we don’t know about Krankl! Soon everyone will know the truth!”

For an instant he was silent, but it was only for an instant. “So,” he cried, in a voice full of venom. “If you’re so interested in Krankl, I can show you where he is lying, and then you can join him there! Keep walking!” he snarled, thrusting the shotgun sharply into my back. My mind reeled. There must be something we could do – we could not simply walk quietly to our deaths – but panic had seized me, and I could think of nothing.

Ahead of me, Holmes walked on steadily, his shoulders hunched against the cold wind, his hands thrust into his coat pockets, as we made our way deeper into the wilderness of the marsh. "Slippery path, this one, Watson," said he over his shoulder. "Mind you don't lose your footing!"

For a brief moment, I confess I was surprised that, in our desperate situation, Holmes should make such a banal remark. Next moment, I realised that he was telling me he wished me to slip and fall to the ground, perhaps as a distraction. How that would help us, I could not imagine, but if that was what he wanted me to do, then that is what I would do.

A short distance further on, as the path breasted a small rise and dropped away into a shallow dip, I saw my opportunity. I deliberately let my left foot slide away in the mud, and, with a loud cry, tumbled to the ground. At once our captor lowered his shotgun and pointed it at me, but in the same instant there came the sharp crack of a pistol-shot. Holmes's hands were still in his pockets, and I realised he had turned and fired his revolver through the fabric of his overcoat. There came a cry of pain from our captor, as the shot caught him on the left arm, and he raised the shotgun towards Holmes. With every ounce of energy in my body, I sprang up and threw myself upon him, forcing the barrels of his gun upwards and to the side. The movement evidently jerked his finger against the triggers, and both barrels discharged with a deafening roar into the open sky above us, then, with a force I would not have believed myself capable of, I swung my fist up and struck him on the chin with the most perfect uppercut I have ever delivered, sending him sprawling backwards into the mud. I quickly picked up the gun which he had dropped as he fell, as Holmes covered him, his revolver held rock-steady in his hand.

"Good man," said my friend to me. "Your swift action saved us all. Are you all right?"

"I think I may have depressed the knuckle of my third finger," I remarked as I examined my right hand, wincing with pain as I touched the spot. "It will probably need setting. I am not much used to fisticuffs."

There came a cry from behind us. I turned, to see a young man hurrying towards us down the path from The Wild Goose. "Stop! Stop!" he cried, waving his arms in the air. As he came nearer I recognized him from pictures I had seen in the illustrated London papers as Prince Otto himself. "Stop at once!" he cried as he came up to us, breathing heavily, his cheeks flushed with effort. "I want no more violence on my account, Schnabel. I have decided to make a clean breast of everything. After all, it *was* an accident."

"Be quiet, you fool!" said the other man in a harsh tone, as he struggled unsteadily to his feet. "How did you get here?"

"I learned late last night in London where you had gone, and caught the first train I could this morning."

"Tell us about the accident you referred to," said Holmes, covering both of them with his pistol. "It is, I take it, to do with Krankl, and Waldenstein's foreign policy."

"Don't tell them anything," said Schnabel quickly, but Stamm ignored him.

"You appear well informed already," said he to us, "so you may be aware that my country has recently been in discussion with Austria, with a view to linking our future to theirs. This is the course long favoured by my father and his chief minister, Franz Krankl. However, Herr Schnabel here has been arguing on behalf of the German Empire that the better course is for us to favour his country. My father is frail and may not have much longer to live. When he dies and I succeed him, the decision will of course be mine, so it is something I must think about now.

"I was in this part of the country anyway, for some duty I had to perform, so Herr Schnabel and I arranged to meet for secret discussions at the most remote spot we could find, The Wild Goose. Unfortunately, Herr Krankl, who was also in

England, got wind of what we had planned, and hurried here to try to dissuade me from this course of action. He arrived one evening and we quarrelled. I had had too much to drink, I admit, and was quite drunk. In the heat of the quarrel, I am ashamed to say, I lost my temper and struck out at him, he fell from his chair and hit his head so hard on the corner of the hearth that it killed him. Herr Schnabel here ushered me from the room – I was in no fit state to do anything sensible – and said he would deal with the matter. He disposed of the body somewhere on the marsh, and later bribed the inn-keeper, Trunch, to say that we had never been here, and that Krankl had hired his boat, put out to sea alone in it, and appeared to have been lost overboard."

"You have made a serious mistake," said Holmes.

"I know," returned Stamm. "I am ashamed of myself, both for being drunk, and for losing my temper with Krankl."

"That was not my meaning," said Holmes. "Your mistake was in permitting Schnabel to dispose of the body. Don't you see that that places you completely in his power? At any time in the future he could, by threatening to expose the truth, blackmail you into doing precisely what he wished you to do."

"Don't listen to him, your Highness," cried Schnabel.

"I imagine that that has been his intention all along," continued Holmes, ignoring the other man's outburst, "to have this hold over you, so that he could force you to do his bidding, as a puppet-master controls his puppets. On the night Krankl was here, he saw his chance and seized it."

"It's a lie!" cried Schnabel.

"You don't even know for certain that Krankl was really dead when you left the room," Holmes persisted. "Perhaps he was only stunned, and was finished off later by Schnabel, after you had gone to bed. It would of course suit his purposes perfectly to be rid of Krankl, who was a staunch proponent of the Austrian alliance."

"That's lie number two!" interrupted Schnabel, his voice hoarse, but Holmes's words had evidently plucked a cord in the young nobleman's memory.

"I had wondered about that," he said, "wondered if I had really killed him or not. For even in my shamefully drunken state, I had noticed that Krankl's wound did not appear to be bleeding at all, and nor was there any sign of blood on the floor the following morning."

Abruptly, the infuriated Schnabel attempted to launch an attack on Holmes, but the latter levelled his pistol at him and he gave it up at once.

"The only way to decide the matter is to examine the body," said Holmes. "Schnabel says it is buried out this way on the marsh. Will you show us where it is?" he asked, turning to the German.

"No. You can find it yourself," Schnabel responded.

"Your lack of co-operation is disappointing," remarked Holmes. "I had only permitted you to drag us out here in the hope that you would lead us to where the unfortunate Herr Krankl lies buried. However, we shall find it soon enough. First, though, I think we'll all get back to the inn, and notify the authorities of what has occurred."

When we reached The Wild Goose, Trunch was nowhere to be seen, but his absence was soon explained, as the serving-girl informed us that he had gone to fetch the local constable, after declaring with great vehemence that he wished he had never become involved with these people. Just a few minutes later we heard a trap pull up outside the inn and Trunch entered, with a policeman who was almost as massive as Trunch himself. Holmes quickly explained to the policeman all that had taken place. This interview ended with Schnabel in handcuffs, and he and von Stamm going off with Trunch and the constable.

"I can't imagine what Mr. and Mrs. Whittle will think when they learn what you have discovered," I remarked to Holmes later that day, as we took lunch at a hotel in Cromer.

My friend chuckled. "Yes, it will certainly be strange for them to discover that as their honeymoon was taking its no doubt blissfully happy course, they were, all unaware, sharing a roof with international intrigue and murder!"

I heard later that the body of Franz Krankl had been recovered from a shallow grave on the marsh, but the medical examination and inquest which followed proved inconclusive. The cause of death was established with certainty as being the wound to the head, but the medical examiner stated that he could not be certain whether Krankl had been struck once, or more than once, and in the end a verdict of accidental death was recorded. Trunch, Schnabel and von Stamm were all convicted on their own admission of attempting to conceal the death, but taking various circumstances into account, and with no doubt half an eye on the diplomatic aspects of the case, the court took a lenient view and handed down relatively light sentences. Trunch therefore returned, no doubt a chastened man, to the inn on the marsh where he continued to cater for the needs of keen bird-watchers, and von Stamm and Schnabel returned to their homelands, and never, so far as I am aware, visited these shores again.

THE GREEN UMBRELLA

IN THE EARLY SPRING OF 1888, a remarkable series of bizarre and perplexing cases was laid before my friend, Mr. Sherlock Holmes, for solution. Among the headings in my notebooks for this period, I find recorded the singular problem of "The Oaken Door"; the baffling affair of "The Second Stair," a case in which several of the oldest families of the kingdom were involved so intimately; and the mysterious disappearance from the Scottish Express of the Barrington brothers and the Star of Golconda diamond, *en route* from London to Glasgow. Even in a period such as this, there were occasional days of frustrating inactivity, but for much of the time my friend was as busy as I had ever known him.

As might be expected, there were among these many cases a few which were not entirely successful from Holmes's point of view, but they nevertheless constitute an admirable wealth of material for his biographer, to the extent that it is only with the very greatest difficulty that I am able to select those which are to be included in these memoirs. In one respect, however, my task is simplified; for several of the more important cases have already received due prominence in the press, and little would be gained by my re-telling them. I am therefore inclined to draw for my present narrative upon that large number of cases which have previously been unreported, and which remain unknown beyond the circle in which the events took place. Among these latter cases is the story of the singular adventure which befell Mr. Horace Barclay, antiquary and collector of sporting prints, of Bedford.

Sherlock Holmes was fond of remarking on the unrivalled possibilities for mystery and confusion which the complex kaleidoscope of life in London offered so plentifully: the unimaginable crossing and re-crossing of separate threads of life which were inevitable in a city of four million souls, and which might lead, through the unseen workings of chance, to the most surprising and *outré* results. Few cases that I can recall have illustrated his thesis more vividly than the one which is forever associated in my mind with the green umbrella.

My notebook records that it was a cold and blustery day towards the end of March, in that period of the year when the harshness of winter begins at last to give way to the fresh delights of the spring, and even in the very heart of the brick fastness of London, the trees acknowledge the inevitability of the seasons, and show here and there the first green shoots upon their bare branches.

My friend had been without a case to engage his energies for a day or two, and already the idleness had begun to throw a visible strain upon his keen, active temperament. Several times that morning, as he had prowled about the rooms, for all the world like some caged, frustrated beast, I had watched with foreboding as his bright eyes had rested thoughtfully for a moment on the corner of the mantelpiece, where lay the small morocco case which contained his hypodermic syringe. Thus far, he had resisted the temptation, but I knew that even Holmes's iron will could not resist much longer the evil blandishments of the needle. After lunch, he had spent some time sifting through the stacks of old books which had accumulated in the corners of the room, tossing most of them aside with a groan, until he at length settled himself in a chair with a copy of Plutarch's *Moralia;* but he read little, and the expression of *ennui* never left his face. I had known him long enough to recognize the danger signals, and if he as a detective was in urgent need of a case upon which he could expend his energies, I as a medical man desired it no less on his behalf. Thus it was that when a sharp ring at the doorbell interrupted my thoughts, I listened with unusual attention to the sound of voices in the hall, and experienced an almost macabre sense of relief when, moments later, there came the step of an unfamiliar foot upon the stair.

A soberly dressed man was shown into the room. His dark frock-coat and top hat, and the solemn expression of his face, all indicated a man of conservative and serious-minded inclinations, and although he could scarcely have been more than two-and-thirty years of age, he had about him the grave air of one almost twice that age. The dark, expensive-looking valise which he carried in his hand served to confirm the general impression, but a singular and incongruous note was struck by his other item of luggage, a very large cotton umbrella, of a vivid emerald green, which he carried under his arm. He bowed slightly, and introduced himself as Horace Barclay.

"Pray, take a seat, Mr. Barclay," said my friend, putting down his book. "You appear a little fatigued by your railway-journey from Bedford."

Our visitor looked up sharply, as he lowered himself wearily into the armchair, and raised one eyebrow quizzically. "How do you know where I have travelled from?" he enquired, a tone of deep suspicion in his voice. "How came you by this information?"

"Tut, tut," said Holmes. "I have no information: I merely observe. When a man walks into my rooms with a slight but unmistakable trace of railway soot upon his hat, and a fresh copy of the *Bedford Gazette* rolled up in the handle of his travelling-bag, it is not so difficult to divine his origins."

A look of relief passed over our visitor's face, but there was still a frown of perplexity there, and he made no immediate response. After a moment, Holmes continued, in a thoughtful, pleasant voice:

"And yet," said he, "the journey from Bedford to London is not generally such a long one as to cause fatigue. Perhaps it is events since your arrival in London which have wearied you so. Yes? I thought as much, for I see that you have been in town for some time – perhaps an hour or two – and have had some walking to do – tut! there is no mystery; your shoes, my dear sir, tell their own story – which must have been tiring if you were obliged to carry that heavy bag with you the whole time, and on such a windy day as this! I think a strong cup of coffee would be of benefit to us all! If you would be so good as to ring for the maid, Watson!

"Now, Mr. Barclay," he continued: "You appear, if I may say so, a man of neat and methodical habits, yet you have come to consult me without having previously made an appointment – not at all, my dear sir! It occasions no difficulty: I mention the fact merely as a link in the chain of reasoning – and it therefore appears that your decision to consult me is a very recent one."

"Less than half an hour old," returned the other. "I was given your name and address by an official at King's Cross station – the only helpful person I have so far encountered since I arrived in London!"

"Quite. Let us see if we cannot swell the numbers of the helpful, then. If you would be so good as to explain in what way we may assist you? You hesitate. Perhaps I can help you? You have, I should say, the appearance of one on a pleasant trip up to town, intending to stay a night or two, perhaps with friends, perhaps at your club. No? With friends, then. But you bring with you a very large green umbrella, which appears more suited to outdoor pursuits." Our visitor's eyes rested momentarily on the umbrella with a look of distaste "Ah! I see! The umbrella is not yours. I suspected as much. You are bringing it for someone, then – for a friend – perhaps the friend you are coming to stay with? He left it at your house, perhaps, when last he was there? Yes? But you have not gone to his house, but have, rather, been tiring yourself, walking on London's crowded pavements. Why is that, I wonder? Perhaps you do not know his present address? Yes? You had arranged to meet, but you have somehow missed each other, and now you are at a loss as to what to do? In short, Mr. Barclay, you wish us to help you find your friend?

"You see, Watson," said Holmes with a chuckle, as our visitor nodded his head wearily, "we progress all the time! Soon we shall be able to dispense with interviews altogether. When clients call to consult us, we shall merely need to look them over to divine the problem, provide an answer and pocket the fee –

nothing could be simpler! Thank you, Mary," he said gaily as the maid brought in the coffee. "If you would place the tray close to hand, I will do the rest.

"Now, Mr. Barclay," he continued, handing his visitor a cup. "I can let you have the names of three reliable private enquiry agents who specialize in matters of this sort. Fairclough is the best, but Parker and Richardson are also competent."

"I had hoped that you would undertake the job yourself, sir. I was told you are the best man in London."

"I am a consultant, sir: I do not usually undertake such simple tasks as this – and my fees reflect that fact."

"Nevertheless, Mr. Holmes, I should deem it a great favour. I do not feel I can drag myself, umbrella and bag round to any further addresses."

"Very well," said Sherlock Holmes, with a note of reluctance in his voice. He reached for his note-book from the side-table. "Pray, let us have the details, then: the name, if you please, of your friend – or acquaintance, perhaps, as you appear to be less than fully intimate with his movements, and do not know enough about him to trace his whereabouts for yourself."

"'Acquaintance' would indeed be more accurate, Mr. Holmes. His name is James Chambers, but there is little more that I can tell you about him. Therein lies the difficulty."

"We can at least make a start," returned Holmes. "Tell me," he said: "is Mr. Chambers a sportsman? When he stayed with you, was it for the fishing in the Ouse, perhaps? No? Nothing of the sort? Well, well, that is interesting. His umbrella is that of a sportsman, and hardly one for everyday use, and yet he did not engage in any activity which might have required it. We cannot trace him in that way, then."

Holmes tapped his pencil on his note-book in a thoughtful manner. "Perhaps," said he at length, "before you tell us all you can of Mr. Chambers, you could explain how you came to miss each other this morning. Was he not waiting for you at the meeting-place?"

"Of that I have no idea," replied our visitor. "I left King's Cross station rather hurriedly, and cannot say whether he was there or not."

"One moment," Holmes interrupted. "You say King's Cross station, but I take it you mean St. Pancras station."

"No; King's Cross."

"But surely the direct trains from Bedford arrive at St. Pancras?"

"Indeed they do, Mr. Holmes, but there were special circumstances which obliged me to travel by a different route today. Once at the station, I made a mistake, and left with the wrong person." His voice faltered as he spoke, and his face coloured bright red, to the roots of his hair.

"Oh?" said Holmes, a slight smile on his face.

"It is nothing," said the other in embarrassment. "It is quite irrelevant, and has no bearing on the matter. As a matter of fact, I left with a woman – a young lady, I mean – who, I believed, had come to meet me. I thought she must be Chambers's sister, and she seemed to mistake me for someone else, too. She was a very engaging, very pressing young woman. It was an unfortunate misunderstanding, but I suppose these things happen in London all the time. By the time we had realised our error and parted, Chambers was nowhere to be seen."

Without warning, Holmes burst out into a roar of laughter, and I must confess that I, too, found it difficult to suppress a chuckle.

"Pray forgive me, my dear sir," said he after a moment, almost choking in his mirth, "but your story is a singular one!"

His client's face assumed a look of annoyance.

"I am not used to being treated as a source of merriment," said he in a heated voice, and seemed about to stand up. But then the lines of his face softened, and he almost smiled. "I suppose it does sound a trifle absurd," said he after a moment, in a reflective tone. "Nothing like it has ever happened to me before. I am a bachelor, and live an extremely quiet and secluded life, as you will appreciate if I tell you a little about myself and how I came to meet James Chambers. My home, 'The Poplars,' lies on the outskirts of Bedford, where I devote much of my time to the study of prints and paintings of the last century, particularly those depicting sporting scenes, upon which I have written a couple of trifling monographs. My own collection of sporting prints is ranked among the best in the country, and although I deal, in a small way, in etchings, mezzotints and so on, it is scarcely a serious business, and chiefly consists of my selling on items which I have acquired at auction, and do not wish to keep for my own collection. I come to London only occasionally, generally in connection with this interest, but over the years I have made one or two friends here with whom it is my pleasure to dine from time to time. These friends are, in the main, those whose interests lie in the same fields as my own, and I might mention that they include Sir Basildon Wemyss and Lord Steeples among their number.

"It was at the house of Lord Steeples, a month or two ago, that I made the acquaintance of a young man by the name of Chambers. His manner was extremely pleasant, and when we discovered that our tastes in prints were very similar, we naturally fell into a deep and prolonged conversation on the matter. The upshot was that we attended an auction together, a few weeks later, during the course of which he asked if he might pay me a visit, and see for himself my collection, which he said he had heard described as 'the most complete panorama ever assembled of man and horse in the eighteenth century.' I was delighted to accede to his request, for I receive few visitors, and I invited him to stay for a couple of days. The thought of a fellow-collector to brighten my weekend was indeed a pleasant one. As a consequence of our discussion, he came to stay with me upon the following Friday, that is, two weeks ago, remaining at my house for three days.

"Shortly afterwards, I received a letter from him, addressed from the *Poste Restante* at Charing Cross post office, expressing his desire to return the compliment and put me up for a few days at his house in London. I wrote back agreeing to this proposal and suggesting a suitable date, whereupon I had a second letter from him, confirming the date and describing the arrangements which were to apply for my visit. He was in dispute with his landlord at the moment, so he informed me, over some unsatisfactory repairs which had been carried out to the roof of his house, and it had been suggested that the dispute might best be resolved by his moving to another of the landlord's properties. Because of this, he could not be certain of his address from one day to the next, which was why he was writing from a post office, but he assured me that the matter would be settled by the time of my visit, and suggested that he meet me at the railway station when I arrived in London. He added in a post-script that he believed that he had left an umbrella at my house, and asked me, if I found it, to bring it with me when I came."

"This is the umbrella in question, I take it," said Holmes, eyeing the gaudy object which lay upon our carpet. "It is certainly a bright object to overlook. One might have supposed that even if your friend forgot to take it with him when leaving, you would have noticed his omission."

"I did not know he had it with him. He must have had it inside his large bag when he arrived, and he never used it while there."

"Ah!" said Holmes, a note of interest in his voice. "Where did you find it?"

"It was pushed behind the wardrobe in the room Chambers had occupied when he stayed with me."

"Excellent!" said Holmes with a dry chuckle. "Pray continue with your most interesting narrative, Mr. Barclay!"

"In the week which followed, we exchanged a perfectly absurd series of letters. I wrote to advise him of the time my train would arrive at St. Pancras station, and added that I had indeed found his umbrella. He then replied that I should come to King's Cross station, which was far more convenient for him than St. Pancras. I wrote again immediately, explaining that to arrive at King's Cross at a reasonable hour I should have to start earlier, make a longer journey across country, and change trains at Sandy. I further pointed out to him that it was manifest nonsense to say that King's Cross was more convenient to him than St. Pancras, for the two stations stand side by side in the same street, and there can be no two railway termini in the world which are closer. Back came his reply by return of post. He acknowledged the sense of what I said, and apologized for having misled me, but added that he had feared to weary me with the true explanation of why he could not meet me at St. Pancras. He had once had a dispute with the Midland Railway Company, who had treated him, so he said, with the most odious discourtesy, as a result of which he had vowed never to use their trains nor enter their premises again. This struck me as a trifle absurd, especially as it was not he but I who would suffer by the arrangement, but, anxious only to draw the correspondence to a close, I wrote back finally, agreeing to his request."

Our visitor paused then and took a sip of coffee, and as he raised the cup to his lips, I observed that his hand trembled slightly.

"Today is the day I was to visit James Chambers," he continued after a moment, "but, as you can see, I have got no further than Baker Street, despite the fact that I arrived at King's Cross over two hours ago."

"The details of what has delayed you, if you please."

"It has absolutely nothing to do with my not being able to locate my friend."

"I think we should reserve our judgment on that question, Mr. Barclay. I find it a useful rule of thumb that when several surprising, but apparently separate incidents occur within a short space of time, there is often a connection between them. We have here, on the one hand, certain unusual features in the arrangements Mr. Chambers made with you, and his leaving his umbrella at your house in somewhat odd circumstances, and, on the other hand, your surprising encounter with a stranger at the railway station. I think we ought to hear the details of the latter before we attempt to reach any conclusions."

"Very well, I will tell you exactly what happened, although it is perfectly absurd. When the train pulled into the station, I alighted quickly, in an attempt to beat the crush at the ticket-barrier. Nevertheless, by the time I reached it, the platform seemed to be swarming with people, and it was some time before I could extricate myself from the throng. As I did so, and as I surveyed the vast sea of faces around me, which seemed to contain an example of every known species of humanity, a handsome and well-dressed young woman dashed suddenly through the crowd towards me, and, flinging her arms round my neck, gripped me in a passionate and unseemly embrace. Burdened as I was, with my heavy bag and this ridiculous umbrella, I was unable to fend off her advances, and, in any case, the speed at which she had executed her attack would in itself have been sufficient to preclude resistance.

"As I attempted to disentangle myself from her embrace, painfully conscious that I was the object of mirth in the crowd around, and convinced that the woman must be a monomaniac of some kind, and quite possibly dangerous, she suddenly spoke, in a gay but urgent voice, and I was surprised to hear that her accent and tone were of the most respectable and refined.

"'Come quickly,' said she. 'I have a cab waiting outside the side-entrance.' I evidently showed the resistance I felt to her entreaties, for she slipped her arm through mine and gave me the most winning of smiles. 'I am so glad you were able to come,' she continued in an excited voice, 'and that you were able to bring the umbrella. I confess that I should hardly have recognized you without it. James will be so pleased! He was sorry not to be able to meet you himself, but something cropped up at the last minute which prevented his coming, and I said I should be glad to take his place.'

"So saying, she took the umbrella gently but firmly from my grasp, and, still with her arm in mine, led me rapidly through the throng and out into the street, where the driver of a four-wheeler took my bag from me and leapt aboard his vehicle with it. For a moment I hesitated, but what was I to do? Bewildered as

I was by the rapidity of events, I could see plainly enough that if I dawdled on the pavement I stood to lose both valise and umbrella, for the young lady had released my arm and was already inside the cab. Meekly, I followed her, and within seconds we were away and rattling at a furious rate up the dismal street beside the station.

"The expression on the young lady's face was tense and thoughtful, and several times she put her head to the window and glanced with a furrowed brow at the road behind us. When I attempted to do likewise, however, she suddenly and abruptly engaged me in conversation.

"'It is some time since you have been to London, is it not?' she asked, in a light, distracted voice.

"'Indeed,' I replied; 'several weeks.'

"'Very good,' said she, in a tone which indicated very clearly that she had not paid the slightest attention to my reply. I tried again to see what it was behind us that filled her with such anxiety, but she quickly spoke again and prevented it. 'Mother will be so pleased you have arrived,' said she with forced gaiety.

"'Mother?'

"'Did James not tell you? The whole family is to be there to greet you. We would not miss it for the world, as you can imagine. We have so much to tell you, and you, no doubt, have much to tell us, too.'

"I confess I knew not what to make of this prattle. Although the young lady was evidently Chambers's sister, her manner was quite unlike his, and I was beginning to wish I had never left home, when she abruptly leaned from the window of the cab and called something to the driver. Seizing the opportunity, I looked quickly from the window on my side, back the way we had come. The road was quiet, and almost deserted, but some fifty yards behind us was a hansom cab. At that distance I could not be certain, but it seemed to me that it had but one occupant, a man with a low, round hat, and a great black beard.

"At that moment, our cab lurched suddenly round a corner and I was flung back into my seat. We had passed through an area I did not know at all, and had now turned into a broad, quiet thoroughfare of handsome modern villas, which led into an attractive square. Along the side of this we rattled, at a terrifying speed, then suddenly pulled up with such abruptness that I was flung onto the floor of the cab, at my companion's feet. She threw open the door, stepped over me and leapt down, taking the umbrella with her.

"'Oh, do come quickly!' she cried in great earnest.

"So affecting was her tone that I scrambled after her obediently, and with absolutely no regard for my dignity. The cabman thereupon threw down my bag with such excessive violence that it struck me a terrific blow on the chest and quite knocked the wind out of me, but I still retained sufficient wit to look back along the road as she hurried me through a gateway, and I saw that, not forty yards away, our pursuer had stopped, and was apparently watching us. Who could this black-bearded villain be, I wondered? Into what dark and evil feud had I unwittingly intruded? Clearly the man in the hansom was an enemy of my new acquaintance, but what could have occurred, that we were pursued so remorselessly in broad daylight?

"We hurried up the short garden path to the house, and, breathless as I was, I felt a flood of relief wash over me at the sight of its stout and imposing front door. Once inside, we should be safe, I felt sure, and all would be explained to me. All at once, however, when we were almost at the door, my companion turned aside and scurried down a short flight of stone steps to a lower path. Puzzled, I nevertheless followed her, and as I did so I observed with surprise that the windows of the house were uncurtained, and thickly smeared with dirt. Clearly the house was unoccupied, and had been so for some time.

"In a moment we had reached a side gate. She unlatched it hurriedly, and we passed through, into a long back garden. Without pausing for breath, we continued our headlong flight, she tripping lightly ahead, the front of her skirts gripped tightly in her hand, I puffing and panting with my heavy bag in the rear. Through a decayed and desolate vegetable-patch we ran, beside a stable, through a second gateway, and out into a narrow, grass-grown cobbled lane. Still our hectic progress was not complete, for with neither a check in her stride nor a word to me, she hurried off again up the lane, and I followed, some yards in the rear. A cab came into view at the head of the lane, where it met the street; she called out, and the driver reined in his horse, although it seemed to me that he was stopping before ever she called to him. She opened the cab-door and climbed quickly in, and as I plunged through the open doorway after her, I recognized that the driver was the very same man who had dropped us off just round the corner, scarcely a minute before.

"'Drive on!' she cried, and away we raced, rocking wildly from side to side, until we reached a busy main road. Here the traffic was dense, and our rate of progress thus much reduced, but this did not seem to worry the young lady, whose face was flushed as much with triumph and exultation as with exertion, so it seemed to me. She still glanced at the road behind us from time to time, but her brow was unfrowning, and a smile played about her lips."

"The bearded man did not pursue you further?" queried Holmes.

Barclay shook his head.

"I never saw him again. We had evidently given him the slip. 'Well,' said I to my companion, when my breath was quite restored, 'I little thought when I left home today that I should have such an adventure!' I spoke with a jollity which I did not really feel, for I wished to indicate my friendship, in the hope that I might learn more of this mysterious and distressing business.

"For a moment she smiled silently at me, but when at last she spoke, her response stunned me like a blow on the head, so that my mind reeled, and my eyes seemed to blur.

"'I should think not,' said she gaily. 'I doubt that such things occur very often in Lincoln, Mr. Thompson!'

"'"Thompson"?' I returned. 'Did you say "Thompson"?'

"'Why, yes. You are, are you not, Mr. Thaddeus Thompson, of Tofts House, Lincoln?'

"'I most certainly am not!' I cried, attempting to rise to my feet.

"She called to the cabman, who reined in his horse and pulled in to the side of the road. The expression on her face was one of utter mortification.

"'My dear sir,' said she in a subdued voice. 'There seems to have been some dreadful mistake. I went to the station to meet my brother's old school chum, who once bounced me upon his knee when I was scarcely old enough to walk. Do you mean to tell me that you are not that man, and that you do not remember little Effie?'

"'My name is Barclay,' said I, feeling more than a little annoyed at the situation in which I found myself. 'I have never in my life known anyone by the name of Thompson, nor, for that matter, anyone called Effie!'

"'But you carried Thaddy's umbrella. He said in his letter that he would carry a bright umbrella, so that we might recognize him easily; for it is a long time since he has been to see us, and he feared, he said, that he had changed so considerably in the intervening years that the Weatheralls would find him a stranger. It is very difficult to persuade him to leave Lincoln, you know.'

"'Is it indeed?' I remarked with some asperity. 'The umbrella is my property, I can assure you, madam. I am bringing it for a friend.'

"I put out my hand and she gave me the umbrella, but with some reluctance, so it seemed to me.

"'Well,' said she. 'We are at Camden Town station, sir, so I will alight and trouble you no more. I regret very much that this mistake has occurred, but I must say that it has been a pleasure to meet you, however brief our acquaintance has been.'

"She spoke so sweetly, and with such an expression of kindness upon her face, that I felt my annoyance quite melt away. I returned her compliments, but insisted that I should be the one to alight and take the train. I stepped from the cab, it rattled quickly away, and I breathed a deep sigh of relief that the matter was at an end. These strange people, with their mysterious and sinister ways, were not connected with my friend, Chambers, after all. I did worry for a moment for the lady's safety, but she seemed well able to take care of herself, and, in any case, she had with her the cabman, who seemed something of an ally. What the mystery was which surrounded her, I could not imagine. She had offered no confidences on the matter, and I had not pressed her to any."

"It is a remarkable tale," said Sherlock Holmes, as our visitor finished speaking. "It is both interesting and suggestive. I am most grateful that you have shared it with us."

"I had no desire ever to share it with anyone," returned Barclay without enthusiasm. "I am not much of a man for mysteries, Mr. Holmes, and should have quite forgotten the matter except that it meant I had missed my friend."

"Quite so," said Holmes, nodding his head with a smile. "Pray continue, then, Mr. Barclay."

"I bought a ticket at the station, intending to return to King's Cross, or as near to it as the train would take me, in the hope that Chambers would be there still, waiting for me. I boarded the wrong train, however, and did not discover my error until I was somewhere on the other side of Hampstead. This set me back a further forty minutes, and when I finally arrived at King's Cross, Chambers was nowhere to be seen.

"Not knowing his address, I was for a while at a loss to know what to do, but then it occurred to me that I could probably discover his address from one of the friends we had in common. I immediately called into the telegraph office and wired everyone I could think of. The replies came back promptly enough, but were utterly disappointing: no one knew his address, and that ass, Lord Steeples, even went so far as to deny having ever heard of either of us. My own resources being at an end, I sought advice, and someone gave me your name, Mr. Holmes."

He paused. "My only thought at first was to locate my friend, but now, as I have narrated the whole matter to you, it begins to strike me in a more suspicious light: I wonder now if the secrecy surrounding Chambers's whereabouts is purely coincidental, or if in fact he and the girl are somehow in league against me, although to what end, I confess I cannot imagine."

"There are indeed some curious and striking features in your story," said Holmes, reaching for his pipe. "A number of possible explanations suggest themselves, of course. When you were sending your wires, did you send one to your own house, in case Chambers had left any message there for you?"

"There would have been no point, for the house is empty. I have given Mrs. Dempster, my housekeeper, the weekend off, and she has gone to visit relatives of hers in Northamptonshire."

"Had you ever seen Chambers before the evening when you conversed so amicably together at Lord Steeples's house?"

"I think I may have seen him somewhere, but only at a distance; I had never before spoken to him."

"If I might make a suggestion," I ventured, "it seems to me that far from being in league, Chambers and this young woman who calls herself Effie might in fact be opposed to each other in some enterprise."

"Why so, Watson?"

"For one thing, she whisked Mr. Barclay away from the station before he had had a chance to see if Chambers were there or not; for another, she seemed keen to get hold of the umbrella – which belongs to Chambers – and reluctant to part with it when once she had it."

"Yes," said our visitor. "That is true. I had not looked at the matter in that way, I confess. In that case, the man following in the hansom might have been an agent of Chambers's, and the charming young woman sitting beside me the real villain in the matter."

"But she does not appear to have acted in a very villainous manner," observed Holmes, a slight smile playing about his lips. “Oddly, yes; even bizarrely; but not, from your account, with any great evil in her heart.”

“Perhaps, unlikely as it may sound,” I suggested, “Mr. Barclay has stumbled accidentally into the activities of some kind of criminal gang, and perhaps there is some secret concealed in the umbrella which is of vital importance to them. That would explain the woman’s great interest in the umbrella, and why the man in the hansom was following them.”

“It is certainly a singular thing,” returned Holmes, smiling, “that a weekend guest should forget to take such a bright object as this umbrella home with him, and the matter becomes doubly curious when the umbrella is found wedged behind a wardrobe.”

“Are you suggesting,” said Barclay, “that he left it at my house on purpose?”

“That is certainly one reading of the matter. But there are great difficulties for your theory, Watson, the chief being that the woman did not in the end keep the umbrella, but seemed content to let Mr. Barclay walk off with it. I assume from your account, Mr. Barclay, that she would have had no opportunity to remove anything which might have been concealed within the umbrella?”

Our visitor shook his head. “I had the thing in view the whole time,” said he, “and it was never unfastened.”

Holmes frowned for a moment, then with a dry chuckle he leaned from his chair, picked up the umbrella and passed it to me. “Let us not deny ourselves the pleasure of examining the thing, then,” said he.

I unfastened the clasp, and opened the umbrella out; I turned it upside down, shook it and examined it fully, but to my disappointment, there was nothing within. I rolled it up again, and we sat for some time in silence, while Holmes, with his eyes closed, and puffing slowly on his pipe, considered the matter. Then, abruptly, our visitor spoke:

“I have had a disturbing thought,” said he in a quiet voice. “It has just occurred to me that I may have been deliberately lured to London so that my house can be burgled in my absence. My collection of prints is extremely valuable."

"Great Heavens!" I cried. "Such a possibility had not occurred to me!"

"But it had occurred to me," said Holmes drily, opening his eyes. "Indeed, the possibility of such a scheme was one of the very first explanations I considered. But it occurred to me with equal rapidity that the very last thing which the perpetrator of such a scheme would desire is that his victim's suspicions be aroused in any way. The ideal state of affairs from a burglar's point of view, would be for Mr. Barclay to spend a perfectly ordinary weekend away, in peace and quiet. Instead of this, however, he is subjected to such a series of alarms and perplexities, immediately upon his arrival in London, that it would have been no more than natural had he returned home there and then, which is the last effect any aspiring burglar would wish to achieve, as I am sure you would agree. Fortunately," Holmes added with a twinkle in his eye, "Mr. Barclay did not return home, but chose the more sensible course, and consulted me."

"And yet it is still just possible, is it not," I persisted, "however unlikely it may be, that burglary is indeed the motive behind it all?"

Holmes laughed. "Really, Watson, you are becoming as tenacious in your grip on a theory as our old friend, Inspector Lestrade. But, yes," he conceded, putting down his pipe, and rising to his feet, "one would have to allow that it is barely, logically, possible – in London all things are possible – despite the fact that Chambers could scarcely have done more to ensure that suspicion would fall upon him immediately should anything happen to Mr. Barclay's collection; despite the fact that Effie's efforts to keep Mr. Barclay occupied flagged after only half an hour, when there are dozens of perfectly elementary ruses which she could have adopted to keep him busy for the rest of the day; despite the fact that the burglary theory provides no adequate explanation of the bearded fellow in the hansom, the premeditated detour through the garden of the empty house, and the odd instructions concerning the railway stations; despite all these considerations, it is, I admit, just possible that Chambers, or someone else, intends to burgle 'The Poplars.' Perhaps the best thing, then, to set Mr. Barclay's mind at ease on the matter, would be for you to take him down to see our friend, Inspector Bradstreet. Explain to him that you are concerned about a possible burglary, Mr. Barclay – I should not trouble him with all the details – and he will make contact with the Bedfordshire force and get an officer sent out to your house at once. Will that suffice?"

"And what will you do, Mr. Holmes?"

"No more questions for the moment, Mr. Barclay, if you please. Time is slipping away as we sit here talking. If you will call back at seven o'clock this evening, I think we may have some positive news for you." He had been drawing on his overcoat as he spoke, and now, with a glance at his watch and a brisk nod to his client, he was away, his footsteps clattering rapidly down the stair. I suggested to Mr. Barclay that he might leave his bag and umbrella in our chambers for the time being, a plan with which he was very willing to comply, and a few minutes later we descended to the street and hailed a cab to take us to the police station.

At half past six that evening, I was reading the evening paper by the fireside; but there was little of interest in it, and my thoughts soon strayed back to the strange story we had heard earlier in the day. I could make no sense of it at all, and was inclined to conclude that the bizarre events in which Horace Barclay had found himself an unwilling participant were, in truth, quite unconnected, when my eye fell on the green umbrella, leaning up against the sofa, and I found myself wondering if it might not, after all, contain some secret which we had missed earlier. It could do no harm to have another look. I opened it up and subjected both the inside and the handle to a careful examination for several minutes, but found nothing hidden there, nor any place where anything could previously have been hidden. I was just about to close it up again when my eye was caught by the small white label which bore the manufacturer's name. Beneath this name a pair of initials, presumably those of the owner, had been written with an indelible pencil. These initials, however, were not those of James Chambers, but were, to my unutterable amazement, 'H B', the initials of Holmes's client, Horace Barclay.

I was still staring at the label in stupefaction, unable to comprehend what it might mean, when my thoughts were disturbed by a sudden sharp ring at the door-bell. To my surprise, a rough-looking man was shown in a moment later by the maid. His name, he said, was George Milburn, and he had come in response to a message left by a Mr. Sherlock Holmes at the cab office at King's Cross, promising half a sovereign for information about a certain fare he had had earlier that day. As I had had no word from Holmes as to when he might return, I decided to conduct the interview myself. I judged that I was sufficiently familiar with my friend's methods to extract any information which the man might have, although, in the event, this amounted to very little.

He worked, he said, out of Woodham's Yard, King's Cross. It was outside that station that he had been hailed that morning by a well-dressed young woman with curly blonde hair, who had instructed him to wait at the side-entrance and be ready for an immediate and rapid departure when she returned. She had given him a sovereign, and told him that there would be another for him if he followed her instructions precisely. He was to drive with all speed to a certain house in Camden Square, where she and her companion would alight, then to wait round the corner, at the head of a lane, until they re-emerged, whereupon he was to make for Camden Town as fast as possible.

So far his testimony merely confirmed the story of Holmes's client, without adding any fresh information, although it did establish for certain that the young woman had foreseen the pursuit which took place, and had planned the route in advance, including the detour through the garden of the empty house.

"Where did the young lady finally alight?" I asked.

"Corner of Camden High Street and Crowndale Road," he replied; "about a quarter mile after the gentleman."

This information made it certain that the woman had made no attempt to return to King's Cross station, so that the story she had told Mr. Barclay, of having gone there to meet a Mr. Thompson from Lincoln, was therefore a complete falsehood. I handed the cabman the half-sovereign, and was about to dismiss him, when there came the sound of rapid footsteps upon the stair. A moment later the door flew open and Holmes hurried into the room. The cabman quickly repeated his scanty information.

"Did you observe in which direction she walked after she had alighted?" Holmes asked when the man had finished.

"She crossed the road towards Mornington Crescent, sir."

Holmes nodded. "And no doubt she was wearing gloves?"

"Yes, sir. Grey cotton."

"Hum. Perhaps she removed them when she was paying you?"

"Yes, sir; that's exactly what she did."

"Ah! And as she did so, you observed upon her left hand a wedding-ring, and also another, jewelled ring, with a dark stone in the centre, and half a dozen small diamonds around the edge."

"'Pon my word, sir! You have described the ring exactly!"

"Thank you," said Holmes with a smile of satisfaction. "You can always rely on a jarvey to observe jewellery, Watson," he remarked when, with a little salute, the man had left us, a broad grin upon his face. "After a while they become quite skilled at assessing the worth of their customers from such little details." He had been rummaging in the drawer of his desk as he spoke, and now he took from it his revolver, and slipped it into the pocket of his overcoat. "Now," said he, glancing at the clock, "there is time, I think, for a stirrup cup. Let us take something warming, then, before venturing out once more into this chilly evening!"

"Where are you going?"

"To pay a call on James Chambers. Will you come?"

"Certainly, if you wish it. Do you anticipate danger?"

"Events sometimes take a surprising turn," said he after a moment, in a considered tone. "You will recall the arrest of Mary Monteith, no doubt? The pistol is a precaution, Watson; that is all. I should be obliged if you did not mention it to Mr. Barclay. It might alarm him. But, unless I am much mistaken, that is our client's cab outside now. If you would be so good as to bring the gamp and bag, we can be off."

"One moment, Holmes," said I, as I remembered my recent discovery. I quickly told him of the label inside the umbrella. "It bears the initials–"

"'H B', I should imagine," my friend interrupted.

I confess I was stunned with surprise. "How on earth do you know that?" I cried.

"It is as I thought," said he simply. "Perhaps, Watson," he added in a thoughtful voice, "you could enquire about those initials when I give you a sign."

I threw on my coat, and, picking up the umbrella and Mr. Barclay's bag, hurried after Holmes as he ran downstairs. A moment later, we had joined his client in the cab and were rattling away through the darkened streets. Barclay sat huddled in the corner, his eyes unhopeful and his expression one of fatigue. Holmes, by contrast, was alert and vibrant with barely suppressed energy. His eyes glittered, and his whole face seemed sharpened and thrust forward, like an excited hound who has the scent in his nostrils and is impatient to be off the leash.

"You spoke to Inspector Bradstreet, I take it?" said he, when we had gone some way.

"Indeed," Barclay replied. "He was most helpful, as were the Bedfordshire Police. They were soon able to inform us that there had been no untoward occurrences at 'The Poplars,' and no strangers had been seen in the neighbourhood; but they say they will keep the house under observation, nevertheless."

Holmes nodded his head. "Now," said he, "to explain matters to you: I have found Mr. Chambers, although, in truth, he was scarcely lost. It had struck me that a man with a knowledge of old prints sufficient for him to be able to engage such an authority as you in conversation, Mr. Barclay, might well be known to the London dealers, and so it proved. Half an hour with a trade directory, followed by a few enquiries at picture-galleries and sale-rooms, gave me the information I required. In truth, I was almost disappointed at the ease with which the facts fell into my lap; it was as if a mountaineer who has prepared himself for an arduous and difficult climb discovers before he has gone ten paces that there exists an easy path to the summit, up which he can stroll without effort. Of course, there is a lesson in everything if we care to take it," he added with a dry chuckle, "and the lesson of this is clearly that satisfaction comes not from the end achieved, but from the struggle to reach that end.

"What I discovered," he continued after a moment, "is that Chambers himself has an interest in a small gallery in Davies Street, which trades under the name of Lambert. There is an extremely garrulous young assistant there, who seemed to have nothing better to do than answer my questions, and I was soon able to learn Chambers's home address, which is in Highbury Fields, and also most of his life history and that of his immediate relations, which is not, I might add, in the first rank from the point of view of general interest."

It was clear that Holmes was not inclined to say more for the moment, and I did not press him. As for his client, he seemed to have settled into a state of passive acceptance of whatever Fate might have in store for him. He and I had earlier passed a pleasant half-hour, while waiting at the police station, in discussing the history of racing; and although I did not know the direction his thoughts had taken since then, it was clear from every line on his face that his spirits had fallen somewhat, and that he wished he had never left his home that morning. The cab rattled on in the darkness, as I pondered further the curious circumstances surrounding his arrival in London, past the great bulk of the buildings along the Euston Road, through Pentonville, and so on towards Islington. The night was very clear, and bitterly cold, and the dark and gloomy streets were almost deserted. Only the noisy and brightly-lit public houses at the street-corners gave any indication that there throbbed a hidden, persistent life beneath the darkened and forbidding exterior of the city. Of Mr. Barclay's adventure I could make nothing, and nor was I very hopeful that in finding Chambers we should get to the bottom of it. Probably, Chambers had simply tired of waiting for his friend at King's Cross, and was as mystified as to his whereabouts now as his friend had been mystified about him; and perhaps the woman Barclay had encountered was indeed some kind of monomaniac, inhabiting a world of her own imagination. Perhaps she made a habit of meeting trains at King's Cross, and subjected a new victim each day to her strange ways. But there were certain features of the matter which I could not so easily explain away in this fashion, and I was still pondering the problem without having reached any conclusion when we turned at last into Highbury Terrace.

Chambers's house lay in the middle of a long, tall, flat-fronted row, which faced onto a large, open square in which I could just make out the shadowed shapes of trees. Darkened, and in complete silence, the house presented a cold and unwelcoming appearance, and I feared that our journey might even yet prove a fruitless one. Eventually our ring at the bell was answered, however, and a young girl showed us into a pleasant, tastefully decorated drawing-room at the rear of the house. Pictures and bric-a-brac of all kinds were displayed upon the walls and upon every available surface, and over all there was an air of solidity and permanence, and certainly no indication of any recent domestic upheaval, such as Chambers had mentioned in his letters to Mr. Barclay. But for the crackle of the fire blazing in the grate, and the ticking of a clock on the mantelpiece, all was silent and still, although, as we stood there, the faint, distant sound of voices came to my ear, and somewhere above us a door closed softly. Moments later, the door of the drawing-room was opened, to admit a tall young man with wavy hair and round, ruddy features.

"My dear Barclay!" he cried, rushing up to his friend and wringing his hand vigorously. "How very glad I am to see you! I had quite given you up, I am afraid. But who are these gentlemen?"

"This is Mr. Holmes and Dr. Watson, who have assisted me in finding you when my own efforts had proved unavailing."

"Thank goodness you were able to help," said Chambers, shaking us both by the hand. "You will take a sherry, gentlemen?" He rang for the maid. "I waited at King's Cross for over an hour and a half, Barclay, and met twenty-three trains before I gave it up. Then I sent a wire to your house, but it was returned to me undelivered. They said there was no one there to receive it. I could not think where you had got to! When did you arrive in London?"

"At twelve-forty-seven, as we had arranged," returned Barclay, appearing a little uncomfortable. "But I was distracted. I had a slight adventure, which took me away from the station, and I did not get back for two hours. I'll tell you about it later."

"Well, well!" said Chambers, clapping him on the shoulder. "All's well that ends well, eh?"

"Yes, thank goodness," said Barclay with a sigh of relief.

"And I see that you found the umbrella, too–"

"One moment," interrupted Holmes. His tone was authoritative and cold, and the other two men looked at him in surprise, the smiles frozen upon their faces. "I am not satisfied."

"Excuse me," said Chambers in a testy voice, "but I don't understand."

"I am not satisfied with your account, nor with your conduct towards my client."

"I do not see that it is your place to express dissatisfaction," returned Chambers, a note of anger in his voice. "You have assisted Mr. Barclay in finding me, and you have manifestly succeeded. I'll ring for the maid to show you out."

"You will do no such thing," said Holmes coldly; "for if you do, the matter will be placed in the hands of the police within half an hour."

A look of alarm came into Chambers's eyes. "How dare you threaten me!" he cried in a blustering voice. "Your part in the matter is at an end."

"We wish," said I boldly, in response to a slight sign from Holmes, "to know about the initials 'H B.'"

The two men looked at one another. "What are you talking about?" said Chambers in a strained voice. "Why, this is 'H B' – Mr. Horace Barclay!"

"There is another," said Holmes, taking the umbrella from me: "the owner of this." He tossed the umbrella onto the floor. "His initials are on the label."

There was a moment of utter silence, in which Holmes remained perfectly motionless, Barclay's features assumed a look of complete stupefaction, and Chambers's eyes darted about the room, as he clenched and unclenched his hands spasmodically. Again I thought I heard slight sounds from outside the room: soft footsteps, and the creaking of a floor-board.

"The umbrella was not new when I acquired it," said Chambers at length, in a breathless tone. "'H B' must have been a previous owner–"

"Do not waste our time further, Mr. Chambers," said Holmes. "Do you recall the Stillingfleet case, Mr. Barclay? – about four years ago, in Croydon?"

"The name means nothing to me, I'm afraid."

"No? It created quite a sensation at the time, I remember. A Dr. Alfred Stillingfleet murdered his wife and buried her body in the garden. Shortly afterwards, her relatives became suspicious when they failed to receive the usual letters from her, for she had previously been a prolific correspondent, and they therefore hired a private enquiry agent to watch the house. Stillingfleet, however, quickly became aware of this fellow, who was a singularly incompetent operator by all accounts, and he therefore arranged for his maid, who had been his partner in the crime, to dress in such a way as to impersonate his late wife and parade up and down the streets of the district until the agent went away satisfied, and wrote his erroneously reassuring report. By this ruse, which was repeated from time to time, and by the forging of letters, Stillingfleet was able to postpone the discovery of the crime for almost two years."

"It is an unpleasant and distressing story," said Barclay; "but I fail to see its relevance."

"It is by no means unique. There was a similar case in Brussels two years ago, and an almost identical one in Hamburg just last year. I believe that the man with the beard who followed you this morning was almost certainly a detective, and as it is apparent for various reasons, including the evidence we have heard from the cabman, that the woman you were with fully expected to be followed from the station, it seems likely that her every action was performed with this man in mind."

"But to what end? And, in any case, what have I to do with those people?"

"If you will consider the matter for a moment, it will surely be obvious to you," returned Holmes, a trace of impatience in his voice. "What does this woman do first? She makes a great, unnecessary scene at the station, thus drawing the attention of everyone there to the fact that she has met you. She then hurries away with you and shakes off the pursuit by a simple but ingenious ruse. Clearly she wishes you to be seen, but not too closely; she wishes anyone who is interested – which means the man with the beard – to know that you have left the station in her company, but not that you have later parted in Camden Town."

"But why, Mr. Holmes, why?" cried Barclay, a look of utter bewilderment upon his face. "Why should anyone wish to see me, or see where I go?"

"Because, Mr. Barclay, that person wished to be certain that you were who he thought you were."

"And who on earth did he think I was, then?"

"Let us suppose for the sake of argument that this woman, 'Effie,' has done away with her husband, and has so far managed to allay the suspicions of his relatives and friends by telling them that he is out of town for a while. The day will arrive, sooner or later, when she must produce him once more, especially if she knows she is being watched by a hired detective. If she has a suitable male confederate, there will be no problem. But let us further suppose that she has no suitable confederate. What is she to do? Clearly she must find some stranger who can pass, at a distance, for her husband. Do I make myself clear?"

Barclay nodded glumly, but the puzzled expression never left his face. "So you believe that everything which that strange woman told me was untrue?"

"I am certain of it. And the purpose of the umbrella, which Mr. Chambers deliberately left at your house, so that you would have to bring it with you–"

"Oh, this is preposterous!" cried Chambers, who had been standing in silence all the time Holmes had been speaking. "I have listened to enough of this nonsense!" He stepped to the bell-pull, a determined expression on his face. But before his hand had touched it, the door of the room burst open, and a pretty, blonde-haired young woman swept into the room with a swishing of her indigo silk evening-dress.

Horace Barclay took a quick step backwards, and raised his arm as if to fend her off. "You!" he cried, a look of stunned recognition in his eyes.

"Violet!" cried Chambers, in a tone of alarm.

"It is no use, James," said she in a firm voice. "I have been listening outside the door. These gentlemen have somehow discovered our little ruse, and now suspect us of something far worse than the truth. We have little enough to be ashamed of. We must tell them all, so that they can understand the position in which I found myself. Pray, take a seat, gentlemen," she continued, turning to us, as Chambers himself sat down heavily in a chair by the fire, like a man finally admitting defeat. "I will explain everything. But first I must ask you a question, and I must beg of you that on your honour as gentlemen you will answer me truthfully."

I nodded my head, mystified as to what she might be going to ask us.

"Are you," said she, "in the employment of Lord Crosspool?"

"Lord Crosspool?" said Holmes in surprise. "The gentleman who was brought before the magistrates a couple of years ago for discharging a fowling-piece at the local rector? I seem to recall that he insisted upon being tried by the House of Lords until persuaded that he was merely making an ass of himself; but, other than that, I know nothing of the man."

"I have never even heard of him," said I.

For a moment she looked keenly into our eyes, then, evidently satisfied, she nodded her head.

"Very well," said she. "I will tell you all. But do not blame James, I implore you! My brother acted only to help me. He had wanted no part in the matter, and only became involved because I begged him."

I glanced over to where Chambers sat by the fire, his elbows upon the arms of the chair, his head sunk in his hands.

"My maiden name was Violet Chambers," she continued. "Eighteen months ago, however, I was married, and became Mrs. Henry Beauchamp. At that time my husband had recently completed his studies at Oxford. He is the second son of Lord Crosspool, of Crosspool Park, Shropshire. To his elder brother, Ronald, will naturally devolve in due course all the duties and privileges of the estate, and it was the wish of Lord Crosspool that Henry's career be made in the local regiment, the

Shropshire Fusiliers, in which Lord Crosspool himself had served as a young man. But Henry's inclinations have always been elsewhere, and this has led to considerable friction between them, I am afraid. Henry's great interest is in the ancient world, and he wishes to devote his energies to archaeology. Lord Crosspool has scarcely left his estates all his life, and his views are very narrow and rigid. He sees no merit in Henry's ambitions at all, and he absolutely forbade him to speak of the matter again, on pain of being utterly disowned, cut off completely from his family, without a penny to his name. What was my husband to do? In a year's time, so he had every reason to believe, he would be able to secure an excellent position at the British Museum, but for the moment he was entirely dependent upon his father for his livelihood. He begged for a little time in which to consider his future, and to continue for the moment his education in London, to which request Lord Crosspool eventually, with extreme reluctance, assented.

"Then, late last August, Henry was offered the chance of joining an archaeological expedition to Egypt, under the guidance of Flinders Petrie. He had to make a decision quickly, as the opportunity had only arisen because of another man's incapacity through illness, and the party was to leave in a few days. All one night he stayed awake, considering the proposition from every aspect. At length, in the morning, when I told him that it was my wish that he should go, he made his decision. He left England on the fifth of September last year, and has spent the winter at Karnak, on the Nile. He has written regularly to me, and it has been a source of great pleasure to me to hear of the great work he is doing, and the experience he has gained. Now, in his last letter but one, he informs me that he has been offered a post on the research staff of the Museum, to begin in June, so that it seems our future is at last assured.

"All this time, it was essential that his father did not learn that he was away from England. There seemed little difficulty in this at first, for Lord Crosspool rarely comes to London; but one Saturday in February some matter concerning the estate had brought him up to town to see his legal advisers, and he arrived quite unannounced at our little house in Mornington Road, where I was quite alone. On the spur of the moment, I told him that Henry was away for a few days, visiting an old college friend in York, and he seemed at first to be satisfied with that explanation for Henry's absence. But something must have aroused his suspicious nature, for I discovered later that he had questioned the servants closely when I was not present. I do not believe he learned anything definite from them, but two weeks later a man with a black beard, piercing eyes, and the smell of beer about him called at the house. He gave his name as O'Donnell, and said he had some confidential information for my husband, which he was obliged to deliver personally, and he asked me when Henry would be returning. I did not believe his story, and suspected that he was an agent of my father-in-law's, and this suspicion was in some measure confirmed when I subsequently saw him loitering in the street at odd times of the day, with a note-book in his hand. No doubt he would soon be reporting back to Lord Crosspool that Henry was nowhere to be seen. What could I do? I was sure that if Henry were here to explain matters to his father, all might still be well. But if his father discovered the truth while Henry was absent and thus unable to defend himself, Lord Crosspool might in his rage carry out what he had threatened. Henry was to leave Alexandria in two weeks' time, but by then it might be too late, the damage might already have been done. If only there were some way I could convince the investigator that Henry was here, in London!"

"I do not see that any further deception was necessary," interrupted Sherlock Holmes. "Your husband's father could hardly take any decisive step unless he knew for certain that his son was abroad, and how could he learn that?"

"Oh, if only I had had your advice before, sir," Mrs. Beauchamp responded after a moment. "I see now that you are right. As it was, I saw then only that ruin awaited us unless I could throw Lord Crosspool's detective off the scent! It was as I was pondering the matter, in my agitation, that I remembered James's telling me of an odd coincidence. A gentleman he had met recently, he said, not only had the same initials as my husband, but bore a strong resemblance to him, from a distance at least. That gentleman was Mr. Barclay, and I found myself wondering, as I recalled James's words, if it might be possible to pass Mr. Barclay off as my husband. I put it to James, and his first reaction was to utterly reject the idea as preposterous; but gradually I managed to convince him that it might work, so long as this man, O'Donnell, did not get too close a look at Mr. Barclay, and would harm no one. In the end, reluctantly, he agreed to it.

"The plan, then, was that James would invite Mr. Barclay to London, where I would meet him in such a way as to convince Mr. O'Donnell – who I knew would be following me – that he was my husband. In order to make it appear as if Henry were returning from York, we had somehow to arrange it so that the meeting occurred at King's Cross Station, which is where the express trains from Yorkshire arrive, and, as a final touch, it was contrived, as you have no doubt realised, that Mr. Barclay would be carrying Henry's umbrella. It is an article which anyone who knows Henry would instantly associate with him. He has had it for years, and takes it everywhere, and I thought that if Lord Crosspool's spy mentioned the umbrella in his report it would make it seem conclusive. The intention was that we should give Mr. O'Donnell the slip, and then part, so that Mr. Barclay could return in the cab to King's Cross, where James would be waiting for him. Unfortunately, I had not thought the matter through sufficiently, and I had not foreseen that Mr. Barclay is too much of a gentleman to have remained in the cab while I alighted, but would insist upon being the one to alight. Alas! He was somehow delayed, and although James waited for nearly two hours, it was not enough! James has been beside himself with concern for his friend ever since. I, meanwhile, returned straight home to learn from the maid that another stranger, a tall man whose name she did not catch, had been asking for me earlier this afternoon. Suspecting another of Lord Crosspool's spies, I left Mornington Road at once and came straight here to my brother's, to avoid being seen alone. There! Now you know everything."

As she finished her account, delivered in a rapid, breathless tone, her breast was heaving with emotion. There followed a long silence. At length, Sherlock Holmes spoke.

"It is an interesting story, madam," said he, "illustrative of the truth that one lie leads on to another, and that what begins as a small deception frequently ends as a very great one. If what you say is true, then, at the very least, you owe Mr. Barclay the most profound apology; but is it true? How are we to judge? You have already today given one demonstration of your abilities as an actress, and you will therefore understand if we now hesitate before granting you our full credence."

The lady bit her lower lip, and put her hands to her face.

"What I have told you is the truth," said she after a moment in a quiet voice; "although I can hardly blame you for your incredulity. I know I cannot expect your forgiveness, although I am sincerely sorry for the trouble my schemes have caused, so I ask only your belief. One moment!" she cried abruptly, as an idea struck her. "Perhaps you could show these gentlemen the press-cuttings, James."

Her brother nodded eagerly, and hurried from the room. In a minute he was back, bearing a small sheaf of papers in his hand.

"Here are a couple of letters which Henry has sent me from Egypt," said he, "and this is a scrap-book I have been keeping."

He opened the latter near the beginning, and showed us a newspaper cutting, dated the sixth of September, 1887, which described the embarkation of the Egyptian Archaeological Party, in which the name of Henry Beauchamp was mentioned.

"Will his father not have seen this report, or a similar one?" I queried.

Mrs. Beauchamp shook her head. "There is little fear of that," she returned. "He reads nothing, except *The Field*, and military and naval reports."

Sherlock Holmes sifted through the papers for some moments, then he looked up, tapping his fingers on the pile before him, and gazed steadily into the lady's eyes. "If we agree to let the matter rest here for the moment," said he at length, "you must bring your husband to see us upon his return. What say you, Watson?"

I nodded my assent, and was about to speak, when Barclay rose to his feet, and cleared his throat.

"Whatever is decided about *that*," said he in a stiff voice, "my position here is clearly a false one. It seems that I have served my purpose, so if you will ask your servant to summon a cab, I will trouble you no more."

"No, no, my dear fellow," cried Chambers, putting out his arms as if he would physically prevent the other man from leaving the room. "I would not have you go for the world! If our foolish plots should cause a rift between us, I should never forgive myself!"

"You can hardly suppose that it is of any moment to me whether you choose to forgive yourself or not," returned Barclay coldly. "I have been used most despicably."

"We did not think–" began Mrs. Beauchamp, her face the very picture of regret; but the severity of Horace Barclay's expression evidently deterred her, for she broke off, and did not complete the sentence.

A heavy silence fell upon the room, and for several minutes there was nothing to be heard but the crackle and splutter of the fire in the grate, and the ticking of the clock above it. Then, with an abruptness which made me start from my chair, there came the fierce jangling of the front-door bell. A moment later, the maid opened the door to announce Mr. Ronald Beauchamp.

A tall, athletic-looking man strode briskly into the room. He was about thirty years of age, I judged, with large, clean-shaven features, and flaxen hair. He stepped quickly to Mrs. Beauchamp and took her hand.

"Violet!" said he. "How good it is to see you again! I've had the devil of a job finding you! I've been calling at your house all day, but your maid denied knowing where you had gone. Eventually I guessed that you might be at your brother's house. James!" he cried, turning to Chambers, and the two men exchanged greetings. "Henry not here?" he enquired, then he laughed. "I thought perhaps not. That rather explains one or two things! I've come up to town as soon as I could, especially to see you, Violet. I have something important to tell you." He glanced in our direction.

"You may speak freely before these gentlemen," said Mrs. Beauchamp.

"Very well. I discovered recently – quite by chance – that my father had employed a private detective to spy on you and Henry. Knowing what I did of Henry's plans and intentions, I guessed that it was something to do with digging, or with Egypt, or both. Well, I don't mind telling you that I told the old man precisely what I thought of his spying. I didn't mince my words, and there was a blazing row. Then, as soon as I was able to leave the estate, I hurried to warn you. So, here I am! Quite frankly, I think that having my strong disagreement made so clear to him, the old man will think again, and you may find that he is a bit more amenable to Henry's plans from now on. But, who are these gentlemen?" he continued. "They must think me terribly rude, to burst in upon your party and ignore them." He glanced round, and then his eye fell on Holmes's client, who had been standing in silence by the door all this time. At once, his eyebrows shot up in surprise. "Why, if it isn't Horace Barclay!" he cried. "Whatever are you doing here, my dear fellow? I didn't know that you were acquainted with my relations!"

Horace Barclay took a step forward and blinked in surprise.

"Bless my soul!" he cried. "Ronald Beauchamp! I'm afraid I did not recognize you, old man. When this young lady introduced herself earlier as Mrs. Beauchamp, I never thought to connect her with you!" He shook the other heartily by the hand. "This is my dear old friend, Ronald Ignatius Beauchamp," he explained, turning to us. "We were at Oxford together. Indeed, we were on the same stair at St. Matthew's for two years. It must be nearly ten years since I've seen you, Beauchamp! What a very happy chance! How have you been keeping? And how are your charming young sisters, Beth and Phyllis, who used to come with their aunt to visit us in College?"

The two men conversed gaily for several minutes, and seemed set for several hours, but Chambers interrupted them.

"You will all stay and have supper with us?" said he. Beauchamp assented with enthusiasm, but Barclay hesitated and frowned, as if endeavouring to weigh against each other several conflicting emotions.

"Oh, very well, then," said he at length, his mouth broadening into a smile. "But I insist – absolutely insist – that my old friend here hears all about this afternoon's adventure while we eat. I will recount it, and 'Effie' can correct me if I go wrong!"

"'Effie'?" queried Beauchamp in surprise.

"I will explain all over supper," said his sister-in-law, laughing.

"It is pleasing," said Holmes, rising to his feet, "that matters appear to have resolved themselves to everyone's satisfaction, for the present at least. I think, Watson," he continued, turning to me, "that we might most profitably return to Baker Street."

"You will not take a little something with us?" said Chambers.

"Thank you, but no," returned Holmes. "Our cook has promised us fowls of rare distinction this evening, so we are under some obligation to put in an appearance at the dinner table. It has been a diverting, but tiring day. Do bring your husband to see us when he returns, Mrs. Beauchamp. I have followed

Flinders Petrie's work with the utmost interest, and should be pleased to have a first-hand account of the latest findings!"

Holmes was in a light-hearted mood as we returned to Baker Street, chuckling as he expressed his pleasure that his worst fears had not been realised.

"I am particularly glad that the pistol proved unnecessary," he remarked with a smile, patting the bulge in his overcoat pocket. "It may be, Watson, that my professional experience has inclined me always to expect the worst possible outcome, but I by no means welcome it, and it is indeed a delight to be mistaken for once. I must confess that when I learned from the young assistant at Chambers's gallery this afternoon that his employer had a sister whose description exactly matched that of the woman Mr. Barclay had encountered at King's Cross, I did fear the worst. It made certain, you see, what we had suspected, that the two of them were in it together. Her occasional visits to her brother's gallery had evidently left a strong impression upon his assistant, incidentally, for he was able to give me the most detailed description of her, even down to the appearance of her ring, which enabled me to confirm the matter beyond doubt with the cabman, as you saw. The assistant also informed me that she had been married the autumn before last, to a Mr. Henry Beauchamp, which is why I fully expected the initials you had found in the umbrella to be 'H B.' I seemed then to see a crime unfolding before me on the very model of the Stillingfleet case, and I think I can be forgiven for judging it so."

"Certainly," said I, "but thank Heavens you were wrong, Holmes! In fact, your reading of the deception being practised was correct in every detail; but, fortunately, in this case, there was no great evil behind it all, and no one is harmed by it. The treatment of Mr. Barclay was perhaps a little callous–"

"Oh, his pride will recover," Holmes interrupted in a gay tone, "and the story of his adventure will establish him for life at the dinner-parties of London!"

Thus ended the singular adventure of Mr. Horace Barclay. And yet, for him, it was not an end, but a beginning; for, some eighteen months later, I heard that he had married Elizabeth Beauchamp, the sister of his old college friend. Perhaps the most surprising aspect of this was that in so doing he had become related through marriage to the young blonde-haired stranger with whom he had once shared a cab in such surprising circumstances, and whom he could not have imagined he would ever see again. That lady did pay us a visit with her husband shortly after his return from Egypt, when we were pleased and interested to hear of the latest discoveries there, and to hear, also, that the disagreement between Lord Crosspool and his son had at last been resolved amicably, and that the two were reconciled once more.

A week after the events I have described, a parcel arrived one morning at our chambers in Baker Street. It contained a cheque and a letter of thanks from Horace Barclay, and also a handsome pair of matching prints, which he hoped would be of interest to us, depicting Champion's unprecedented double triumph in the Derby and St. Leger of 1800. With a chuckle, Holmes passed these to me. I accepted them gladly, and hung them that very day on the wall above the dressing-table in my bedroom, since which time they have never ceased to give me pleasure.

THE JET BROOCH

DURING THE YEARS I shared chambers with Mr. Sherlock Holmes, the well-known criminal investigator, he handled many cases which involved the intimate private concerns of families whose names would be recognized by most readers of the daily press. I have included but few of these in this series of records I have lain before the public, for obvious reasons. I would be guilty of gross indiscretion and a very great breach of confidence were I to even hint at the nature of some of these cases, let alone provide a detailed account. Occasionally, however, when some time has elapsed since the events in question, and when I am able with a few little changes to disguise the identities of those involved, it is possible for me to give an account of one or two of these cases, if I judge that the facts of the matter are of sufficient interest to warrant it. Such a case is the one I shall now recount, an odd little tangle with a mysterious package at one end and a well-known song at the other.

It was the week before Christmas. The weather was cold, and I had awoken that morning to the rapid rat-a-tat-tat of hail against my bedroom window. Our breakfast finished, Sherlock Holmes had pulled the sofa a little nearer to the fire, and now lounged there in his old mouse-coloured dressing-gown, examining a small, flat package, about an inch in depth and three or four inches square, which had been delivered that morning.

"I wonder what this can be?" he remarked, turning it over in his hand, as I sat down on the other side of the fireplace. "I was not expecting anything today, so it is probably from a stranger."

"Why do you not open it and see?" I suggested.

"All in good time," said he. "I prefer to examine the outside first. It is easier to extract any information that may be there while the package is still intact. What do you make of it, Watson?" he asked, tossing it across to me.

"It is a little lighter than I had expected," I said, weighing it in my hand. "I thought it might have been a tin of tobacco, but I don't think it is heavy enough for that. It is wrapped in rather dull brown paper. This is not gummed in any way; it is simply fastened with string. It feels as if there is a small cardboard box inside the wrapping," I added, as I gave the package a gentle squeeze.

"Anything else?"

"Not that I can see."

"The address?"

I looked again at the address. "Why," I said in surprise, "the house number has been missed off. It simply says 'Mr. Sherlock Holmes, Baker Street, London'."

"Precisely. We benefit from the fact that the postman has delivered so many letters to me in the year we have been living here that he knows where to find me even when the address is incomplete. Now, I can't imagine that anyone who knew it would forget to include the house number in the address. It therefore seems likely that it was not known by the sender, who just trusted to luck that the parcel would find me. This supports my initial supposition that it is from a stranger, and someone, moreover, who was not in a position to find out my full address. Are there any more clues in the wrapping?"

"I don't think so," I replied after a moment.

"What about the string?"

"It is just a commonplace piece of thin twine," I said as I examined it.

"Not quite," said Holmes with a shake of the head. "It is certainly commonplace, but it is not one piece but three, which have been knotted together to make a suitable length."

"That is true, but is that of any significance?"

"Well, it suggests either someone who is very parsimonious with his string – using short pieces which most people would probably have thrown away – or perhaps a servant or other employee who has used discarded string – perhaps rescued from a waste-paper basket – to avoid being accused of using his employer's property for his own purposes."

"It is possible."

"Next we come to the handwriting itself, which, as you see, is in pencil. It seems to me it is a woman's hand. Why the handwriting of men and women should differ in so distinctive a way, I do not know – it is a mystery I have not yet solved – but that they do so differ is undeniable. Of course, each hand has its own idiosyncrasies and not all women write in this way, but I have never yet encountered a single man whose hand was like this. Therefore we are probably justified in saying it is the hand of a woman. It is clear enough, but not very regularly formed, so it may be the hand of a young person, although that inference cannot be drawn with the same degree of confidence. As to what you describe as dull brown paper, I think it is simply ordinary brown paper turned back to front, with the shiny side on the inside and the dull side on the outside. This suggests someone using old paper, and accords with the inferences we drew from the knotted string. Let us now open the package and see what it contains!"

He took a small pen-knife from the little table by his elbow, neatly cut the string and slipped it from the packet. Then he unwrapped the brown paper and examined it closely for a moment. "This piece has been cut – rather hurriedly to judge from the irregular shape – from a larger sheet. It is indeed a used piece of paper, for on the other side there is another address, written in ink, in a different hand. I rather fancy that my mysterious correspondent has used this ingenious method to indicate where the package has come from."

He passed me the paper and I saw that the address on the back of it was "Sir George Datchett, 8 Cumberland Gardens, Kensington", although the name on the first line had been crossed through with a pencil. Holmes, meanwhile, was carefully lifting the lid from the cardboard box which had been wrapped in the paper. As he did so, he let out a cry of surprise, and I saw that the box was full to the brim with some white powder. He licked his finger, pushed it into the powder and tasted it.

"It is flour," said he, "perfectly ordinary flour. If you would pass me a piece of paper from the desk, Watson, I will tip it out and see if there is anything else beneath the flour."

I laid the sheet of paper on the hearth-rug and watched as my companion carefully tipped the flour onto it. All at once, a small, dark object fell out onto the little heap of flour. He picked it up, blew off the loose flour, then rubbed it on the sleeve of his dressing-gown. As he held it up, I saw that it was an ornate brooch. In the centre was a circular black disc, the size of a large coin, its surface faceted so that it caught the light with each slight movement, and around the edge was a golden rim in which the metal was teased into fantastic little twirls and curls.

"The stone in the middle looks like jet," I said.

My friend nodded his head. "Yes, and the setting is gold. It looks quite a valuable piece of jewellery." He passed me the brooch, and lifted the lid of the box to his nose. "There is a distinctive smell to this box," he said.

"Of what?"

"Soap. Scented soap. Quite expensive, I should say, as might be used in a fairly well-to-do household. Now, why should anyone send me a jet brooch without explanation, packed in flour in an old soap-box? Ah!"

He leaned over and extracted a tiny scrap of paper from the little heap of flour on the floor. The paper was of a rough, irregular shape and appeared to have been torn from the edge of a sheet of newspaper.

"Perhaps this will make things clearer," said my companion, but his face remained impassive as he examined it, and, with a frown, he passed it to me.

Upon the scrap of paper, just three words were written in pencil: "Please help me".

"That does not tell us much," I remarked.

"No," said Holmes. "It is written in the same hand as the address, and with the same pencil, but that is no more than one would expect."

"I wonder why the box has been filled with flour."

"Presumably to prevent the brooch from rattling about. The use of flour suggests someone who has access to a kitchen, or, to look at it another way, someone who does not have access to any more usual packing material, such as cotton wool. To sum up, then, our mysterious correspondent is probably female, probably young, and probably a domestic servant in a well-to-do household, who has read or heard my name somewhere and believes I may be able to help her. In what way she requires help we cannot say. It may have something to do with this brooch, but that is not certain. The brooch may be simply a deposit to secure my services – although it seems an unlikely piece of jewellery for a young housemaid to have in her possession."

"I was just thinking the same," I remarked. "It looks like something an older woman might wear."

As I was speaking there came a ring at the front doorbell. A few moments later our landlady appeared in the doorway to inform us that a lady had called to see Mr. Sherlock Holmes, but had declined to give her name.

"One moment, Mrs. Hudson," said Holmes, springing to his feet. "I shall just restore a little order, and then you can show her up." Carefully, he picked up from the floor the sheet of paper on which lay the little heap of flour and carried it over to his desk. I gathered together the brown paper, string and cardboard box and handed them to him. These, together with the brooch and scrap of paper, he also placed on his desk and closed the lid. "Now," said he, as he pulled the sofa back from the fire, "I think we are ready to receive our visitor."

The woman who was shown into our room a few moments later was tall and stately in her bearing. Although of middle age she had retained the figure and posture of a younger woman. She was wearing a very smart dark blue costume with yellow piping on the edges.

"Pray, take a seat," said Holmes, indicating the chair beside the hearth, "and let us know what we can do for you."

"No, thank you," returned our visitor in a firm tone. "I shall not be here for more than a few moments. I have simply called to collect something."

"Oh?" said Holmes in surprise. "And what might that be?"

"A brooch," said she. "My brooch. It has been sent here in error. The wrong address was written on the package."

"Did you address it yourself?"

"No. Someone else did."

"To whom should it have been sent?"

"To the jeweller. The clasp needs repairing."

"Well," said Holmes, "so far as I am aware, we have received no misaddressed parcels here."

"You must have; it was posted yesterday."

Holmes shook his head. "It is but a few days to Christmas, madam," said he, "and you must know what that means for postal deliveries. The sorting-offices have mailbags piled up to the ceiling, and everything takes longer than usual. If you would give me your name and address," he continued, taking up his note-book and pencil from the table, "I shall let you know if any misaddressed parcel arrives here."

The woman hesitated. "No," said she. "I shall call again tomorrow."

She had turned to leave us, but stopped as Holmes spoke again.

"It seems strange to me," said he, "that you should have my address at all. Do you – or anyone in your household – wish me to look into some problem for you?"

"Absolutely not," she returned sharply. "It is no concern of yours how the mistake was made. I simply wish you to return to me the package when I call again. Do you understand?"

"Understanding is not the issue here, madam," returned Holmes in an urbane tone. "Rather, it is a matter of proof. You will call again and expect me to hand over to you something I have received in the post. But how do I know you have any right to the object in question? For all I know, the brooch may have been stolen – possibly by you. If so, the rightful owner would scarcely thank me for handing it over to someone I have never met before and who refuses to give me her name."

Our visitor's face blanched perceptibly. "How dare you make such an impertinent remark!" she cried in a sharp tone. She appeared about to say more, but bit her lip and was silent for a moment, breathing very heavily. "I shall return tomorrow," she said at length, scarcely able to get the words out as her breast rose and fell with emotion, "and shall bring a pair of ear-rings with me that you will see exactly match the brooch." With that, she turned on her heel and left the room, slamming the door as she did so.

"What a very entertaining interview!" said Holmes after a moment.

"She appeared to be one used to having her instructions obeyed," I remarked, "but she also seemed very emotional about something."

Holmes nodded his head. "More than that," said he; "she is in a state of extreme anxiety. About what, I do not know – but I intend to find out. Of course, what she told us is a tissue of lies: There is nothing wrong with the clasp on the brooch, as I could see when I examined it."

"Will you follow her, to see where she goes?" I asked.

Holmes shook his head. "I am confident that the address on the reverse of that brown paper is pertinent to the matter. That is where I shall go."

He disappeared into his bedroom and did not emerge again for fifteen minutes. I looked up from the newspaper I was reading as he did so and received a shock. In the place of the neatly turned out fellow-lodger I had expected to see, there stood a disreputable-looking figure with a tangled beard, wearing an old, threadbare jacket and cap and a pair of ill-fitting corduroy trousers. The appearance was completed by a bright check muffler that was knotted round his neck.

"Is that you, Holmes?" I queried, not entirely in jest.

"Yes, Watson, it is I," returned he. "It is not only villains who can adopt disguises in order to pursue their ends. I am off to do a little research, and have adopted the character of Jack Brown, itinerant knife-grinder, which I believe will serve me the best."

"Knife-grinder?" I cried with a chuckle. "But you haven't got a grinding-wheel!"

"True, but that is not an insuperable obstacle. I have a small grindstone, at least," he continued, producing a cylindrically-shaped stone from an inside pocket. "That may suffice for my purposes. Now, I can't say when I shall be back, but I should be obliged if you would save me a little bread and cheese from your mid-day meal, as I may not have much opportunity to eat while I am out!"

With a little salute he was gone, and I was left to wonder what it was he intended to do. For a time I tried to distract my thoughts with the day's newspapers, but they contained little of interest and I soon found my thoughts returning once more to the strange business my companion was involved in.

It seemed likely to me that the brooch really did belong to our morning visitor, but as Holmes had remarked, it did not appear to be in need of repair. Why, then, had it been sent anywhere at all, and why, in particular, had it been sent to Holmes? Our visitor did not appear to have sent it herself, but how, then, did she know it had been sent to our address? Who had sent it and why? Did our visitor know who had sent it or not? Why was she so determined to withhold her own name?

One thing that seemed evident was that she did not want Holmes to learn anything of the facts surrounding the brooch, but Holmes, it was clear, was equally determined that he would uncover these facts. He had had a tiny message in the package he had received, pleading for his help, and he needed no further persuasion than that. As I was beginning to learn, it was only rarely that he refused his help when it was sincerely requested. This generosity of spirit put enormous demands upon his constitution, demands that would have quite exhausted another man, but which seemed only to spur my friend on to greater industry.

I should not wish my readers to think that I was excessively self-absorbed, but as I reflected on my fellow lodger's intense and energetic activity, I was led inevitably to a consideration of my own contrasting circumstances. Little more than a year had passed since I had been invalided home from the war in Afghanistan, and I had stepped onto the jetty at Portsmouth with my health seemingly ruined forever. That had, in truth, not proved to be the case: I was definitely in somewhat better health now than I had been twelve months previously; but the slightest over-exertion was still likely to reduce me to the state of a limp rag. In these circumstances, I had come to look to Sherlock Holmes and his work to provide the zest and interest in my life which I could not provide for myself. I had begun to keep notes of his cases and had on a few occasions been able to accompany him on his investigations, although that was not always possible. Now, as I pondered the mystery of the jet brooch, I found myself glancing frequently at the clock on the mantelpiece, wondering when my friend would return, and if he would have managed to learn anything of the matter.

It was the middle of the afternoon before I heard Holmes's characteristically rapid footsteps ascending the stair. I could see at once, from the expression on his face, as he burst into the room like a whirlwind, that he had had some success.

"The bread and cheese is on the table, under the cloth," I said.

"Good man!" said he. "I am famished! I shall just remove this beard, which has begun to irritate me, and be with you in a moment. Do you know if we have any beer in the house at present?"

"Yes," I said. "There are some bottles of pale ale in the cupboard. I'll open one for you."

A few minutes later, he returned from his bedroom. The beard had gone, along with the grimy jacket and cap, and he had donned his old dressing-gown once more.

"Now," said he, as he laid into his simple meal with gusto, "I dare say you are wondering what I have discovered."

"I have been able to think of little else."

Holmes laughed. "Yes, it is an intriguing little problem, is it not! You will be interested to know, then, that I have learned a great deal – although there are still one or two small points that are not clear to me.

"I made my way to Cumberland Gardens, in Kensington. It is a short, handsome street, with plane trees along the sides. The houses are very smart, all in white stucco, and clearly the homes of the wealthy. I began my investigation by simply loafing about there and striking up a conversation with anyone who seemed likely to respond. I make a grand loafer, Watson, even if I say so myself. It seems to come naturally to me. Gradually, through conversation with some of the ostlers in the nearby mews, a man delivering vegetables from his cart and numerous other people, I was able to accumulate information about the occupants of number eight. Needless to say, I also gathered information about the occupants of numbers two, four, six and ten, which I endeavoured to forget as soon as I had heard it.

"Head of the household at number eight is Sir George Datchett, who was one of the founders of the Sea Eagle Marine Insurance Company, and who was knighted just two months ago for his services to commerce. His wife is Lady Hilary Datchett, and from the description I was given of her, I am fairly certain it was she who called upon us this morning. The family is completed by a son, Michael, aged about twenty, who is up at Oxford but returned home for the Christmas vacation two weeks ago, and a daughter, Olivia, who is seventeen and in her final year at the Cheltenham Ladies' College. She returned home last week. The domestic staff at the Datchett household numbers four. There is a butler, who organizes the household, a cook, a kitchen-maid and a chambermaid.

"Having amassed this information, I abandoned my loafing about and called at the tradesman's entrance of number eight, where I offered my services as a knife-grinder. This was rejected, much as I had expected, but I did not give up.

"'My dear lady,' I said to the cook, who had answered the door to me. I was about to extol the benefits of having sharpened knives, but she interrupted me.

"'Don't you be so bold,' said she. '"Dear lady" indeed!' But she laughed nonetheless and I could see that by amusing her I had gained a small foothold. I thereupon offered to sharpen a pair of scissors for her free of charge, 'to demonstrate the worth of my technique' as I put it. This she assented to, in grudging fashion, and I had thereby gained a few more minutes of standing in the kitchen doorway, which was of course my aim.

"As I did my best to sharpen the scissors a little, I chatted with her and watched as she and the kitchen-maid – who appeared to be called Lily – bustled about their work. When I'd finished, I declared that it was 'thirsty work' and asked if I might have a cup of water, which she brought me. Up to that point, to speak frankly, I hadn't really learned anything very useful, but all at once things changed. Another girl came into the kitchen in a maid's uniform. She was there for only a few moments, picked something up and left again, but in that few moments I thought I might have found my way to the heart of the mystery. I was already fairly confident, if you recall, that the brooch and the request for help had been sent to me by someone who was young, female and a domestic servant. Neither the cook nor the kitchen-maid looked likely to be so imaginative or enterprising, and the butler could surely be ruled out. But in the few moments the other housemaid had been in the kitchen, she had glanced across to where I stood, in the doorway. For half a second, our eyes had met and in that half-second I had seen an unusual depth and intelligence in her eye. Surely, I thought, this was my mysterious correspondent! I might also add that she was quite attractive."

"I thought you always said," I interrupted, "that the appearance of your clients was a matter of complete indifference to you."

"Yes, of course, that is true when their appearance is irrelevant to the case, as it generally is; but there are odd occasions when a woman's appearance is not simply an irrelevant, peripheral matter, but a central feature of the case, and I found myself wondering if this might not be one such instance. Sometimes, a pretty face in a household or other group of people can have an effect akin to the tossing of a small pebble into a placid mill-pond: ripples are created which, although sometimes scarcely discernible, can reach a long way.

"'That girl who was in here just now,' I said to the cook as I sipped my cup of water: 'I believe I may know her. Is it not Susan, who used to be in the household of Lady Darlington?'

"'No, it ain't,' said the cook. 'It's Jane, who didn't use to be in anybody's household.'

"'Of course,' I said, 'but I do know her from somewhere. Is it Jane Robinson?'

"'No it ain't. It's Jane Page – and how would a shabby-looking fellow like you know someone as sweet as Jane?'

"I was saved from having to answer that question by the reappearance of the girl herself.

"'Here, Jane,' said the cook. 'This dirty-looking scoundrel reckons he knows you from somewhere. Do you know him?'

"The girl looked across the kitchen at me, a very dubious expression on her face. 'I don't think so,' she said.

"I glanced at the cook. She had turned away to put something in the sink, and I took the opportunity to take a card from my pocket and held it out so that the girl could see it.

"She took a step closer. 'You don't look like I thought you would,' she said in a doubtful tone.

"I leaned in at the kitchen door. The cook and the kitchen-maid were still occupied at the other side of the room. I dropped the rough accent I had assumed in my guise as a knife-grinder and, lowering my voice, I said 'I'm in disguise. I've come in answer to your request for help. Quickly! Tell me what has happened!'

"She came to the kitchen-door and stuck her head out so that she would not be heard by the others. 'That brooch–' she began.

"'Yes? Is it Lady Hilary's?'

"'Yes. Someone put it in my box.'

"'Where was that? At the foot of your bed?'

"'Yes. And then Lady Hilary found it was missing from her jewellery case, and asked me if I had seen it anywhere. I said I hadn't, but it was in my pocket. I was walking round all day with it in there, trying to think what to do with it. I couldn't tell her where I'd found it – she'd just think I'd stolen it. But I couldn't just put it back in her room, either, as she told me she'd looked all round there – on the dressing-table and on the floor underneath it. Then I thought of you. Mr. Boardman–'

"'Is that the butler?'

"'Yes. He'd read us out a report in the newspaper one evening of how Sherlock Holmes of Baker Street had solved some mysterious burglary when nobody else could, and I thought perhaps you could help me.'

"'I'll try. Who do you think might have put the brooch in your box? Are any of the other servants jealous of you?'

"'Oh, no,' she returned in surprise. 'We all get on famously. Hardly ever a cross word.'

"'Your master and mistress?' I asked: 'do they treat you well? Are you happy here?'

"'Oh, yes,' she replied quickly. 'It's like heaven. Sir George is the kindest man I've ever known.'

"'And Lady Hilary?' I asked as she paused.

"'She can be a bit sharp sometimes,' Jane replied, lowering her voice a little more, 'but I think she's quite nice underneath.'

"'The children?'

"'I never see much of Miss Olivia. She's been away at school all the autumn and only came home at the end of last week. She seems nice enough.'

"'And the son?' I asked as the girl hesitated.

"'He's very good-looking, and they tell me he's quite clever.'

"'But?'

"'He's a bit bold sometimes. One night last week, I think he'd had a little too much to drink and got a bit over-familiar with me, if you know what I mean. I told him it was wrong, but he wouldn't take 'no' for an answer and I had to push him away. I was worried after that that I'd get into trouble.'

"'When did you find the brooch in your box?'

"'Just yesterday morning. Then, about tea-time, Sir George gave me some letters to post for him. I put them on the hall table and went downstairs to get my hat and coat. While I was downstairs I had the idea of sending the brooch to you, so I put it in an old soap-box, filled it up with flour to stop it rattling about, and wrapped it up.'

"'Could anyone have learned where you sent it? Did anyone see you writing the address?'

"'No, I'm sure they didn't.'

"'Did you perhaps leave it somewhere unattended for a few moments?'

"'No – wait! – I did! When I got back up to the hall, I realised I'd not got my gloves, so I put the little packet on top of Sir George's letters and ran back downstairs to get them. It was only for a few seconds, though, and there was nobody about in the hall.'

"'But someone might have passed through the hall, and seen the packet lying there?'

"'I suppose so. But I didn't see anyone.'

"At that moment, the butler, Boardman, entered the kitchen and put an end to our discussion by asking what I wanted. I told him I was a knife-grinder, he said they didn't need any knives grinding and that was that. I thanked them for the water, gave the cup back to Jane, and wandered off.

"I then loitered near the end of the street for some time, sitting on a low wall, smoking my old clay pipe. I was just deciding what to do next when my mind was made up for me. The front door of the Datchett's house opened and out stepped a smart and fashionably-dressed young man who proceeded along the pavement, tapping his cane as he went. I followed him until I judged we were far enough from the house that our encounter would not be visible from there.

"'Excuse me,' I said.

"'No, I haven't got any small change that I can spare,' he responded, scarcely glancing in my direction, and evidently taking me for some sort of beggar.

"'I don't want any,' said I.

"'Then you should be very happy that I'm not going to give you any,' said he without breaking stride.

"I could see that the only way I could halt his progress long enough to speak to him would be to surprise him, so I again dropped my rough accent and in my ordinary voice simply said 'Michael Datchett?'

"He stopped abruptly and turned to me. 'Who the devil are you, and how do you know my name?' he demanded.

"'It is my business to know things,' I said, and gave him my card.

"'Well, Mr. Sherlock Holmes,' said he as he handed back my card, 'what is it you want?'

"'I am looking into a matter concerning Jane Page.'

"'What, Jane the housemaid?' he cried in surprise. 'What has she done?'

"'She hasn't done anything. On the contrary, things have been done to her.'

"'Such as?'

"'You have recently forced your unwanted attentions upon her.'

"'Oh, I see,' said Datchett. 'That is what she told you, is it? Well Mr. Sanctimonious Holmes, you don't want to believe everything you are told.'

"'Do you deny it?'

"'No. Why should I? What I dispute is the term 'unwanted.' The whole matter is, in any case, an utter trifle.'

"'And now someone has stolen something from the house and placed it among Miss Page's possessions, with the evident intention of getting her accused of theft and thus dismissed, or even charged with the matter in a court of law.'

"'Surely it is more likely, if anything is stolen, that she has stolen it herself.'

"'If so, she would hardly have told me about it.'

"'You might think that, but you can never tell what people might do. Look, if she's taken a silver teaspoon from a cutlery drawer in the kitchen, or whatever it is, just tell her to put it back where she found it and no one will be any the wiser. I certainly won't mention it to anyone. Now I really must be off.'

"He turned away, but I persisted. 'It would be natural to wonder if the attempt to incriminate her was a form of revenge, perhaps perpetrated by someone whose advances had been rebuffed.'

"'Revenge?' he repeated in an incredulous tone, then burst out laughing. 'Why on earth should I want dear Jane dismissed? Christmas is coming. In two or three days, there will be bunches of mistletoe hanging up, and then she will be obliged to accept a kiss from me. You can't go against the venerable traditions of antiquity, you know! You'll see – or, at least, she will!' With that, he turned away once more and I was left to ponder the matter further."

"With any result?" I asked.

My friend shook his head. "There are several possibilities," he replied, "with little in the way of evidence to indicate which is true."

"What will you do, then?"

"I really think I shall have to go round to the Datchetts' house this evening and try to force matters to a conclusion. If I don't, Lady Hilary will call here again tomorrow morning and I shall have to give her the brooch. She will then take it away with her and the mystery will remain unresolved. For all we know, Miss Page might then be dismissed from her position, and that is not something I can contemplate with equanimity."

Holmes fell silent then for several minutes, and it was apparent he was considering the matter from every different point of view. "Would you care to accompany me?" he asked abruptly.

I was somewhat taken aback by this sudden and surprising invitation. "I think I should like that," I replied, "if I would not be in your way."

"Not at all," said my friend. "I think it would be interesting for you to see what I hope will be the final act in this little drama. It will be best if we call when the family is all present, but before they sit down to dine, so be ready to leave just after six. Make yourself as neat as possible, Watson, and I will do the same. We must make a favourable initial impression or we may not be seen at all."

It was starting to snow as we took a cab from Baker Street, and as we rattled along through the dark, raw evening, the street lamps we passed served only to illuminate the whirling and tumbling snowflakes which filled the air. By the time we reached Kensington, just after half past six, I could see that the snow was beginning to settle.

The front door of the Datchetts' house was opened to us by a large and imposing-looking butler who took Holmes's card into a room on the left while we waited in the hall. A moment later the door opened and the butler re-emerged, followed by a pleasant-faced, grey-haired man of about fifty, who held Holmes's card in his hand.

"What is this about, gentlemen?" he enquired in a puzzled tone, as he closed the door behind him.

"Something odd has happened to a member of your household," replied Holmes, "and I have been trying to help. I am here to conclude the matter."

Datchett frowned. "Perhaps we should continue this discussion in the study," said he, indicating a door on the opposite side of the hall.

"Excuse me, Sir George, but are your family members all in the drawing-room?"

"Yes, they are, as it happens. We were just chatting, and are about to dine shortly. Why do you ask?"

"I think it would be better if I said what I have to say in front of everyone. It will not take very long."

"Who is principally concerned in the matter?"

"Your maid, Jane Page."

"Has she done something she shouldn't have?"

"No."

"Very well," said Datchett after a moment's hesitation, "if you think it best. But be aware that I am only agreeing to this because I have heard something of you, and your reputation is that of a gentleman. I do not want any unpleasantness. My wife detests anything of that sort, and my daughter is still a schoolgirl. Do you understand?"

Holmes nodded his head but did not reply, and, after a moment, Datchett opened the drawing-room door and we followed him into the room.

"This is Mr. Sherlock Holmes and his colleague, Dr. Watson," said Datchett, as his wife, son and daughter turned towards us, their features expressing surprise. "They have something to tell us. Go ahead, Mr. Holmes," he continued as he seated himself on a sofa.

"I will be as brief as possible," Holmes began. "Your maid, Jane, found a valuable piece of jewellery – a jet brooch – among her own possessions the other day, which she recognized as belonging to her mistress. She had no idea how it got there. Before she could do anything about it, Lady Hilary found that the brooch was missing. Frightened that she would be accused of stealing it and unable to think what to do with it, Jane, on the spur of the moment, parcelled it up and sent it to me. This removed the immediate danger from her, by getting the brooch out of the house. No doubt she also thought that my involvement might lead to the truth being revealed.

"Unfortunately for her, Lady Hilary learned where she had sent the brooch. I assume, madam," he continued, addressing Lady Hilary, "that you saw the package lying on the hall table."

"That is correct. I happened to pass through the hall, and as I did so I glanced at some items on the table that were awaiting posting. Most of them, I could see, were letters my husband had written, but there was also a small package which appeared to have been addressed in a different hand. When I mentioned it to my husband later, he said he knew nothing about it."

"You then conjectured that it might have contained the brooch?"

"Yes, from the size and shape of the package."

"When you called at my chambers this morning, and gave me some rigmarole about the brooch needing repair, you did not assume I was involved in the theft of the brooch, or consider calling the police?"

"No, of course not. Like others, I have heard of you as one who solves crimes, not commits them."

"And yet you presumably felt sure by then that it was Jane who had sent the brooch to me."

"Yes. What of it?"

"Do you believe that Jane stole the brooch?"

"No."

"Why not?"

"Because I don't believe it is in her character to do such a thing."

"Well, if Jane did not place the brooch under her own pillow, then someone else did. She was led, understandably, to the conclusion that someone had deliberately tried to incriminate her, so she would be accused of theft and dismissed, a conclusion with which I entirely concur. If you did not believe that Jane had stolen it, you must surely have reached the same conclusion. There is no other possibility."

Lady Hilary hesitated a moment, and glanced at her husband as if for support, but the expression on his face was one of complete mystification, and it was evident she could receive no assistance from that quarter.

"I repeat," Holmes persisted, "if Jane did not remove the brooch from your jewellery-case, then someone else did, and I believe you know who that someone is, which is why you were so keen to hush the matter up, and had no intention of pressing charges against Jane."

"Oh, all right," said Lady Hilary abruptly in a sharp tone, rising to her feet. "I took the brooch myself. I was looking for a way of dismissing her. I felt my husband was becoming too fond of her, and that she was almost eclipsing his own children in his eyes."

"What nonsense!" cried her husband.

"But when I realised she had sent the brooch to you," Lady Hilary continued, ignoring the interruption, "I decided it had all got out of hand. I just wanted to get the brooch back, brush the whole business under the carpet and forget about it."

"So, let us be clear about it," said Holmes. "You yourself took the brooch from your jewellery case, and you yourself placed it under the pillow on Jane's bed?"

"Yes, I did. So now you know everything."

"Unfortunately, I do not."

"What do you mean?"

"Madam, you are not speaking the truth."

"How dare you call me a liar in my own house!"

"The house is irrelevant. I know you are not speaking the truth, madam, because you say it was you who placed the brooch under Jane's pillow, and I know you did not do so. I know you did not do so because no one did so: Jane did not find the brooch under her pillow, but in the box at the foot of her bed."

"It is no good, Mother," said Olivia Datchett, speaking for the first time since we had entered the room. "He has tricked you." She rose to her feet. "Mother is trying to protect me," she said, addressing Holmes, her voice breaking with emotion. "It was I who took the brooch, and I who placed it in Jane's box."

"Olivia!" cried her father. "Surely you would not stoop to such a low, mean trick!"

At this, the girl burst into tears. "It's true," she said, between sobs. "It was mean of me, and stupid, and I am very, very sorry."

I took a handkerchief from my pocket and passed it to her, as no one else seemed to be doing so, and she dabbed her eyes.

"Can this really be true, Hilary?" asked Datchett.

"Yes," replied his wife. "Olivia came to me and asked if I had seen the jet brooch recently, as she said she had been trying to find it and couldn't see it anywhere. But there had been an odd expression on her face as she spoke to me, and all the time I was looking for the brooch I suspected that she herself had had something to do with its disappearance. Eventually, in the evening, I confronted her with my suspicions and she admitted the truth. I then remembered the package I had seen on the hall table, and told her I was fairly certain I knew where the brooch had gone. I said I would try to get it back the next morning, so we could put the matter behind us and forget it had ever happened. Unfortunately, things did not work out so simply as that."

The room fell silent for a moment then, until, with a bewildered shake of the head, Datchett addressed his daughter. "Whatever can have possessed you, Olivia, to do such a thing? What has Jane ever done to cause you displeasure?"

"Mother told me in a letter that you have arranged for a special tutor to come in to coach Jane in English and arithmetic."

"And you were jealous of the attention? It is only one afternoon a week, Olivia – I am not sending her to the Cheltenham Ladies' College! She is an intelligent girl, and works very hard. I thought it was the least I could do. She has great potential and could make someone a good housekeeper one day – or a good wife."

"Then in Mother's last letter she said that Jane had been singing so beautifully that it had made you cry."

"Oh, that!" Lady Hilary interrupted. "I only put that in the letter to amuse you, Olivia. You know what Father is like; he cries when he hears sad songs; he cries when he sees a sad play; and sometimes he even cries when he sees a happy play! It is just his way, and I am sure we would not want him any different!"

"He never cries when I sing," said Olivia through her sobs.

"Ah! I see!" said her father in a tone of enlightenment. "Now I think I understand! Sit down, sit down, both of you – and you, too, gentlemen – and I will tell you something you do not know. Perhaps then you, too, will understand matters a little better." He closed his eyes for a few moments, as if gathering his thoughts, before continuing.

"When Jane was just a tiny baby," he began at length, "she was left at the foundling hospital. Neither she nor anyone else has any idea who her mother and father were. She was simply left one morning on the doorstep in a little wicker basket. A few months later, she was adopted by an elderly couple called Page from the East End, who gave her the name of Jane. The man worked as a cobbler, and apparently did all right for himself, but just a few years later both Mr. and Mr. Page fell ill and died within a few months of each other. Thus the only family little Jane had ever known had been taken from her. She was only five years old at the time. Mrs. Page's sister took her in for a little while, but she herself was elderly and could not cope with the child, and less than a year later she gave her up and she was placed in an orphanage. After a time, she was moved from that orphanage to another, and, later, to a third. In all, she remained in such institutions for nearly ten years.

"Two years ago, when we needed a new chambermaid, Jane was recommended to me. I agreed to take her almost as soon as we had met, for I could see at once that she showed great promise, and I have not been disappointed. Despite her unfortunate and unhappy childhood – which might have embittered or spoiled the character of some people – she has fitted into our household very well, and gets along well with everyone.

"Now I come to what occurred two weeks ago. I was in my bedroom early one evening, changing for dinner. My bedroom, as you know, overlooks the back garden, and through the window I could see that it was a dark, cold evening. All at once, as I stood before the mirror, buttoning my shirt, I heard someone singing in the garden below. I looked out, and there, illuminated by a light from the kitchen window, was Jane. She was putting some rubbish in the dustbin – not the most pleasant of jobs at the best of times – and singing softly and sweetly to herself. And do you know what she was singing, this girl who has never had any family, nor anywhere she could ever call her home? She was singing *Home, Sweet Home* – 'Mid pleasures and palaces though we may roam; be it ever so humble, there's no place like home.'

"As I stood there listening, I knew that the home she referred to was our house, that we had, without particularly intending it, given Jane the first real home she had ever had in her life. At that realisation, as much as at her voice, I admit I began to weep, but I am not ashamed of it. Your mother came into the room then, and asked me why I was crying. I told her I had been listening to Jane singing, but it was getting late, we had visitors coming, and there wasn't time for me to explain all the circumstances to her. There," said Datchett in conclusion, "that is the story of how Jane's singing brought me to tears, and I hope, Olivia, that you will understand the matter a little better now."

The room had fallen silent, save for the girl's quiet sobbing, and remained so for several minutes. Then Sherlock Holmes rose to his feet and took from his pocket the jet brooch, which he handed to Lady Hilary.

"That, I believe, concludes the matter, from my perspective at least," said he.

"Thank you for unravelling it all for us," said Sir George Datchett as he stood up and shook my companion by the hand.

We had turned to leave when there came a sharp pull at the front doorbell, and I heard the sound of singing from outside the house. A moment later, the butler entered the room to announce that the carol-singers from St Mary's had called, collecting for the parish charity.

"Oh!" cried Olivia. "I forgot it was tonight. I wanted to go with them! May I go? Please, Father? I can get a bite to eat later."

"Of course you may," said Datchett. "But you must wrap up warm, Olivia. It is a very cold night."

"And may I take Jane with me?" she asked. "I know from something she said to me this morning that she would dearly love to go carol-singing."

"Certainly, certainly," said Datchett, "but see that she, too, wraps up well. Now I must speak to the carol-singers."

With a cry of delight, the girl ran from the room, and I heard her footsteps clattering down the stair to the basement. We followed her father to the front door and stood for several minutes, listening to the carol-singers. Behind them in the cold night air the snow was now falling heavily. As they finished their carol, Datchett spoke to their leader, but I was distracted by the arrival behind me in the hall of two girls in overcoats, hats and mufflers. I turned to see them, but they slipped quickly past us and ran down the steps to join the carol-singers outside.

Presently, as the carol-singers made their way out of the gate and along the street, Sir George Datchett turned to us and thanked my friend again for his help. "Please send me your account for the trouble you have been put to," he said.

Holmes shook his head with a smile. "That won't be necessary," said he. "Sometimes the elucidation of the truth is itself more than adequate recompense."

As we made our way down the street, we came to where the carol-singers had stopped before another house, and paused a moment to listen. A girl at the back of the group glanced our way and I had an impression of a pair of bright, piercing eyes in a happy face, framed in tight dark curls. Holmes made a little gesture and she left the group and ran over to where we stood.

"I am confident everything will be all right now, Jane," said he, leaning over to speak closer to her.

"Yes," she returned in a breathless voice. "Miss Olivia has explained it all to me. It's all right now."

"But," he continued, "if at any time you find yourself in difficulty once more, do not hesitate to write to me again."

She nodded her head, then, raising herself on her tip-toes, she gave my companion a little peck on the cheek. "You look better without your beard," said she in a gay tone, and ran back to re-join the carol singers.

"I feel I should point out to you, Watson," said Holmes in a tone of embarrassment, as we resumed our progress down the street, "that that is not a regular occurrence at the conclusion of my cases."

I laughed. It amused me greatly to see my logical friend, usually so cold and unemotional, discomfited by a young girl, and I confess that I teased him about it for some time afterwards. Trivial incident though it may have been, I thought it worthy of mention here as being the only occasion in all of my records when my famous friend received payment from his client in the form of a kiss.

THE MAN IN THE GREEN TWEED SUIT

MY MORNING MEDICAL ROUND being finished earlier than usual, I had called upon my friend, Mr. Sherlock Holmes, on a pleasant day in October and found him lounging full-length on the sofa in his old mouse-coloured dressing-gown, apparently staring at the ceiling. On the floor beside him lay crumpled heaps of newspapers, like so much flotsam washed up against the sofa by some unseen tide.

He acknowledged my presence with a slight wave of his hand, but did not move, and, aware as I was of his occasional weakness for artificial stimulants when he found life too boring to contemplate, I feared for a moment that he was in the poisonous grip of some powerful narcotic. But, abruptly, he swung his legs to the floor and sat up, with a sparkle and clarity in his eyes which told me that my fears were groundless.

"My dear fellow!" said he. "Do forgive my rudeness! My thoughts were elsewhere. It is always a pleasure to see you here, Watson, as I'm sure you know."

"I take it you have no case in hand at present," I remarked as I sat down in my old arm-chair.

"On the contrary," he responded, as he reached for his pipe and the slipper in which he kept his tobacco, "I have a singularly puzzling business to consider. Our old friend, Inspector Lanner, called round last night to consult me on the matter."

"Were you able to help him?"

Holmes shook his head. "Not in any very decisive way. Of course, I have my own theory – one cannot help but form a preliminary hypothesis, even against one's own better judgement – but I cannot prove it, and did not feel inclined to trouble Lanner with it. I was just running over the facts of the matter again in my mind, when you entered."

"I would be very interested to hear about it," said I, "if it would be helpful to you to repeat it aloud to someone."

"Very well," said he. "It's the Wentworth case. You have perhaps read something of it in your newspaper."

"Very little, other than the barest outline. I have been kept very busy lately with my professional duties, and have not had time to study the papers in the way I used to."

"All the better!" cried my friend, as he put a match to his pipe. "Then your judgement will not be biased by what you have already read. As I have often remarked to you, one cannot hope to solve a case merely from reading an account of it in the daily press. Such accounts are generally lacking in the very details one wishes most to know about. In this case, we have, at least, Inspector Lanner's account, which is a little more detailed than that in the papers. Indeed, because of the nature of the case, Lanner's account may be all the material we shall ever have, so we must make the most of it.

"The case, Watson, as you probably know, is one of murder, the murder of a gentleman by the name of Piers Wentworth, of Links House, Woodside Lane, Bickley, a man well known in the more Bohemian circles of London Society, who was found shot dead in his own study."

"One of the papers," I interrupted, "the *Daily Chronicle*, I think it was, reported that when the body of the unfortunate man was discovered, all the doors of the house were found to be locked on the inside."

Holmes chuckled. "That is true," said he, "but the fact is of no significance. That item of information represents, I take it, an attempt by the *Daily Chronicle* to add a little more mystery to a crime which is in no need of such embellishment. The back door of the house, and the French window which gives directly from the study onto the back garden were indeed both locked on the inside. The front door, however, has a sprung latch, so that anyone leaving the house that way merely has to pull the door shut behind him and the lock is engaged. It is therefore practically a certainty that the murderer left the house by the front door, but the point is of no importance. Of somewhat greater interest is the question as to how he had entered the house in the first place – but I shall come to that in a moment.

"Now, to give you a little more general information about the victim of this crime: He seems to have been moderately well off; not what might be described as significantly wealthy, but, still, sufficiently comfortably placed that he was not obliged to pursue any particular profession. He did, however, have an interest in a couple of commercial enterprises, one a brokerage house in the City, the other a wholesale drapers in Holborn, at both of which he spent one day a week.

"He was not married, and lived alone in a fairly isolated house near Bickley, which, as you are no doubt aware, is in Kent, just the other side of Bromley. His sole domestic servant was an elderly widow, Mrs. Barnham, who acted as cook, housekeeper and maid-of-all-work, although her duties, according to her own testimony, were not very exacting.

"Wentworth's recreation seems to have consisted chiefly of two activities. The first of these was golf. He was a very keen golfer and was able to indulge his fondness for the game without difficulty, as his house adjoins the local golf course. There is in fact a gate at the bottom of the back garden which gives directly onto the course. Except in bad weather, he played most days of the week, save those days he was obliged to go up to town on business.

"His second great interest in life and probably the more important, both from his point of view and from ours, was the fair sex. Of course, most men have an interest, to a greater or lesser degree, in the opposite sex, but Wentworth seems to have been one of those in whom this interest has become the ruling passion of their lives. He was, in short, something of a Don Juan, and, by all accounts, a very successful one. For this information, as with the rest of what we know, we must thank the indefatigable researches of Inspector Lanner. Wentworth had never been married, he had never even been nearly married, and seemed unlikely ever to be so. It is said that he valued his independence and his bachelor establishment at Bickley too highly for that. But the chase, the pursuit and conquest of whichever female he had set his sights on at any given moment, that, it seems, was the source of the very greatest pleasure for Wentworth, and the mainspring of his life.

"He was no longer a young man – he was not far short of his fortieth birthday – but the passage of the years does not seem to have brought any noticeable alteration in his habits. He would go up to town, to a theatre or music-hall, at least once a week and often more frequently than that, where he would endeavour to strike up an acquaintance with some pretty girl or other and invite her to dine with him. He was also a member of Tilbury's Club, in the Haymarket, where he would call in at least once a week, to play cards and the like. He was well known there, and had a fairly large circle of acquaintances, but does not seem to have had any really close friends.

"And that," said Holmes after a moment, "gives you the main points of the antecedents to the case." He leaned over, struck a match on the hearth and put it to his pipe, which had gone out while he was speaking. "Is that clear so far, Watson? Do you have any questions?"

"Clear enough," I replied, "but I do have one question: Did the murdered man have any other place of lodging, an apartment in town, for instance?"

Holmes shook his head. "He had had such a place when he was younger, a small *pied-a-terre* in Knightsbridge, but had sold it about ten years ago. The train-journey from Victoria down to Bickley is a fairly quick one and the service is frequent, so I imagine Wentworth found it just as easy to go home at night as to stay in town. He did occasionally stay at his club, but not very often, and if the evening had got late, he sometimes put up with one of his cronies. He had also been known to borrow someone else's apartment in town for a few days when the owner was away.

"Now, on the day in question, which was just over two weeks ago, on the twenty-fifth of September, Wentworth did not come up to town. He had played a round of golf in the morning with Colonel Stockley, another member of the local golf club, who states that there was nothing in either Wentworth's speech or manner which was at all unusual. He had then spent the rest of the day at home, reading, attending to business correspondence and so on. That day being a Wednesday, Wentworth's housekeeper had the afternoon off, as was usual, but before she left to visit friends, at about twelve o'clock, she had prepared a cold luncheon, which she had left, under covers, on the dining-room table. The weather all that week was pleasant and mild, and when Wentworth had informed her, a few days earlier, that he was expecting a visitor on Wednesday, he had mentioned that they might take lunch in the open, at Frog's Heath, a popular spot locally for walking and taking picnics. But he seems to have dropped this idea, as he did not mention it on the Wednesday. Nor did he mention who the visitor he was expecting might be. The departure of Mrs. Barnham, by the way, was the last time that Wentworth was seen alive. She was just going out of the front gate when he called to her, then he followed her down the path and they exchanged a few words by the gate concerning what she had left for luncheon. The nearest house is some considerable distance away, but it has a very large garden which comes close to that of Links House, and at that time a gardener was working there. He overheard the brief conversation between Wentworth and his housekeeper and states that it was as Mrs. Barnham describes, and that there seemed nothing unusual in Wentworth's manner.

"The housekeeper returned at about half past five, and let herself in with her latch-key. After hanging up her coat, she went into the study to inform her master she was back and to ask if there was anything he required. There, she was shocked to find Wentworth lying on his back upon the floor, the front of his clothes soaked with blood. She at once ran to fetch the local doctor, who pronounced him dead, shot through the heart at close quarters about four hours previously with a small-calibre pistol.

"The police were quickly notified of the crime, and Inspector Lanner was assigned to the case. The first significant fact he discovered was that there was a considerable sum of money on both the desk and table in Wentworth's study; not a huge amount, but certainly enough to tempt a thief. That this had not been touched suggested, therefore, that the motive for the crime had not been theft, but something else. There was also no indication that a struggle had taken place in the study, which suggested that Wentworth had been taken by surprise by his assassin. The question then arose as to how the murderer had gained entry to the house. There seemed to be two possibilities here: either Wentworth himself had admitted him at the front door, or the French window of the study had been standing open when the murderer arrived and he had gained entry to the house that way. If the former, then Wentworth probably knew the identity of his murderer; if the latter, then the inference is not so clear.

"Energetic enquiries were at once instituted in the district, to try to learn if anyone had seen this assassin, but these enquiries largely drew a blank. None of Wentworth's immediate neighbours had seen any strangers on the road that day, and nor had they seen anyone at all entering Wentworth's property by the front gate. However, two members of the local golf club – a Mr. Ould and a Mr. Poulter – had been playing a round that afternoon, and they state that at about one o'clock they had seen a man crossing the golf course from right to left some distance ahead of them. He was about fifty yards away – too far for them to give a very accurate description of him, but close enough for them to be sure that it was no one that they had ever seen before. He had a beard, they say, was wearing a green tweed suit, with a soft, wide-brimmed felt hat upon his head, and was carrying a light-brown overcoat folded over his arm. They had just finished the third hole at the time, and were about to tee off on the fourth when they saw him, and as the man was crossing the fairway ahead of them, one of them called 'fore' to warn him. He turned, raised his arm and waved in acknowledgement of the warning.

Then he paused, glanced up at the sky, slipped on his overcoat and proceeded on his way. The last they saw of him was when he passed behind a clump of bushes to the left of the fairway. As the path he was on leads directly to Woodside Lane, passing the back garden gate of Wentworth's house as it does so, they assumed that that was where he was going, and gave him no more thought. They never saw him again.

"As the only person seen in the vicinity of Wentworth's house on the day he was murdered, the man in the green tweed suit naturally became the focus for all the police enquiries, but he proved somewhat difficult to track down. No one seemed to have noticed him as he passed along the road from the centre of Bickley towards Wentworth's house, and no one at the golf club had noticed him either, save only the two men I mentioned before. Enquiries at the railway station proved a little more fruitful, however. There, a porter, who was busy on the platform during the afternoon, recalled seeing a young man in a green tweed suit sitting on one of the platform benches, smoking a cigarette. A light-brown overcoat was flung over the back of the bench beside him. The porter says he did not give the man much consideration. He did think, however, that with his well-cut clothes and the languid way he was lounging on the bench, the young man seemed something of a 'swell.' When the train for Victoria rolled in, the young man rose to his feet, slipped on his overcoat, although he didn't bother to fasten it, and made his way to a smoking carriage.

"From the description of the young man, the police understandably thought it more likely that he would have been returning to the West End, rather than anywhere in the suburbs, and, accordingly, concentrated their enquiries at Victoria station. Here, however, they again drew a blank. None of the officials there could recall seeing such a traveller on the day in question. The police then widened their enquiries to Ludgate Hill and the other stations on the City branch, thinking that the young man might have changed trains at Herne Hill, but with an equal lack of success. They also asked Wentworth's housekeeper if her master had ever had a visitor answering to the description given by the two golfers and the porter at Bickley station, but she could not think of anyone.

"Now, as the young man seen on the golf-course had also been seen at the railway station, it seemed a reasonable assumption that he had arrived in and left the district by train, but the police were puzzled at first as to why he had chosen the route he did from the station to Wentworth's house. You see, the road from the railway station towards Links House forks as it comes away from the centre of Bickley. The left-hand branch, Woodside Lane, has a number of houses on it before passing the front of Wentworth's own house. The right-hand branch, Links Lane, which goes up to the golf club-house, is much narrower, has no houses on it, and is little frequented save by those bound for the golf-course. The left-hand branch is the shorter, more direct route from the station to Wentworth's house. The right-hand branch is longer, but much quieter. That the gentleman in the green tweed suit had chosen the latter route therefore suggests certain conclusions. First, that as he was familiar enough with the district to know that it was possible to get to Wentworth's house by going up Links Lane and then crossing the golf-course, he had almost certainly visited Wentworth's house before, or had been instructed by someone who had. Second, that as he had chosen the way which was longer but quieter, it must be supposed that his intention was to avoid being seen. This in turn suggests that the murder was not an accident or the result of a spur-of-the-moment decision, but had been planned in advance.

"There the matter rested for a couple of days, until one of the officials at Bromley station – which is, of course, the very next station on the line towards London after Bickley – came forward with a fresh piece of information, having read of the crime in his newspaper. No enquiries had up to then been made at Bromley, it being the almost universal belief that the murderer – if that is what the young man was – must have travelled from Bickley to Victoria, or somewhere close to it. The idea that he might have travelled just one stop on the line before alighting had been assumed to be so unlikely as to be not worth considering. That, however, is precisely what the railway official's information suggested. The official in question, a man by the name of Badger, had been in charge of the left-luggage office at Bromley station on the afternoon of the day of the murder. He states that a young man in a light-brown overcoat and a soft brown hat called at the office at about half past three in the afternoon to collect a medium-sized carpet-bag which had been deposited there earlier that same day. As to the green tweed suit, he can't be certain, as the young man's overcoat was buttoned up. But, aside from that, he has provided the best description so far. The man, he says, was certainly young, of medium height, with light brown hair and a sandy, almost gingery beard. He also states that the young man did not say very much, seeming preoccupied as he handed over the ticket relating to the carpet-bag. Mr. Badger says that he himself made some remark about the fine weather, at which the other smiled in a pleasant enough fashion, nodded his head in agreement, and made some observation in a quiet voice, which Mr. Badger did not catch. After collecting the bag, the young man simply walked away, and was not seen again by anyone. He may have caught the next up train, he may have caught the next down train, he may have left the station altogether: no one knows."

"As he had a travelling-bag with him," I interjected, "could it be that he was not going home, but was on his way to somewhere else, perhaps in Kent or Sussex?"

"The police certainly considered that a possibility."

"He may even have been making for Folkestone or Dover," I added, "to take a boat to the Continent."

"That, also, was considered possible. However, although enquiries have been made at all the ports, they have met with no success. The man in the green tweed suit has become somewhat like the 'x' in algebra – the unknown quantity. Do you have any further observations?"

“I have at least some questions,” I responded. “First of all, is it known who deposited the carpet-bag that the young man collected on the afternoon of the murder?”

“No. All that is known for certain is that the bag was deposited on the same day as it was collected; the time and date are on the ticket. But a different official was on duty there in the morning, someone not as observant as Mr. Badger, and he cannot recall who it was that left the bag there.”

“It seems to me,” I remarked after a moment, “that even if these three sightings are all of the same person, as seems more than likely, we still cannot say for certain that he is definitely the murderer of Piers Wentworth.”

“Why do you say that?” asked Holmes, a note of curiosity in his voice.

“It seems to me possible,” I replied, “that even if the young man crossing the golf-course was indeed making for Wentworth’s house, as appeared to be the case, he may not have committed any crime. It is possible that when he reached the house he found that Wentworth had already been shot dead by someone else. Then, seeing that there was nothing he could do for the dead man, and fearing that he himself would be accused of the crime, he decided to make himself scarce and deny ever having been there.”

“That would certainly be possible,” conceded my friend, “although no one else was seen in the vicinity of Wentworth’s house on that day, and it is difficult to see why, if he is innocent, he should fear being accused of the crime unless (a) he had a good motive for committing it, and (b) he had arrived armed with a pistol of his own. Still, I am glad to see that you are keeping an open mind on the subject. You are becoming a more careful reasoner in your mature years, Watson!”

“I don’t know about ‘mature years,’” I returned with a chuckle; “but all the years I spent lodging here with you have no doubt had an effect upon my investigative abilities.”

“Any other questions?”

"Yes. What of Wentworth's luncheon guest? You have said nothing about him. Was that the young man in the green tweed suit, or was it someone else? Surely that person, if not the murderer himself, was more likely than anyone else to have seen the murderer."

Holmes shook his head. "The person Wentworth was expecting may have been the man in the green tweed suit or it may not. No one knows. The fact is that no one else came. The meal which Mrs. Barnham had laid on the dining-room table remained perfectly undisturbed when she returned at half-past five. However, what *is* known is who the luncheon-guest was originally supposed to be. One of the performers at the Frivolity Theatre in the Strand, a singer and dancer who goes by the name of Belinda Lee, came forward the day after the murder – when news of the crime was in all the morning papers – to say that she had been invited to Links House for lunch on the 25th. There is no matinee performance at the Frivolity Theatre on Wednesdays, and she had often visited Links House on that day, although not for several weeks. On the day before, however – that is, Tuesday the 24th – she had arrived at the theatre in the early afternoon to find that among the letters which had come for her that morning was one from Wentworth, expressing regret that their Wednesday luncheon appointment would have to be postponed, as he had had notice that someone else proposed to call on him that day and he could not get out of the arrangement. He said he was very sorry about this, and he looked forward to seeing her on another day."

"Did he mention who this other visitor might be?"

"No, he didn't. In Wentworth's study, Lanner found a diary or appointment-book. On the page for Wednesday, 25th September, a single letter – 'B' – is inscribed. This probably refers to Miss Lee, her first name, as I mentioned, being Belinda, but we can't say for certain. It might also be someone else's initial."

"I suppose if he had just heard, on the Monday, say, that someone else intended to pay him a visit, he would be unlikely to forget it, and there would thus be little point in recording the fact in his appointment-book."

"That is certainly possible," said Holmes. "It is also possible, however, that he had some other specific reason for not wishing the appointment to be recorded."

"Such as?"

"I don't pretend to know. I am merely stating that it is a possibility."

"And Wentworth's housekeeper could shed no light on the question of his likely visitor?"

"None whatever. Apparently, it was only rarely that he told her who he was expecting, and she, like the good, discreet housekeeper she was, never asked. That illustrates one of the problems of this case: although Wentworth's habits were, in a general sense, well known to everyone, no one really knows any details, particularly of what he intended to do on the day he was murdered. Without such details, it is very difficult to solve a case such as this, and I fear that Lanner is finding it an uphill struggle."

"Is that the end of the matter, then, from your point of view?"

"Not quite. Lanner is calling round this morning, to conduct me to interviews he has arranged with some of Wentworth's associates. He has questioned them all already, without eliciting any information of interest, but thought it might be worthwhile for me to see them for myself and form my own opinion of them. Having nothing better to do, I agreed to accompany him, although I shall probably take no part in the questioning. Will you come? You can leave your medical case here."

I had opened my mouth to reply when there came a peal at the front-door bell. A moment later, Inspector Lanner was shown into the room. There was a look of anxiety upon his features, but his expression brightened up considerably when he saw me.

"Why, Dr. Watson!" he cried, greeting me like a long-lost friend. "It seems a long time since our paths have crossed! You are coming with us, I take it. It will be good to have another opinion on the matter."

I had been about to tell Holmes that I could not spare the time, partly, I admit, because I could not see that we were likely to learn anything fresh if Lanner had already questioned all the people we were going to see; but the policeman appeared so pleased that I might accompany them that I didn't have the heart to disappoint him. "I should be delighted to come," I said, and a few moments later, the three of us set off.

"I imagine Mr. Holmes has given you an account of the case," said Lanner to me as we walked along. "You will understand, then, that we have believed right from the start that Wentworth's murderer was someone known to him."

"That must have narrowed the field down considerably."

"Yes, but it was still a large one. Wentworth seems to have had a very wide circle of acquaintances. However, we have managed to eliminate from our enquiries all those people he knew at the golf club, and most of those connected with his business activities, too. He did have a quarrel, the week before he died, with someone at the stockbroking firm in which he has an interest, but that doesn't seem to have amounted to much. In any case, the whereabouts of all these people on the day of Wentworth's death are all accounted for. With his personal friends and acquaintances it has been a different story. We have had the devil of a job trying to establish their movements on that day. In the last few days, however, we have eliminated most of them, leaving us with just three young men whose account of their activities cannot be satisfactorily verified – George Redfearn, Alexander Wychwood and Albert Maitland. As these three men were also three of Wentworth's closest acquaintances, had visited his house several times and knew his habits well, they are, in my opinion, our chief suspects – but I can get no further than that. It is they we are going to see this morning. We shall also pay a visit on Miss Belinda Lee, who knows these three particularly well, for a view from the other side of the fence, as it were."

Our first call was at a modern apartment building in New Cavendish Street, near the corner of Marylebone Lane. This was, Lanner informed us, the residence of George Redfearn. He had been a regular crony of Wentworth's in the last two or three years, although they had apparently fallen out over a woman, and had not been so close recently as they had been before.

Our ring at the bell was answered by a middle-aged woman in the uniform of a housekeeper, who showed us into a light and airy drawing-room, Lanner having introduced Holmes and myself as consulting detectives. For several minutes we sat waiting in silence, before Redfearn himself at length appeared, clad in a dressing-gown, unshaven and bleary-eyed.

"Well?" he demanded in an aggressive tone, as he dropped into an armchair. "What do you want? I've already told you all I know."

"We simply wish to clarify one or two points, sir," returned Lanner placidly.

"Clarify? I should have thought it was clear enough already – as far as I am concerned, anyway. The rest of it may be as clear as mud for all I know, but I neither know nor care. Somebody's shot Wentworth and it wasn't me: that's all I know."

"It doesn't sound as if the thought of it troubles you very greatly," observed Lanner.

"It doesn't" returned Redfearn.

"You didn't care for Wentworth?"

"Not particularly. I wouldn't have shot him, if that's what you're driving at – that's a pretty drastic step to take – but I'm not going to grieve about it. He wouldn't have shed any tears if the boot were on the other foot."

"Do you own a pistol?" Lanner asked after a moment.

"No, I don't," returned Redfearn. "You have already asked me that."

"But I have learnt since that you are a member of the 'Sharp-shooters' Society at your club."

"That's true. We have a range in the basement. But I use one of the society's pistols."

"I see. Can you suggest who might have shot Mr. Wentworth?"

"No, I can't. You might do better to ask Sandy Wychwood or Albert Maitland that question."

"Are you suggesting that either of those two gentlemen might have had something to do with the crime?"

"Certainly not. Please desist from trying to twist my words. I simply mean that they have had more to do with Wentworth in recent months than I have."

"Is there anyone you can think of who might have had a grudge against Mr. Wentworth?"

"Not really. It depends what you mean by a grudge. I mean, everyone has enemies of some sort or another, don't they?"

"I'll give you an example, to show you what I mean," said the policeman, ignoring the other's question. "I understand that you were very friendly at one time with Miss Belinda Lee, but that she subsequently became somewhat less friendly with you and more friendly with Mr. Wentworth. That's the sort of thing a man might bear a grudge about."

"I suppose he might, in certain circumstances, but it's hardly a shooting matter. In any case, your example is not entirely accurate, Inspector. Any connection I had with Belinda Lee ended a long time since – several months ago. And it wasn't Wentworth who relieved me of her, either, but Albert Maitland. I do believe that Wentworth later extended the same courtesy to Maitland, but by then it was a matter of complete indifference to me."

I glanced at Sherlock Holmes. He had remained silent throughout this exchange, but I could see from the expression on his face and frown of concentration, that he was taking in all this information and carefully docketing it somewhere in his brain.

"On the day of Mr. Wentworth's death," Lanner continued after a moment, "you were, you informed us, with your brother, Lewis."

"That's right," replied Redfearn. "As I told you, he had come up to London from the depths of Shropshire. He doesn't get up very often, so I felt obliged to give him a guided tour. We wandered about town for a while, then took a boat down the river to Greenwich, where we had something to eat. Afterwards, we meandered slowly back. But I've told you all this already."

"Yes, sir; but we have not been able to find anyone, either on the boat or at the restaurant in Greenwich, who definitely remembers you and your brother."

Redfearn snorted. "You can hardly blame me for other people's poor memories, Inspector. That's not my problem."

A few minutes later, Holmes, Lanner and I were making our way along New Cavendish Street.

"Despite Redfearn's protestations of indifference," said Holmes to the policeman, "I rather fancy that your reference to Miss Lee stung him – and more than a little, too."

"I had the same impression," I remarked. "Do you think that Redfearn's ill-feeling might be what lies behind this crime?"

"We cannot yet say, Watson. Let us wait until we have heard the testimony of all the others in the case before we draw any conclusions. One thing we can say with confidence, however, is that human nature does not change. For all the affectations of careless indifference by those such as Redfearn – and, no doubt, all his cronies, too – there remain few things quite so mortifying as being deserted for a rival by a member of the opposite sex."

A walk of twenty minutes brought us to Bloomsbury and the address of Alexander Wychwood's lodgings in a pleasant house in Montague Street. He was seated at a writing-table as we were shown in, but he put down his pen, stood up and greeted us cordially.

"I was just writing a letter to my mother," he volunteered with a wry smile. "Mothers always want to know what one is doing, down to the last detail! Now, gentlemen, what can I do for you? I assume it's about the Wentworth business."

"Just a few more questions for you, sir," said Lanner, nodding his head. "I wondered – now you've had more time to think about it – if you could think of anyone who might have had a grudge against Mr. Wentworth."

"No, absolutely not. I still think it's most likely that the motive for the crime was robbery."

"That is always possible, of course, sir; but there was money in Mr. Wentworth's study which was not touched."

"Then perhaps the gun went off accidentally, and the robber lost his nerve and fled when he realised that Wentworth was dead."

"Yes, but on the other hand, if anyone did have a grudge against Mr. Wentworth," Lanner persisted, "that also might explain the crime."

"I suppose so," Wychwood conceded, "but it would have to be a pretty strong grudge. I can't believe that of anyone I know."

"But one or two people perhaps did have a grudge against Mr. Wentworth? I understand he wasn't the most popular man in London."

Wychwood paused, ran his hand through his hair and sighed. "That can't be denied," he said at length. "Wentworth was always very popular with the ladies, but somewhat less so with the men."

"Indeed, so I understand. I've heard that this was part of the problem, that Wentworth was a little too popular with the ladies."

"What do you mean?"

"I understand, for instance, that Miss Belinda Lee had been particularly friendly with George Redfearn for some time, but later switched her affections to Mr. Wentworth."

"That's not quite true, Inspector. She certainly switched her affections: not to Wentworth, though, but to Albert Maitland. However, you're right in a sense, as her dalliance with Maitland didn't last long, and then she did fall in with Wentworth. That's some time ago."

"Miss Lee seems a very popular woman," Lanner remarked after a moment in a dry tone. "Did you ever harbour hopes in that direction yourself, Mr. Wychwood?"

"Me? Hardly, Inspector. Belinda Lee has been popular for some considerable time, and not just with Wentworth and his cronies, either, but with the general public, too. She is altogether too grand for me, I'm afraid, even if I were interested, which I'm not. Besides, I have other irons in the fire, as it were, irons that are more approachable and unlikely to burn one's fingers so badly."

"Without wishing to seem too inquisitive about your private affairs," Lanner continued after a moment, "might I enquire who these other 'irons in the fire' might be?"

"Certainly," Wychwood replied in a careless tone, although he appeared a little embarrassed at the question. "There is no secret about it, though I must say I can't see the relevance to your enquiries. I have recently been paying court, as you might say, to a young lady by the name of Maria Monkley. You may have heard of her."

"Is she also employed at the Frivolity Theatre?"

"Yes, she is a singer and dancer there, although she is a more recent arrival there than Belinda Lee, and her name is not yet so well known. Apparently, she was very popular in Liverpool, and I am sure she will soon become so in London, too. She is a very attractive girl."

"I don't doubt it. It would not be surprising, then, if you had had rivals for Miss Monkley's favour."

"That is true. but I think I have seen off the competition – for the present at least."

"Would George Redfearn be one of your rivals?"

"Yes, I suppose that is so. I think that – whatever he might say – he was a little bitter at losing out in the case of Belinda Lee, and tried to make up for it by buzzing like a bee around Miss Monkley. But all to no avail, I am pleased to say, as she seems to prefer me."

"And Albert Maitland?"

"The same applies to him."

"And Piers Wentworth?"

Wychwood paused. "Look, Inspector, I know you're looking for someone with a strong grudge against Wentworth, so you can close your case, and move on to something else, but, speaking for myself at least, I can assure you that that doesn't apply in this case. Any annoyance I might have felt in his direction was only temporary and has been quite expunged by the fact that if it had been a challenge competition – which it wasn't – I would have won."

"So Mr. Wentworth *did* annoy you then?"

"Yes, he annoyed me. He annoyed everybody."

"He tried to push himself forward with regard to Miss Monkley?"

"Yes, of course he did. With a man like Wentworth, it would have been surprising if he hadn't. She had scarcely arrived in London from Liverpool when he began making obvious overtures to her. Apart from trying to elbow me aside with his fatter pocket-book, speaking to her in my presence as if I were not there at all and as if he knew her much better than I did anyway, he also invited her down to his house at Bickley."

"Did she go?"

"Yes, eventually. She went twice, both on Wednesday afternoons, the first time four weeks ago and then again three weeks ago."

"That must have been annoying for you."

"Yes, of course it was," Wychwood responded quickly. "I wouldn't deny it." He paused a moment, then continued at a rush. "Under normal circumstances, I wouldn't repeat the content of a private conversation, but on this occasion I'll make an exception, so you will understand the situation clearly. Miss Monkley said to me after she had visited Wentworth that she found his attentions both unwelcome and boring. She said she had at length accepted his invitation to go down for lunch to Links House just so that he would stop badgering her about it in the future.

"'I must have been a great disappointment to him,' she said to me, 'as I resisted all his overtures to me, and told him I was not interested. On both occasions, we had lunch, we discussed the musical theatre, and then he read me some poetry. This was obviously meant to put me in a romantic mood, but I just found it stupid and tedious, like having a love-song read out by the man who shouts out the train-times at the railway station.'

"She laughed when she was telling me, and said that Wentworth seemed old enough to be her father and she thought he ought to be pensioned off. So you see, Inspector, I had no reason to hold a grudge against Wentworth."

As we made our way down to Holborn, I considered what Wychwood had told us.

"Wychwood was certainly somewhat more forthcoming than Redfearn," I remarked to Lanner. "What do you think about his testimony?"

The policeman shook his head. "I don't know, Dr. Watson," said he. "He seems a pleasant enough young man. But he's no fool, and quite capable of lying if it suited his purposes to do so. I'm not sure I entirely believe him, and not sure he entirely believes Miss Monkley – if she did say what he claims she did. What do you think, Mr. Holmes?"

"I am simply watching and listening for the moment, Lanner," responded Holmes, "and should rather not pass any detailed judgement on what any of them say, until I have seen and heard all of them."

The traffic in High Holborn was dense, but we managed at length to thread our way through it, and plunged at once into the warren of streets which lies on the south side. Left and right and left again we turned, until I was quite lost, but eventually we stopped before a small cobbler's shop just round the corner from Drury Lane.

"Maitland has rooms above this shop," said Lanner, giving a sharp rap on the door-knocker. This was answered by a maid, who conducted us up a narrow and steep staircase to the first floor. There, in a pleasant if cramped sitting-room, Albert Maitland was waiting for us. He was a pale-faced, thin young man, who stood very erect in the middle of the room.

"I assume this visit is something to do with the death of Piers Wentworth," said he, as he waved his hand vaguely in the direction of some upright chairs which stood by the wall. "I hope it will not take too long. I have a number of things to do this morning, and several important appointments."

"We just wished to clarify a few points," returned Lanner.

"I'm sure I don't know anything other than what I have already told you."

"That may be so, sir, but we are re-interviewing everyone connected with the matter, in case they have remembered anything which might be helpful to us."

"I haven't."

"Perhaps not, sir, but I wonder – now that you've had time to give the matter more thought – if you can think of anyone who might have borne a grudge against Mr. Wentworth?"

"No," returned the young man with a firm shake of the head.

"Not anyone?"

"No."

"Had anyone, to your knowledge, quarrelled with Mr. Wentworth recently?"

"No."

"I understand that your cousin, William Maitland, has a position at the stockbroking firm in which Mr. Wentworth had an interest."

"Indeed he does. What of it?"

"Nothing, sir. I am merely verifying the fact. You are familiar, I believe, with Mr. Wentworth's house at Bickley."

"That is so. I have stayed there on one or two occasions and he stayed here with me once or twice."

"I have in my notes that you are the owner of a small revolver," said Lanner, consulting his note-book.

"That is surely hardly surprising, Inspector, considering that I myself gave you that information."

"Quite so, sir. Have you lent it to anyone recently?"

"No."

"Do you know if anyone else has borrowed a revolver – from the club, say?"

"No. I am not in the habit of monitoring the actions of my friends and acquaintances."

"I am aware, from the information you provided before, that you do not possess a green tweed suit, but I wonder now if you can think of anyone else who does?"

"No, I can't. You asked me that before."

"Finally, Mr. Maitland, I wonder if you could tell us something of your relations with Miss Belinda Lee?"

"I don't see why I should. What the devil has that got to do with you?"

"Just this, sir, that Miss Lee was associated with you in the eyes of others for some time, but was subsequently associated with Piers Wentworth."

"What of it? You might as well point out that prior to being 'associated' with me, as you so quaintly put it, she had been 'associated' with George Redfearn for some time. This all proves nothing whatsoever, except, I suppose, that Miss Lee has always been very popular and that Piers Wentworth always got what he wanted in the end."

"And Miss Maria Monkley? Do you have an interest in that direction, sir?"

"Not particularly. As far as I understand it, she was making some sort of decision between Wentworth and Sandy Wychwood. You know what they say, Inspector: a man can put all the effort he wants into his wooing, but in the end it's the woman who will make the decision, usually for reasons the man doesn't even understand."

"Indeed, sir. I suppose that Mr. Wentworth's death clears the field in that respect for Mr. Wychwood."

"Yes, I suppose it does."

As we made our way down Drury Lane towards the Strand, Lanner and I discussed the case, but neither of us could reach any worthwhile conclusions. Holmes took no part in the discussion, appearing lost in his own thoughts.

The doorman at the Frivolity Theatre admitted us without demur, and we were shown in to Miss Lee's dressing-room. She turned as we entered, but did not rise, being busy at her dressing-table, in front of a very large mirror, assisted by a small, middle-aged woman.

"You must excuse me, Inspector Lanner," said Miss Lee. "I had expected you a little earlier. We have a matinee performance this afternoon, and I must begin to get ready now. But I am all ears, and I am sure if I can help you I will. You may go and get yourself a cup of tea, Alice," she added, addressing the other woman. "I shouldn't think we'll be more than five or ten minutes. Now, Inspector, what is it you wish to know? I'm sure I've told you all I can think of."

"I simply wish to clarify a few points," replied Lanner. "In the first place, about visitors to Mr. Wentworth's house at Bickley. You yourself had paid visits there, I understand."

"Yes, numerous times."

"Were you by yourself on these occasions, or were others present at the same time?"

"Both. Sometimes there was quite a crowd there, some of whom had to stay overnight at the Station Hotel, as Links House was not very big. At other times there were just one or two other people there, and sometimes I was there alone."

"When was the last time you were there?"

"Towards the end of August."

"About a month before Mr. Wentworth's death?"

"Yes, that would be about right."

"Did you happen to observe, Miss Lee, on those occasions when there were others present, if any of them approached the house by way of the golf-course?"

Miss Lee considered the question for a moment. "No," she replied at length, "I don't believe so. On some occasions, though," she added, "when he had invited his friends down for a game of golf, I think they would meet up at the clubhouse and I suppose when they had finished their game they would walk back to Links House across the golf-course."

Lanner nodded. "Now," he said: "about three gentlemen in particular: George Redfearn, Alexander Wychwood and Albert Maitland: did Mr. Wentworth ever fall out with any of them?"

"I really have no idea," returned Miss Lee. "He may have done, for all I know. They could all be a little quarrelsome on occasion, when they had had too much to drink."

"Are you aware that any of them ever fell out over *you*?"

"Absolutely not. Well, not in my presence, anyhow. What they may have done at other times, I really couldn't say, but I never had any indication of anything like that."

"You don't think that any of the gentlemen I named might have had a grudge against Mr. Wentworth for any reason?"

"I doubt it. I don't think they are the grudge-bearing kind. Well, George Redfearn might be, but I don't think he'd ever bother to do anything about it, even if he did bear someone a grudge. Sandy is a lovely boy, but he's an incurable romantic, and sees the world through a prism of romantic ideals. I don't think he could possibly bear a grudge against Piers, especially as – so I understand – he'd recently come out on top in a tussle with Piers for the affections of Maria Monkley."

"Miss Monkley is also employed here, at the Frivolity, I understand."

"Yes, that's right. She's a sweet girl, but another one who's a hopeless romantic, like Sandy Wychwood – so I think they were probably meant for each other."

"What about Albert Maitland?"

"What, Bertie? He wouldn't hurt a fly. He puts on a very stiff front – frightfully correct, and all that – but behind that front he's as soft as a brush, really. He does have rather strong views on what's right and what's wrong, but they are just his own personal views, and I don't think he'd ever try to impose them on anyone else."

"I see," said Lanner. "Finally, then, Miss Lee, as to the note you received from Mr. Wentworth the day before he died, which I have here." He took a folded slip of stiff, cream-coloured paper from an inside pocket and opened it out. "It says 'Very sorry, Belinda, but our plan for tomorrow will have to be postponed. Someone is coming here that I can't put off. Will see you at the end of the week as usual, when we can make a fresh arrangement. Yours as ever, P.'"

Lanner handed the note to Miss Lee. "Are you sure," he asked, "that that is Mr. Wentworth's hand?"

For a moment she studied the note. "I believe so," she responded at length, looking up. "Of course, when I received it I had no reason to suppose it wasn't from Piers. The possibility that it might not be from Piers never even crossed my mind. And now I see it again, I feel much the same. I'm sure it's his hand. Do you have any reason for supposing it might not be?"

"Nothing in particular," returned the policeman. "The stationery certainly seems the same as some blank sheets we found in Mr. Wentworth's study. It simply occurred to us that although the letter appeared to be from Mr. Wentworth, it might not have been. If, for instance, someone planned to do harm to Mr. Wentworth, and was aware that you were due to go down that particular day, he might have sent this letter to put you off from going, to leave the field open for himself. Had you ever had letters of this sort from Mr. Wentworth before?"

"Yes, a number of times."

"Did he always sign himself simply with the initial 'P'?"

"Not always. Sometimes he would put 'P W', and, on rare occasions, 'Piers'. There didn't seem to be any significance to this, one way or the other. Piers was a very discreet man, who had a horror, I think, of his correspondence falling into the wrong hands. So his communications were always fairly anonymous, if you know what I mean."

Lanner nodded, as he took back the note from Miss Lee. "Thank you for your help," he said. "I think that that is all for the present."

"Have you made any progress with the case?" she asked as we prepared to leave.

"A little," the policeman returned. "We are still looking into one or two possibilities."

Outside, Holmes, Lanner and I stood for a few moments on the pavement in the Strand, as the unbroken stream of traffic rattled past us.

"And that, gentlemen, is that," said the policeman with a sigh. "You see the difficulty? We have so little evidence upon which to found a solution to the mystery. We cannot narrow down who had an opportunity to commit the crime, and nor can we establish who might have had a motive. Unless some new information comes to light, I fear we may never solve the case."

"So," I said, "your remark to Miss Lee about looking into one or two possibilities was, I take it, the merest humbug."

Lanner looked abashed. "I should not have put it so bluntly myself, Dr. Watson," he returned, "but, yes, I admit it. As a young man in the police force, I was instructed by my superiors to always answer enquiries from the public in a positive, optimistic manner. 'Negativity upsets people,' they said, 'and achieves nothing.' I can certainly see the point of that as a general rule, but it's hard sometimes to be optimistic when there's nothing but negative thoughts in your head."

"What of your enquiries at Bickley?" I asked. "Have you had any success in your search for the young man in the green tweed suit?"

Lanner shook his head. "None whatsoever," he replied. "He has disappeared without trace. And, of course, I still do not know for a certainty whether he had anything to do with the crime or not. He certainly doesn't resemble any of our chief suspects very closely. What do you think about it all, Mr. Holmes?" he continued, turning to my friend. "If I may say so, I have never known you so silent in all the time I have known you. Do you have any insight into the matter? Or are you as puzzled as the rest of us?"

"One could postulate several hypotheses," returned Holmes, "but, as you say, the solid evidence for any view is somewhat lacking. I regret that I cannot yet give you a conclusive solution to the problem."

With that, we parted, Lanner returning to Scotland Yard, and Holmes and I to Baker Street. My friend was as uncommunicative back in his lodgings as he had been earlier, and after a little while I abandoned my efforts to try to get him to discuss the case, picked up my medical bag and prepared to leave. As I had my hand on the doorknob, however, he looked up and spoke.

"I should like to bring the Wentworth case to a close," he remarked in a matter-of-fact tone. "To that end, I intend to make a few more enquiries this afternoon and, I hope, interview Wentworth's murderer. If you wish to know how I got on, pray feel free to drop by this evening and we can discuss the matter."

"What!" I cried. "I thought you told Lanner that any number of hypotheses were possible and you could not venture an opinion as to which might be correct."

"That's not quite right," returned my friend. "Of course, it is always possible to suggest different possible solutions to any problem, and that is what I said to Lanner. But that does not mean that I do not have a theory of my own. In fact, I do have such a theory, which I hope to put to the test this afternoon."

"Then why did you not inform Lanner? Why give him such a misleading impression?"

"You know how much I dislike indulging in idle speculation, Watson. It would have gained us nothing. Besides, I cannot yet prove my own hypothesis, and may never be able to."

With that unsatisfactory conclusion, I left him then and made my way home, but I was determined to return later and learn more of my friend's theories. The unfathomable nature of the case fascinated me, and having had so many years' experience of my friend's successes, I could not doubt that if he had formed his own theory of the matter, it was very likely to be the correct one, or, at least, very close to it. Lanner was convinced that Piers Wentworth had been murdered by someone known to him, and could see no other motive for the crime, but did Holmes agree with him or did he see some other possibility?

I was intrigued, also, by the note Miss Lee had received, the day before the murder. She seemed fairly sure it really was from Wentworth, as it purported to be. If so, the clear inferences were, first, that Wentworth was expecting someone to call; second, that this was someone he knew; and third, that it was this person that shot him. If, however, the letter was a forgery, and had not been written by Wentworth, then he must have still been expecting Miss Lee to call on the Wednesday, and must have been taken by surprise by the arrival of the other visitor. In either case, it seemed to me, we were brought back to the man in the green tweed suit. Did Wentworth know this man, or was it someone he had never met before? It was impossible to tell, and although I wasted some considerable time in considering the matter, I got precisely nowhere with this conundrum.

Keen though I was to hear Holmes's conclusions on the case, various tasks, both professional and domestic, delayed me, and it was not until a quarter to eight that I reached my friend's lodgings that evening. I found him busy at his chemical bench, and although he acknowledged my presence with a nod of his head and a murmured word of greeting, he appeared preoccupied by what he was doing.

"Well?" I demanded at length, unable to contain my curiosity any longer. "Any success to report?"

"Hardly," he replied in a dry tone, as he measured some dark liquid from a small glass bottle into a test-tube. "I have only just begun. The fact is, I misplaced my small stock of silver nitrate. You will never guess where I found it, Watson. In my sock drawer, of all places!"

"Never mind that," I said. "What about the Wentworth case? You said you would have something more to tell me about it this evening."

"Oh, *that*," said he in a dismissive tone, as if I were raising some long-forgotten and unimportant issue. "I have been trying to put that out of my mind."

"Have you solved the case?"

"Yes. I thought I had made that clear."

"No, you didn't. Is the villain under arrest?"

Holmes paused, put the test-tube in the rack and came over to where I was standing by the fire. "Do take a seat, Watson. Your standing about in that fashion suggests that you have only called in for a minute or two in order to upbraid me!"

I laughed as I seated myself in my old arm-chair. "I simply wish to know the results of your enquiries, Holmes. The Wentworth case seems such an unfathomable puzzle!"

As I spoke, my friend flung himself into his own chair, then leaned over and took his pipe and tobacco from the hearth. "It is not really such a puzzle if one understands human nature," said he as he filled his pipe. "There were clear indications from the very beginning for anyone prepared to read them. However, building a case which could stand up in court is another matter. But I shall tell you in order what steps I took, and you can then compare my views with your own – and upbraid me if you wish."

"I very much doubt I shall wish to," I responded.

Holmes shook his head. "I think you should reserve your judgment on that point until you have heard my report, Watson," said he. "I fear I have not handled the case well." He put a match to his pipe, and I settled back to listen to his account.

"I decided after we spoke earlier that the first thing I would do would be to go and interview Miss Belinda Lee again. Apart from any other consideration, it was clear that she was a central figure in the case, for she was the one actor in this little drama who had intimate knowledge of all of the others – their characters, habits, propensities and so on."

"I did think, when we spoke to Miss Lee earlier," I remarked, "that she could have said more if she would. Although, to be honest," I added, "I think I thought something similar about all of them."

"You are probably right," said Holmes with a chuckle. "When questioning the actors in a drama such as the present one, you must always remember that although they will answer your questions – with a greater or lesser degree of honesty – they tend not to volunteer information which is outwith the scope of your questions. Therefore, the questions you ask are as important as the answers they give to them. Anyhow, having managed to catch Miss Lee in the short interval between the matinee performance and the evening one, and having little time at my disposal, I decided to omit all preliminaries and get straight to the point.

"'You will have heard, I imagine,' I said to her, 'about the man in the green tweed suit.'

"'Of course,' she returned. 'Who can have read anything of the case who hasn't also read about that mysterious gentleman? It has been in all the papers. But, as I understand it, it is not yet clear whether he had anything to do with the death of Piers Wentworth or not.'

"I nodded. 'And yet,' I said, 'despite all the publicity the matter has had, no one has yet come forward to state that he is that man, and to explain what he was doing at Bickley that day, which would have cleared him of all suspicion and enabled the authorities to eliminate him from their enquiries.'

"'Yes, that is true,' she said, 'but perhaps he has gone abroad and has heard nothing of the case: I understand that on the day of Mr. Wentworth's death, the man in the green tweed suit was seen in the district with a small travelling-bag of some sort.'

"'It is possible; but two weeks have now passed. You would think he would have heard something of the matter by now. Besides, if he had nothing to do with the crime, and was not making for Wentworth's house when he was seen crossing the golf course, then where was he going? For the police have interviewed all Wentworth's neighbours, and not one of them saw such a man on the day in question.'

"'Then it is a mystery. But I do not quite understand why you are discussing this man at such length with me; I thought you had come back to ask me some more questions.'

"'I thought perhaps the young man's description might put you in mind of someone.'

"She frowned. 'Well, it doesn't,' she said. 'Why did you think it might?'

"'Because it puts me in mind of someone – not so much what the young man looked like, as what he did. However, let us leave that for the moment. Do you know of anyone who possesses such a distinctive tweed suit – perhaps someone in Wentworth's circle of acquaintances?'

"'No,' she replied with a firm shake of the head. 'The police have already asked me that, more than once.'

"'But I suppose it might be possible to hire such an outfit for a day or two?'

"She looked surprised. 'I wouldn't know,' she said. 'I suppose it might be. But I think the gentlemen's dress-hire establishments deal mainly in formal wear, rather than tweeds.'

"'But tweeds might be available somewhere else,' I persisted, 'somewhere such as a theatrical costumiers, or the costume department of a theatre.'

"'Perhaps,' said she, 'but, again, I wouldn't know. I believe that most of the big costumiers only hire out complete sets of costumes, rather than odd ones, as you are suggesting. And I don't think that most theatres ever hire out their own costumes at all.'

"'No, but if someone were employed at a theatre, or had some other regular connection with it, he might, I suppose, be able to borrow such a costume – "unofficially", as it were.'

"'I suppose he might. I really wouldn't know.'

"'Is there such a green tweed suit in the stock here, at the Frivolity?'

"'I have no idea. There may well be, but I can't recall seeing any of the actors wearing such an outfit.'

"'I see,' I said. I had hoped to shake her composure a little, and extract a little more information from her, but she remained perfectly calm and self-possessed, so I decided to take a yet more direct route to my destination. 'Very well,' I said. 'I will now make a conjecture, Miss Lee. I believe, despite what you say, that there is indeed such a green tweed suit in the costume stock here. Yes, and a wide-brimmed brown hat and light-brown overcoat, too, not to mention materials for making up a gingery beard. I believe that, in a sense, the man in the green tweed suit both started and finished his journey here, at this theatre.'

"She frowned again. 'If that is what you believe, should you not inform the police?'

"'Perhaps I should. What would you do then?'

"'I? Why should I do anything?'

"'Because, Miss Lee, you yourself were the man in the green tweed suit, a disguise you adopted for one day only, in order to murder Piers Wentworth. Having arrived at Bickley and made your way up Links Lane, you crossed the golf-course – where, unfortunately for you, you were seen by two golfers – passed up the back garden of Links House and entered the study directly through the French window which, it being a fine day, was standing open. No doubt Wentworth sprang to his feet in surprise, not recognizing who you were, but you raised your pistol and shot him through the heart before he could make any further move. You then closed and locked the French window, left the house by the front door, and returned the way you had come.'

"'What nonsense!' she cried, although her voice faltered a little. 'If you have come here only to make these wild and absurd accusations, I must ask you to leave at once!'

"'An accusation it may be,' I returned, 'but there is nothing absurd about it. You and I both know it is the truth.'

"For a long moment we sat there, looking at each other in silence.

"'I repeat,' said she at length, 'that what you say is complete and utter nonsense, and is moreover a gross slander which I'm sure is actionable at law. However," she continued, a little smile playing about her lips, 'I am intrigued as to why you should be advancing this ridiculous theory. What do you hope to gain by it?'

"'The truth.'

"At this, she laughed out loud. 'Well, if that is your aim I rather fancy you will be disappointed,' said she. 'And if you hoped for celebrity as a great reasoner, I am sorry to tell you that you will only gain celebrity as a pitiable eccentric.' There was a gleam of triumph in her eye now, and I could see that she thought she had me at a severe disadvantage. 'Let us examine your ludicrous theory, then, Mr. Holmes. Why, to start with, do you think I would wish to murder Piers Wentworth?'

"'I was hoping that you might tell me that,' I returned.

"'Well, I can't, because I didn't. Besides, it was undoubtedly a man who went to see Piers that day, a man wearing the green tweed suit. Everyone is agreed upon that point.'

"I shook my head. 'No, they are not,' said I. 'I do not agree. What anyone else might think is of no importance. It was a woman who went to see Wentworth that day, a woman dressed as a man.'

"'You are forgetting,' said she, 'that I received a note from Piers, the day before he was killed, postponing my own visit to him, as he was expecting someone else.'

"'I am not forgetting that,' I said. 'You wrote that letter yourself, Miss Lee.'

"'Nonsense! The letter was written on his own notepaper, and in his own hand.'

"'The hand would not be difficult to imitate for someone who had received numerous letters from Wentworth in the past, as you mentioned earlier. As to the stationery, there is no difficulty there: you simply took a sheet of it from Wentworth's study.'

"'But how could I?' she demanded. 'I hadn't been to Mr. Wentworth's house for a month or more before that day, before the week he was killed – unless you are going to claim that I planned his murder far in advance, and took the paper months ago.'

"'Such a claim is unnecessary, and the solution to the problem is simpler, if a little more subtle: you took the sheet of notepaper from Wentworth's study *after* you had killed him. You wrote the letter to yourself later, at your leisure, and subsequently claimed to have received it in the post on Tuesday.'

"'That is a clever theory,' said Miss Lee after a moment with a little smile, 'but you have still not explained why, if you were correct in your reasoning, I should have committed the crime at all.'

"'Perhaps you were annoyed that Wentworth had dropped you in favour of Maria Monkley,' I suggested.

"At this, Miss Lee threw her head back and laughed loudly again. 'So,' she said, 'you are not so clever as you imagine, Mr. Holmes. Piers got nowhere with Maria, that I know for a fact. Not only that, but she told him in no uncertain terms that she never wished to see him or visit his house again.'

"'Perhaps so,' I responded. I could see from her expression and the look in her eye that what she said was almost certainly true, and it also accorded with my own view of the matter. 'But, still,' I ventured, 'he treated you badly.' I watched her face closely. She was trying to conceal her emotion, but I could see that I had touched a nerve. 'Ah!' I said. 'I think I see now. When Miss Monkley came along, Wentworth dropped you abruptly, without ceremony and without any thought for your feelings. This was a blow to your pride, but was perhaps bearable. But then, when Miss Monkley rebuffed him so firmly, told him, in effect, to ‘sling his hook elsewhere,’ as they say in some parts, he turned once more to you, and expected you to simply take up where you had left off before, as if nothing had happened. This, I imagine was an insult you could not bear, this treating of you as a disposable commodity, and perhaps expecting you to show gratitude for another invitation to Links House, despite all that had happened.’

“Again we sat in silence for some time. Then Miss Lee stood up, opened the door of her dressing-room and looked out into the corridor. Evidently satisfied that there was no one there who might be listening, she closed the door again and resumed her seat.

“‘Perhaps you do have some perception after all, Mr. Holmes,’ she began in a tone of amusement, although there was a wary look in her eye, ‘and what they say of you is true. You are right to use the word “gratitude” in connection with Piers Wentworth. I admit nothing, but I shall tell you something now, something you do not know. Piers Wentworth was an odious and obnoxious man. Of course, no one is perfect, and in his case there were, at least, some compensations. He was wealthy and could be quite free with his money when he wished to be. But always, underlying his apparent open-handedness, was an unpleasant expectation that the recipients of his largesse should show gratitude. This was a constant irritation and annoyance, for it cost him little to spend his plentiful money, and, moreover, he himself never showed the slightest shred of gratitude for anything that anyone else did for him. It was as if, having spent his money, he considered it his right to expect such generosity from others.

“‘Yes, he treated me badly, very badly, in many ways which you cannot imagine, and which I shall not go into. He made promises to me which turned out to be like pledges written on water. And all the while, as he continued to humiliate and disparage me, he expected me to show gratitude that he was seeing me at all. His treatment of me over the last month or two was not an isolated incident, but was, rather, the latest in a chapter of such incidents. I do not blame Maria Monkley; she is, as I mentioned to you earlier, something of a romantic, and decidedly naive in the way she perceives the world; all the blame lies with Piers Wentworth.'

"'So you killed him.'

"For a moment, her eyelashes flickered, and, almost imperceptibly, she nodded her head in silence. Next moment, this mute admission of guilt had vanished, and she spoke in a firm, defiant tone.

"'My tongue will never confess to such a charge,' said she. 'Should the police make any further enquiries of me, I shall say the following: I know nothing of Piers Wentworth's death, I have no idea who might have killed him, I have never known any man who possessed a green tweed suit, I do not own a revolver and I have no knowledge of anyone who does.'

"'And the carpet-bag?' I interjected.

"'What carpet-bag?'

"'The carpet-bag which the man in the green tweed suit collected from Bromley station and took away with him.'

"'I know nothing of that. I myself once owned such a bag, but that has gone to glory some time ago. I think it was burnt on the fire.'

"'Then there is nothing more you can tell me?'

"'No.'

"'I think you have made a mistake, Miss Lee.'

"For a brief moment there was a flicker of alarm in her eyes, but when she spoke, it was in a defiant tone. 'I think not,' said she, but then added 'What did you have in mind?'

"'Not in the execution of your plan; that, for all I can tell, may be flawless; but in your decision to commit the crime at all. Wentworth may, as you say, have been odious, or worse, but you could have found some other way to drive him from your life, and put distance between the two of you.'

"'Such as ?'

"'You could have simply told him, as Miss Monkley did, that you did not wish to see him again.'

"'It would not have been sufficient. You do not know what he was like. He would not leave me alone. He would spread foul, vindictive rumours about me, as he had done in the past when I would not do as he wished'

"'Well, then, you could have moved away from London. With your reputation, you could have secured employment at any theatre in the country.'

"'No doubt, but for a much-reduced fee. Where I am now is at the very summit of the English musical theatre. To go anywhere else would be to drop far, far lower in every conceivable way. People would think I had gone mad.'

"'So, instead of that slight blow to your pride, you have sentenced yourself to a lifetime of guilt, self-recrimination and remorse.'

"'I think not.'

"'Perhaps not now, but in the years to come. You have taken a man's life, which was not yours to take, however unpleasant he may have been. Your conscience will not let you forget that. And unlike Piers Wentworth, your conscience cannot be destroyed, for it grips you not from without, but from within.'

"'We shall see, Mr. Holmes, we shall see.'

"I left her then, Watson, certain that I had solved the case, but equally certain that I would never be able to bring Wentworth's murderer to justice."

For some time we sat in silence. I confess I was shocked at what my friend had told me, shocked at the violence which seemed to lurk just beneath the glittering surface of London society.

"Have you informed Lanner?" I asked at length.

My friend shook his head. "There would seem little point."

"What!" I cried. "You know who it is that has committed this terrible crime and you are not going to do anything about it? I find that almost as shocking as the crime itself, Holmes! Where is your sense of justice?"

"My dear fellow! You interrupted me. I was about to say that there would seem little point in telling Lanner my theory, as I cannot prove it, and he would probably give it no credence, anyway, but of course I must do so. However unpleasant Wentworth may have been, he cannot now defend himself. It is therefore the duty of anyone who claims to uphold justice and truth to act on his behalf. But I fear it will be a fruitless task."

"Is there nothing you can do to prove your case?"

"It is difficult to feel optimistic, Watson. Had I been consulted earlier, I might have searched through the costumes at the Frivolity Theatre until I found the green tweed suit – for I am sure it is there – and examined it for any threads or other traces upon it which might suggest who had worn it most recently or if, for instance, the sleeves or trouser-legs had recently been shortened. I might also have examined the pockets to see if any of them showed traces of gunpowder where a pistol had been carried."

"What about the carpet-bag that you mentioned to her?"

"She is not stupid. Her planning of the crime seems to have been exceptionally thorough. If she now says that her old carpet-bag has been burnt on the fire, then I am sure that that is so. Similarly, I have no hope now of discovering the pistol that was used in the crime. You know how much I hate to guess at anything, Watson, but if I had to guess, I should say that the pistol is probably at the bottom of the Thames."

"What was the point of the carpet-bag, anyway?" I asked. "Was she simply hoping to suggest that the murderer had gone abroad, as we wondered earlier?"

Holmes shook his head. "Not at all. The bag, which she had deposited at Bromley station earlier that day, was a crucial part of her plan, for it contained her change of clothes. It is what enabled the young man in the tweed suit to vanish so completely after leaving the station, and enabled Miss Lee to journey unsuspected back to town."

"What do you mean? She could hardly change her clothes in Bromley High Street."

"Of course not. But if you were to study the map, as I have done, you would see that between Bromley and Shortlands, the next station on the line, from where I believe she caught a train back to town, there are several rural areas, including a small wood, where she could easily have slipped out of sight and changed her appearance in a matter of a minute or two."

"Surely it would take longer than that."

"Not at all. She would have had a large skirt in the bag, which she could have slipped on over what she was already wearing. That would have taken scarcely thirty seconds. Another thirty seconds to remove the suit jacket and replace it with a smaller, lady's jacket, thirty seconds more to exchange the man's hat for a more feminine item, letting her hair fall more loosely about her head, and she would be practically finished. Then, into the bag would go the tweed jacket, the overcoat and the hat, together, of course, with the false beard. She may even have had a large folded canvas bag with her, to conceal the carpet-bag itself from public view. All done in less than two minutes, and then she could walk on to Shortlands, to catch the next train unnoticed."

"I suppose you are right, Holmes. But what was it that made you suspect Miss Lee in the first place? You seem to have been very sure of it, but I cannot imagine why."

"The actions of the supposed man in the green tweed suit rather gave it away."

"His actions? But I can't recall that he did anything very notable, except lounge on a bench on the platform at Bickley station and stroll across the golf-course waving to the golfers there."

"But in both cases, if you remember, Watson, he put on his coat. It was a mild, pleasant day. We know this from the weather records, and from the testimony of witnesses, but even if we didn't, we could infer it from the fact that the young man was not wearing the coat he had brought with him. On the golf course, he was carrying it over his arm, and at the railway station he had placed it over the back of the bench. Yet when the golfers made their presence known to him by calling out, he slipped it on – his glance at the sky, as if he thought it might rain, was, I take it, the merest humbug – as he did when he stood up on the railway platform to walk to the train which had just arrived. What does that suggest to you?"

"Nothing whatever, unless he was simply tired of carrying the coat."

Holmes shook his head with a chuckle. "As I considered the matter, I was convinced it was a question of anatomy. You, as a medical man must surely appreciate the point, Watson. The fact is that a woman may readily pass for a man with suitable clothes and a little cosmetic attention to the hair and facial features. But she will only ever be entirely convincing when she is sitting down or standing still. As soon as a woman begins to walk – or run – she will almost always give herself away, unless she is completely covered up – with a large overcoat, say. Or perhaps you have never noticed that a woman's swaying gait is somewhat different from that of a man?" he added with a twinkle in his eye.

"Yes, of course I have," I responded with some heat.

"Very well," said Holmes. "You will understand, then, why I was convinced that the supposed 'young man' in the green tweed suit was in reality a woman. There was simply no other satisfactory explanation for the putting-on of the overcoat only when he was walking under the observation of others. It only remained for me to discover who the woman might be. Lanner's interviews with Wentworth's acquaintances this morning clarified that question considerably. Wentworth had invited Maria Monkley down to his house at Bickley on two consecutive Wednesdays. I think we may take it that if he had made the progress with her that he had been hoping for, he would have invited her down again the following week. However, he didn't, so I think we are justified in assuming that Wychwood's account of the matter was correct, and that Wentworth had not got anywhere with her. In that case, I judged, Miss Monkley, having rebuffed Wentworth in no uncertain terms and being apparently fond of Alexander Wychwood, had no real motive for the crime, but Belinda Lee certainly did. She had been intimate with Wentworth for some considerable time, but had been pushed unceremoniously aside when Miss Monkley appeared on the scene. That must have been a severe blow to the pride of a woman who had no doubt revelled in the general popularity she had enjoyed for so long. Then, on top of that, when Wentworth was snubbed by Miss Monkley, he seems to have expected Miss Lee to be grateful for another invitation to his house at Bickley, an invitation she must have known she would never have received if there had been any prospect of his getting Miss Monkley to visit him there again. How that knowledge must have embittered her!"

Sherlock Holmes duly notified the authorities of his view of the case, and his reasons for holding that view, but despite extensive enquiries, and despite their questioning Miss Lee closely several times, no conclusive evidence was ever found which might link her with Wentworth's murder. Acting on Holmes's suggestion, the police questioned the officials at Shortlands station, and one man there thought he remembered seeing Miss Lee at that station on the day of the murder; but she flatly denied that she had been there and, as several weeks had by then passed, the man's testimony was not given with any great conviction. Clothes which might have been the tweed suit, the overcoat and the hat worn by the murderer were indeed found in the costume department of the Frivolity theatre, as Holmes had predicted, but as the theatre's wardrobe was a very large one, that was not so surprising and proved nothing. From the perspective of the police, then, the matter remained unresolved and the case was never closed. Although I was convinced that Holmes's analysis of the matter was correct in every respect, it could not be proved, and Miss Lee was never arrested for the crime. Much to my regret, therefore, I was unable to include the Wentworth case in that series of sketches of my friend's professional career which I laid before the public some time ago.

A year or two later, however, I chanced to see a small item in the *Globe* which described how Miss Belinda Lee had fallen out acrimoniously with the management of the Frivolity Theatre, as a result of which her employment there had been terminated. Some months after that, I read somewhere that she had sailed for Australia, in the hope, it said, of rekindling her career in the antipodes. After that, she passed quite out of my knowledge and had not crossed my mind for several years when a brief paragraph in the *Telegraph* one morning caught my eye. Under the heading "Mysterious death of former 'Frivolity' singer", it described how Miss Belinda Lee had been shot dead in her dressing-room at a theatre in Sydney. She had apparently had a very wide circle of male acquaintances in Sydney, many of them disreputable and suspected of criminal activities, but, despite extensive enquiries among these men, the police had been unable to make any progress in the case. Of course, I knew nothing of the matter other than the bare outline I have indicated here, but I could not help but think as I read the account that in that mysterious way which does sometimes occur, a sort of blind justice or retribution had been meted out to Belinda Lee for the terrible crime she had committed in the Wentworth case.

AN UNUSUAL INTERVIEW

I HAD KNOWN SHERLOCK HOLMES, the well-known criminal investigator, for some years at the time of those incidents associated with Henry Barton and the *Dulwich Weekly Post.* During this time, I had become so accustomed to his every pronouncement on a case being precisely correct that the thought of his making a mistake had ceased to enter my head. It came as a surprise to me then, when, on this occasion, my friend revealed himself to be as fallible as the rest of mankind, and not immune, as I had supposed, from reaching a hasty and unwarranted conclusion. Fortunately, this uncharacteristic lapse did not prevent the truth of the matter from being discovered, as I shall describe.

It was boisterous, blustery weather in the early part of October when Mr. Henry Barton paid a visit to the chambers I shared with Holmes in Baker Street. He was a young man, no more than two-and-twenty, I judged, well dressed but with a somewhat dishevelled air about him, as if the strong autumnal winds had blown him along the street and into our rooms just as they were whirling and scattering the leaves from the trees.

We had finished our lunch and Holmes had returned to his commonplace book, into which he was pasting a heap of newspaper cuttings he had amassed over the preceding two weeks, but now he put down his pasting-brush and addressed our visitor.

"What can we do for you, Mr. Barton?" he asked, waving the young man to a chair by the fire.

"I have heard that you can extricate people from difficulties," said Barton as he sat down, "and free them from false charges."

"I try," returned Holmes. "Have false charges been made against you?"

"Not yet, but I strongly suspect they will be," Barton continued in a rush, his voice almost breathless, his chest heaving with emotion. "If anyone was ever in difficulties, Mr. Holmes, then I am."

"Very well," said Holmes in a calming tone, "take a few deep breaths and recover yourself, then tell us precisely what has occurred to discomfit you in this way."

Barton did as Holmes suggested, and, a few moments later, began the following account:

"You should know first that I am a junior reporter on the *Harrow and Wealdstone Telegraph*, one of the weekly newspapers in that district. It is a comfortable enough lay and in general I have no complaints in that direction. As I am the most junior member of staff, though, it means that I am given all the jobs that no one else wants, and I seem to spend half my working life reporting on flower shows. I sometimes think I could write the reports in my sleep. Indeed, I have even dreamed about flower shows at night recently – Mrs. Blenkinsop winning the prize for best dahlias for the third year in a row, Mr. Rogers winning the prize for biggest sunflower after being beaten into second place last year by Mr. Smithers, and so on. I may be wrong, but I feel I have the talent to go on to somewhat greater things." He paused and shook his head.

"Fortunately," he continued after a moment, "my mother's cousin, Mr. Wilfred Langwith, has always been involved with local newspapers in and around London. Indeed, it was partly as a result of his help and advice that I secured my present position. I therefore went to see him last week, to tell him of my boredom with having to do flower shows and the like, and to see if he had any suggestions to make.

"He greeted me very cordially, I must say, and listened sympathetically to my complaint before responding.

"'Do not dismiss flower shows out of hand,' said he with a chuckle. 'They are very important to some people, my boy, and the experience you have gained from reporting on them will be very valuable to you in the future. However, I can see that you are now ready to move on to greater things. As it happens, I believe that a friend of mine, Thurston Withers, who owns the *Dulwich Weekly Post*, is looking for a bright young man to add to his staff there. I think, Henry, that you might be just the sort of person he is looking for! The newspaper business in south London is extremely competitive, you know, and any advantage old Withers can gain over his rivals would be like finding gold dust to him. Of course, as you know, the papers make a certain proportion of their income from the commercial advertisements they contain. The competition for this advertising is very intense, especially with the recent launching of one or two new, upstart papers, such as the *Streatham Star*, the *Wimbledon Courier* and others, all fishing from the same pool. But local businesses will only advertise in a paper if the circulation is strong, and the circulation will only be strong if the standard of reporting is high and the reports consistently interesting. So, ultimately, a paper's prosperity depends on people like you, Henry. But apart from these considerations, there is also a strong family rivalry in south London.'

"I asked Mr. Langwith what he meant and he explained:

"'Mr. Withers's grandfather used to own two newspapers in those parts, both of which he had founded, the *Dulwich Weekly Post* and the *Dulwich and Norwood Echo*. His two sons assisted him, but they could never agree on anything and were constantly quarrelling, so when he died he stipulated in his will that his newspaper "empire" was to be divided up – somewhat like that of Alexander the Great – and his two sons were each to have one of the papers. Later, these papers passed to his grandsons, Thurston Withers having ownership of the *Dulwich Weekly Post* and his cousin, Seymour Withers, the *Dulwich and Norwood Echo*. The rivalry between the two of them is just as fierce now as it was between their respective fathers. Thurston Withers has the better paper, I believe, but his cousin has recently raised queries about the interpretation of their grandfather's will, and claimed that the *Post* should rightfully belong to his side of the family, a claim which

Thurston Withers hotly disputes. All in all, it has been a worrying time for Withers, and the last time I saw him, his nerves seemed very much on edge. He told me that the stress and worry of the business was upsetting him so badly that he had scarcely been able to sleep at night, and had recently begun taking some kind of sleeping-powders prescribed for him by his doctor. So you will appreciate, Henry, that Thurston Withers will only want to take you on if he is convinced that you show real promise. He only wants the very best! Anyway, leave the matter with me, my boy, and I'll arrange an appointment for you to see old Withers as soon as possible.'

"A few days later, I had a letter from Mr. Langwith, informing me that he had made an appointment for me to see Mr. Withers at his home, at ten o'clock on Friday the tenth."

"Today, in fact," said Holmes.

"Precisely, Mr. Holmes. Mr. Langwith said he would come with me, to introduce me and support my case, which I thought was jolly decent of him. 'However,' he said, 'we must not be late, for there is nothing old Withers hates more than poor time-keeping.' He gave me Mr. Withers's address, but said we should meet outside the front of Dulwich railway station at a quarter to ten, from where we could walk together to Mr. Withers's house, which was not far away, and prepare ourselves for the interview as we went.

"You can imagine how pleased I was at this, Mr. Holmes. This morning I rose earlier than usual, to make myself as smart as I could and put my best suit on. Unfortunately, I spent so long getting ready that I ran out of time and had to hurry off without any breakfast. Still, that is not so unusual an occurrence for me and I did not give it a thought. I was too excited at the prospect of meeting such an important man as Mr. Withers to care about breakfast, and all the way down to Dulwich in the train I practised the answers I should give to his questions.

"I was a little early reaching Dulwich, and there was no sign there of Mr. Langwith. This did not trouble me, however, and I passed the time usefully by continuing to rehearse answers to the questions I expected to be asked. All the time, as I paced back and forth before the station, with my 'Not at all, Mr. Withers', 'I could not agree more, Mr. Withers', and all the rest of it, the station clock was ticking towards ten o'clock. Another down train had called at the station since the one I had arrived on, but I looked in vain for Mr. Langwith among the passengers who alighted there.

"As the clock reached the hour, I became seriously concerned, bearing in mind what Mr. Langwith had said about Mr. Withers's dislike of people being late, and I decided I could wait no longer. I could not think what had happened to Mr. Langwith, and wondered if he had arrived earlier than I had and had left the station just before I got there. Fortunately, I had studied a map of the Dulwich area the evening before, and was confident I could find Mr. Withers's house by myself. I set off at a smart pace, and, about seven minutes later, arrived, somewhat breathless, before Banstead House, the address which Mr. Langwith had given me.

"It was a large house, surrounded by its own garden, in a quiet, tree-lined road. When I had recovered my breath and ordered my thoughts a little, I marched up to the front door and gave a couple of bangs on the large brass door-knocker. Even as I did so, I heard sounds of movement in the house, and a moment later the door was opened, not by a housemaid as I had expected, but by a tall, broad-shouldered and well-dressed middle-aged man. He was clean shaven, save for a dark, waxed moustache, and had a pair of dark, piercing eyes. His whole expression was one of thrusting impatience, as of one used to issuing orders and having them obeyed, and altogether he was a very imposing figure.

"'Yes?' he enquired abruptly. 'What is it?'

"'Mr. Withers?' I asked, somewhat taken aback by his forceful manner.

"'Yes. What do you want?'

"'May I enquire if Mr. Langwith is here?' I asked.

"'Yes, you may, and no, he isn't.'

"I quickly explained to him who I was and my connection with Mr. Langwith.

"'I thought you weren't coming,' said he, in a voice full of annoyance.

"'I'm sorry I'm a bit late,' I returned, and started to tell him how I had waited for Mr. Langwith at Dulwich station, but he cut me short.

"'That doesn't matter,' said he in a peremptory tone. 'You may as well come in now you're here. You'll have to excuse the disorder,' he continued, as I followed him in and along the hall. 'The whole house has recently been re-painted. They did the outside last month, and in the last couple of weeks they have been doing the inside.'

"In fact that was already apparent to me, for the smell of fresh paint was so strong as to be almost overpowering. 'I'm afraid the servants are all lodging elsewhere this week,' Mr. Withers continued, 'as I am myself. I only came back to collect something, so you're fortunate to find me here. However, I'll put the kettle on and make us a cup of tea. If you just wait in here,' he continued, pushing open a door at the end of the hall, 'I'll be back in a moment.'

"The room into which he ushered me was some kind of drawing-room. The painting appeared to be finished in this room and the curtains had been re-hung, although some of the furniture was still covered with dust-sheets. I perched myself on a sofa in the centre of the room and waited, somewhat apprehensively, for Mr. Withers to return. As I did so, I heard doors banging and what sounded like a violent oath from Mr. Withers, as if he was intensely annoyed about something or had banged his head on a cupboard door or something of the sort. All in all, my appointment was proving a somewhat surprising one.

"Abruptly, the door opened and Mr. Withers strode into the room.

"'The tea will be ready in a minute or two,' said he. 'We may as well get on with it. You are a reporter on the *Harrow and Wealdstone Telegraph*, you say?'

"'Yes, sir,' I responded smartly.

"'But you now wish to spread your wings, and think the *Dulwich Weekly Post* might be a suitable next step in your career?'

"'Precisely.'

"'Hum. As it happens, we are in need of another reporter at the moment – a fresh pair of eyes and a fresh pen.'

"My heart rose at this promising information. 'What might the new man's duties be?' I enquired.

"'To begin with,' he replied, 'you – or whoever we took on – would be the chief reporter of flower shows and the like.'

"My heart sank heavily at this, and my face must have betrayed my disappointment, for he hurriedly continued:

"'Of course, that is not all you would be responsible for. There are many other things which would fall within your remit – vegetable shows, for example.'

"'I see,' I said, trying to look interested.

"'Yes,' he continued. 'You'd be amazed how obsessed some people are with growing the largest marrow in the district and that sort of thing. Lord knows why!' he exclaimed with a harsh laugh. 'I can't stand marrow myself! Then there are the general "nature notes" columns – there is one every week, describing the wild flowers to be seen at that time of the year, and so on. Of course, it's all humbug, really. Most gardeners in Dulwich regard these things as weeds, and spend all their time pulling them up. Incidentally, you don't need to concern yourself with the wild-flower illustrations. They are done for us by a nun at the local convent – Sister Euphorbia – who has a gift for that sort of thing. As a matter of fact, there is another one, too, who sometimes stands in for Sister Euphorbia when she is indisposed. That's Sister Gonzaga,' he added. He shot me a keen, penetrating glance. 'You don't have any objection to working with nuns, I suppose?'

"'No,' I said, 'not at all. To be honest, Mr. Withers, it's not something I've ever really thought about.'

"'Good. Only you know how it is, Mr. Barton. Some people get beaten by nuns when they first start school, and after that they can't see a nun without a feeling of bitterness overcoming them.'

"'I assure you I don't harbour any such thoughts,' I insisted. I certainly did not want to lose the job on account of a supposed antipathy to nuns.

"'Very well,' said Mr. Withers, 'but you will appreciate that I have to ask these questions. One can't be too careful! Now I'll go and see if that kettle has boiled yet. While I'm away you can be thinking of any questions you wish to ask me.'

"I let out a very deep breath when Withers had left the room. My interview was not proceeding quite how I had expected, but, on the whole, it seemed more positive than negative. I tried to think of some intelligent-sounding questions to ask him, but I had not got very far when the door was flung open again with great force and Mr. Withers entered with two cups on a small tray.

"'You're not a tea fanatic, I hope,' he said as he put the tray down on a low table by the sofa.

"I shook my head, unsure as to his meaning.

"'That's good,' said he, 'because I've made a pot of coffee instead. The milk has gone off, so I've had to use some tinned muck, which I always think is disgusting in tea, but just about acceptable in coffee.'

"I took a sip from my cup. It was recognizable as coffee, although it was not very good, and it certainly had an odd flavour.

"'Now, about your questions,' said Mr. Withers in an impatient tone: 'Have you got any?'

"'Yes, sir,' I returned promptly, and proceeded to put to him what I hoped would strike him as intelligent and knowledgeable queries. He answered me in a very brief and brusque manner, I must say, his responses to my involved and careful questions sometimes consisting of only one or two words, after which he would say 'Next question?' We proceeded in this way for a few minutes, the rapidity of the questions and answers so great that I began to feel quite exhausted. Indeed, I was so overcome with mental weariness that I had the irresistible urge to yawn, which I managed to disguise by pretending to cough.

"Presently, Mr. Withers rose to his feet. 'I think that that just about covers everything,' he said with an air of finality. 'I like a young man who asks sensible questions.' he added, although I had become so muddled by the rapid questions and answers that I could scarcely remember anything I had asked, or the answers he had given. 'I've got something to do for a minute or two,' he continued. 'You just sit here and finish your coffee, and I'll be back in a little while.'

"When Withers had left the room and closed the door behind him, I sat for some time staring at the carpet. I was glad the main part of the discussion was over. I felt so exhausted that I really didn't feel I could carry on with it any longer. I looked down at the coffee-cup I was holding in my hand. I had drunk very little of it and didn't much fancy drinking any more. I glanced round the room. In a corner, in a raised stand, was some kind of large green plant with thick, leathery leaves. I struggled to my feet, made my way unsteadily over to the plant-stand and tipped the remainder of my coffee into the plant-pot. Then I resumed my seat on the sofa, supported my head on my hand, and–"

Our young visitor fell silent then.

"And?" prompted Holmes after a moment.

"And nothing," returned Barton. "That's just it. I can't remember anything else. Incredible though it seems, at eleven o'clock in the morning, or whatever it was, I think I must have fallen asleep. I've never felt quite so exhausted in all my life."

"What happened next?" Holmes enquired.

"I woke up abruptly. I don't think I'd been asleep very long. I looked at my watch. It was just after half past eleven. The house was in complete silence, although I was conscious of a faint hissing noise, and there was a smell of gas in the room.

"I rose to my feet, wondering where Mr. Withers was. I hoped he hadn't come in and found me asleep – that would hardly have done much for my job prospects. I decided the best thing to do was to go and find him – at least that would show a bit of initiative. I shook my head to try to clear the cobwebs away, and made to open the door. To my great surprise, the door would not move, and it was clear that it was locked.

"'Mr. Withers!' I called out, and banged on the door, but there was no answer and I could hear no sounds of movement anywhere in the house. I called again, several times, but to no avail. I thumped on the door, I pulled at the door-knob with every ounce of strength I possessed, but it was no use: I was locked in. Meanwhile, the smell of gas was becoming stronger by the minute, and, as soon as I stopped banging on the door, I could hear again the hissing noise.

"There were two gas-jets in the room, one on the wall by the window and one on the wall opposite that. The latter was properly turned off, and was not the source of the hissing or the escaping gas, but when I examined the one near the window, I could see at once that it was slightly turned on. I made to turn it off, but found that the tap was jammed. A closer examination revealed that it was stuck fast with paint. I put all my force into twisting the tap off, but made no impression on it whatsoever. In desperation, I took off my boot and, using it like a hammer, thumped the tap with it. This achieved nothing, so I tried again and again, hitting it harder each time. Suddenly, with a snapping noise, the gas-tap broke off completely and fell to the floor with a clatter. At the same moment, the sound of the gas escaping from the jet increased tremendously. It was clear that there was only one thing to be done. I must light the gas or I should die of gas-poisoning within a few minutes.

"With some trepidation, I struck a match just in front of the gas-jet. I had expected that it would flare a little at first, but I was not prepared for what in fact happened. The instant I struck the match, there was an almighty flash and bang in the air all around me and the distinctive smell of singed hair assailed my nostrils. Not only that, but the explosion had extinguished the match without lighting the escaping gas. Somewhat dazed, I quickly struck another match, and applied it to the gas-jet. To my horror, this resulted in a huge flame licking up the wall, half-way to the ceiling. I should have to find the main gas-tap in the house and turn it off as quickly as I could. but how could I get at it, prisoner as I was in that room? No sooner had I posed this question to myself than the obvious answer presented itself: if I could not get out through the doorway, I should have to get out through the window.

"The window in the room was a large one, of the sash-cord variety. I quickly opened the catch, and, for what seemed an age, struggled with the window, trying to push the bottom half upwards or pull the top half downwards, but I couldn't move it even a fraction of an inch, and it was clear that, like the gas-tap, it was stuck fast with paint. There was only one thing for it: I picked up my boot from where I had flung it onto the floor, and attacked one of the panes of glass with it.

"There was a terrific smashing noise as the glass splintered and fell to the ground outside, and a strong gust of cold, fresh, air rushed into the room. That was certainly an improvement on the foul air I had been breathing before, but my problems were hardly over. I could not possibly squeeze through the single broken pane. I should have to smash a second pane and try to break the wooden bar which separated them.

"With a heavy heart – I loathe wanton destruction of this sort – I struck the second pane with my boot-heel and smashed it to smithereens. then, replacing the boot on my foot, I kicked with all the strength I could muster at that part of the window-frame which separated the two broken panes of glass. It was only a slim-looking piece of wood, but was surprisingly sturdy, and resisted my efforts for some time. At length, however, with a loud crack, it snapped off at the top and I was able to remove it completely. I then spent several minutes picking out the jagged shards of glass which remained embedded, like dragon's teeth, in the hardened putty round the edges of the broken panes, until I thought it safe to attempt to climb through the gap. As I was doing so, being careful to avoid lacerating my hands on the many shards of glass which littered the window-sill, I saw that there was a housemaid in the next-door garden. She had been beating a carpet which was flung over a washing-line, but was now standing with mouth agape, staring at me over the low fence which separated the two gardens.

"'I have been trapped in the house,' I called out to her, by way of explanation for what no doubt struck her as extraordinary behaviour. She did not respond, but remained by the fence, staring at me. I had no time to give any further thought to her, however, as it was imperative I got back into the house as quickly as possible, to turn off the gas supply.

"Re-entering the house proved every bit as difficult as getting out of it. I ran round the whole building, but could find no easy way in. The front door was locked, the back door was locked, and all the windows were firmly closed. There was nothing for it: I should have to break in just as I had broken out. I made a quick survey of all the ground-floor windows. Some of them were too high for me to be able to scramble into them, and I eventually selected the window to the left of the front door, which gave on to what looked like a study. Again I took my boot off and began smashing the lowest panes of glass. As I did so, I glanced over to where the next-door housemaid had been standing, but she was no longer there. By the time I had snapped off the wooden frame and cleared the glass, however, and was about to climb in through the gap, the girl had returned, accompanied by a tall, distinguished-looking man with white hair and moustache. He called something to me as I clambered into the house, but I didn't stay to listen, as I could think of nothing but that great flame roaring up the wall in the back room.

"I made my way out of the study, which appeared to be in a state of great disorder, ran down the hall and glanced into the kitchen, but there was no smell of gas there. All the gas-taps were evidently turned off correctly. I then found the cellar door and clattered down the stone steps in the dark. It was almost pitch black down there, the only illumination coming from a small grating high in the wall ahead of me. I struck a match and lit a candle which was standing on a shelf below the grating. There were two chambers in the cellar. To the right was a coal-cellar, with a huge heap of coal beneath a large grating. To the left was a chamber for provisions with a stone table in the middle of the floor. I glanced about, and at once saw where the main gas pipe came into the house and where the main tap was. Having turned this off as tightly as I could, I ran back upstairs and made my way to the drawing-room in which my meeting with Mr. Withers had taken place.

"The key was in the lock. I turned it and pushed the door open. The gas-jet near the window was no longer alight, thank goodness, but I gave little thought to that, as the window-curtain was now on fire, and blazing away. It was clear that the strong gusts of wind through the broken window had blown the curtain into the flame from the gas-jet. I tried to extinguish the burning curtain by smothering it with a chair-cushion, but it was not easy, and I only succeeding in burning my hands. In a blind panic, I leapt up and grabbed the curtain above where it was burning, to try to pull it down, so that I could stamp on it on the floor. I pulled with all my weight at it, and suddenly, with a terrific crash, the whole curtain-rail came down and struck me a terrific blow on the head. Oblivious to the pain, I stamped furiously on the burning curtain, grinding the smouldering remains of it into the carpet, until I was satisfied that all the flames were out and the charred fabric held no heat.

"I had returned to the hall, and was making my way towards the front door when I heard voices. The door to the study was ajar, and I peeped through the crack between the door and the frame. A large group of people had assembled outside the window which I had broken to re-enter the house, among whom I saw the distinguished-looking man from next door.

"'It must be one of those window-smashing lunatics,' he was saying. 'He'll probably climb onto the roof next – that's usually what they do. I'm sure the constable will soon have the matter sorted out when he gets here.' As he spoke I saw a policeman approaching in the distance, in the company of the housemaid I had seen earlier.

"For a second I considered explaining to these people what had happened, but only for a second, because I got the distinct impression that they would not believe me and I should undoubtedly be arrested by the policeman and taken off in handcuffs to the nearest police station. I hesitated no longer. I ran to the back door, unlocked and opened it as quietly as I could, then slipped out into the back garden. I took the key from the lock and re-locked the door from the outside, taking the key away with me so that they should think I was still inside the house and spend time looking for me there while I made my escape. Then I ran like a hare in a straight line down the back garden, pushed my way through a thick hedge and found myself in the large garden of a house which I could see was on a different road altogether.

"As unobtrusively as I could, I made my way round the edge of this garden, out through a gate and into a quiet, tree-lined road. Up this road I set off at a fast rate. I had no idea where I was or where I was going to; I just wanted to put as much distance between Mr. Withers's house and myself as I could. Up roads, down roads, round corners I ran, and did not stop until I came to a small railway station, which turned out to be Lower Norwood. Quite where this station was situated, relative to Dulwich or anywhere else, I hadn't the faintest idea, but I was able to buy a ticket there for Victoria, which is all that I wanted, and forty minutes later I was back in town. From Victoria I came straight here to seek your advice and assistance, Mr. Holmes. That is my story, and here I am!"

Sherlock Holmes sat in silence for some time when our visitor had finished speaking.

"Your account is a fascinating one, Mr. Barton," he remarked at length. "It raises many questions, and I would not have missed it for the world! But I feel you may have made a mistake."

Barton looked surprised. "I cannot think what else I could have done at any stage in the day," he returned. "Did you have anything particular in mind?"

"Your fleeing the scene of these upsetting events may make it more difficult to convince those concerned of your innocence."

"Perhaps so, but I could see from their faces and hear from their words that they had already decided that I was as guilty as any villain could be, and that the only mitigating circumstance they would allow me was that I was probably a lunatic."

"I appreciate the point – I have been in similar situations myself – but you have certainly convinced me of your veracity, so perhaps you could have convinced others, too. Still, what is done is done, and we must work from the situation in which we find ourselves."

"You will take my case, then?" asked Barton, an imploring look in his eyes.

"Most certainly," replied Holmes. "What I propose is that we return to Dulwich at once. Do not fear, Mr. Barton," he added, as our visitor's face fell. "I shall act as your defence counsel, and I am confident we shall quickly get the whole business straightened out. Let us postpone any further discussion of the matter until we are on our way," he continued, as Barton made to speak. "Will you accompany us, Watson?"

"I should be delighted to," I replied. "I am keen to see how you propose to 'straighten out,' as you put it, such a very odd affair."

Five minutes later, the three of us were in a cab and rattling along through the crowded streets towards Victoria station.

"The surprising and alarming events at Mr. Withers's house," said Holmes, "have had the effect of eclipsing and putting out of consideration what should really be the first mystery in this business."

"What is that?" queried Barton in surprise.

"The failure of your cousin, Mr. Langwith, to turn up as arranged."

"That's true," said Barton. "I wonder what can have become of him."

"We can only speculate," said Holmes. "Perhaps he fell ill, or suffered some kind of accident on his way to meet you at Dulwich station. But both of those explanations would require a singularly unfortunate coincidence to have occurred. More likely, as it involves no such coincidence of events, is that he simply learned in the last few days that the appointment with Thurston Withers could not take place as arranged after all, and there was thus no point in his going."

"Then why did he not write and tell me of this?" objected Barton.

"Perhaps he did, and you did not receive his letter," replied Holmes. "You left home in a great hurry this morning, without taking any breakfast. Does your landlady usually place your post on the breakfast-table?"

"Yes, she does. It is always beside my plate."

"Then perhaps there was a letter from Mr. Langwith there this morning, which, in your haste, you failed to see."

Barton clapped his hand to his head. "Of course!" he cried. "That must be it! But," he added after a moment, "the fact that Mr. Langwith was not present does not even begin to explain why Mr. Withers acted and spoke so strangely to me – he was not at all as I had expected him to be – nor why he left the house so abruptly, leaving me locked in the drawing-room with a leaking gas tap which I could not turn off."

"It is certainly a singularly absurd and confused affair, although I don't imagine it struck you that way at the time. But some aspects of it seem clear enough: first of all, that the man you met in Dulwich was not Thurston Withers."

"I suppose that that is possible," remarked Barton after a moment, "but how can you be so sure? He was, after all, in Mr. Withers's house, and when I first arrived there and addressed him as Mr. Withers, he did not appear at all surprised. It is true that some of the questions he asked me were a little eccentric, but I put that down to his strong, forceful character."

"'Eccentric' is not the word I would choose to describe him," returned Holmes. "I think if we described him as an accomplished liar we should be nearer the truth. In any case, consider for a moment the point you yourself raised, that he left you locked in the drawing-room when he disappeared from the house: It is surely inconceivable that the real Thurston Withers would have done such a thing; for if it really were his house, he should have to return to it at some time, when you would still be there. It seems to me much more likely that the man you saw had no right to be in the house at all. I imagine he only answered your knock at the door because he thought it might be a neighbour of Withers's who had seen him enter the house and he did not wish to arouse suspicion. But when you first addressed him, he would at once have realised that you did not know Thurston Withers by sight, and he probably judged that the best course of action for himself was to continue the pretence of being Withers for a short time until either he could get rid of you or make his own escape. Mr. Langwith had mentioned to you that Thurston Withers had been suffering from insomnia recently, and had had recourse to some kind of sleeping-powder. It seems likely from your account that this stranger had come across this in the kitchen and had added a dose to your cup of coffee, obviously thinking that you would fall fast asleep and he could leave the house and be far away before you woke up again."

Barton nodded his agreement to this analysis. "Fortunately for me," he said, "I drank very little of the coffee, on account of its odd taste. Had I drained the cup, I might have slept for an hour or two, I suppose, and might very well have died from gas-poisoning. The mere thought of that makes me feel quite ill," he added with a shudder. "Do you think this strange man intended to murder me?"

Holmes shook his head. "I think that very unlikely. I imagine that what happened was this, that when he went to boil the kettle, he discovered there was no gas available in the kitchen, so he turned on the main gas-tap in the cellar, not realising that it had been turned off deliberately because of the leaking tap in the drawing-room. As he did not stay for long in the drawing-room with you after he brought in the coffee, he probably did not notice the smell of gas there."

"That may be true. He drank his own coffee quickly while we exchanged a series of rapid questions and answers, as I mentioned to you, then he left, saying he had something to attend to. The smell of gas was not noticeable then; it only became so when I awoke from my nap."

"I wonder who this person could have been," I remarked, "if it was not, indeed, Mr. Withers?"

"Of course we cannot say for certain," said Holmes, "but I suspect we need look no further than Thurston Withers's own cousin, Seymour Withers. We have heard that the two men are, as their fathers before them, bitter rivals in the newspaper business. We have also heard that there was some dispute over which of the two newspapers each son should have inherited. No doubt Seymour Withers learned that his cousin and his domestic staff would be absent from the house while it was being redecorated and thought to take advantage of that fact to rifle through his cousin's private papers in the hope of finding something of benefit to his own cause."

"But how could he have got into the house?" I objected.

Sherlock Holmes shook his head dismissively. "Pooh!" said he. "I see no great problem in that, if a man is determined enough. Cousin Seymour may have purloined a key during some previous visit to the house; he may have had a duplicate key made at some time; he may, for all we know, have entered the house through the coal-cellar grating. But, here we are at Victoria, so further speculation will have to wait!"

A stopping train for Bickley was just about to leave as we dashed onto the platform, and we sprang aboard as the guard blew his whistle. Twenty minutes later, we had alighted at Dulwich, and were making our way down a tree-lined avenue towards the house in which Holmes's client had had such a strange experience.

As we approached, we saw that there was a small group of people, including a policeman, in front of the house, watching two workmen affixing a piece of plywood over a broken window.

"There is Mr. Langwith," cried Barton: "just to the left of the constable."

The man in question, a tall elderly gentleman, turned at that moment and saw us.

"Why, Henry!" cried he. "Here you are at last! Where on earth have you been?" A large, stout man, standing by his side, turned to follow his gaze, and Langwith addressed him. "This is the young man – my cousin's son – that I mentioned to you, Withers," he explained. Then he turned once more to our companion. "You won't believe what has been happening here, Henry! Mr. Withers has had a lunatic in the house, who has gone round smashing all the windows and setting fire to the curtains!"

Before Holmes's client could respond, a distinguished-looking man, standing just behind Langwith, let out a cry of surprise and recognition. "That's him!" he cried. "That's the villain I saw trying to destroy the house! Constable! Arrest that man at once!"

"One moment," returned Holmes in an authoritative tone, as the policeman took a step forward. "So far from arresting this young man, you should consider giving him an award. His quick thinking and decisive actions undoubtedly saved the house from burning down or being utterly destroyed in an explosion, as a result of a serious gas leak."

The stout man beside Langwith shook his head, a look of great annoyance on his face. "I am Thurston Withers," said he in an angry voice, "this is my house, and I know all about the gas leak, thank you very much! A plumber is coming tomorrow to deal with the matter. Until then, I have had the gas turned off at the mains."

"But what you don't know," returned Holmes, "is that someone turned the main tap back on again. This young man is Mr. Henry Barton, who arrived this morning for an interview with you, and managed to save your house."

"Did you not receive my note, Henry?" Langwith interrupted in a tone of surprise. "I wrote to tell you that Mr. Withers was otherwise engaged this morning and that our appointment was therefore postponed until this afternoon."

Barton shook his head. "I came at ten o'clock, as we had previously arranged, and had an interview with someone who pretended to be Mr. Withers. But he put some kind of sleeping potion in my coffee-cup and locked me in a drawing-room where the gas was leaking."

"What!" cried Thurston Withers in a tone of disbelief. "What a preposterous and unbelievable story!"

"At least hear Mr. Barton's account before you dismiss it," said Holmes. "You are an experienced newspaperman, Mr. Withers, so you, if anyone, must know that every man must be given the opportunity to state his own case."

There came a grudging assent to this observation from Withers, and, at a sign from Holmes, his client launched into a brief account of all that had happened to him since he left home that morning.

"Can this really be true?" exclaimed Withers, as Barton finished speaking.

"Every word of it, Mr. Withers," returned the latter.

"But who could this stranger be?" asked Withers.

"I think," said Holmes, "that taking everything into account, including the fact that the intruder seems to have been well informed about you, and that he rifled the private papers in your study, which are, I take it, more concerned with personal affairs than business matters, the chief suspect must surely be your own cousin, Seymour Withers."

At this, a small man with a grizzled moustache who had been standing beside Thurston Withers, but who had not previously spoken, stepped forward, a look of great anger upon his features.

"How dare you!" he cried. "How dare you accuse an honest man of such deceitful behaviour! It is an outrage! I am Seymour Withers, and I know nothing whatever of this business!"

There was a moment's uncomfortable silence, during which the workmen behind us banged nails into their sheet of plywood.

"Describe the man you encountered this morning," said Holmes to Barton, "and let us see if anyone recognizes the description."

"He was a tall man," began Barton, "broad-shouldered and powerful-looking, with very penetrating eyes. He had very dark hair and eyebrows, and a black, waxed moustache. He was a well-spoken gentleman, but very abrupt and impatient in his manner."

Thurston Withers looked at his cousin, who nodded his head. "That sounds very much like Lancelot Woodhouse," said Seymour Withers.

"I agree," said Thurston Withers. "It must be he. The description is exact."

"Who on earth is Lancelot Woodhouse?" asked Barton.

"I believe, Henry," said Langwith, "that he is the owner and editor-in-chief of the *Streatham Star*. Is that correct, Withers?"

"Yes, and a more ruthless fellow you are never likely to meet. He has put a lot of energy recently into trying to persuade many of our commercial advertisers to switch their allegiance to his paper. I have become increasingly concerned of late about leaks from our newspaper office of confidential correspondence on the subject, and have taken to keeping such correspondence here at home. No doubt Woodhouse has learned of this and his intention this morning was to find something among my private papers which he could turn to his advantage. I wonder how the devil he got into the house?"

"Has he paid you a visit recently?" asked Holmes.

"Yes," replied Thurston Withers, "as a matter of fact he has, although I wasn't in at the time. The foreman of the painters who have been working here told me that Woodhouse called one day last week. They informed him that I wasn't at home, but he said that he had reason to think I would be returning shortly – which, incidentally, wasn't true – and that he would wait a little while for me. He sat on a chair in the hall, but, after about ten minutes, he called to the painters and told them that he had decided not to wait any longer after all. What he wanted, I do not know, as I have not spoken to him since."

"I think that explains how he gained entry to the house today," said Holmes. "No doubt when the painters left him alone in the hall for ten minutes, he removed the key from the front door and made an impression of it in softened wax or something of the sort, so that he could have a duplicate made. He has evidently been following the progress of your redecoration closely, and was aware that the house would be quite unoccupied this morning. Had Mr. Barton not arrived when he did, Woodhouse would probably have finished his survey of your private correspondence and left the house as he had found it, and no one would ever have known he had been here."

"I am sure you are right," said Thurston Withers in a determined voice. "I shall speak to my solicitor tomorrow with a view to commencing legal proceedings against Woodhouse."

"What of my cousin here, Withers?" asked Langwith. "I know it has been an upsetting business for you, but could we possibly make another appointment for Mr. Barton to see you?"

"No," said Withers, shaking his head in vehement fashion. "There will be no interview. It is not necessary. I have heard your recommendation, Langwith, and Mr. Barton himself has just given a first-class demonstration of his ability to give a report in a pithy and convincing way. That is enough for me." He turned to Barton then, and held out his hand with a smile. "The position is yours, my boy, if you want it. Whatever you were getting at the *Harrow and Wealdstone Telegraph*, I'll give you twenty per cent more. What do you say?"

Barton seized the other's hand and wrung it vigorously. "I accept your offer, Mr. Withers," said he. "I am sure you will not regret it."

Holmes was silent as we walked back to the railway station. "It is something of a relief to me," he remarked at length, "that the circumstances – Barton's being offered the position he desired and so on – had the effect of erasing my own lamentable error with regard to Seymour Withers."

"I shouldn't worry about it, Holmes," I returned with a chuckle. "Everyone makes a mistake occasionally. I shouldn't dwell on it if I were you."

"But I must dwell on it, Watson," said my friend in an emphatic tone. "One can learn more from one blunder than from a hundred successes. I must therefore concentrate all my thoughts upon the blunder in order to reap the full benefit of it."

And that was the last word my friend spoke on the subject, as we made our way back to Baker Street.

THE ZODIAC PLATE

"POISON," SAID SHERLOCK HOLMES, pushing back his chair from the supper table. I looked up from the medical journal I was reading, and watched as he took his old clay pipe from the mantelpiece. "Poison," he continued, "is, in its many and varied forms, one of the greatest benefactors of the human race. We have indeed much for which to thank the poisons."

"I hardly think that many could be found to agree with you," I replied in some amusement.

"Nevertheless, it is true. If you would consider the matter for but five seconds, Watson, you must agree. Where, to take the most obvious example, would medicine be today, but for poisons?"

"I believe I see what you mean. It is true that there are certain substances which would commonly be regarded as poisonous, but which in regulated doses may be useful in the treatment of certain ailments. In some instances, indeed, the physician will deliberately administer one poison in the knowledge that it will drive out another poison which is already present in the body – as in the case of nicotine and strychnine."

Holmes waved his hand impatiently. "Yes, yes; of course, this is true; but it is a trivial point, of little interest to the theorist: that a substance can be found that will drive out another is not so very surprising, and that either of these two, taken in isolation, would have a deleterious effect upon the human system is surely no more than experience might lead one to expect. The point I wish to make, however, is a somewhat more profound one: that it is the chance occurrence of poisons, unfortunate as their effects may be upon the individual, that has given mankind the great knowledge it now possesses. When a poison causes an upheaval of the normal, everyday run of things, it reveals to us as it does so something also of the system it has affected. In this way, little by little, our knowledge has increased. Without such revelations, on the other hand, we should really know very little of the workings of the human body. And it is not only to the realm of medicine that this observation applies: in the sphere of our mental life the situation is the same. As Kant argues in the book I was looking at this afternoon, many of the paradoxical and perplexing notions with which we are inclined to ensnare and befuddle our own minds are in a sense poisons, which, by defeating our intellects, demonstrate to us our own limitations."

"You have been reading Kant?"

"Time has been hanging somewhat heavily upon my hands just lately," replied my friend, "and the *Critique of Pure Reason* is good light reading at such a time."

"Light reading!" I cried. "I understood that Kant's *Critique* was one of the most difficult books ever written!"

"Really? You surprise me; I find it most congenial and refreshing. I suppose it is a question of temperament. There are distinct parallels between the work of the expert philosopher and that of the expert detective. In both employments, the talents of imagination, observation and deduction form an absolute prerequisite. In both fields, too, the admission of exotic poisons into the commonplace progress of life is apt to produce effects which could not have been foreseen."

"As to the philosophical aspects of your thesis, I should not care to advance an opinion," I remarked after a moment; "but upon the medical side of things I think I see a flaw in your argument. For if no poisons existed, then surely, in such a perfect world, we should simply have no need of the knowledge that, on your account, we should thereby be denied. We might not, it is true, have so full an understanding of the complexities of the human body, but we should be not one whit disadvantaged as a consequence, for there would simply be no call for such knowledge."

"Ha!" cried Holmes. "I really cannot believe that that is your considered opinion, Watson. It seems to me a quite fallacious piece of reasoning, to conclude from the fact that our knowledge, whether medical or otherwise, is often of practical use to us, that that is therefore the reason for its existence. You may as well argue, from the fact that the ocean winds have proved of the utmost use to mariners, that the winds owe their very existence to that employment. The situation in my opinion is quite the other way about: Man has an unquenchable thirst for knowledge, which leads him upon an endless quest for answers and explanations, irrespective of whether they will materially affect him either one way or the other; the fact that some of his knowledge proves to be of practical use is simply a bonus. But we will perhaps have an opportunity to take a third opinion upon the matter when my visitor arrives, for he is a medical colleague of yours, a Dr. James Saunders."

"Dr. James Saunders of Harley Street?" I cried in surprise. "He may indeed have an opinion upon the matter, for he is by all accounts one of the most brilliant men in London, and in the very van of medical research. Why, he has a monograph in the journal I have in my hand at this moment! He gives it the title 'Not a Door but a Window'."

"The reference being – ?"

"To the epidermis. He argues that it is an area of study which has been lamentably neglected and misunderstood in recent years, and one which could make a far greater contribution to general diagnosis than has hitherto been supposed. He is undoubtedly one of the foremost authorities upon the subject – I wonder what on earth he can want with us?"

"Your thirst for knowledge upon the point should be satisfied in just five minutes," remarked my friend drily, with a glance at the clock. "His appointment is for half-past-eight."

Our visitor was punctual to the minute. A tall, upright man, a little over forty years of age, he had a broad, intelligent face, in which his dark and thoughtful eyes seemed to gleam with intellectual power. A greying of the hair about the temples was the only sign that the famous specialist was as susceptible to the passage of the years as the rest of his human brethren. He took a seat by our cheerily-crackling fire, and rubbed his hands gently together in the warmth.

"Well, sir," said Holmes after a moment. "What brings Dr. James Saunders from Harley Street to Baker Street on so dark a night as this? It has meant your going without your supper, I perceive. May we offer you a sandwich and a glass of wine?"

"Thank you, Mr. Holmes," replied the other, "but I have a cold chicken waiting for me at home – but how on earth do you know that I have not yet eaten this evening? I should not have thought that my appearance would strike anyone as especially undernourished!"

"I observed that your overcoat is suffering from a swollen pocket, occasioned by the medical instruments which I see protruding from the top. You have evidently not come here direct from home, then, but have been out upon a professional call. At this time of day, and upon an evening when you already have one engagement, it seems likely that your journey was not premeditated, but the result of an unexpected summons. It has certainly occupied you some time, for the fresh mould adhering to your boot is peculiar to the Surrey side, and is found there only in certain parts. Would I be correct if I were to suggest that you have been out to Norwood?"

"As near as makes no difference," our visitor replied, a look of amazement upon his face. "I have heard of your powers, of course, Mr. Holmes, but I hardly expected to receive a demonstration of them so promptly! You have, also, a reputation for discretion," he continued after a moment, "which, if one considers it, must be so difficult an achievement as to be almost a contradiction in terms." He smiled slightly at his own jest, his eyes sparkling, and Holmes bowed his head in acknowledgement of the compliment. "It is this that brings me here tonight; for I require something to be done which may be both difficult and unpleasant – yes, and perhaps shameful, too."

"Pray be explicit."

"Very well. My sister, Winifred, who is some years older than I am, is the widow of Sir Douglas Harford Joyce, who, as you will probably recall, was our ambassador at the time of the Bucharest incident. She has one son, my nephew, Robert. He was just eighteen years old when his father died, and, to speak perfectly frankly, has sorely missed the influence of a father since that time. It is not that he is a bad lad, but he is wild and undisciplined, and shows no sign of taking any particular direction in life. As his only near relative, I have felt some responsibility in the matter of his upbringing and education, but my own work keeps me so continuously occupied that I have not always been able to devote the time to the task that I should have wished. His mother naturally thinks the world of him, and wants only what is for the best; but just as he has only one parent, so she has only one child, and she has as a result, I am afraid, tended to concede every point of contention which has arisen between them. This has not, as you will appreciate, been conducive to the formation of those manners which society expects of its members, and Robert has thus tended to gravitate to the company of those whose behaviour is as reckless and unprincipled as his own. I have done my best to arrest this downward progress, but have succeeded only in making myself a figure of stuffiness and gloom in his eyes, if not, indeed, a figure of derision.

"About a year ago he began to gamble heavily, which threw a further strain upon the already stretched resources of the allowance he receives under the terms of his father's will. Since that time he has continually approached me in my capacity as a trustee of his father's estate and begged for advances on the money he can expect to inherit upon his twenty-fifth birthday. I have, I regret to say, acquiesced more often than I have refused. When he came to me last week, however, and demanded five hundred pounds to pay off some money-lender or other, I flatly refused.

" 'You must learn to curb your excesses,' I told him. 'You cannot expect simply to do as you wish, and then presume that someone will always come along to settle your account for you.'

" 'I shall not need to, after September,' he retorted. 'When the money is under my own control you will have no further opportunity for these sermons you so enjoy delivering, Uncle James; that is something I can promise you. Now, as there is so little time remaining for you to get upon my good side, perhaps you had better reconsider, and let me have the money after all.'

" 'I shall not give you a penny!' I cried. 'In seven months' time you will be free to do whatever you wish with the money. You may gamble it away, drink it away, or throw it in the river if it pleases you to do so, and I shall not be able to stop you. But until the time I am obliged by law to relinquish control of your financial affairs, I shall not be a party to such profligate and reprehensible waste. You will not, I repeat, get another penny out of me until the appointed day, on the first of next month.'

" 'You may regret it, Uncle,' said he, with a hard, bitter look upon his face, such as I had never seen there before.

" 'You are the one that will know regret,' I responded, but, with a foul oath by way of farewell, he left the room, slamming the door hard behind him. I worried afterwards lest I had been too severe upon the young man – I have all along sought to strike a balance between guidance and friendship – but events since have convinced me that I have not, in the past, been firm enough.

"I received a note yesterday morning from Lady Harford Joyce's butler, Milner, a man who has been in the family's employ for over a score of years, and upon whose discretion and good sense one could pledge one's life. He informed me that – well, that the very worst thing I could have conceived has taken place."

"Pray be specific," said Sherlock Holmes impatiently. "What, precisely, has happened, and in what way can I assist you?"

"I must tell you first of the Harford Joyce Plate," replied the great specialist. "It is the family's one great heirloom, and has been in their possession for generations. It is approximately twelve inches wide and eighteen in length, and is roughly oval in shape, although the corners are squared off. It is quite a heavy piece, for it is fashioned of solid silver. In the centre, depicted in relief, is a representation of the sun; and in a circle around it, also in relief, are the various traditional creatures of the Zodiac – crabs and scorpions and rams, and so on. Inset into the metal, representing the stars whose configurations first inspired men's minds with the idea of the Zodiac creatures, are scores of precious and semi-precious stones. While these certainly have a considerable intrinsic value, they are not, so I understand, of the very finest. It is rather the skill of the setting, the remarkable craftsmanship which has gone into the execution of its unique design, which gives the plate its value."

"Which is?" interjected Holmes.

"At a conservative estimate, twelve thousand pounds. A few years ago, my late brother-in-law had it valued, for insurance purposes, and I believe that the figure agreed upon was of that order. It may be worth considerably more now, for all I know. In one sense, of course, it is priceless, for there is not another like it in the world. To my sister, also, it has a value far greater than any price which it might fetch at auction; for, since Sir Douglas's death, the things which attached to him and to his family have become most dear to her; and the Zodiac Plate is, of course, of all such things, the very *non plus ultra.* Indeed, she has become almost obsessive about it: only last year she turned down an invitation from the British Museum for the Plate to be included in an exhibition of such artefacts which they were mounting, giving as her reason the wish of her husband that the Plate remain forever in the family home."

"And your nephew has threatened to sell this plate unless you advance him the money he requires?"

"Worse than that, Mr. Holmes; he has already given it into the hands of the money-lender he had mentioned to me, as security against the loan which is still outstanding. This was the news which Milner conveyed to me yesterday."

"I am not quite clear why it fell to the butler to be your informant," remarked Holmes, a note of curiosity in his voice. "Is Lady Harford Joyce ignorant of this recent transaction?"

"She has been in ill-health for some years, Mr. Holmes," replied Dr. Saunders, with a shake of the head, "and has been virtually bed-ridden this last nine months. She knows nothing of what occurs downstairs, other than what she learns from her son or from her domestic staff. In this case, Robert of course told no one what he was about, and Milner, having discovered what had happened, thought it wiser not to break the news of her son's idiocy to his mistress unless he was obliged to do so. With this judgement, I agree: The shock of such a disclosure might very well have appalling consequences upon her precarious state of health. Instead, he at once sent a note to me."

"Your intention, then, is to get the Plate back without your sister's knowing that it has ever left the house?"

"Precisely."

"Who has legal ownership of the Plate?"

"At present it is held in trust, the trustees being my sister, her solicitor in Gray's Inn and myself. When Robert attains the age of twenty-five, in seven months' time, it becomes his property absolutely."

"But your object, I take it, is less to remedy a legal wrong than to protect your sister, Lady Harford Joyce, from distress."

"That is correct; and, also, I might add – although he would sneer if he heard me say it – to protect my nephew from future remorse at the foolish actions of his youth. I do not imagine for one moment that his coming of age will mark any great change in his character, but I feel sure that something will one day bring him to his senses. Then, if he has inherited but one scrap of the dignity and sense of honour of his parents, he must surely hide his head in shame at the recollection of the life he is leading now. My only wish for him is that his memories should not be unbearably painful."

"Quite so. I can understand the scandal which would be aroused if it became generally known that the family's chief heirloom had been pawned to pay gambling debts. But the situation does not seem so very serious. Have you had a word with your nephew?"

"I spoke with him yesterday afternoon, and pointed out that if he had intended by his action to spite me, then he had badly misjudged the matter, for it was he himself he would hurt most. At this he only laughed. Eventually, seeing that there was no other way out of it, and with his mother's condition at the forefront of my mind, I offered him the five hundred pounds he had asked me for last week, on condition that he use it to redeem the Plate. At this he laughed still louder.

" 'It will take more than that to get the Plate back now,' he cried, a jeering note in his voice. 'I have already borrowed another thousand on the strength of it.'

"I was aghast at this, for I realised at once his intentions."

"To continue borrowing against the plate until September, presumably," observed Holmes. "Did you offer him any further money?"

Dr. Saunders nodded his head slowly, a defeated look upon his face.

"But he turned you down?"

"He did. It is evident that no amount short of his full inheritance will persuade him to alter his plans. I could see as we spoke that he felt that he had scored over me, and this only made him more obdurate. Then, in the heat of the moment, I said a foolish thing."

"You threatened him with legal action of some kind," said Holmes with a sigh, resting his chin upon his hand.

"I am afraid that I did, Mr. Holmes. Of course, the very idea is ridiculous. A legal suit would be guaranteed to stir up precisely the sort of scandal that I most wish to avoid – "

"And would likely enough not reach the courts before September in any case," interjected Holmes, with a grim smile.

"At any event," continued our visitor, "all that my threats achieved was to harden my nephew's heart yet further, and turn his cold scorn into hot anger. His response to my threat was swift:

" 'The Harford Joyce Plate is mine, to do with as I please,' cried he angrily.

" 'Not until September,' I returned, attempting to speak calmly and thus remedy the damage my unconsidered threat had caused.

" 'It is morally mine now,' retorted Robert, 'and you know it. There is no other male Harford Joyce alive but me, so whose else could it be?'

" 'But your father, in his wisdom – '

" 'Leave my father out of it, if you please.'

" 'Very well, Robert: if you will not consider your father's wishes, consider at least your mother's feelings.'

" 'She need know nothing of it,' replied the young scoundrel with a smirk of superiority, ' – unless, of course, you tell her yourself. And now, Uncle, I really must be off; I promised some fellows that I would meet them at Gates' this afternoon.' With that he left the room and our interview was at an end."

"If he is losing money at Gates' Club, then he is undoubtedly losing a great deal of it," observed Holmes after a moment; "and the arrangement with the money-lender regarding the Plate will of course only encourage him to lose yet more." He paused for a moment, his brows knitted with thought. "Tell me," he said at length; "to which of the Society parasites is he indebted?"

"A man by the name of Oscar Morley."

"Ah! That is bad, very bad! He is the most odious man in London. We can hope for little assistance there, I am afraid. Indeed, his involvement raises the possibility of a yet greater calamity."

"Whatever do you mean?" asked Dr. Saunders quickly, a note of alarm in his voice.

"I have no desire to raise fears unnecessarily," replied Holmes gravely, "but it is my duty as an expert in these matters to apprise you of all the possibilities, however unpleasant. Oscar Morley has no principles but one, the principle of ruthless self-interest. Should he judge that his interests were best served by selling the Zodiac Plate to some third party, and pocketing the proceeds, then no consideration on earth would weigh against it."

"Good God!" cried our visitor, clapping his hand to his head. "I had no idea our position was so perilous! But, wait! Surely you exaggerate the danger? Surely he cannot sell the Plate without exposing himself to criminal charges? For by no interpretation of the circumstances could he claim that the Plate was his; it is merely in his keeping as a temporary security."

Holmes shook his head, the severity of his expression offering no comfort to the imploring eyes of the other. "Unfortunately," said he, "it is not so simple as you imagine. These things are rarely arranged with full legal propriety. He has given your nephew five hundred pounds – or fifteen hundred, as it now is – and your nephew has given him the Zodiac Plate. That is all there is to it. Should anything happen to the Plate, neither your nephew nor anyone else would have the slightest legal recourse – unless, of course, you are prepared to demonstrate in a court of law that your nephew had no right to take the Plate in the first place."

"But surely there must be some signed documents, some record of the transaction between the two of them?" Dr. Saunders persisted.

Again Holmes shook his head. "If there is such a record, whom would you expect it to favour? The man who has recourse to such a transaction but once or twice in his life, in moments of desperation, or the man whose every day is spent in such dealings? But very likely there are no papers in existence at all, save a couple of simple, bald and unconditional receipts. To the lawyers it is known as a debt of honour, and, as such, outwith their purview."

"A debt of dishonour, more like!" cried our visitor, thumping the chair-arm with his fist.

"However that may be," said Holmes after a moment, in a measured tone, "it is imperative that the pledge be redeemed, and redeemed as quickly as possible. You have approached your nephew without success, so I take it you wish me to approach Morley directly."

Our visitor nodded his head. "It is a task, I readily confess, for which my education has not well fitted me."

"Very well, then," continued Holmes; "but I cannot promise success. I tell you now that Oscar Morley has not an atom of decency in his whole being, and that he is susceptible to no persuasion but that which is withdrawn from a bank vault."

For answer, the eminent specialist reached deep within the recesses of his coat and produced a thick brown leather purse, which he tossed across to my friend. "There are bank-notes there to the value of fifteen hundred pounds, which I withdrew this afternoon."

"It will not be enough."

"I shall also give you a blank cheque. Please keep it locked in your desk. When you have fixed a price with this vile man, fill in whatever amount is necessary, up to five thousand. My bankers are Drummond's, at Charing Cross. They will pay over the counter there without question." He took a cheque-book from his pocket, I passed him a pen, and he wrote out a cheque upon his knee.

"You had best give me a fuller description of the Harford Joyce Plate," said Holmes, as he took the cheque and placed it in his drawer. "I would not put it past Morley to attempt to swindle us in some way."

"I can do better than that," replied Dr Saunders, glancing at his watch. "At the time my brother-in-law had the Plate valued, an extremely good photograph was taken of it, showing its every detail in great clarity. This photograph hangs in the family home; if we go along there now, the chances are that my sister will be asleep and will thus not know that we have called. I sent a note to Milner earlier, to say that such a visit might be made, so we should be able to get in quietly enough."

"Excellent!" cried Holmes, springing from his chair. "You appear to have anticipated our every need!" He disappeared into his room, but was back again in a few seconds, his heaviest overcoat in his hand. "Are you up to a trip through the fog, Watson?" he called to me.

"Certainly," I replied, "if my presence would be of any value to you."

"Good old Watson!" said my friend with a dry chuckle. "Your presence is always of value, old fellow. Where does your sister reside, Dr. Saunders?"

"In the Campden Hill area. It should not take us more than half an hour."

The night was cold and dark, and the dense and swirling fog deadened all noise and hid all but the faint glimmer of the streetlamps from our view, so that, for all our senses could tell us, we might have been the last men in London. Indeed, so silent and deserted was the dismal, dripping world through which we passed that night, that were it not for the muffled clatter of the horse's hooves and the constant silvery jingle of the harness, one could have believed that the four walls of the cab marked the very bounds of existence itself. No word passed between us to dispel this gloomy monotony, and it seemed a long half-hour indeed before our cab finally halted. But at length the driver reined in his horse, and we stepped down into a broad road, lined with stark, leafless plane trees, which loomed up like sentinels out of the fog as we approached, only to vanish once again a moment later, as the fog wreathed its ghostly fingers about them. Beyond the trees lay the dark, solid masses of the large houses, dimly seen through chance rifts in the greasy brown curtain.

"This is Campden Hill Crescent," said James Saunders, clapping his gloved hands together vigorously. The words were scarcely out of his mouth, when there came the crack of a whip, the shrill whinny of a horse, and, with a sudden and startling rattle and crash, a carriage emerged at a rush from a gateway a few yards ahead of us. An iron-faced driver sat upon the box with his coat collar turned up; and as the carriage passed us with a clatter, I saw a frowning face within. For a second our eyes met, and I had the impression of a young and arrogant face, the thin line of a moustache above a curling, disdainful lip; a moment later and the carriage had vanished from sight into the dense and silent fog-bank.

"This is most annoying," remarked our guide with chagrin, as we stepped forward once more. "That was my nephew, Robert, and he evidently saw us. I had made arrangements with Milner for the side-door to be left unlocked for us, that we might enter in as unobtrusive a manner as possible, to lessen the chance of our presence becoming apparent to my sister; but as Robert may well mention to his mother that he has seen us, perhaps we had best appear like honest men and use the front door after all."

The butler, a tall, spare figure, whose bald head gleamed in the bright lights of the hall, directed us in silence to a large warm room at the rear of the house, and turned up the gas. The fragrant aroma of Turkish tobacco which hung in the air there told me that Robert Harford Joyce had only recently quit the room, and in the hearth I observed a number of dark cigarette-stubs. Upon the white cloth of a small table was a broad red stain, in the middle of which stood a bottle of wine and a half-emptied glass. Dr. Saunders stepped at once to a tall lacquered cabinet beside the fireplace and took from the top of it a large silver-framed photograph.

"The Harford Joyce Plate," said he, holding the picture for us beneath the light. It did indeed appear a splendid example of the silversmith's art, its surface embossed with gentle, graceful curves and lines, and set with a great number of gems, in its exquisite depiction of the mythical creatures of the Zodiac.

"Of course, the real thing is far more impressive," remarked our guide after a moment. "The stones were chosen for their purity of colour, and are extremely well matched. They say – "

The door opened abruptly, and we were joined by the butler. "Her Ladyship has heard you and would speak with you, Dr. Saunders," said he. The two of them left the room together, but scarcely a minute had passed before Milner returned to inform us that our presence, too, was required. We ascended the broad, thickly carpeted stairs, and followed him into a warm and stifling bedroom, where a frail, sickly looking woman was sitting up in bed, propped up on pillows. What little of her was visible, above the mound of blankets, was swathed in thick plaid shawls, and there was a woollen bonnet upon her head. Her brother was seated upon a chair beside the bed, but rose to his feet as we entered.

"Allow me to introduce you," said he. "Lady Harford Joyce, this is Dr. John Watson, a medical colleague of mine, and his friend, Mr. Sherlock Holmes. I was just telling my sister, gentlemen, of your interest in her collection of Ming vases. It is an excellent collection, is it not?" We nodded our heads and murmured our assent, and he continued, addressing Lady Harford Joyce. "I feared to disturb you, Winifred, and knew you would have no objection to my showing these gentlemen your collection."

We then exchanged a few pleasantries about pottery in general, the London museums and the weather, and it seemed that the interview was about to end, when Lady Harford Joyce spoke suddenly in a different, agitated tone.

"Why are you telling me these lies?" she demanded abruptly, addressing her brother with all the power of her faint, weak voice. He took a step backwards in surprise, and did not reply. "I have heard Mr. Holmes's name," she continued. "He is an enquiry agent or lawyer of some kind; he was involved in the settling of that unpleasantness at Delvoir Castle, the year before last. Furthermore, you have not so much as glanced at the Ming since you entered the house – your movements have been perfectly audible to me, and I am well aware that you have entered no room but the drawing-room."

There followed a long moment during which no one spoke. Dr. Saunders cleared his throat, and seemed about to reply, but then lapsed once more into silence. Evidently the story of the Ming vases had exhausted his powers of invention for the present. I shot a swift glance at Holmes, but it was evident from the expression upon his face that he was disinclined to take any active part in the deception being practised upon Lady Harford Joyce.

"Madam," said I, almost before I knew what I was doing; "permit me as a medical man to express my pleasure at the fact that both your sense of hearing and your memory for names remain unaffected by your bodily infirmity. You are perfectly correct in all your observations. Your brother naturally did not wish to alarm you, but the fact of the matter is this: there has been a spate of burglaries in the Notting Hill area recently, and he was concerned that these premises were not as secure against intruders as they perhaps ought to be, especially in view of the numerous objects of value which are kept here. I therefore recommended that he take the opinion of my friend, Mr. Holmes, who is an acknowledged expert in this field. Our intention was to make our survey of your doors and windows without your knowledge, in order to spare you anxiety upon the matter."

As I finished speaking, I realised that I had hardly taken a breath since I began, and I stood with heaving chest as Lady Harford Joyce replied. Fortunately, she addressed herself to James Saunders, and did not observe my discomfort, nor the flush which I felt burning upon my cheeks.

"Is this correct?" she asked her brother.

He nodded his head. "Theft is, indeed, the subject of our visit," he replied.

"How like you it is, to be concerned on my behalf," she remarked. "Dear James! I do not know what I ever should have done without you since Douglas's death!"

Five minutes later the three of us were descending the front steps of the house.

"You demonstrated a remarkable turn of speed in your thoughts, there, Watson," said Holmes, in an appreciative voice. "I must congratulate you; I thought for a moment we were undone. But you do not look very happy, old fellow!"

"I have never lied to a woman before."

"It is all in a good cause," remarked Dr. Saunders, but there was little enthusiasm in his voice.

"I only hope that that proves true," I replied.

"And I," remarked Holmes, "that what little reputation I now possess is not forever destroyed by the enterprise of some thoughtless and inconsiderate burglar!"

At breakfast the next morning, Holmes was uncommunicative. It was clear enough from his brisk manner that he had formulated some plan of approach to the money-lender, Oscar Morley, but what it might be, I could not guess. As he was donning his hat and coat, however, he turned and addressed me.

"How is your leg, today, old fellow?" he enquired. "Is it up to an hour's standing about on the pavement, would you say?"

"I imagine it could manage that," I returned with a smile, my egg-spoon poised half-way to my mouth. "Is there something you wish me to do?"

He nodded. "I shall give you the details later. I should be back at lunchtime. *Au revoir!*"

As it turned out, my friend returned well in advance of lunch, his features crestfallen.

"You have seen Morley," I remarked, looking up from my newspaper, "and he would not agree to your terms."

"Such an outcome would have been a relative success," replied Holmes sardonically. "He refused even to see me."

He tossed off his hat and coat, poured himself a glass of beer, and stood before the fire in silence for several minutes.

"I should derive a quite singular degree of pleasure," said he at length, "from completing this commission successfully. Do you know this man, Morley, Watson?"

"I have heard the name; that is all."

"He is a man who lives off the folly of youth – aye, and lives handsomely off it, too. Each year a fresh complement of young men reaches the age at which the attractions of gambling and general high-living seem irresistible, each year a fresh complement spends more than it should, and is forced to borrow to remain active in these wastrel activities. After a season or two of living in this way, the majority of these young men discover that there is more to life than spending money and rendering oneself insensible with alcohol, and they drift away into other pursuits, generally with little regret. But by this time a fresh complement has arrived to take their place. Thus, while the cast is constantly changing, the play runs continuously – and waiting in the wings each year to claim his share of the profits is one of the managers, our friend Oscar Morley. His presence is constant, his influence malign. Without his encouragement, his ready offers of money, the folly and the waste would be decidedly less, and the all-too-frequent tragedies of which one reads would very likely not occur at all."

Holmes drained off the glass of beer and banged it down upon the mantelpiece."Do you know," he cried angrily, "there are men of forty who now live quietly and studiously in respectable homes up and down the country, whom one would take for the very models of propriety and sensible decorum – as indeed they now are – but who are yet paying off the debt which Morley encouraged them to run up in a few months of madness, twenty years ago. I am not a vindictive man, Watson, but I tell you that the satisfaction of knowing that I had discomfited Oscar Morley would last me a long time indeed!"

"You have a plan of some kind?"

"I have. It is risky and uncertain, but I see nothing better. This morning, when I called at his house in Hill Street, I was obliged to give a preliminary account of my purpose to his servant – a man who seemed every bit as odious as his master – and was then kept waiting for half an hour in the morning-room, until the reply came back from upstairs that it was not convenient for Mr. Morley to see me today."

"The nerve of the man!"

"Unfortunately, he holds the best cards at present, Watson, and there is little we can do about it. I made it perfectly clear to his man that I acted at the request of the family, and that I was prepared to pay a considerable sum for the return of the Plate, but the response was nil."

"I cannot understand why such a man should turn down the opportunity to make a fat profit so quickly and at so little trouble to himself," I remarked.

"It may be simply that he prefers to curry favour with the younger Harford Joyce, no doubt seeing that as likely to be the more profitable line of business in the long run; or it may be that he has other plans – which brings me to this afternoon: it is vitally important that a watch be kept upon Morley's house, and as I shall not myself be free to undertake the task, I should be most obliged if you would stand in for me."

I readily agreed to this request, for I welcomed any opportunity to escape for a while from the confines of our chambers. When I asked if there were anything in particular for which I should watch, Holmes nodded his head.

"A man, Watson, a specific visitor to friend Morley. What other callers he may have, I neither know nor care, but there is one man in London at present whose appearance upon the scene can only spell trouble, and I have good reason to believe that he may show himself this afternoon."

"Who, then?"

"His name, when last I heard, was Dmitri Theokritoff, but that may not be what he is calling himself at present; for it is not the name he was born with, and he is a man who has in the past shown a distinct aversion to retaining any one name for very long. He is an Armenian by birth, but lives everywhere and nowhere. He is an international dealer in works of art, curios, antiquities and so on, most of which find their way into his hands by means which would not pass muster at Sotheby's or

Christie's. Indeed, he is wanted for questioning by the authorities in at least three countries on the Continent, in connection with certain transactions in which he was involved last year. He has been lying low of late, but the Zodiac Plate is just such a prize as might tempt him to emerge into the open once more. If he does come, as I strongly suspect he will, it would be greatly to our advantage to have some knowledge of his whereabouts. But, come, let us take lunch now, and I can give you a description of the fellow as we eat."

At two-thirty that afternoon, I was standing beside a lamp-post near the corner of Hill Street and South Audley Street. The day had brightened up a little since the morning, but there was a damp heaviness in the air which made me hope that my vigil would not be a long one. From where I stood I was able to observe anyone who might call at Morley's house, which was on the opposite side of the road and about twenty yards to the east. In the first half-hour he had two callers, a fashionably dressed young man, and a tall woman dressed in black, her face concealed behind a veil. Neither of them stayed for very long. At ten past three I took a walk along the street in the direction of Berkeley Square, in order to give some exercise to my leg, which was beginning to throb painfully from the old wound I carried there. When I had gone perhaps a hundred yards, I chanced to glance back along the street, and it was fortunate that I did so, for there upon the step of Morley's house was the very man whose description Holmes had given me. Even at that distance there could be no mistaking the dark, oily complexion and the stoop to the shoulders. He was clad in a heavy overcoat, of an unusual shade of dark olive green, and upon his head was an uncommonly tall hat. I began to retrace my steps, but before I had gone ten yards the door had opened and he had passed inside, and out of my sight. I returned to my former position, reasoning that as he had evidently entered the street from the Park Lane end, he would very likely return that way, also, and, if so, I should be able to observe him more closely as he passed me.

For fully half an hour I waited, feeling the cold more keenly with each minute that passed. The throbbing in my leg had settled to a dull, persistent ache, and my mind had wandered far from the matter in hand, when Morley's front door opened suddenly and Theokritoff stood once more upon the step. He glanced swiftly up and down the street, then set off at a brisk pace towards Berkeley Square, tapping his cane upon the pavement as he went. I waited until there were thirty or forty yards between us, then set off after him. Holmes's instructions were that I should follow him as far as I could, in the hope of discovering his present abode. As I drew level with Morley's house, the door opened again, and a small, sharp-faced man emerged, clad in a top hat and a heavy black coat which reached almost to the ground. He, too, looked about him in a furtive manner, then abruptly bent down and began to adjust the laces of his boots. Ahead of me, my quarry had increased the distance between us, so I lengthened my own stride. Along Hill Street I followed him, across the angle of Berkeley Square, and up Berkeley Street to Piccadilly. At the corner he paused a moment, looked this way and that, and then turned to the east and set off once more at a brisk rate. When I reached the corner he was some distance ahead, but although the pavement was thronged with passengers, the unusual colour of his coat and his tall hat made it less difficult than it might otherwise have been for me to keep him in view.

We had gone some three hundred yards when Theokritoff abruptly stopped, and stared with great intensity across the street. I followed his gaze, but could see nothing there which might account for his sudden interest. A moment later, I was disconcerted to see that he was staring back the way he had come, and I feared for a moment that my pursuit had been discovered. As I looked again, however, it seemed, so far as I could determine, that his attention was not fixed upon me, nor upon anything in my immediate vicinity, but on something, or someone, much further back down the street. I did not turn, but put my head down and continued walking. When I looked up again, I was just in time to see him turning quickly into Sackville Street.

There seemed something more rapid and determined in his movements, and, fearing that he might give me the slip, I hurried forward to the corner. To my surprise I saw that he was already three-quarters of the way to the other end of the street. I quickened my stride, but had not succeeded in reducing the distance between us to any appreciable extent before he had reached the corner and turned left into Vigo Street. Cursing myself for my carelessness, I increased my pace still further. His route was certainly an odd one, I reflected as I hurried along: unless he altered his direction drastically, he might very well end up back in Hill Street.

I was quite breathless by the time I reached the corner. There, my worst fears were realised: there was no sign whatever of my quarry. He had evidently perceived that he was pursued and taken deliberate steps to escape. Fool that I was to have let him get so far ahead of me! I almost shouted aloud in my annoyance, as I hastened to the corner of Savile Row, and desperately scanned the pavements there, and along Burlington Gardens to the west. It was no use; Dmitri Theokritoff had demonstrated that guile which my little knowledge of his past career should have led me to expect. Once more he had sunk without trace in the very centre of this vast metropolis, once more we had no resource but to watch and wait patiently for him to reappear of his own volition.

But, no! I could not give up my commission so easily. I ran back along Vigo Street to see if there were any doorway or shop into which he might have slipped. Perhaps even now he was standing in the shadows, waiting for me to abandon my search; perhaps I had passed him without seeing him, and he had then slipped from his hiding-place and returned the way we had come, back down towards Piccadilly. At the corner of Vigo Street and Sackville Street I ran straight into a man who was hurrying in the opposite direction. I apologized, although the fault was as much his as mine, and, as I did so, I recognized him as the man who had been attending to his boot-laces outside Oscar Morley's house. My courtesy was wasted upon him, for he answered it only with a vile oath, as he pushed his way past me. Down towards the south end of Sackville Street, I descried a man with a tall hat, and with a sudden uprush of hope I hastened forward. But I had not gone ten yards before I saw that it was not the man I sought. Utterly dejected at my failure, I made my way down to Piccadilly and caught a cab home, wondering what Holmes would say when he learnt that I had found Theokritoff only to lose him again.

My colleague returned at half-past-five. He seemed in good spirits, and I hesitated to inform him of my own failure.

"My plans go as well as I could have hoped," said he in answer to my query. "You have been back some time, I see – the teapot is distinctly on the tepid side. I'll chance a cup, nevertheless, and you can tell me how you fared this afternoon."

"I have failed you, Holmes," said I.

"Oh? How is that?" said he in an unconcerned manner, as he stirred his tea.

"I watched Morley's house, as you directed, saw Theokritoff, and followed him half-way round the West End, but he gave me the slip, I am afraid to say, and I am no wiser now as to his whereabouts than I was this morning."

"Do not be concerned; you have done very well," said my friend, to my great surprise.

"I would rather you reserved your praise for those occasions upon which I have earned it," I remarked.

"But you most certainly *have* earned it," he returned with emphasis. "You identified your quarry and you followed him, which is all that I had asked you to do. You followed him well – along Hill Street, up Berkeley Street, along Piccadilly and into Sackville Street. No man could have done better, and some not so well."

"Holmes!" I cried. "This is amazing! How on earth? – Holmes, you were following me!"

"On the contrary," replied my friend in a languid and careless tone: "It is you who were following *me*"

I sprang from my chair in anger, as I perceived the meaning of his words.

"Holmes! Do you mean to tell me that Theokritoff was simply another of your wretched disguises?"

"But a reasonably effective one, would you not say?" he replied, a chuckle in his voice.

"This is unworthy of you, Holmes!" I protested. "What purpose you may have in deceiving Oscar Morley in this way, I do not know; but it seems a mean trick to play upon your oldest friend, I must say, to have him standing about in the cold all afternoon to no purpose whatever."

"My dear fellow!" cried he, a look of anxiety upon his face. "Pray calm yourself! Your presence this afternoon was absolutely vital, of that I can assure you. I should not even have considered subjecting you to this dank and dismal weather under any but the most compelling of circumstances."

"Forgive my obtuseness," I retorted, "but I fail to see what could possibly be vital about such a fool's errand as I have been sent upon! As for your assurance, I seem to remember your assuring me that it was vital we discovered Theokritoff's hiding-place, which, considering that he exists nowhere but in your own head, must rank as the most futile and pointless commission ever given by one man to another!"

"I can see that it must strike you in that light," said Holmes after a moment, in a quieter tone.

"We are agreed upon one thing, then, at least."

"I do apologize, Watson. I have been so absorbed in my own plans that it did not occur to me that what was clear to me would not be clear to you; but if you will permit me to describe to you how matters stand, I am sure that you will see the worth of it all."

I sat back down in my chair, crossed my legs and lit a cigar. "You have my full attention," said I.

"In the first place," said he, "Morley would not deal with me this morning. This was no more than I had expected, and merely confirmed my opinion that it was only upon the side of his bank account that he was accessible. Unfortunately, the funds at my disposal are limited, and incapable of taking the trick. My only chance, therefore, lay in pretending to greater wealth than I in fact possessed. Clearly I could not do this with any conviction as myself, and it was therefore necessary that I assume a fresh identity. Now, I happen to know that Dmitri Theokritoff – whose career was approximately as I sketched out for you at lunchtime – was stabbed to death in Marseilles, two years ago, and thus I could see no objection to my assuming for a short while his identity, which is precisely what the occasion required."

"Will Morley not be aware of his death?"

"Not unless he is a student of foreign criminal reports, which is so unlikely a possibility as to be beneath consideration."

"You intend, then, to offer him a large sum of money, in the hope that he will hand over the Plate," I suggested. "You will give him a worthless cheque, perhaps?"

"Hardly that, Watson. Friend Morley is no fool. He may be the most odious man in London, but he is also one of the smartest. As a matter of fact, I have offered him the crown jewels of one of the independent Arabian tribes."

"You have offered him *what!*" I cried incredulously.

"The prize must be a large one to tempt him. I have given him a dark account of how I acquired my treasure, and stressed that were it not that there are agents all over Europe actively pursuing it at this very moment, I should not even consider parting with it for less than twenty-five thousand. Under the circumstances, however – so I informed him – I am prepared to trade it for a certain object which I have reason to believe has recently come into his possession."

"What a preposterous story! Surely you invite disaster by such an overblown tale?"

"On the contrary, it is very often the biggest lies which enjoy the greatest success. Human nature is an odd thing, Watson, and does not always operate in the most perfectly logical manner. Morley showed considerable interest in my proposition, so it seemed to me, and intimated that he might not be averse to parting with the Zodiac Plate if the terms were right. However, it does not really matter whether he believed me or not, for it is my intention that he be informed tomorrow that the story of the crown jewels is, indeed, a complete tissue of lies."

My face must have betrayed the utter bewilderment I felt at Holmes's complex, and, as it seemed to me, nonsensical scheme, for he chuckled as his eyes met mine.

"All will become clear!" said he, with a broad smile upon his face.

He pulled a handful of tobacco from the old slipper in which he kept it to dry beside the fire, and stuffed it into his long-stemmed, cherrywood pipe.

"You see," he continued after a moment, "one must always think ahead. I have offered Mr. Morley something which I do not possess. What do you suppose would happen, then, were we to come to the point of exchanging our wares?"

I did not reply, and he continued:

"Precisely, Watson! You perceive the difficulty! It is necessary, then, for us to amend the course of events. I have interested him in the crown jewels; now I must interest him in something even better."

"I cannot think what could be better," I remarked; "nor, in that case, why you should have mentioned the jewels in the first place."

"You are an honest man, Watson, but Morley is not. He has a devious, scheming brain, and our plan must therefore be equally devious if it is to succeed. Of just one thing can we be certain: whether Morley believes the story of the crown jewels or not, he will suspect Theokritoff of duplicity."

"Why should he?"

"Chiefly because he is a dishonest man himself, and tends to regard everyone else in the same light. We must therefore turn this fact to our advantage. I have left with him – ostensibly as a token of my good intentions – a few quite worthless imitation diamonds which I picked up this morning at Silverstone's in Oxford Street – you know the sort of thing: 'a twenty-guinea stone for only one and fourpence.' He will also be aware that there was an agent following me in the street this afternoon. This was your role, Watson, to make my activities appear as suspect as possible."

"He may not have noticed me," I remarked.

"On the contrary, I made certain that he did. I stared at you from the window of his study; he naturally enough followed my gaze, and could not have failed to see you, standing alone beside the lamp post."

"But why, then, the later charade in the street? Morley could have seen nothing of that."

"No, but his agent certainly did. Did you observe an odd little fellow, wearing a coat a size too large for him?"

"We nearly knocked each other over at the corner of Vigo Street," I replied. "He left Morley's house just a few moments after you did."

"That was Leveritt, Morley's right-hand man; he was following me, too, as I had expected he would. Here your presence served a second purpose, for it made it necessary for this man – who would perceive that you were following me – to hang back somewhat further than he might otherwise have done. This made it significantly easier for me to effect my escape – which I achieved, incidentally, by simply jumping into the first empty cab I chanced to come across."

"But why, then, could you not inform me of your plans beforehand?" I protested. "Had I known what you had in mind, surely I could have played my part all the better?"

Holmes shook his head. "I am sorry to have had to play this trick upon you, my dear fellow, and I very nearly did tell you all, but I judged in the end that your actions would appear most convincing if you were performing them in earnest."

"Should you ever require such assistance again," I responded, somewhat tartly, "I should prefer that you made me privy to your plans. I cannot promise, however, that I shall understand them any more than I understand the present ones, which appear, so far as I can see, to achieve precisely nothing. What do you intend to do next?"

"An agent of mine will call upon Morley tomorrow. He will present himself as having been upon Theokritoff s trail for many months, and will inform Morley that a considerable reward is offered for that villain, who is wanted on numerous charges of theft and fraud, from Constantinople to Amsterdam. He will tell Morley that Theokritoff was seen entering his house yesterday, and will ask him if he was offered any 'Arabian crown jewels,' giving the impression that this is one of Theokritoff s most tried and trusted lines of chicanery. As Morley will already have his own suspicions and doubts, this speech will, I hope, have a convincing ring of truth about it. It is always shrewd to play to a man's own prejudices if you wish to impress him – indeed, most society conversation consists of little else."

"Who is your agent?"

"Tilham Fox, the actor. I helped him once, and he is quite agreeable to returning the favour. If Morley has not by tomorrow discovered for himself that the gems I left him are bogus, then Fox will apprise him of this fact, also, which will of course add one further turn of the screw to the establishment of his own *bona fides*. He will then tell Morley that the only impediment to Theokritoff's immediate apprehension is that he has so far committed no crime in England. If he could be caught in some criminal act, and charged by an English court, then the foreign authorities would be able to get their hands upon him, and they would at once pay up the reward. Morley is therefore to let him have whatever it is he is after – which is of course the Harford Joyce Plate – when next he calls, and to let him carry it to the door, as if believing his story of the crown jewels.

Immediately he is past the front door, he will be arrested and charged with the theft of the Plate."

"When is Theokritoff s next appointment with Morley?"

"On Monday, at ten o'clock. When I pay my call, you and Fox will be positioned in the street below – if, that is, you have forgiven me for this afternoon. Good fellow! I knew you would! Your presence, which Morley will be watching for, should reassure him that all is going as planned, and that Theokritoff will get no further than his front doorstep with the Plate. I shall hand over a few more of my bogus gems, and inform Morley that I wish to have the Plate examined by an acquaintance of mine who is an expert on such things. I shall then slip the Plate into a cardboard box which I have purchased specially for the purpose, seal up the box and descend with it to the front door. When you see me there, you will rush across and arrest me, after which Fox will return the box to Morley, who will sign a prepared statement, accusing me of attempting to swindle him. I shall then climb with my captors into a cab, and we shall depart, apparently for the nearest police station. After that, Morley will never again clap eyes on any of us as long as he lives."

"What in Heaven's name will be the point of all that?" I cried. "For Morley will still have the Plate!"

Holmes threw back his head and laughed aloud. "He will have a china plate," he replied at length. "For the one thing he will not know is that there are two cardboard boxes, identical in every respect, one of which will be snugly concealed inside my large green coat. As I descend his stairs – which are poorly illuminated, as I discovered today – I shall exchange the box in my hand with that inside my coat. It is of the utmost importance, you see, that Morley's suspicions are never for an instant directed at you or Fox, and if it seems to him that the Plate – or its container – has hardly left his sight for an instant, then that should be sufficient to allay his fears. Besides, if I know my man, he will be so pleased with himself for over-trumping

Theokritoff's deceit with his own that he will never suspect that there is yet a higher card remaining to be played."

"It seems a somewhat over-complex plot," I remarked after a moment.

"But it must be, Watson, if it is to succeed," replied my friend in an earnest tone. "Without the story of the crown jewels, I should stand very little chance of gaining entry to Morley's inner sanctum – for he is, as we already know, rather selective in the visitors he receives. Even then, it is unlikely that he could be persuaded to remove the Plate from his safe until I produced my own treasure. After Fox's story, however, which will seem to promise a financial gain quite free of the risk and criminality of Theokritoff's scheme, he should feel far less anxiety upon the point, especially as he will feel assured that the Plate will scarcely pass beyond his front door. This last point is crucial: without some such contrivance, the possibility of the Plate's passing beyond even his study doorway must be considered remote. He is a man who keeps arms about the house, and who is quite prepared to use them. But, come! This game is in the future. Let us banish for a while the complexities and deceits of this mundane sphere, and turn our thoughts to the pure sweetness of a higher existence!"

He took his violin from its case and adjusted the strings. "It is a little thing by de Beriot," he murmured, as he began to play a perfectly exquisite and melancholy air. I had closed my eyes and allowed the music to surround me in the soft, dream-like folds of its beauty, when I was abruptly roused from peace by the voice of the maid. Holmes stopped playing, and put down his bow with a sigh.

"This was pushed through the letter-box for you, sir," said the girl, handing him a cream-coloured envelope. He took it from her, tore it open and scanned the contents. As his eyes reached the foot of the page they returned once more to the top, and he read it through a second time, a look of amazement upon his face. With a whistle of disbelief, he tossed the sheet over to me and threw himself back in his chair, his eyes upon the ceiling, his brow creased with thought. It was a plain cream sheet, with neither monogram nor address. The message, in black ink, was terse and to the point:

"MR. HOLMES," I read. "Further to our meeting today, I have decided after all to agree to the terms you offer on behalf of the Harford Joyce trustees. If you will bring the amount outstanding (one thousand and five hundred pounds) we can conclude the business this evening. Please be at the lamppost by the south-western corner of Primrose Hill, at eight o'clock sharp, where my agent will meet you. I shall bring the Plate. O. M."

"You observed when it was written, no doubt?" said Holmes, as I finished reading.

I glanced again at the top of the sheet.

"It is dated the twenty-third, at six-thirty p.m.," I replied. "Half an hour ago!"

"Precisely. Now, what on earth can it mean, Watson? What has wrought this sudden change in friend Morley's disposition? Why should he be now so desirous of obliging those he earlier treated with such disdain?"

"He refers to your meeting," I remarked, "but I understood you to say that he did not deign to see you."

"That is so; it is a curious slip, but perhaps it signifies nothing. He may simply be referring to the conversation I had with his servant."

"Perhaps Morley himself was eavesdropping upon that conversation in some way," I suggested.

"That is possible. There is something else which is odd about this message: he is claiming no interest upon the money he advanced to young Harford Joyce. For a man of Morley's persuasions, that is certainly the most unlikely omission he could possibly make. What can have happened, to shake his customary composure to this degree? Why is his summons so abrupt, and the rendezvous he suggests so singular? He has not used headed note-paper, he has not signed his name, and he has arranged to meet us neither at our house nor his own."

"It is almost as if he wishes to be able to deny in the future that the meeting ever took place at all," I suggested. Holmes nodded his head slowly. "Do you suppose," I added, "that it can have anything to do with your visit as Theokritoff?"

Holmes shook his head in silence, an expression of puzzlement upon his face. "I can suggest nothing," he said at length, "to account for this latest development. I do not believe that I have ever been so surprised at anything in my life." He glanced at the clock, and sprang from his chair. "Come, Watson; let us fortify ourselves with a little bread and cheese; the hour of our assignation draws near."

At half past seven we donned our coats. Holmes took his pistol from his desk and carefully loaded the chambers, glancing at me as he did so.

"I sincerely advise you to do the same," said he, in answer to my querying look. "There is no telling what adventures may await us in the darkness of the night. Many a man has answered a summons to a secret appointment and been heard of never again."

A few minutes later we left the warmth of our chambers, and stepped into a raw and foggy night. An empty hansom was trundling past, and I stepped forward to stop it, but Sherlock Holmes put his hand upon my arm and drew me back.

"One cannot be too careful," said he in a tense whisper. "We are responding to Mr. Morley's summons quite upon his terms, both as to time and as to place. Let us at least be sure that our carriage is of our own choosing."

Up Baker Street we walked, our footsteps sounding dully upon the pavement, and as we did so the greasy, swirling mist seemed to thicken around us and enclose us in its dark and unhealthy reek. A second empty cab passed us with a clatter of hooves and a jingle of harness, its lamps a momentary glimmer in the darkness, but Holmes ignored it. At the Metropolitan Station he selected a hansom which had just deposited a fare, and we were soon rattling up Park Road towards St. John's Wood, and, from there, along the north side of Regent's Park, beside the canal. Presently the driver reined in his horse, and we stepped down into the silent sea of mist. Holmes passed the driver a half-sovereign with the instruction that he should follow us at a distance of twenty-five yards wherever we should go, and come at once upon our whistle.

It wanted two minutes to eight o'clock when, as we stamped our feet and clapped our hands together in the freezing air, a dark figure stepped forward from the bank of mist which hid the other side of the road from our view. As he approached us, I saw that he was dressed in the livery of a coachman, a large cloak about his shoulders with the collar turned up high, and a top hat upon his head.

"Mr. Holmes?" said he, his voice harsh and sudden in the enveloping silence.

My friend nodded. "This is my colleague, Dr. Watson," said he, "who has an interest in this matter."

"That is all right," said the other shortly. "Please follow me." With that he turned upon his heel briskly and began almost at once to disappear into the fog. Holmes gave a last instruction to our cabbie and we set off after the muffled footsteps ahead of us.

"There is something decidedly odd afoot here," said my friend in a low voice, as we hurried after the dark retreating figure. "Be upon your guard at all times, Watson!"

My fingers closed around the pistol in my pocket, and I was glad to feel its reassuring shape and solidity. A loaded revolver was a good friend to have on one's side in doubtful and threatening circumstances.

Presently our guide turned in through a gateway by the zoo, we crossed the canal on a narrow footbridge, and found ourselves upon the Outer Circle of the Park. Still he did not pause, but pressed on through the blanket of darkness, around the long curve towards Gloucester Terrace.

"He has cut us off from our cab," said Holmes in a sibilant whisper. Even as he spoke, the figure ahead of us stopped abruptly and turned to face us, his arm upraised.

"We are almost there," said he in a gloomy and sepulchral voice. "Have you the money? Very good. If you will give it to me, I will fetch you that which you have come for."

"I am to deal only with principals," returned Holmes, making no move to withdraw the money from within his coat.

For a moment we all three stood in silence, then, with a shrug of his shoulders, our guide turned on his heel once more. Motioning us to follow him, he resumed his brisk pace. We had gone but a little further, however, when a sudden slight gust dissipated the fog and revealed to us the twin spires of St Katherine's upon our left hand, and, ahead of us, a four-wheeled carriage, the feeble glimmer of its lamps encircled by haloes of mist. The side-window of the carriage was lowered, but no lamp was lit within, and a heavy curtain veiled the interior from our view.

"They have brought the money," said our guide into the darkness.

In answer a gloved hand emerged from behind the curtain.

"The Plate," said Holmes, without moving.

The hand withdrew without a sound, and re-appeared after a moment bearing a large oblong object, which gleamed dully in the faltering light of the carriage-lamp. That it was heavy was evident, for it slipped a little in the fingers which held it. The dark man who stood beside us quickly took the weight and passed it over to us. Holmes examined it carefully, his eyes running rapidly over the details of its design; but there could be little chance of mistaking so unusual an object. At length, evidently satisfied that it conformed to the photograph he had seen, he glanced at me and raised his eyebrows questioningly. I nodded my head, and he reached deep within his coat and drew out Dr. Saunders's leather satchel. The coachman took it from him, and spoke once more to the silent figure within the carriage.

"Do you wish me to count it?" said he.

The disembodied hand waved from side to side in a dismissive gesture, and as it did so the sleeve fell back an inch or two, revealing a bare wrist which was so excessively thin and fleshless that I almost cried aloud in surprise. The skin was wrinkled and blotched, and seemed to hang loose upon the bones. It was only for a moment that I saw it, for as soon as the coachman had handed over the leather bag the hand vanished from sight once more behind the curtain; but so startling was the sight that I was as sure of what I had seen as I had ever been sure of anything in my life. As the coachman leapt aboard his seat and lashed the horse into a gallop, I looked across at my friend. It was plain from the expression upon his face that he was as surprised and perplexed as I was.

In a moment the carriage had disappeared into the darkness, south towards Park Square, and seconds later the clatter and rattle which indicated its direction had ceased to be audible, and we stood alone in the thick fog. Holmes put his hand upon my arm; "Come," said he; and we began to retrace our steps.

"Do you understand the purpose of this strange manner of meeting?" I asked, after we had gone a little way.

"Not I," said he. "It appears quite pointless, so far as I can see. "You recognised the coachman, I take it?"

"I don't believe I have ever seen him before," I replied in surprise.

"It is the Harford Joyce groom. He was just leaving with young Harford Joyce last night, as we arrived at Campden Hill Crescent."

"The Harford Joyce groom?" I repeated incredulously. "Surely you are mistaken?"

"There could be no mistaking the fellow."

"What on earth can it mean, then?" I cried. "Is the man in Morley's pay, or what?"

"There would be little point to such deceit," replied Holmes, shaking his head; "Morley needs no spies in the house to persuade young Harford Joyce to sink further into his debt. Besides, it was not Morley with whom we were dealing tonight."

He was about to say more, when a bulky figure materialized abruptly out of the gloom ahead of us. For a moment I tensed, and put my hand to the pocket which held my revolver, but when he spoke I recognized the voice of our own cabbie.

"There you are!" said he in evident relief. "I was wondering where you two gentlemen had got to. The cab is this way."

"Good man!" cried Holmes, clapping the cabbie upon the shoulder. "I feared that this fog would part us for ever! Back to Baker Street, then, and a hot toddy all round!"

As our cab was crossing the Marylebone Road, however, Holmes abruptly flung up the trap and directed the driver to take us to Campden Hill. Then he settled once more into the deep and frowning silence in which he had passed the journey back from Primrose Hill.

What was passing in his mind then, I could not begin to guess. To me, the events of the evening were incomprehensible. I had supposed that the meeting would shed some light upon Morley's sudden and surprising change of heart in accepting our money in settlement of young Harford Joyce's debts; in the event, however, our strange, fog-shrouded meeting by St. Katherine's had explained nothing, but had instead added further mysteries of its own. Why had the carriage been driven by the Harford Joyce coachman, and who was its unseen occupant?

"What can you hope to learn at Campden Hill?" I asked my friend, as our cab rattled along Sussex Gardens. "Do you intend to interview the groom?"

Holmes shook his head. "The coachman was simply carrying out his orders. I think it unlikely that he could tell us anything of interest. The one I wish to speak to is the one who gave him his orders, took our money, and handed over the Plate: the one with the weak, thin wrist, which startled you so much, Watson."

"You have some notion, then, who it was?"

"It was Lady Harford Joyce," said he simply.

"But that is absurd, Holmes! In the first place, she is not only ill, but virtually bed-ridden; in the second place, she was not even in possession of the Plate, which was in the hands of that odious fellow, Morley – a fact of which she was totally unaware; and in the third place, if, by some miracle, Lady Harford Joyce *had* regained possession of the Plate – the family's most prized heirloom, and the possession which we are told she values above all others – what conceivable reason could she have for handing it over to you for a mere fifteen hundred pounds? The idea is utterly fantastic!"

Holmes had nodded his head in silence as I spoke, and when he replied it was in a tone of some perplexity.

"You state the case fairly and accurately," he remarked, his chin resting heavily upon his hand; "and yet it *was* Lady Harford Joyce – the markings upon her wrist, which I had observed yesterday evening at Campden Hill, were quite unmistakable. Indeed, your own reaction upon seeing her wrist in the Park this evening led me to suppose that you, too, had recognised it." With a deep sigh he leaned back in his seat, and lapsed once more into silence. When he at length spoke again, it was in an altogether different, almost careless tone of voice.

"But perhaps we should simply make an end of the matter, and return to Baker Street, Watson. We have, after all, recovered the Plate, which is all that we were required to do – and that without recourse to the good Dr. Saunders's blank cheque, for which he will no doubt thank us effusively. All in all, it seems to me a job well done: what concern is it of ours to know how many strange and varied hands the Plate has passed through before coming into our own safe-keeping? It is scarcely knowledge which will add appreciably to the sum of human happiness – and certainly not to that of our client. *'Cui bono?'*, eh, Watson?"

For a moment I was quite dumbfounded. Never before had I known Sherlock Holmes elect to close a case which held still an unresolved riddle at its centre. Had one of the famous Nile explorers declared his total lack of interest in the whereabouts of that river's sources, it could scarcely have been more astounding to me.

"Holmes!" I cried at length. "You amaze me! You have the Plate, it is true, and so, to that extent, your commission is complete; but surely your mind cannot rest at ease in the midst of such puzzlement, while ever you possess the power to end it? If you tell me that it can, then I must confess that every conclusion I have reached regarding your character has been wrong. Surely there are some further enquiries you can make to throw some light upon this mystery?"

"It will not help Dr. Saunders," replied my friend laconically, with a shrug of the shoulders.

"But, Holmes! Consider, then, your own professional records! An unfinished case can be nothing but a blemish upon them!"

"Admit it, Watson," rejoined Holmes in a soft voice, a sly smile spreading across his features; "it is as much for your own mental satisfaction as for mine that you require this mystery to be uncovered. If you deny it, I shall not believe you."

"Very well, then," said I somewhat heatedly, for I was nettled by his tone of superiority. "I admit I would wish to get to the bottom of this riddle, if it were at all possible."

"Even if it benefited our client not one whit?"

I nodded my head.

"And if our investigation were therefore merely to satisfy your own curiosity?"

"I fail to see what you are driving at, but, if you insist on putting it in that way, then, yes, I admit it."

"Aha! I take it you therefore concede the point to me that man has an unslakable thirst for knowledge, irrespective of whether it will be of any use to him? It was, if you recall, a point upon which we differed in our discussion the other evening."

I saw then that his whole careless manner had been assumed simply for the purpose of forcing me to yield this abstract point to him. In any other man such a pretence would have irritated me beyond words, but I had become so inured to

Holmes's odd character over the years of our friendship that I simply shook my head and sighed.

"You never had any intention, then, of dropping the case?"

"Certainly not," said he in a more vigorous tone. "Besides, one can always find some justification or other for one's innate curiosity. It could be argued with some plausibility, for instance, that unless we understand the meaning of this night's events, we cannot in all honesty return the Plate to Dr. Saunders with the assurance that his troubles are now at an end."

"Indeed, that argument has perhaps a greater validity than you allow," I remarked after a moment's thought. "For, on reflection, it strikes me that we have a genuine duty not simply to recover the Plate, but also to apprise your client of any other danger with which it may be threatened; and unless we understand all that has taken place, we cannot swear that no such danger exists. To take your own metaphor, Holmes: the poison which entered the life of Dr. Saunders with such strange and unforeseeable consequences has not yet been extirpated. The consultant cannot yet claim his fee."

"Well said, my dear fellow!" cried Holmes merrily. "You would make a fine advocate, Watson. The issue is settled, then, and we confront Lady Harford Joyce tonight."

We left the cab at the foot of Campden Hill Crescent with the instruction that he should await our return, and walked slowly up the hill in the oily murk.

"There is one thing that troubles me still," I confessed. "You say you recognized the coachman, you say you recognized the mottled wrist; but if by any chance you are wrong, and Lady Harford Joyce is not involved in the matter in any way, then our visit will set at nought the whole purpose of our original mission, which was to keep her in ignorance of her son's shameful conduct."

"Perhaps a third piece of evidence, pointing in precisely the same direction as the other two, will convince you, then," replied Holmes, a trace of irritability in his voice. "I took the opportunity outside St. Katherine's of remarking any distinctive feature of the carriage that I could later use to identify it. Upon the panel to the right of the door there was a deep scratch, with a smaller scratch crossing it at right angles, close to one end, forming the shape of an elongated letter *'t'*. If that scratch is present on the Harford Joyce carriage, even you can scarcely argue against our proceeding, Watson!"

In silence we entered the gateway and made our way along the side of the house and to the stables, which lay in darkness, some distance to the rear. The door was not locked, and we slipped inside quietly. Holmes struck a match. In a stall at one end stood a glossy black horse, which shifted its feet uneasily and whinnied slightly at the sudden light. Holmes put his hand upon the animal's neck.

"He, at least, has had a busy evening," said my friend, wiping the moisture from his hand. "So far, so good." He struck another match and bent to the panelling on the side of the coach. In a moment he was pointing in triumph to a ragged scratch which ran for a foot or more across the centre of the panel. It formed the clear shape of a recumbent letter *'t'*.

The front door was opened to us by the butler, Milner. It was evident from the look of surprise upon his face that he recognized us at once, and equally evident that we were the very last two he had expected to find upon the doorstep that evening. Clearly nonplussed, he hesitated, then informed us flatly that his mistress had retired for the night after a particularly tiring day, and could not possibly be disturbed. We had come too far, however, to be turned away at the last, and Holmes, after a moment's thought, wrote a brief note upon the back of a visiting-card and instructed the butler to convey it to his mistress at once or bear full responsibility for whatever might otherwise occur. Still the man hesitated, and seemed inclined to refuse us, when a sudden and unexpected intervention resolved the situation in a moment. A door upon the right of the hall opened abruptly, and there, framed in the bright oblong of light, stood Lady Harford Joyce, supporting herself unsteadily on a pair of walking-sticks.

"Show the gentlemen in, Milner," said she, in a feeble, cracked voice. She turned round with some difficulty and we followed her into what I judged, from the crowded bookshelves around the walls, to have been Sir Douglas's library.

"Mr. Holmes, Dr. Watson," said she in a weak voice, when the three of us were seated at a large mahogany table in the centre of the room. "I trust it is something of importance which necessitates your disturbing me at this hour." She looked at us with an expression of great weariness in her eyes, and it seemed to me that she had a yet greater air of old age and infirmity about her than upon the previous evening. Involuntarily, my eye went to her wrist, thin and fleshless, and wrinkled with age.

"It concerns the Harford Joyce Plate," returned Holmes in a quiet voice. The old lady's eyes narrowed perceptibly, but she did not reply. "Someone gave it to me in the street earlier this evening," Holmes continued. He unbuttoned his coat and drew forth the object in question. Her hands started up from where they rested upon the table edge and her eyes opened wide with astonishment, as she stammered out a series of half-formed and scarcely intelligible questions, in a voice which trembled with fear and agitation.

"Come, come, Lady Harford Joyce," said Holmes at length, holding up his hand in protest at this uncontrolled outburst. "You and I both know that it was you that put the Plate in my hands, not an hour ago. Why you should take this strange action with an object you revere so greatly?"

He broke off as she waved her hand feebly. The colour had drained from her face as he spoke, and a dry, choking noise came from her throat. I stood up quickly, to render what assistance I could, but she waved me back to my seat with a gesture of impatience. Several minutes passed in silence as she sought to recover herself, and I feared that she would be too weak to speak further that evening. But she rallied remarkably, and when she spoke there was a note both of strength and decision in her voice.

"Gentlemen," said she firmly; "what you say is nonsense. You tell me that I revere that object; I tell you that I revile it. To me it is that most hateful of things—a permanent reminder of the one black cloud which cast its shadow upon my life. You speak to me of the Harford Joyce Plate as if you know something of it, but I, who know far more than you, readily confess that I have no knowledge of where on God's earth it might be."

I glanced across at my friend. The expression upon his face must have mirrored my own, for it was one of astonishment and stupefaction.

"Do not fear that I am raving," continued Lady Harford Joyce quickly, as if reading only too well the thoughts which were passing through my mind. She nodded her head towards the heavy silver object which Holmes still held in his hands: "That is not the Harford Joyce Plate."

Now it was our turn to protest our disbelief and plead our lack of comprehension; but she cut us short.

"It is a simple enough tale to tell," said she, in a tone of bitter resignation. "You are correct in one thing at least, Mr. Holmes: it was I that handed you that plate this evening. I should have known from your reputation that my own attempt at trickery was unlikely to succeed. However, you will understand why I was driven to such lengths when you hear the miserable history of the object you hold in your hand. I trust you on your honour as gentlemen to repeat nothing of what I tell you.

"The Harford Joyce Plate came into the family in the last century, when one of my late husband's ancestors performed some trifling service for an over-grateful Russian Empress, at the time of the Pugachoff Rebellion. The family has always been as intensely proud of its heirloom as of its own name, and my husband was no different from his kin in this respect.

"About a dozen years ago, my husband happened, in the course of his diplomatic career, to spend several years in the eastern lands of Europe. There, he became involved in certain matters which, let us say, fell somewhat short of his family's code of honour, and was led to commit certain indiscretions which he later came to regret most bitterly. Although I am not prepared to enter into the details of these matters, which cannot possibly be of interest to you, I can – and will – assure you that my husband's indiscretions involved neither loss of life nor injury to anyone, no threat to his nation's security or well-being, and absolutely no financial gain to himself.

"The matter passed into history, my husband retired, and we returned to England, to live in this house. He thought then that his past was dead and buried, and could not harm him, especially since certain documents and records had been lost in a fire. But some years later, in the autumn of '81, a certain man – no, a vile, unspeakable reptile! – paid him a visit and made it clear that he was in possession of documents, which, were they to be published, would bring back to life this ancient scandal, and would incriminate my husband quite unequivocally. He also made it clear that unless my husband were to do precisely as he requested, he would proceed with their publication forthwith."

Lady Harford Joyce paused, as a dry cough shook her body. I rose and poured her a tumbler of water from a carafe which stood upon a sideboard. Her voice had begun to tremble again as she was speaking, but when she continued, after taking a sip of the water, the firmness and strength were back once more.

"What was he to do?" said she, looking from Holmes to me, and back again, as if imploring our understanding. "It was not for himself he feared, but his family – or families, rather, for he had not only his own to consider, but also the one into which he had married. If you had known my husband, gentlemen, then you would know that what I say is the truth."

"The price of the blackmailer's silence was the Zodiac Plate?" interrupted Holmes, with a quizzical raise of the eyebrow.

Lady Harford Joyce nodded her head. "He would take nothing else. No amount of money could dissuade him from his wicked desire. At length, Douglas agreed to his terms, but on condition that the transaction be delayed a short while, in order that he might commission a craftsman to make a copy of the Plate. In this way he hoped to conceal its loss from the world. The copy was duly made, in conditions of the utmost secrecy, and the original handed over to this vile man in exchange for the documents he possessed. It is the copy you now hold in your hand, and a poor shadow of the genuine Plate it is, too. It was cast at a foundry in Birmingham, in a mould taken from the original, and afterwards plated. As a result of this process, much of the clarity and definition of the original design was inevitably lost, and the lustre of the duplicate is, of course, quite inferior. The gems, too, are the very cheapest of stones, and do not possess one tenth the fire of those in the true plate."

I saw Holmes look with surprise at the Plate, and shake his head, as Lady Harford Joyce raised the glass to her lips once more before she continued.

"From that day to this," she said at last, "no one has known of this deception save only my husband, our old butler and myself. I have endeavoured to keep that object locked away, out of sight of the public gaze. When you came here with James last night, I could tell by his manner that he was not speaking the truth to me. In my eyes he is still the small boy he was forty years ago, and he can never hope to deceive me. When you had gone it took me only a few minutes to learn the truth from the servants, and I at once saw the great danger into which Robert's foolish action had thrust us – a danger which none but myself could fully appreciate. For if this man Morley were to show the Plate to anyone who knew about such things, or attempt to have it valued, then my husband's secret disgrace would inevitably become public knowledge. It was imperative that the Plate be recovered at once, to save the family name. How that could be accomplished, I could not at first see, but decided in the end that there was no other recourse but to tell Robert the whole story, and make him realise the urgency of the situation. In making this decision, I consoled myself with the thought that he must, at any event, know his father's secret one day.

"To my great pleasure he reacted to the news as I had hoped he would, and was riven with horror at the thought of what he had done. This afternoon I supplied him with sufficient funds to cover his debt, and he called on the moneylender to reclaim the Plate. Apparently, Morley was none too keen to part with it. It seems he had some profitable plan afoot, in which he attempted to interest Robert, involving someone's crown jewels. To cut a long story short, the interview ended with Robert's punching him on the nose. I suppose that that puts an end to all further financial transactions between them, but I cannot say that that is a prospect I view with any great regret. I am glad to see that you are amused, Mr. Holmes."

"Would you tell me," said Holmes, his whole body shaking with silent laughter, "why it was that you felt it necessary to put on that strange performance in Regent's Park this evening?"

"I did not wish my brother to learn anything of my own involvement in the Plate's recovery, and perhaps suspect my motive. He had always had a most high regard and respect for Douglas, and I could not bear my husband's memory to be tarnished in his eyes. I decided, therefore, to let the Plate be returned to the house through his efforts, as he had planned, and when Robert told me of Morley's mentioning your visit to him this morning, it seemed the best idea to send you a note pretending that Morley had changed his mind. I thought it unlikely that you would ever learn the truth. What do you intend to tell James when you see him again?"

Holmes sat a while in silent thought. "I shall tell your brother," said he at last, "that after some initial difficulty, Morley evidently saw the pointlessness of his obduracy, and agreed to our terms."

"That is all?"

"That is all. You need not fear for the safety of your secret, Lady Harford Joyce. It is yours to keep or to reveal as you will."

We had stood up and were preparing to take our leave, when my friend paused.

"One final thing," said he: "I wonder if you would satisfy my curiosity on one point, Lady Harford Joyce: the name of the man who blackmailed your husband, the man with the documents—"

"I cannot bring myself to speak it, Mr. Holmes," replied the other firmly. "It would be an affront to my ears."

Holmes took a card from his pocket and scribbled a word upon it.

"Was it by any chance this man?" said he, handing the card to Lady Harford Joyce.

She glanced at the card for but a moment before crushing it in her hand; then she stared hard at my friend, an expression of amazement upon her face.

"Can it be true, then, what they say of you," said she, incredulously, "that there is nothing you do not know?"

"Not at all," replied Holmes, with a smile and a shake of the head. "But in this field I am a specialist, and make it my business to know all there is to know of those whose prosperity is wrung from the misfortune of others. On silver plate, however, my knowledge is somewhat less profound!"

THE WATCHER IN THE WOODS

DURING THE YEARS I shared chambers with Mr. Sherlock Holmes before my marriage, I was able to experience at first hand the immense variety of cases upon which he was consulted; most of which he succeeded in bringing to a successful conclusion. Among these cases were a great number that were odd or unusual, and not a few that were so strange as to seem at first unfathomable. Among these latter cases I would include that which concerned the singular experiences of Mr. Cuthbert Lidington in the Isle of Apstone and the surprising sequel, and it is this case I now propose to recount.

It was a chilly, foggy morning towards the end of October. The preceding weeks had been moderately sunny, but there had been little warmth in the sunshine, and with each day that passed, the air had seemed to become a degree colder.

Sherlock Holmes had been working his way through the morning papers for some time, alternately groaning and sighing at what he read there.

"It sometimes seems to me," said he at length, tossing aside the last of the papers, "that the daily press has come into existence merely to record all that is banal, ignorant and stupid in our modern world."

"You can scarcely expect profound philosophical reflections on life to appear every day in the morning papers," I remarked without looking up from my own reading.

"Perhaps not, but there must surely be something more intellectually stimulating for them to report than that one group of men kicked a leather ball more efficiently up a muddy field than another group of men, or that the Duchess of Deptford wore a striped hat to the theatre last night!"

I laughed. "Perhaps you will be presented with an interesting case soon," I said, "and then you can bid *au revoir* for a time to the commonplaces of existence."

"I hope so," said he. "I am in need of a case, Watson. I feel like a man who has become accustomed to having a tumbler of rum every morning with his breakfast. The bottle has been empty now for some time, and the absence of my stimulant is making me irritable!"

"So I had noticed," I remarked. As I spoke there came a sharp peal at the front doorbell. "Here is someone," I said. "Perhaps it is a caller for you."

"Yes," returned my friend in a pessimistic tone; "no doubt someone wishing to sell me half a dozen 'lucky' clothes-pegs, or someone come to inform me that if I contribute a shilling to whatever worthy cause he represents I can have my name engraved on a brick!"

A moment later, a slight, nervous-looking young man was shown into our sitting-room, and announced as Cuthbert Lidington.

"Good morning," said Holmes, waving the visitor to a chair. "What can we do for you?"

"I understand you are accomplished at unravelling life's mysteries," the young man began in a hesitant tone.

"I have had some experience of it, at least," returned Holmes. "Do you have a mystery for us?"

Lidington nodded. "If I can't get to the bottom of it, I feel I shall go mad. That may sound a somewhat dramatic, exaggerated thing to say," he added quickly, "but that is the state I have been driven to."

"Pray, give us the details."

"First of all, you should know that I am not one given to fancies or whimsical notions. I studied scientific subjects for some years at London University. I then held a senior position with the South Eastern Railway at Ashford, in Kent. However, my own private reading was leading me in a very different direction. My study of early scientific works had introduced me to the subject of alchemy, in which I developed a very great interest."

"Alchemy?" I cried in surprise. "Is that not the mediaeval pseudo-science that claimed that with the right formula base metals could be turned into gold, and, with some other formula, men could be made immortal?"

Lidington shook his head. "I would not dispute that you enunciate the popular view of the subject accurately," said he, "but there is much more to alchemy than that. It is an all-embracing doctrine of a mystical, spiritual kind. Anyway, to continue: I had been looking for some new lodgings for a while, as the place at which I was staying in Ashford was very cramped, and some of the other people staying there were not to my taste. Then, one day when I was in the house-agent's office, I saw that a house in the village of Apstone was available to rent. When I saw the name of the house, I could hardly believe it!"

"Why was that?" asked Holmes.

"Well, you see, it was Naxon House, and I recognized the name as being that of the residence for many years of Serenus Charling, one of the leading writers on alchemy of the last hundred years. I felt that fate must have placed this opportunity in my hands, to live and work in the very house that had been occupied for so many years by one of the writers I admired the most. Within twenty-four hours, I had taken a two-year lease on the house, and within a week I had handed in my notice to the South Eastern Railway, so that I could devote myself entirely to my alchemical studies. That was just under two years ago.

"The village of Apstone is a very small place, little more than a hamlet, really. It stands on a slight eminence, known as the Isle of Apstone, which overlooks the flat expanse of the Romney Marsh to the east, from which dense, cold mists frequently roll in, shrouding everything in a grey veil. To the west, the countryside is quite different, being hilly and thickly wooded. The village is always very quiet, and becomes even quieter when the mist sits upon it, but that suits my requirements exactly. It used to be a little more important than it is now, and had its own church, but that collapsed during a great storm in the middle of the last century and was never rebuilt. Local legend has it that the church tower was struck by a bolt of lightning and that the rector – who was in the church at the time, and who was killed when it collapsed – was some kind of sinner or heretic, and that it was his misdemeanours that brought this retribution upon his church. The story of the lightning strike may be true, but I think the collapse of the church was almost certainly the result of subsidence, caused by the terrible floods in the area at the time, when the marsh became so completely flooded that the water overflowed onto the surrounding land, washing much of it away. I am telling you these things so you will appreciate what a very quiet place it is in which I live, but one with its own curious history. It is largely untouched by the modern world, but not entirely cut off. It is, for instance, only a ten-minute walk to the larger village of Ham Street, where there are shops and the local railway station.

"To come now to recent events," Lidington continued after a moment: "I receive little correspondence at Naxon House, but two weeks ago I received this puzzling letter." He drew a small envelope from his inside pocket, which he passed to us. I saw that it was addressed to "The Occupier, Naxon House, Apstone." The postmark was that of Ashford, which indicated that the letter had been posted locally. Holmes took out the letter from within, and held it so I could see it. There was no address at the head of the sheet, nor any salutation, and the brief message ran as follows:

> Will come soon, as arranged.
> "Those who have done no wrong have nothing to fear."
> C.

"The date is a very singular one," said Holmes.

I had not noticed the date at the top of the letter. Now I looked again and saw that it read "April 25th 1869".

"How very strange," I said. "What on earth can that mean?"

Holmes shook his head in puzzlement. "According to the postmark, the letter was posted on October 13th," he said.

"That would be right," said Lidington. "I received it on the fourteenth."

"Does the letter mean anything to you?" asked Holmes.

"Nothing whatever. I have not arranged anything with anybody, and know no one with the initial 'C'."

"Very well. Pray continue."

"I leave the house very little – the local carter who calls twice a week supplies most of my needs – but except when it is raining heavily, I go for a walk every morning at ten o'clock, to take a little exercise and think about what I will be studying later. I generally go the same way every day. I was out one morning, about two weeks ago, and was passing along the edge of a large field. All along the other side of that particular field is a dark and dense wood. As I passed along, I chanced to glance across the field, and was surprised to see a man standing there, at the edge of the wood, apparently watching me."

"Was it anyone you knew?" asked Holmes.

Lidington shook his head. "I don't think so. He appeared to be wearing a long black coat or cloak, which reached down to his feet, a low-crowned black hat with a wide brim and – as far as I could make out – dark-tinted glasses. I had never before seen anyone in the district who looked even remotely like that."

"What made you think he was watching you?" queried Holmes. "It sounds from your description as if he would be too far away for you to be certain about that, especially if he was wearing dark spectacles."

Lidington nodded. "Yes, you are right. I suppose it was because he remained so still, and because each time I glanced across at him – which I did several times – his face seemed to be turned my way. When I reached home, I threw myself into my work, and gave no more thought to this strange figure. Two days later, however, I was out for a walk in the same place, at the same time, and there was the man again, standing perfectly still at the edge of the woods on the other side of the field, staring across at me. I considered crossing the field to where he stood – although I admit I felt strangely nervous and disturbed by his appearance – but the field had been recently ploughed and was nothing but a sea of rutted mud. I was not wearing suitable footwear, and judged that if I left the path I should become caked in mud, so I abandoned the idea.

"The field is slightly higher in the middle than at the edges, and as the side I was on dipped down a little, I lost sight of the other side, and of that strange, still figure. As my way rose up again a little, I looked again across the field, but there was no sign of him.

"A few days later, I set off for my morning walk as usual, wondering as I did so if I should again see the sinister dark figure. As I made my way along the lane near my house, I happened to run across one of my neighbours, Colonel Strother, a retired military man who lives by himself about half a mile away. He said he was out to get some fresh air and stretch his legs, as he put it, so we walked along together. I was tempted to ask him if he had seen the dark figure loitering at the edge of the woods on his recent walks, but I resisted the urge. I was aware from remarks my cleaning-woman had made that I was already regarded as something of a reclusive figure, an oddity, in the district, and I did not want to give Colonel Strother or anyone else any reason to regard me yet more oddly. It had occurred to me that I had been putting a strain on myself, working very hard recently, and although I could not really believe that the dark figure I had seen was simply the figment of an overheated brain, I knew that that is what others might think. I thus said nothing to the colonel.

"As our way brought us to the field across which I had seen the figure, I glanced nervously over to the dark woods on the other side. It was at first difficult to make anything out there, as it was a dull and gloomy morning. The woods appeared dense and dark, and a thin mist was drifting about the field in front of the trees. After a moment, however, I saw that the dark figure was standing where I had seen him before, at the edge of the wood, against the trees.

"'Colonel,' I said, interrupting his flow, for he was at the time discoursing at length on the different owls he had seen in the district, 'do you see that man over there?'

"'What man?' he responded, turning and squinting in the direction I had indicated.

"'The man in the black coat and hat, with the dark glasses on,' I said, 'standing just between those two tall trees.'

"'No,' said he at length, shaking his head. 'I can't say that I do. It's probably just a trick of the light, Lidington. Of course, no one likes to think they're imagining things, but sometimes your eyes or brain, or whatever it is that arranges these things, makes you think there's something there when there isn't. I remember one morning when I was in India. I'd had to rise very early – before the sun was up – and had had less than three hours sleep. As I walked down a rural lane in the dark, I saw a man about thirty yards away, coming straight towards me. He was a big, strong-looking fellow, and there seemed something determined and a little menacing in his manner, so I braced myself for a possible attack. Next moment, I looked again, and there was no one there at all. I could hardly believe it. I'd seen him as clearly as I see you now – or thought I had, anyway.'

"'But,' I interrupted him again, 'we've moved on some distance now, and I can still see him. Are you sure you can't see anybody there?'

"He stopped and looked again across the field. 'No,' said he at length. 'I don't think there's anybody there, Lidington. I can see a bit of shadow between two trees. That's probably what you're seeing. Funny things, eyes, the way they play tricks on you. You can't trust them for a minute.'

"I didn't pursue the matter. I don't think Colonel Strother's eyes are very good now, so his testimony was not really of any value, and I could not say for certain whether the man by the woods had really been there or not.

"Mercifully, I did not see him again for several days, and I was able to pursue my studies without the man in the black coat and hat constantly intruding into my thoughts. I did learn something, however, which I found more than a little disturbing. Another of my neighbours, Mr. Meade Taylor, invited me round to take tea with him on Sunday afternoon. He also invited Colonel Strother. Over our tea, we chatted about matters of local interest, and the other two, who had both lived in Apstone much longer than I had, told me some interesting facts about the district.

"'Your residence, Naxon House, has a somewhat odd reputation,' remarked Colonel Strother. 'I wouldn't have mentioned this to you when you were first here, in case it bothered you. But now you've been here a couple of years and got to know the district, I may as well tell you. I have heard it said that the house is built on the site of an ancient temple that predates the Roman occupation by several hundred years, and that the influence of this persists to this day. Of course, that sounds a lot of nonsense, but it can't be denied that odd things have happened there over the years, some of them before my time, but some even since I've lived in Apstone, which is thirteen years last July.'

"'What do you mean?' I asked. 'What sort of things have happened?'

"'At least two occupants of Naxon House have gone mad, for a start,' Strother replied. 'It was lived in for many years by a writer of mystical stuff, Serenus Charling.'

"'Yes,' I said; 'I'm aware of that.'

"'But do you know what happened to him in the end? No? Well, I'll tell you: they found his body one morning, floating in the old Military Canal. It seems he'd gone out in the middle of the night and flung himself in there. No one could explain why, and the general belief was that he'd lost his mind. People said he'd been acting strangely for a while, so in a way it wasn't such a surprise as it might have been. That was about two years before I moved into the district. Then, two years after that, the man who was living at Naxon House when I first came to Apstone was by all accounts a very mysterious, reclusive sort of fellow. I was told that he hid himself away all day, and only ever went out after dark. He had been a friend of Charling's, so I understand, so perhaps he was a bit unbalanced as well. Anyway, they came and took him away early one morning, and that's the last anyone ever saw of him. That was just a month or two after I'd moved here.'

"I can't tell you," said Lidington, "how appalling it was to hear Colonel Strother speaking of these dreadful matters in so off-hand and careless a tone, just as if he were relating the latest racing results from Epsom."

"Did you know already that Charling had lost his life in the canal?" asked Holmes.

Lidington shook his head. "No," said he. "Although I had read several of his books, I didn't really know anything much about the man himself. I did know that he had lived somewhere in Kent, at a place called Naxon House, but I'd never known where that was until the day I had chanced to see the name at the house-agent's in Ashford. Anyway, you will imagine that I returned home in a somewhat disturbed state of mind after the conversation with Colonel Strother and Mr. Taylor.

"That evening I felt horribly nervous, to be all alone in what now struck me as an over-large and gloomy house. I went all round the house twice, ensuring that the doors and windows were all securely fastened. The utter silence, other than the slight noise I myself made as I passed from room to room, I now found stifling and oppressive, and I longed for the sound of another human voice. About eight o'clock, a good three hours after it had gone dark, this silence was suddenly broken in the most dramatic and alarming fashion. I was sitting at my desk, writing, when there came a sudden thunderous hammering on the door-knocker. I picked up the lamp from the desk and carried it to the front door. There is a frosted glass panel in the door, but as it was pitch black outside I could see nothing through it.

"'Hello,' I cried. 'Who is there?', but no answer came, only a complete, deathly silence. 'Who is it?' I tried again, but was met again only with silence. My hands were shaking, I remember, as I made sure yet again that the front door was locked, and returned, consumed by fear and trepidation, to my study. I lay long awake in bed that night, every slight noise from the garden outside setting my senses alert and my nerves jangling. Then, just as I was drifting off to sleep, I heard a creak on the stairs outside my room. I sat bolt upright and listened for a minute, but heard nothing more. Taking the lamp from beside my bed, which I had left burning, I opened the bedroom door. There was nothing to be seen there but the dark, shadowed staircase descending to the blackness of the hall below. I returned to my bed, locking my bedroom door as I did so, but I could not sleep. Sometime later, there came a slight tap-tapping noise, as of a small branch of a climbing plant knocking against my bedroom window in the wind. I left my bed again, drew back the curtain and looked out. It was dark, but I could see that the wisteria on the house-wall was nowhere near my window, and could not have caused the tapping noise. However, the noise had ceased as I opened the curtain, so after a moment I returned to my bed and at length fell asleep.

"The following day I did not leave the house at all. As the afternoon was turning into evening and the light was fading, I was working in my study, which overlooks the back garden, and the curtains were still open. It had been my habit to have them so throughout the summer and early autumn. I dislike closing the curtains before it is absolutely necessary to do so; I like to enjoy the evening light for as long as possible. As I worked away at my desk, making notes from one of Serenus Charling's books, a difficult volume which seemed to lie somewhere on the vague and meandering border between mysticism and magic, I heard a slight noise in the garden.

"I looked up. The light was fading rapidly now, and had almost gone completely. Thin wraiths of mist were drifting across the garden, and at the far end, where a hedge separates the garden from the field beyond, it was difficult to make anything out through a dense grey curtain of mist. Then, as a little eddy of wind stirred the mist a little, I saw, with a sickening shock of horror, that there was someone standing there, perfectly motionless, and staring into the study.

"I sprang to my feet, but could move no more than that, so transfixed was I with terror. It was the man I had seen at the edge of the woods, clad in a long black coat, broad-brimmed black hat, and, on his strange round, pale face, a pair of dark spectacles. At the end of the garden is a large ornamental stone urn on a pedestal, and it was by this urn that the dark figure was standing, staring straight at me. Then, as I remained frozen with fear, the urn began to rock a little on its base, as if by some power of its own, and slowly, very slowly, it toppled over, onto the man beside it. It is a heavy urn, and as it fell it crushed the man beneath it in the most dreadfully gruesome way imaginable. I have never been struck with such horror in all my life. I dashed forward and pulled the curtains closed. Then I think I must have fainted, for I can remember no more.

"When I came to my senses, I was lying on the floor in the study. I had clearly caught my head on the corner of a chair as I fell, for it was bleeding and throbbed with pain. I rekindled the study fire, the only fire in the house still alight, and poured myself a glass of brandy to steady my nerves. Then, taking the poker from the hearth, I made a slow and cautious survey of the whole house, but found nothing amiss, and no sign that anyone had been in there.

"I spent the night sitting in a chair by the fire, with the poker on my knee. I suppose I did drop off to sleep once or twice, but awoke instantly at the slightest sound. I did not open the curtains again until it was broad daylight – about eight o'clock. To my astonishment, the garden outside looked as it had always done. The urn was still on its plinth, and there was no sign that anyone had been in the garden. I was stunned by this. Had any of what I thought I had seen the previous evening really taken place? Or had I perhaps fallen asleep at my desk and imagined the whole thing? No, that could not be, I told myself. I had been so frightened that I had fainted, and the cut on my head, where it had struck the chair, was real enough. Anyway, you will perhaps appreciate why I thought I might be going mad.

"That was yesterday. I eventually fell asleep and slept away much of the day. Then, last night, either because I had slept too long during the day, or because of anxiety at what might happen in the night, I scarcely slept a minute. This morning I was up early, and caught the first train I could from Ham Street, in the hope that you could advise me, and perhaps shed some light on the horrible predicament I find myself in."

Sherlock Holmes sat for some time in silence. "I take it from your account, Mr. Lidington, that you do not keep any resident domestic staff," he said at length.

"That is correct," replied Lidington. "I could not afford to do so even if it were necessary, which it isn't. A local woman comes in twice a week to clean round a little, and comes in other days to prepare a meal for me, which I find sufficient for my requirements. I dislike having people bustling about when I am trying to study."

"Am I also correct in inferring that your two-year lease is shortly up for renewal?"

"Yes, next month."

Holmes nodded. "Have you, or anyone else, seen any strangers in the district recently?"

"I don't think so. No, wait," added Lidington, correcting himself. "There has been a commercial traveller about recently, an elderly, grey-haired man. I have seen him a few times, lugging a suitcase about, and one day we exchanged a few words when I bumped into him on the road to Ham Street."

"A commercial traveller?" queried Holmes. "It did not appear, from your description of Apstone, that there would be any shops there for him to visit."

"That is true. I think he must be one of those fellows that go from door to door with a case full of samples."

"Do you know what he is selling?"

"No. He's not called on me, nor any of my neighbours, so far as I am aware."

"Is there anywhere in Apstone where he might stay?"

"No. But in Ham Street there are several inns, at least two of which cater especially to commercial travellers."

"Look up the trains to Ham Street in Bradshaw, would you, Watson?" said Holmes to me.

"You intend to come down to Kent with me?" said Lidington in a tone of relief.

Holmes nodded. "There are one or two things I wish to see for myself."

"I cannot quite see the drift of your questions, Mr. Holmes – my lease, whether I keep servants or not and your interest in the commercial traveller."

"It is simply a question of ascertaining all the facts," returned Holmes. "The more facts we have, the more likely it is that we shall solve the problem."

"There is a train leaving shortly from Charing Cross," I said, my eye running down the columns of figures. "I think we could catch it if we leave within the next five minutes and secure a cab straight away. There isn't another one for a couple of hours."

"Then we must catch this one," said Holmes, springing to his feet. "Throw your razor and a spare collar into a bag, Watson, and be ready to leave in two minutes!"

The next twenty minutes were a frantic dash through the crowded streets. It was not until we were ensconced in a first-class smoking compartment in the Dover express, *en route* for Ashford, where we would change for Ham Street, that we were able to relax and discuss further Mr. Lidington's alarming mystery.

"Do you see any possible meaning to these recent events, Mr. Holmes?" he asked.

"It is too early to speak with any confidence on the matter," returned Holmes, "although I think the evidence so far permits us to make one or two conjectures. The first sightings you had of your mysterious persecutor were somewhat ambiguous in nature. He appeared to be watching you from the edge of the woods, but that might not have been the case. He might, for instance, have been watching and waiting for someone else. However, the more recent events at your house, especially the performance he put on in your garden the night before last, which you found so disconcerting, can surely mean only one thing."

"What is that?"

"If we set aside any supernatural explanation, we must conclude that someone has been deliberately trying to frighten you."

"He certainly succeeded in that," said Lidington with feeling. "But why should he? What have I ever done to harm anyone?"

"It may not be because of who you are, but because of where you are. You mentioned that your two-year lease on Naxon House is coming to an end. Perhaps someone does not wish you to renew it, because he wishes to rent the house himself."

"It would seem a somewhat elaborate scheme if that is his only aim."

"I agree, but it is possible. However, there is another possibility, which is that someone wishes to frighten you away from the house for just a day or two."

"Whatever for?"

"So that he can break into the house for some reason. If that is his aim, then it is possible that your visit to London today may have provided him with just the chance he has been waiting for. The fact that you have no domestic staff in the house would of course make his task easier."

"Good Lord!"

"Do you have anything of significant value in the house?"

Lidington shook his head. "No, nothing at all that I can think of. But," he added, "I saw the sinister-looking figure crushed flat by that heavy garden urn the night before last. I am sure if you had seen it, you would have been as horrified as I was. Yet in the morning there was no one there, and no sign that there ever had been. How can you explain that?"

"It is not so very difficult," said Holmes, filling his pipe with tobacco and putting a match to it. "The dark suit of clothes – the long coat, hat and spectacles – that you had previously seen worn by the figure in the woods, were in this case, I suggest, hung upon a wooden frame of some sort. An upturned rake or broom would serve the purpose adequately, I should think. Perhaps they had always been on such a frame – you were never close enough to see before."

"But the person in the garden had a head. I could see that clearly enough."

"Yes, but your gaze would inevitably have been drawn to the most prominent feature, the dark spectacles. I doubt you would have scrutinized the rest of it very closely."

"What are you suggesting?"

"That what you thought was a head was in fact some kind of inflatable ball, with the hat perched on top of it and the spectacles secured at the sides."

"I suppose it is possible," conceded Lidington. "The face – what I saw of it – did seem strangely pale and rounded. But the urn seemed to tip over of its own volition, as if by magic."

"I fancy I could achieve the same effect, given the circumstances," returned Holmes, much to Lidington's surprise. "It was, I suspect, an ancient and time-honoured conjuring trick, which is simple but always effective. All the villain would have needed was a large piece of black cloth to hide behind as he pushed the urn over. You were very unlikely to see what was really happening in the late twilight, when, as you described, the light had almost completely gone. The fact that he had all the equipment necessary for the performance suggests that that was his ultimate aim, and that the sightings you had had of the figure by the woods formed a sort of deliberately disturbing prologue."

"You may be right," said Lidington, "but that still leaves unanswered the question of why I am being persecuted in this way."

"There are, as I mentioned, several possibilities," said Holmes. "If I knew which was the correct one, I should not be travelling down to Kent with you, but should be sitting at home with my feet up, having already solved all your problems for you. Let us therefore leave the matter there for the moment and see what we turn up in and around Apstone."

In two hours we had reached Ashford. The branch train stood waiting in the bay platform, but Holmes went to consult a time-table on the wall by the exit.

"This train leaves in eight minutes," he said, "but there is another later this afternoon that we can take. I want first to have a word with the house agent who deals with the rental of Naxon House."

Lidington took us through the streets of the busy town to an office bearing the sign "Sandhurst and Martin, House Agents". Inside, a young man whom Lidington introduced to us as Mr. Carter was seated behind a large desk. He greeted us cordially, but when Holmes asked if anyone had recently expressed an interest in Naxon House, he shook his head.

"No, not at all," said he. "We were rather hoping that Mr. Lidington would renew his lease next month. That would keep things simple from our point of view," he added with a chuckle. "I hope there is no problem – loose tiles, leaks, or anything of the sort?"

"No," said Holmes with a glance at his client. "We are interested in the past history of the property, though. Could you tell us who was in the house before Mr. Lidington?"

"One moment," said the young man. He leaned over, pulled open a large drawer in a cabinet behind him, and, after a moment, took out a large manila envelope. "As far as I recall," he said as he tipped the contents of the envelope onto his desk, "the house had been unoccupied for six months before Mr. Lidington took it, and prior to that the owner himself had lived in it for some years. Yes," he continued after a moment, "the owner of the property is a Mr. Westerton – he lives at Hythe now – Cliff Road, which always sounds a bit dangerous to me," he added, laughing at his own joke. "He lived at Naxon House from '81 to early '84. Before that, it was rented out for about eight years, from '73 to '81, to an officer of the South Eastern Railway, a Mr. Stroulger. Before Mr. Stroulger it was rented to a Mr. Smith for about two years. That takes us back to 1871, which was the first year we had anything to do with the property. I believe it had previously been occupied by the owner, who died in that year. He was probably some relation of the present owner, I should think."

"If I remember correctly," said Holmes to Lidington, "Colonel Strother told you he had lived in Apstone for thirteen years, which means he came in '73. He also said that the incident of the man who had gone mad and been taken away early one morning occurred just a couple of months after he moved there, so that must also have been in '73, and the man in question must be the Mr. Smith that Mr. Carter referred to. Do you know any more details of the matter, Mr. Carter?" he continued, turning to the house agent.

"I'm afraid not," replied Carter. "That was long before my time. My superior, Mr. Martin, might possibly remember. He's been here a long time."

The young man disappeared through a doorway at the back of the office, but reappeared a few moments later. "If you come this way," he said, "Mr. Martin will see you now."

We were shown into a warm office at the rear of the building, where a fire burned merrily in the grate. An elderly, grey-haired man stood up from behind a desk and waved us to the chairs in front of it. "I understand you are interested in our mysterious Mr. Smith, who got taken away from Naxon House one bright morning," said he in a dry tone.

"Among other things," returned Holmes. "Why do you refer to him as 'mysterious'?"

"Well, his name wasn't Smith, for a start," said Martin, "as we discovered after he'd gone. It was Farley."

"Had you not taken up his references?" asked Holmes in surprise.

Martin shook his head. "The whole business was quite irregular, which is why I recall it so clearly. The first time we ever had anything to do with Naxon House was when the owner, Serenus Charling, died. That was an odd business in itself. Of course, he was a fairly well-known local character, being a writer of some repute, but he was also a decided eccentric. He used to wander about the Romney Marsh at all hours of the day and night, wearing a large ankle-length black cape and wide-brimmed black hat, generally talking to himself and ignoring everyone else. Most people thought he was slightly mad, so when he was found one morning, drowned in the Royal Military Canal, no one was altogether surprised. Whether he slipped in or jumped in, no one could say, and the verdict at the inquest was death by misadventure.

"Shortly after his death, we were approached by a distant cousin of his, a Mr. Westerton, who had inherited Charling's property. He himself lived in Ashford at the time, and wanted us to deal with the letting of Naxon House. We had just agreed to this, when he called on us again a few days later to say that an acquaintance of Charling's had turned up at Naxon House while Westerton was there looking round the place. This acquaintance, who gave his name as Smith, said he had been staying with Charling for some time, although he hadn't been there at the time of his death. Now, he said, he was interested in renting the house for himself, and, as an old friend of the dead man, would prefer it if Charling's furniture and other belongings were left in place. This suited Mr. Westerton perfectly, as it meant he would not have the trouble of sorting out his late cousin's possessions, so he told us to go ahead and rent the house to this man, Smith. I was a bit dubious about this, as I didn't much care for the look of Smith, a deceitful-looking, rat-faced man, but it was Westerton's house, to do with as he wished, so I went ahead and wrote out the lease.

"Nothing much happened for the next two years, although I heard occasional reports from people I knew who lived down that way that this Smith fellow was every bit as eccentric as Charling had been, scarcely ever leaving the house until it had gone dark. Then, early in the autumn of '73 I had a visit one day from a police inspector, accompanied by a senior officer from Maidstone Prison. They informed me that they were on the track of a man called Farley, who had escaped from prison three years previously and who, they now had reason to believe, was one and the same person as the man called Smith, who was living at Naxon House. I was astounded at this, although it did confirm that the unfavourable impression I had formed of him in the first place had been correct. I told them what I knew of him – which wasn't much – and gave them my spare key, and the next morning at dawn they entered Naxon House and arrested him.

"I later heard that there was a rumour in the district that Smith had been insane and had been taken away for his own and others' safety. How this rumour began, I cannot say, but I never went out of my way to correct it. From the point of view of letting the house, it was bad enough that it had been occupied by a man who had gone mad. It would have been even worse, I thought, if it were known that the occupant had been a hardened and vicious escaped convict."

"Is there any particular reason why you refer to him as 'hardened and vicious'?" asked Holmes.

"He was a member of the gang that carried out the notorious bullion robbery here in Ashford in the late 'sixties, in the course of which several railway employees were badly beaten. I don't suppose any of you have heard of that."

"I have read something of it," said Holmes. "A quantity of gold bullion – both bars and coins – was being shipped in great secrecy from Dover to London by the South Eastern Railway. One of that company's employees got wind of what was being carried and hatched a plan with his confederates to rob the train just north of Ashford station. As I recall, there were some ingenious touches to the scheme, involving replacing the couplings either side of the wagon containing the bullion with loops of thick rope which could then be cut with a knife – first the back one and then the front one – thus isolating that wagon from the rest of the train. Unfortunately for the gang, the execution of the scheme was not so accomplished as the planning of it had been. They cut the ropes too soon, and too close together, so they didn't remain isolated for long enough to make off with much of the gold."

"Your account of it is very accurate," said Martin in surprise.

"The history of such crimes is a little hobby of mine," returned Holmes. "Could the date of the robbery have been April 25th, 1869?"

Martin frowned as he tried to remember. "Yes, that would be about right," he said at length. "I remember it was in the spring. Anyway, all five members of the gang were soon caught and convicted. Three of them, including Farley, were sentenced to ten years in Maidstone Prison. The other two, who were evidently judged less culpable, got seven years. As far as I remember, most of the stolen gold was recovered, but not quite all of it." Martin paused. "We seem to have drifted quite a long way from your question about previous tenants of Naxon House," he remarked, scratching his head.

"Nevertheless, it is all interesting, and we are very grateful to you for sparing us the time," said Holmes.

As we walked back to the railway station, Holmes was silent, with a look of intense concentration on his features. I knew better than to bother him with questions when he was so deep in thought, and knew he would share his thoughts on the matter when he felt he had reached a worthwhile conclusion, but Lidington asked him if the information we had received from the house agents had altered his views of the matter.

In answer, Holmes shook his head in a puzzled manner. “Sometimes,” said he at length, “a little fresh information can clarify a case considerably. In this instance, however, the new information has served only to complicate the matter further. It now seems very likely that the bizarre and puzzling date on the mysterious letter you received a few weeks ago is in fact the date of this notorious bullion robbery, but what might be the significance of that, we cannot say. Let us therefore possess our souls in patience a little longer before attempting to reach any conclusions.”

We caught the next branch train and a short time later alighted at Ham Street, the first stop on the line. A brisk walk of ten minutes brought us to the hamlet of Apstone, its scattered houses dotted about among the fields and woods. Away to the east, the vast flat and featureless expanse of the Romney Marsh stretched far away. After a moment, following Lidington’s lead, we turned from the main road into a muddy lane. A short distance up this lane an equally muddy track went off to the left, and just beyond this track stood a substantial double-fronted house built of dark red brick, which Lidington informed us was Naxon House.

“If you will wait here in the lane,” said Holmes, “I shall inspect the area around the house.”

We watched as he made a slow and careful examination of the path from the garden gate to the front door of the house, then of the lane outside the garden, and lastly of the side-track. Something there seemed to particularly catch his attention, and he followed the track all the way along the outside of the garden hedge, and beyond the hedge, into the field behind the house.

“It is as I thought,” said he as he rejoined us.

“You have discovered something?” queried Lidington.

Holmes nodded. “Fortunately, it rained here last night. As a result, all the footprints are fresh and clear, and I can be sure that they were all made today. The first thing that happened this morning, Mr. Lidington, is that you left the house, got half-way down the path to the gate and turned back. You then re-entered the house, came out again and made your way out of the garden and down the lane here."

"That is true. I realised that I had come out without any money, having left my purse on the kitchen table, so I went back to get it."

"The second thing that happened," Holmes continued, "is that a man with a nick in the outside edge of his right shoe came up the lane. In several places his footprints overlay your own, going in the opposite direction. Interestingly, he did not proceed to your garden gate, but turned off into the track at the side of your garden. He had not gone very far up the track, however, when he met someone with large feet coming down the track from the field behind your garden."

"That must have been Colonel Strother. He has large feet, I have noticed, and he often comes down that track when he has been for his morning walk over the fields."

"The two of them stood together for a few moments, then both of them came down the track, into the lane, and so down to the main road. In other words, large feet continued on the way he had been going when they met, while the other man, the one with the nick in the side of his shoe, turned round and accompanied large feet down to the road."

"Can you really see all that?" asked Lidington in an incredulous tone.

"Certainly. The footprints are very clear."

"Do you think the two men met by arrangement?" I asked.

Holmes shook his head. "It looks to me as if they met by chance," he replied. "After their brief conversation, which is indicated by the area on the track where their feet shuffle about a little, the man with the nicked shoe evidently changed what he was planning to do, as he turned round and accompanied the other man back down to the road. This suggests that large feet told him something that obliged him to change his plan."

"What could that have been?" I asked.

"Probably that Mr. Lidington was not at home."

"How could the man with the large feet have known that, if he had just walked down from the field behind the house?"

"Probably he had observed that there was no smoke rising from any of the chimneys, and had seen from over the back hedge that Mr. Lidington was not in his study. If large feet were indeed Colonel Strother, as Mr. Lidington suggests, then you must remember that he is an old military man, and would be used to making such observations as a matter of habit. Anyway, although he could not admit it, the other man was no doubt already aware, of course, that Mr. Lidington was not at home. He had probably watched him go for the train at Ham Street. That is why he had not called at the house in a normal sort of way, but was making his way up the little track at the side of the property when he encountered the colonel."

"What do you think he had intended to do?" asked Lidington.

"Probably to break a window round the back of the house and gain entry that way. Only the colonel's chance arrival prevented it."

"What a pity that we do not know who the other man was," said Lidington.

"Oh, there's no mystery about that," said Holmes. "It was undoubtedly the commercial traveller."

"How can you be so sure?" I asked in surprise.

"It is an elementary matter of observation, Watson. Come and see," he continued, leading us up the side-track a little way. "This is where the two men stood together for a few moments, as you can see from the scuffed footprints on the ground. Large shoes has come down the track, nicked sole has come up the track, and they have both stopped here. But what else do you see?"

I looked where he was pointing and saw that at the side of the footprints was a large, square-cornered oblong mark, about two and a half feet long by eight inches wide.

"It is his suitcase!" I cried, as I realised the meaning of the mark. "He has put it down while the two of them were speaking!"

"Precisely! Come, let us now make haste back to Ham Street and see if we can find where this bogus commercial traveller has been staying!"

"It is all very puzzling to me," said Lidington, as we walked along. "When he and I spoke the other day, he struck me as a quite exceptionally pleasant man."

"Perhaps he did," remarked Holmes, "but as a commercial traveller he is certainly something of an oddity. In the first place he appears, from your description of him, to be a little mature for that sort of work. In the second place, he seems to have spent at least a week, perhaps more, wandering about Apstone and the district when it is apparent that there are only enough houses here to occupy him for an hour or two at most. In the third place, considering how few households there are, it is strange that he does not appear to have actually called at any of them."

We were soon back in Ham Street, and Lidington took us first to an inn called the Plough, but the landlord there did not recognize the description he gave him. Lidington then led us down the village high street until we came to a large, imposing inn, painted in a black and white Tudor style. A sign hanging over the entrance identified this as the George. "This is the most popular place with commercial travellers, I believe," said Lidington as he pushed open the door. Inside was a large taproom, with five or six men sitting in lively conversation and another couple leaning on the bar, talking to the landlord. Lidington described to him the man we were looking for, at which he nodded his head.

"That would be Mr. Beresford," said he in a jovial tone. "He's in the back parlour now."

We thanked him and pushed open the connecting door which led to the parlour. There, sitting by himself at a small table, was a grey-haired man in a tweed suit, nearer sixty than fifty, I judged. He had a pipe in his mouth and a tankard of ale before him, and on his face was a far-away, thoughtful expression. As the three of us approached his table, he turned. Upon his face was a look of surprise and also, I thought, of apprehension. He put down his pipe and began to rise to his feet.

"Don't trouble to get up," said Holmes in an affable tone. "Instead, we'll sit down. it's Mr. Beresford, isn't it?"

The man nodded his head. "What can I do for you, gentlemen?" he asked, as we drew up chairs to the table at which he was sitting.

"You could answer a few questions," returned Holmes.

"What sort of questions?"

"First and foremost, you could tell us why you have been persecuting Mr. Lidington here recently."

"I don't know what you are talking about. Why should I answer your questions, anyway? Who are you?"

"My name is Holmes. I am an investigator of mysteries."

"What, another one of those infernal crack-brained and fraudulent alchemists?"

"Not at all. The mysteries I investigate have no such pretensions to profundity, but nevertheless affect people's lives more directly. Such mysteries cause people to become puzzled or anxious, miserable or frightened. That is why I try to solve their problems for them."

"Best of luck with that," said the other in a sarcastic tone, picking up his pipe again from the table, "but I don't see what it's got to do with me."

"Why do you refer to alchemists as 'crack-brained' or 'fraudulent'?"

"I misunderstood you, that is all. It's not important."

"On the contrary, I think it is very important. My client, whom I believe you have met," Holmes continued, nodding his head in the direction of Lidington, "happens to live in Naxon House, which was once owned by Serenus Charling, a noted alchemist, and there you are, bringing up the subject of alchemy without any prompting from me. That seems something of a coincidence, would you not agree? Incidentally, we know that you were out at Naxon House today. Unfortunately for your plan to force an entry to the house, you ran across one of Mr. Lidington's neighbours in the lane beside the house and had to abandon the scheme."

Beresford seemed about to reply, but hesitated and remained silent.

"I might also mention," Holmes continued, "that we know all about the bungled railway robbery of 1869, of Farley's escape from Maidstone Prison the following year and his subsequent recapture at Charling's house."

Beresford remained silent a moment longer, then he turned to Lidington, a bitter expression on his face. "You are, I take it, a relative of that devil, Charling?"

"I?" returned Lidington in surprise. "No, I have no connection with him at all. I just happen to live in his old house."

"I don't believe you," said Beresford sharply. "I made enquiries some time ago, and learned that Naxon House was now owned by a relative of Charling's."

"I believe that that is true," said Lidington, "but I am not that man. I am a mere tenant. The owner of the house lives somewhere else, and I have never even met him. I know nothing whatever about him, nor, for that matter, about Serenus Charling himself. I have read one or two of Charling's books, that is all."

"I made other enquiries locally," persisted Beresford, "and was told that you have spent most of your time in the last two years studying alchemy."

"That is also true," said Lidington. "I had had an interest in the subject for some time, and when I was looking for somewhere to live, I happened to discover quite by chance that Charling's old house was vacant. I thought then that fate must have intended me to move in there, and took a two-year lease on the place. That is my only connection with it, or with Serenus Charling."

Beresford bowed his head, blew out his cheeks and ran his hand through his hair. "It seems I have made a mistake," said he at last, raising his head after a long silence. "I put two and two together and made five."

"More pertinently," said Holmes, "you also frightened the wits out of my client."

Beresford nodded his head slowly. "I wouldn't blame you if you never forgave me," said he to Lidington in a voice full of contrition, "but please believe me when I say I am sorry if I have caused you distress."

"You appear to have some grudge against Serenus Charling or his family," said Holmes. "Would you care to tell us about it?"

"You would not believe me if I told you," said the other after a moment.

"We might if what you told us was the truth," returned Holmes. "I think we are entitled to some sort of explanation."

"I agree," said Beresford. "Perhaps the first two things you should know, then," he continued after a moment in a dignified tone, "is that my true name is not Beresford but Walters, and I, like that man Farley that you mentioned, am an ex-convict."

"I find that difficult to believe," I said in surprise.

"Thank you, sir," said he; "but it is true. I was convicted, along with four other men, of that bullion robbery in '69 that your companion mentioned, although I had nothing whatever to do with it."

"Then how came you to be convicted?" asked Holmes.

"Purely on the lying testimony of others. I will explain, so you will understand the depths of bitterness that have poisoned my soul for nearly twenty years. As a boy I had little formal education, but I was a very keen reader, read every book I could lay my hands on, and thus educated myself in that way. I was born and raised in Ashford, and at the age of thirteen was apprenticed to a small engineering concern there, owned by a very kind and generous man by the name of Beresford. It had begun by making various items of ironwork for farm carts and the like, but the coming of the railway had increased the demand for all sorts of ironwork enormously, and we were very busy. As the years passed, it became clear to me that Mr. Beresford had come to rely heavily on me, but I was taken by surprise one day when he offered me a half-share in the business. He and his wife, who had died by then, had never had any children, and I think he had come to look on me as a son. More years passed, and when Mr. Beresford himself died, I discovered that in his will he had left me the other half of the business, saying that he wished above all for it to continue successfully. I was thus, at a relatively young age, the owner of a prosperous business, comfortably-off and well-respected in the area. Sadly, my wife had not lived to enjoy this prosperity, but she had borne me a child, our daughter, Florence, who was now my greatest source of happiness.

"There is in Ashford – or, at least, there was in those days – I know nothing of it now – a literary and scientific society, whose members would meet once a month to discuss various intellectual matters. Often someone – one of our members or a visitor – would read a paper on some subject or other and then we would discuss it. On one occasion, Serenus Charling, the well-known writer on alchemy, read a paper. In the discussion afterwards, I raised several objections to points he had made, as did some of the others, and a good discussion ensued. A couple of months later, I myself read a paper defending the conventional, scientific view of the world and, I suppose, dismissing alternative 'mystical' views. My criticisms of the latter were not particularly harsh, and I had certainly intended to make them in the friendly, open spirit which usually marked our discussions, but I felt afterwards, from Charling's manner towards me, that I had perhaps offended him and he had taken against me in a personal way. Still, on the surface at least, we remained on good terms, and he invited me to his house on a number of occasions to discuss our intellectual differences.

"I must now mention the one mistake I made in running the firm of Beresford and Walters, as it was still known. Generally speaking, when taking on new men, I prided myself on being able to judge the character of each prospective employee, but on one occasion I erred badly. I took on a man by the name of Seth Woodall, who soon proved to be nothing but trouble. From the very start, he showed a marked reluctance to put any effort into what he was supposed to be doing, and he had been with the firm scarcely two months when he began to complain about everything – the premises, the equipment, the work he was required to do and his fellow workers. None of these complaints was justified and they were generally made simply to explain away his own shortcomings and mistakes. Matters finally came to a head when there were a number of petty thefts, both from the firm and its employees, and after a thorough investigation it became clear that Woodall was responsible. I had no choice but to dismiss him, but it was an unpleasant situation, and he left the premises mouthing the foulest of oaths and vowing vengeance against me.

"I come now to the fateful evening of April 25th, 1869."

"The day of the bullion robbery."

"Exactly, Mr. Holmes. I had gone down to Apstone to see Charling. We had supper together and discussed our differing views on alchemy. Then, leaving with him an essay I had written on the subject, summarising my opinions, I drove myself home to Ashford. The following morning, news of the robbery had spread round Ashford like wildfire. Two of the four criminals had been captured at the scene of the robbery and the other two were being sought in Ashford. By the time the local evening newspaper appeared, all four men were in custody.

"Early that evening, I was sitting at home, having a cup of tea and reading the paper, when there came a ring at the bell. Next moment, three large policemen were shown in, one of whom produced a warrant for my arrest. I was utterly astounded at this, but even more astounded to learn that I had been incriminated in the robbery by one of the captured men. This man was Seth Woodall, the man I had had to dismiss from his job for dishonesty the previous year. That evil, lying rat had told the police that I was 'the clever one' they suspected had planned the robbery. He had evidently seized the chance to wreak vengeance upon me, as he had threatened. His confederates, evidently as foul and depraved as he was, said nothing to dispute his false claim.

"If I had been shocked and astounded by these base lies, I was soon to find that there was a yet greater shock awaiting me. I told the police that I knew no more about the robbery than any other member of the public, and that I had been visiting Serenus Charling on the evening it took place, but when they interviewed Charling he denied ever having seen me that day. I said I had taken him an essay I had just finished writing, as my housekeeper could attest, as she had seen me writing it, but Charling said he had no knowledge of any such essay. My mind was reeling at this, and I could not believe what I was hearing. Surely the man's mind could not be so poisoned with hatred for me just because I had argued against his opinions, so poisoned that he would condemn a perfectly innocent man to a brutal term of imprisonment? But that was how it was, and what was seen as my lie in stating that I had visited Charling on the evening of the robbery only added to my appearance of guilt in the eyes of the authorities. I was convicted and sentenced to seven years' hard labour in Maidstone Prison. For seven years I was locked away from the world, with only the most vicious and brutal of men for company. For seven years I was separated from my only daughter, Florence. She had gone to live with my sister in Canterbury upon my arrest, and it was there she grew from childhood to adulthood, and eventually married, from all of which I was completely cut off.

"I was released back into the world in '76, almost broken both in body and spirit by my time in prison. Florence and her husband invited me to join them in York, where they now lived, and where her husband had a small engineering business not so dissimilar from the business I had once had in Ashford. This I eventually did, and I like to think I have proved myself useful to the business, but first I returned to Ashford, to tidy up my affairs there. I spent some time reading old newspapers, and soon learned that Charling had died five years previously, in '71, and that after Farley's escape from prison in 1870, of which I was already aware, he had lived at Charling's house until he was recaptured in '73. What had become of Woodall and the other lying criminals, I neither knew nor cared. I do remember wondering if Farley had in fact murdered Charling. It did not seem that the authorities had ever considered that possibility, but as I was only too well aware, the authorities were capable of making dreadful errors. However, I did not wish to dwell on the past, so when I had finished my business in Ashford, I shook the dust of Kent from my feet and set off for the North, doubting that I should ever return.

"Several years passed. My son-in-law's business was flourishing, Florence had borne two children, so that I was now a grandfather and in constant demand from that quarter, and the events of the past had almost faded from my memory. Then, one afternoon, as I was walking home and crossing a bridge in the middle of York, I paused to look down at the river, and for no reason I have ever been able to determine, Charling, Naxon House and all the rest of it came flooding back into my mind. As I stood there a moment, almost overcome by the suddenness of these recollections, a fresh thought struck me like the blow from a sledgehammer, something I had never considered before, even in my wildest imaginings. Could it be that there really had been a 'clever one' behind the bullion robbery, as the police had always suspected? It was certainly not me, but could that 'clever one' have been Charling?

"The more I thought about it, the more possible did it seem. It would have given Charling a stronger motive for lying about me than simply his dislike of my intellectual arguments and criticisms. Woodall's initial lies about me would in fact have given Charling the opportunity to use me as a sort of scapegoat, to provide the police with the 'clever one' they were looking for, and take any attention away from Charling himself. Charling's involvement might also explain the whereabouts of the missing gold. Perhaps after I had left him, on the night of the robbery, the two men who remained at large for nearly twenty-four hours had arrived with the gold and it had been hidden for safekeeping at Naxon House.

"Charling's involvement in the robbery would also explain why Farley had ended up at his house after his escape from prison. For, if my speculations were true, one could readily imagine that Farley might have threatened to expose Charling's part in the robbery unless he hid him away at Naxon House. One could further imagine that Farley and Charling had subsequently fallen out – probably over the gold – and Farley had murdered Charling, as I had speculated before.

"But why should Charling have become involved in the robbery in the first place? As soon as I posed myself this question, two possible answers at once suggested themselves, both of which, I judged, could be true. In the first place, I had long suspected that Charling was not so well off as people supposed. Although he adopted the pose of 'the distinguished local author.' and made the most of it in the district, I had long suspected that his books were not, in fact, read very much, and brought him little if any income. If so, the prospect of acquiring a quantity of gold might have proved irresistible to him. In the second place, he had once told me that he had managed to produce a very small quantity of gold by one of his alchemical processes and was hoping to repeat the experiment on a larger scale. I did not believe him – I had come to feel he was both a liar and a fraud – but, out of politeness, I had not expressed my disbelief openly. It now seemed possible to me that he might have intended to melt down some of the stolen gold and pretend that he had produced it by alchemical means.

"Of course, the men who were imprisoned for their part in the robbery would presumably have expected to receive their share of the gold upon their release from prison. But by the time they got out of prison, Charling had been dead some years and his house was in the hands of another, so perhaps they simply abandoned the idea as futile and did not pursue the matter. Anyway, as I considered all these possibilities, I became consumed with the idea of gaining entry to Naxon House in the hope that I might find there something which would prove Charling's guilt, and my own innocence. Unfortunately, I soon learnt that the present occupant of Naxon House hardly ever went out for longer than an hour at a time, so I had to find some way of driving him from the house just long enough to allow me to get in there and look for evidence. The idea I came up with – forgive me – was to try to frighten him away by pretending to be Serenus Charling returned from the dead. The rest you appear to know."

"What made you think that you might be able to find any evidence after all this time?" asked Holmes. "Surely it was more likely that any evidence would be long gone, found by Charling's relative or one of his tenants."

Walters hesitated. "Do you believe all that I have told you?" he asked at length.

"Yes," replied Holmes, at which Lidington and I nodded our agreement. With such intensity and conviction had Walters told his tale that I could not doubt for a moment that it was the unvarnished truth.

"Can I trust that you will pursue the truth, no matter what the consequences?" he asked.

"Certainly you can," said Holmes. "It is in everyone's interest that the true facts be known."

"Very well, then," said Walters. "I will tell you. There is a secret room in Naxon House which I doubt anyone knows about but me. Charling himself had it constructed many years ago so he could have somewhere private in which to conduct his secret alchemical experiments. I only learned about it by chance: I had called round to see him in the early days of our acquaintance, and, finding the door open, assumed it had been left so for me. I walked straight in, calling a greeting to him as I did so, but either I was earlier than he expected, or he had forgotten I was coming, for just as I walked in, he emerged from the entrance of the secret room. He showed it to me then – he could hardly do otherwise – but asked me not to tell anyone else about it. I very much doubt he would have shown it to Farley or anyone else, and it is very unlikely to have been discovered by chance. It is just possible that there is something in there which will shed some light on what happened all those years ago."

Holmes rose to his feet. "Let us get down to Apstone, then, before the daylight goes," said he.

The sun was setting as we left the inn, and, by the time we reached Naxon House, twilight was well advanced. Cold air was drifting off the marsh, and on its surface small clouds of evening mist were forming. Lidington unlocked the front door of the house and we followed him inside.

"Where, precisely, is the secret room?" Holmes asked.

"It is in the attic," Walters returned, "but one cannot get into it up there. I believe there was originally a large trap-door between the attic and one of the bedrooms when Charling was first moving furniture up there, but that was later sealed up, and the only entrance now is in the study. I'll show you." He led the way towards the back of the house and we entered a room which overlooked the rear garden. As I looked out of the window, I saw the large urn on its pedestal at the end of the garden, as Lidington had described it to us. Wisps of mist were drifting about the foot of the pedestal and the hedge behind it.

"You see how peculiarly thick the walls are here," said Walters, standing beside the window. "That is because there is a steep and narrow staircase within the wall."

In the corner of the room, between the fireplace and the window, a large, tall cupboard had been constructed, as high as the picture-rail. Walters opened the doors of this, to reveal broad wooden shelves on which were piled numerous books and documents. "May I move these out of the way?" he asked Lidington, who nodded his head. I lent a hand, and soon all the books and papers were piled upon the floor by the desk. Then Walters lifted up the shelves in the cupboard, which were not fastened to the brackets upon which they rested, and stacked them all against the wall by the window. "This side panel inside the cupboard conceals the staircase," he said. "One of these little brackets is actually attached to a latch on the other side, and if we lift it, it should release the panel. Yes, there we are." He had lifted the bracket slightly and pulled it forward, whereupon the whole wooden side-wall of the cupboard hinged forward, revealing a steep and narrow staircase behind it.

Holmes had lit a lamp which stood on the desk. This he handed to Walters, who set off up the stairs holding the lamp in front of him, as we followed behind. It was so very cramped that one's shoulders brushed the side-walls as the staircase twisted round in a tight spiral, and so extremely steep that our ascent seemed almost as vertical as climbing a ladder. At the top of the stair we entered one of the strangest chambers I have ever seen. It was surprisingly large, and must have occupied half of the loft space. That we were immediately beneath the roof-tiles was apparent from the steeply-sloping ceiling. All about us were large, highly-coloured and mysterious-looking pictures, covered with strange figures and symbols, and in the centre of the room were various chests, cupboards and tables, on some of which stood items of chemical equipment and bottles of vividly-coloured chemicals. Over everything was a thick layer of dust, and uncountable numbers of old, dusty cobwebs.

"A little more light would be helpful," said Holmes as he lit two lamps which stood on one of the tables. "Now let us see what we can find," he continued, pulling open a drawer in a small bureau which stood by the wall. "There are a lot of papers in here," he said, "and a number of newspaper cuttings relating to the bullion robbery. Ah! Charling's vanity may have betrayed him! He has underlined those parts of the newspaper reports that say what an ingeniously planned robbery it was! And here is something in a different hand: 'A Critical Examination of the Claims of Alchemy'."

"That is my essay!" cried Walters in delight.

"I wonder why he kept it," I said.

"I cannot imagine," said Walters, "but perhaps it was because he recognized that the arguments it contained were valid, and he had never succeeded in countering them. Anyway, it's the essay I brought him on the evening I was supposed to have been involved with the robbery."

"May I have a look at it?" asked Lidington.

"By all means," returned Walters. "What is it, Mr. Holmes?" he asked, as Holmes let out a cry of surprise.

"There is a drawer full of gold coins here," replied Holmes.

"These look like gold, too," I said as I opened the lid of a small chest and lifted out two small bars, each stamped with an assay symbol.

Thus we continued searching this strange room until we were certain there was no hiding-place we had missed. Then Holmes stood for some time in silence, his chin in his hand.

"What are you thinking?" asked Walters.

"I am considering what to do about all this," replied Holmes. "I think you had best let me handle the matter, Mr. Walters. I may not yet have much of a reputation in Ashford, but I am well known to some of the senior officers at the headquarters of the Kent Constabulary, and am very well known in London. If I give an account of what you have told us and what we have found here, I am more likely to be believed straight away than you are. We don't want to run the risk of your being suspected of knowing about this gold all along and simply wanting to get your own hands on it."

"Good Lord!" cried Walters. "I had not thought of that! You do believe what I have told you, don't you?"

"Of course," said Holmes. "I believe every word you have spoken. I have never doubted you for an instant."

At this, much to my surprise, Walters abruptly put his hands up to his face and burst into tears. "Do excuse me, gentlemen," he said, taking a handkerchief from his pocket. "Do forgive my weakness."

It is always a surprising and striking thing to see a grown man weep, and is nearly always of some special significance. In this case, it was evident that Holmes's prompt and unreserved declaration of belief in Mr. Walters had completely undermined the hardened natural defences of one who had been disbelieved, abused and vilified for so long.

"No apology is necessary," said Holmes, ushering the other to a chair. "Sit down here and compose yourself for a moment. Courage, Mr. Walters! Fate certainly dealt you a bad hand, but it may be that some of the cards in it are not quite so weak as they appeared. Tomorrow we shall go to the best solicitor in Ashford and swear an affidavit of all that we have learnt, and then present the facts to the authorities."

Once we had completed all the formalities, and the police had examined and searched Naxon House to their satisfaction, Holmes and I returned to London. As our train sped along through the Vale of Kent, Holmes was in a thoughtful, reflective mood, and when I remarked how deeply moved Walters had been by Holmes's generous expression of confidence in him, he turned to me in surprise.

"I had no intention of being 'generous', as you put it," returned my friend; "I was simply stating a fact."

I asked him then why he had been so confident in Mr. Walters's veracity.

"It is an instinctive thing," said he at length, "and not easy to put one's finger on. You may as well ask me how I know that two and two make four. That they do is instantly clear, but explaining precisely why they do takes a little longer. I suppose his eyes played a part in it."

"His eyes?"

"Well, the look in them, at least. One can generally tell an honest man by the look in his eyes."

"I seem to remember your saying that one should never trust to generalized impressions, as they can be misleading."

"There is no contradiction, Watson. I had already moved beyond my first general impression of Walters when I looked into his eyes and knew at once he was an honest man. It has been said, as you are no doubt aware, that the eyes are the windows of the soul, and when you have scrutinized as many faces as I have, you know that to be true."

The wheels of justice are sometimes very slow to turn, and it was many months before Mr. Walters's attempt to clear his name received a proper hearing. Even then the result was indecisive, and the matter was passed on to a higher court. Eventually the case reached the House of Lords. There, the judicial committee declared at length that although his original conviction had not been unreasonable on the evidence available at the time, it was now clear that it was mistaken, and should be struck from the record. Mr. Walters was at last, therefore, granted a complete and unconditional pardon.

As for Mr. Lidington, whose mystery had brought us into the case in the first place, he did not renew his lease upon Naxon House. He also gave up the study of alchemy, which he said he had quite lost the taste for, and, the last I heard, he had applied for and succeeded in regaining his former post with the South Eastern Railway.

THE YELLOW GLOVE

"IF ONLY CRIMINALS would occasionally display a little imagination," remarked Sherlock Holmes, as we sat in conversation after breakfast, one morning towards the end of the summer, "it would surely make life so much more interesting for everyone, and – who can say? – the criminals themselves might find that they derived an increased satisfaction from their work."

"The general opinion, I fancy, would be that criminals show quite enough imagination as it is," I responded with a chuckle. "They imagine that what is in someone else's pocket might be in their own, and then take steps to bring their imagined vision to reality!"

"Tush!" cried my companion, waving his pipe in the air in a gesture of dismissal. "You must not confuse simple activity, however energetically it is pursued, with the creative application of the imaginative faculties. Of course, oafs will continue to hit their victims over the head with lumps of wood, and hurl bricks through windows in pursuit of their aims. Every day brings fresh accounts of such crude and uninspired villainy. But where today is the carefully conceived plan, the enterprise so daring and subtle that it leaves the authorities baffled, and the victims themselves half admiring of the crime?"

"You have an unusual point of view," I ventured. "Indeed, some might describe it as beyond the bounds of eccentricity."

"Perhaps so," my companion conceded. "I'll own my view is coloured somewhat by professional considerations. I long for that spark of originality in the criminal which might kindle a little interest in my own slumbering intellect. As it is, I fear that my brain is in danger of suffering atrophy from lack of use."

"Might I enquire if anything in particular has prompted these reflections?" I asked after a moment.

For answer he picked up a sheet of note-paper which lay on the floor beside his chair, and passed it to me. "I received this note by the first post," said he.

I took the sheet from him and read the following:

> MY DEAR MR. HOLMES – I wish most urgently to consult you. I have had the most bizarre and inexplicable experience of my life. What it means, I simply cannot imagine, but I fear that it may have some sinister implication for my employers, for whom I am at present acting in a senior capacity until our principal returns from abroad. I shall call at ten-thirty in the morning, and hope that that is not inconvenient for you. – MICHAEL ELDER

"I do not understand," I remarked in some puzzlement, as I finished reading the letter. "For one who laments the lack of intellectual stimulation, this letter is surely a cause of hope rather than the opposite!"

"Ah!" said my companion. "There, my dear fellow, you put your finger on the very nub of the matter! It does, I agree, appear to afford some justification for hope, and for a moment, as I read it, my spirits rose accordingly. But next moment I recalled how frequently my hopes have been dashed, how many times that which a correspondent describes as 'bizarre' or 'inexplicable' is revealed upon inspection to be so commonplace that the most egregious imbecile at Scotland Yard might be expected to fathom it. Thus, I fear that what appears to promise hope, presages instead only disappointment!"

"You are a pessimist!" said I, smiling at my companion's forlorn countenance.

"Not at all," returned he quickly. "On the contrary, Watson, I am by temperament a perennial optimist. But experience has taught me – alas! – that my optimism is very often unwarranted. However, we shall soon learn what it is that Mr. Elder finds bizarre and inexplicable, for that is probably his hand on the bell now!"

The front doorbell had jangled as he had been speaking, and a moment later our landlady showed a neatly dressed young man into the room, whom she announced as Mr. Michael Elder. He was youthful in appearance, scarcely more than twenty years of age, I judged, and was of slight build, with a pale, clean-shaven face.

"Pray take a seat, and let us know how we can help you!" said Holmes, vacating his own chair by the hearth and ushering the young man into it.

"Thank you," returned the other in a pleasant tone. "I'll come straight to the point," he continued after a moment, but then paused, and stroked his chin in silence. "The facts of the matter are these," he resumed eventually: "I am in the employment of a highly respected firm, somewhere in London. Our principal, who also happens to be my cousin, is away at present, in consequence of which I have had to assume a little more responsibility than I had before. I am confident that I have done nothing wrong, but am concerned, nevertheless, that something which has occurred, for which I must accept some responsibility, may have compromised the confidentiality of our business. I therefore wish to discover – simply for my own peace of mind, you understand – whether or not this is so. There," he concluded, breathing heavily; "that is the matter in a nutshell."

Sherlock Holmes raised his eyebrow, and regarded the young man for a moment.

"Really, Mr. Elder," said he at length; "you can hardly suppose that I shall be able to offer you any sensible advice, if the details of the matter, on which, perforce, my advice must be founded, are kept from me!"

"I beg your pardon," returned Elder. "I am a little afraid lest I endanger the commercial confidentiality of the company yet further. It is difficult to know what to do," he added, scratching his head.

"Then let me make it a little easier for you," said Holmes. "Your employers, I believe, are Elder and Kemp, the well-known engineering firm, of Southwark. The principal of the firm is your relative, Sir George Elder, who was knighted two years ago for his contribution to the engineering feats of the century. He has been in Russia for some time, where he has been supervising the construction of a new railway bridge across the river Volga, but is presently on his way back to England. His ship docks in London on Saturday afternoon. You therefore have three days in which to resolve whatever it is that is troubling you."

The young man's mouth fell open in astonishment. "How do you know all this?" he asked.

"I observed as you sat down that you had a small slide-rule in your pocket. Who but an engineer would carry a slide-rule about with him? From that observation, and knowledge of your surname, it is scarcely a super-human feat of intellect to associate you with the engineering firm of which Sir George Elder is the head. As to his activities in Russia, and his imminent return, there was an interesting report on the matter in this morning's *Times*."

"Well, I'll be blowed!" exclaimed the young man. He scratched his head for a moment before continuing. "You appear to know so much of my business already, that any further attempts at discretion on my part would seem pointless."

"That is something upon which we are agreed, then," said Holmes in a dry tone. "Pray, proceed!"

"Very well. You should first know a little of my own personal situation, for it has some bearing on the matter. I may carry a slide-rule in my pocket, as you observed; but I am not yet, I regret, very advanced in engineering expertise. I am still in the early stages of a training that will continue for some years before I am able to put any letters after my name.

"My father is a solicitor in Guildford, and the original idea was that I should follow him into that game. I did my best to stick it out for a couple of years, but it was all torts and contracts, parties of the first part, and that sort of nonsense, and I didn't really seem to be getting anywhere with it. Of course, I didn't want to disappoint the old man. He seemed so keen to see me in his dusty old chambers, and you know how touchy parents can be when you tell them you don't really care for something they've spent thirty-odd years at. I did my best to humour him, but it was no go in the end. He saw it as well as I. So, to cut a long story short, he offered me to his cousin, old George Elder, to train as an engineer. To be frank, I don't think my cousin was quite so enthusiastic to receive me as my father was to give me away, but he was civil enough about it, and took me under his engineering wing, as it were. When I came to London, I lodged for a while at Sir George's house, out Holland Park way, but we didn't always see eye to eye about what time I should come in of an evening, and other things, so eventually it was agreed that it might be better if I had diggings of my own, so that we could each keep the hours we wished without either of us putting the other out. I therefore took up lodgings in Notting Hill, an arrangement which seems to suit us both. Sir George's carriage passes the end of my road every morning, I wait there and get into it when it comes, then travel with him to Southwark. Once or twice, perhaps, he has had to send his coachman to look for me, when I didn't appear to be waiting there in the morning as he expected, but on the whole the arrangement has proved satisfactory.

"However," our visitor continued after a pause, "–and this will bring me to the point of the matter – I have reason to know that my cousin is an irascible man, and should he feel that I have fallen significantly below some standard of conduct that he keeps in his head, along with all his engineering standards, I might find myself obliged to seek other employment." Elder paused again and scratched his head. "Have I explained myself clearly, gentlemen?"

"I believe we understand the situation," responded Holmes. "What is it that has occurred, to cause you to fear your cousin's disapproval?"

"I'm not sure that 'disapproval' quite does the matter justice," returned Elder in a wry tone. "'Unappeasable wrath' might, perhaps, be nearer the mark. Anyhow, I'll tell you what's happened and see if you can offer any suggestions.

"The construction of the Volga bridge is a very big job, as you will imagine, and has been going on for a couple of years. Although Sir George has had to hop over to Russia every now and then, he has, for the most part, been content to leave the matter in the hands of subordinates. However, the completion was planned for this summer, so it was necessary for him to be there to supervise the final stages, to officially hand the bridge over to the authorities, and to collect the payment for the job. Just before he left, he took me aside. 'Michael,' said he to me in his gravest tone; 'I shall, as you know, be away from England for several months, and I am looking to you to uphold the good name of the firm in my absence.'

"'Yes, sir; of course,' I returned promptly, wondering why he should have selected me to receive his thoughts on the firm's good name, when there are many in his employ who are far senior to me, and, I dare say, much more important to the business.

"'I am addressing these remarks to you,' he continued, as if reading my mind, 'because you, Michael, are the only man here that bears the name of Elder, and that is a not insignificant matter.'

"'No, sir,' I responded, wondering where the conversation was leading.

"'I do not, as you know, have a son of my own, Michael. That being so, I have come to look upon you in that capacity. Although we have had our little disagreements, I entertain hopes – keen hopes, I might say – that you will one day make your own mark in the world of engineering, and perhaps succeed me as head of this firm. I have recently requested a report on your progress from Mr. Troughton, and he informs me that your work has been satisfactory. This encourages me to hope that my confidence in you will not be disappointed. Do I make myself clear?'

"'Certainly, sir,' said I, in as reassuring a tone as I could muster. But I don't mind admitting I felt a little oppressed by my cousin's weighty manner. It seemed to bear a remarkable family resemblance to that of my father. It is no uncommon thing for a father to have two sons; it is somewhat less common, I should imagine, for a son to have two fathers, and the responsibility of it weighs a bit heavy, I can tell you. I was pleased, anyway, that old Troughton had given me an acceptable report, even if it was not exactly glowing in its praise. He's the senior draughtsman at Elder and Kemp, and a grim, humourless fellow if ever there was one. He always gives me the impression of looking down upon me from a great height, which is no doubt how he sees the relations between us.

"Anyhow, things have been fairly quiet over the last couple of months, so the good name of the firm has been in no danger. Sir George very thoughtfully instructed his coachman to call for me every morning and evening as usual, so I've been on time every day, and given no cause for complaint. Recently, however – just this week – a very strange thing has occurred. I don't know how to explain it, and I am anxious in case I have inadvertently done something wrong."

"The details, please!"

"Two days ago, that is, on the thirtieth, Mr. Wade, the company secretary, called me into his private office. He had received a letter that morning, he informed me, from a Señor Fernando Rodriguez, a Chilean gentleman resident in London, who proposed to call that afternoon at three-thirty. He wished, he said, to consult Mr. Elder upon a civil engineering project in South America, which he described as of the very first importance.

"'I expect by "Mr. Elder" he means Sir George,' I remarked.

"'No doubt that is so,' returned Mr. Wade; 'but he makes it clear that his business is so important he will speak to no one but 'Mr. Elder.' He is evidently one of those people who sets great value upon seeing the principal. As Sir George is absent, it might be best if you stood in for him, Elder. You at least bear the same name, and that may suffice to satisfy Señor Rodriguez. You will probably only need to take preliminary details of the matter. Sir George can deal with it in greater depth upon his return. Of course, this Señor Rodriguez may be a puffed-up, self-important fool, and his business of no interest to us. On the other hand, however, the project he mentions may be every bit as important as he implies, and, if so, we should not wish to lose what might prove a lucrative commission, simply because Sir George is not here. Do you think you could cope with the matter?'

"'Certainly,' I responded; 'so long as the man speaks English.'

"'That should be no problem,' said Mr. Wade. 'His letter is written in perfect English.'

"I must say I felt thrilled and honoured to be in charge of this business. I had spoken to clients of ours before – and some most important ones, too – but only ever in the company of my cousin, Sir George. I had never before conducted such an interview on my own. Nevertheless, I told myself, of those that were there that day, I was undoubtedly the best qualified to deal with the matter. Old Mr. Wade is red-hot on legal issues and the like, but knows as much about bridge abutments as I know about solicitors' deed-boxes. It is the same with Mr. Goreham, the chief accountant: he is, I am told, a veritable wizard with figures, but knows practically nothing of engineering. Only Mr. Troughton, the senior draughtsman, is my superior in engineering knowledge, and he is a man of such gloomy aspect and manner that his involvement with any prospective client would be highly likely to lose us the business altogether. When I returned from Mr. Wade's office, Mr. Troughton asked me what was afoot, and as I described the matter to him, in as careless a manner as I could muster, I confess that I had difficulty keeping the excitement from my voice. I seemed to detect in his eyes a look of annoyance that I had been given charge of the matter, and I don't mind admitting that I was not entirely displeased to see him discomfited for once.

"'If you get into difficulties with the client,' said he, 'or feel that you are getting out of your depth, you can always ask me to join the discussion.'

"'Thank you, Mr. Troughton, I shall remember it,' I returned, in a tone which I hoped conveyed that I had no intention whatever of taking up his offer.

"At half past three, I was informed that Señor Rodriguez had arrived and had been shown into the conference-room, on the top floor. We generally see important clients there, for the room has a large table in it, which is useful for spreading out maps and plans. I hurried upstairs to meet him, and found him already seated at the table, sorting through a sheaf of papers that he had taken from a large leather valise. He rose to his feet as I entered, and I saw that he was a short, stocky man, with a very swarthy complexion, and a large dark moustache. He was elegantly clad in a light-grey suit, and upon the table lay a low-crowned, broad-brimmed hat of the same hue.

"'Señor Rodriguez?' said I, extending my hand.

"He shook my hand, but there was an expression of surprise upon his features.

"'You are somewhat younger than I had expected, Mr. Elder,' said he, in a very strong foreign accent.

"'Our principal, Sir George Elder, is unfortunately abroad at present,' said I. 'I am Michael Elder. I have been deputed to act for him in his absence.'

"Señor Rodriguez's eyes narrowed under his bushy eyebrows.

"'You are a member of the Elder family?' said he in a suspicious tone.

"'Certainly.'

"'A close member?'

"'I am Sir George Elder's cousin, his only relation in the firm, and have his full confidence.'

"For a moment he hesitated, then he nodded his head. 'Very well,' said he. 'You must excuse my caution, Mr. Elder, but the matter is an extremely confidential one, and I have found it wise to deal only with the heads of business. I represent the very highest interests in my country, and although my presence in London has not been generally advertised, we suspect that our enemies may have got wind of it, nevertheless. There are those who would stop at nothing to thwart our plans. Peru, for one, has spies everywhere. Do you understand?'

"'I believe so. You need have no fear as to my discretion, Señor Rodriguez.'

"Again he nodded his head. 'You are no doubt aware that the state of Chile has in recent years extended its territory to the north?'

"'I am not fully conversant with the details of the situation there,' I admitted.

"'No matter,' said he with a little smile. 'Why should you be? What is Antofagasta to you, eh? Or you to Antofagasta?'

"'Quite so.'

"'Suffice it to say, Mr. Elder, that it is desired to connect these newly occupied northern territories with the rest of the country, by a continuous line of rail. The terrain through which such a railway must pass is, in places, very severe, and will require considerable engineering works, including at least two very substantial bridges near Antofagasta. Do I make myself clear?'

"'Perfectly so.'

"There had been some slight noise behind me as Señor Rodriguez had been speaking. Not wishing to appear rude, I had not turned my head away from him, but he seemed to sense my distraction.

"'I take it you have no objection to my wife's being present?' said he.

"I turned now, and saw to my very great surprise that a lady was seated, in perfect stillness and silence, on a chair by the wall behind me. The chair was immediately behind the door, and as I had entered, and greeted Señor Rodriguez, I had closed the door behind me without looking, which is why I had not observed her. Although she was seated, I had the impression that she was somewhat taller than her husband. She was of a slim figure, dressed all in black, with a black bonnet upon her head, and a heavy veil covering her face. Señor Rodriguez explained to me that his wife was of a very nervous disposition. She did not speak English, and was unfamiliar with London, as a consequence of which she suffered great anxiety if ever he left her alone for any length of time. I assured him that his wife's presence occasioned no difficulty, and our interview proceeded. He explained to me at the outset that he had no technical knowledge of engineering matters, and would be guided by my opinions on the various difficulties likely to be encountered in the construction of the proposed railway line. This lessened the anxiety I had been feeling lest the limitations of my own technical knowledge became too evident to our client, and the consultation proceeded without difficulty for some time.

"All the while we were in discussion, I was conscious of the dark, silent figure of Señora Rodriguez behind my back. She never spoke, but occasionally coughed, or shuffled her feet on the floor. After a time, however, there came a strange, low moaning noise from behind me. I looked round in surprise. Señor Rodriguez stood up and went across to his wife. Then, leaning down close to her, he spoke softly in her ear. She, in return, whispered something back to him. So soft was her voice that no words were audible. Only the sibilance of her whisper carried to my ears.

"'My wife has abnormally sensitive faculties,' said Señor Rodriguez to me, coming to the table and leaning over in a confidential manner. 'In many ways, this is a rare gift; but sometimes – alas! – it is a curse. She is suffering at present from a very bad headache, Mr. Elder, a condition to which she is, regrettably, somewhat prone, and our conversation is, I fear, making her condition worse. When she has such attacks, the only effective cure is complete silence. Is there another room in which she could sit while we talk?'

"'Certainly,' said I. I should explain that on the top floor of the building are two large rooms, side by side, the conference-room, in which we had been sitting, and the boardroom, between which there is an interconnecting door. The boardroom was not in use at the time, so I opened the door and gestured to Señora Rodriguez, but she did not move. 'Your wife may sit undisturbed in here,' I suggested to her husband, 'if she does not object to the solitude.'

"'On the contrary,' said he, 'the solitude will be to her as balm to a wound. She will know that we are close at hand, and will not be anxious.' He took his wife's arm, and escorted her into the other room. Then he closed the door and rejoined me at the table, and we resumed the consultation.

"Barely five more minutes had passed, however, before our conversation was again interrupted. Out of the corner of my eye, I saw the door from the boardroom open slowly and quietly. I turned and saw Señora Rodriguez, standing perfectly still in the doorway, her veiled face turned in our direction. Señor Rodriguez stood up and conversed very softly with her again for a few moments.

"'Señora Rodriguez craves pardon for troubling you, but finds the air in the other room somewhat dank and still,' said he to me. 'Would it be possible for the window to be opened a little?'

"'Certainly,' said I. This interruption wasted a further five minutes, for the windows at Elder's have locking metal gates upon the inside, composed of vertical iron rods, and the casement windows cannot themselves be opened until the metal gates are open. I was thus obliged to hunt about for the key for a time, but eventually the iron gates and the window were open to the lady's satisfaction, and Señor Rodriguez and I resumed our discussion.

"It was becoming increasingly clear to me that his proposals were of a very ambitious nature indeed. If our firm could secure but a quarter of the engineering work involved it would still be a very good piece of business for us. One feature of the route in particular appeared to concern Señor Rodriguez above the rest, where the railway line was to cross a broad, canyon-like river-valley, a few miles south of Antofagasta. The river was practically dry for much of the year, he explained to me, but could become a raging torrent after heavy rainfall, or when the snows upon the mountains melted in the spring. A particular difficulty for any bridge constructed across this valley was that although one bank of the river was composed of very hard and stable rock, the other was chiefly composed of unstable shales, which could not support the weight of a bridge pier with any safety, and which were, in any case, at constant risk of landslip. By chance, our firm has been recently drawing up plans for a bridge across the Muchty Firth in the West Highlands of Scotland, the design of which has had to overcome a very similar problem. When I mentioned this to Señor Rodriguez, he showed great interest, and asked if he might see the plans. The matter is a highly confidential one, as we are in competition with several other firms for the contract, including our keen rivals, Gibbs and Wakefield of Birmingham, but I could see no objection to showing the plans to Señor Rodriguez. I hurried downstairs to the drawing-office, and explained the matter to Mr. Troughton. He was somewhat reluctant to release the papers at first, but I at length persuaded him.

"When I returned to the conference-room, Señor Rodriguez was pacing about the floor in an impatient manner, and as I spread out the papers on the conference-table he pounced upon them eagerly. Scarcely had I been able to point out to him the chief topographical features of the Muchty Firth, however, when we were interrupted yet again. The door from the boardroom opened slowly once more, and once again Señora Rodriguez stood there in silent entreaty. Her husband turned, and the professional enthusiasm quite vanished from his features and was replaced instead by a soft, husbandly tenderness. I could only marvel at the respect and solicitude shown by this man towards his wife. What might perhaps in another man have produced irritation, evoked in Señor Rodriguez only tender concern. Again he spoke to her in low tones, again she answered him in a soft sibilant whisper. Then he turned to me once more.

"'My wife bitterly regrets the inconvenience she is causing you,' said he, 'but wonders if it would be possible for her to have a glass of water. She unfortunately suffers from dryness of the mouth. Many medical men have investigated the case and made suggestions, but all – alas! – have been unavailing.'

"'Kindly inform Señora Rodriguez that she occasions no inconvenience whatever,' I returned as I hurried off to fetch the water, wondering to myself if there were any complaint that the lady did *not* suffer from.

"When I returned, Señor Rodriguez was poring over the maps and plans of the Muchty Firth bridge, making very copious notes.

"'This is very interesting, Mr. Elder,' said he, when he had passed the glass of water to his wife.

"'Of course,' I observed, as I looked over the notes he had made, 'some of the figures you have noted down are specific to the Muchty Firth bridge. The calculations for the Antofagasta bridge might be quite different.'

"'I appreciate that fact,' returned he, 'but these figures will enable me to understand more fully the mechanical principles involved, which will be the same for both bridges.'

"Thus we discussed the matter further, for another twenty minutes or so. Then Señor Rodriguez declared himself satisfied, and said that he would report back favourably to his superiors, and write to us again when the matter had been thoroughly discussed by them. With that he prepared to take his leave.

"I glanced at the clock. The afternoon had flown by, and it was almost time for us all to be leaving. I knew that Sir George's carriage would be waiting for me downstairs, so I offered to take Señor Rodriguez and his wife to wherever they were going.

"'We are staying in Eaton Square at present,' said he. 'It is kind of you to offer, Mr. Elder, but quite unnecessary. We can easily take a cab.'

"'Not at all,' I insisted. 'I pass close by Eaton Square on my way home. It will be no trouble at all to take you there.'

"It was certainly an odd little journey. Señor Rodriguez was very animated, crying out with a visitor's delight at the Houses of Parliament, Westminster Abbey and other notable buildings that we passed on our way. His strange, veiled wife, meanwhile, sat in perfect silence the whole way, scarcely moving her head an inch, and giving no indication that she was conscious of anything beyond the confines of the carriage.

"Presently we reached Eaton Square, and our driver drew the carriage to a halt at the address Señor Rodriguez had given him, a large house near the corner of Belgrave Place. Señor Rodriguez and I shook hands warmly as he and his wife alighted, and as the carriage drew away he waved to me from the doorstep of the house, his wife standing silently beside him. I sat back in my seat with some satisfaction, then, I don't mind admitting, for I was confident that I had laid the groundwork for a very good piece of business for our firm. I had, I felt, dealt in a professional and assured manner with all the questions Señor Rodriguez had put to me, and had persuaded him, I felt certain, of the unrivalled skill and experience which Elder and Kemp could bring to the various problems the proposed railway was likely to encounter. Already, I began to imagine the discussion I would have with Sir George Elder on the matter, and to imagine, too, his beaming face and words of praise for me.

"We were passing along the side of Belgrave Square, which is very little distance from Eaton Square, and I was reflecting in this fashion, when I noticed one of Señor Rodriguez's gloves on the floor of the carriage. It was yellow, and made of soft kid leather. I picked it up. It was undoubtedly his. He must have dropped it when alighting, probably when picking up his valise, which had stood on the floor beside his seat. I called to the coachman, and instructed him to return to Eaton Square.

"'I shall only be a moment,' I called to him as I sprang from the carriage, ran up the front doorsteps, and pulled at the bell. A moment later the door was opened by the imposing figure of a large, bald-headed butler.

"'Yes, sir?' said he, looking somewhat down his nose at me.

"I held up the yellow glove. 'Señor Rodriguez dropped this in my carriage,' I explained.

"'Did he, sir? How very unfortunate!'

"His tone puzzled me. 'Well, it's not so unfortunate now,' said I, 'as I have found it.'

"'Quite so, sir,' said he. 'I am sure that Señor Rodriguez will be most relieved.'

"'Right-ho, then,' said I, proffering the glove; but he made no move to take it from me. 'Are you not going to take it?' I asked in surprise.

"'No, sir.'

"'Why ever not?' I queried. 'Señor Rodriguez will be very glad to have it back.'

"'Then may I suggest that you give it to him, sir?'

"'Why can you not give it to him, may I ask?'

"'Because, sir, I am not acquainted with the gentleman to whom you refer.'

"'But he lives here,' I protested.

"'I can assure you, sir, that he does not.'

"I stepped back to verify that I had come to the right house. Yes, there could be no doubting it; this was the door at which I had last seen Señor Rodriguez and his wife. Then it occurred to me that their presence here might be a closely guarded secret, and that the butler might be on his guard for enemy agents trying by a ruse to learn their whereabouts. I leaned closer to him and lowered my voice.

"'I am not a Peruvian spy, you know,' said I.

"'I never supposed for one moment that you were, sir,' returned he.

"'Señor Rodriguez has been consulting me in confidence about the construction of a railway line,' I explained.

"'Has he indeed, sir? How very interesting for you!'

"It was clear that I was not going to get anywhere by such an approach. I offered the glove once more, the butler again declined it, and as a last attempt I tried a different tack.

"'Although you say that you don't know Señor Rodriguez,' said I, 'he should, nevertheless, be informed that his glove is in the possession of Michael Elder. He will recognize the name.'

"'I am sure he will, sir. Should I ever be introduced to the gentleman in question, the news that you have his glove will be the first information upon my lips.'

"With that, I gave it up. My day's work, which I had shortly before deemed such a triumphant success, seemed tarnished somewhat by this surprising and unsatisfactory codicil. I said nothing about it to anyone, and hoped that the next day would bring an explanation of some kind. Perhaps my conjecture had been correct, and the household in Eaton Square had been warned of possible enemy agents and instructed to deny all knowledge of Rodriguez. Perhaps I had, after all, approached the wrong house upon my return with the glove; or, more likely, I thought, perhaps Señor Rodriguez himself, being unfamiliar with his surroundings, had inadvertently mounted the wrong front steps as I left him, and, realising his mistake, had repaired to the correct house whilst I was driving up through Belgravia. At any event, I hoped to hear something from him the next day. In this hope, however, I was disappointed.

"It was then that I recalled the great care with which my visitor had copied down the figures from the plan of the Muchty Firth bridge, figures which related to our own unique solution to the engineering problems that the bridge presented. A cold, clammy hand seemed all at once to grip my vitals, as I realised that I had shown these highly confidential calculations to a man whom I had never met before, and of whose antecedents I really knew nothing. Gone from my imagination in a flash was the beaming figure of Sir George Elder, showering me with praise; replaced now by a stern and vindictive Sir George Elder, kicking me out into the street.

"I asked Mr. Wade if I might see Señor Rodriguez's letter. The address at the top of the sheet was indeed that of the house at which I had called the day before. But the address was only hand-written, not printed on the sheet, and I thought it possible that he had made a mistake as to the house number. In a state of some anxiety, I left work early, and took myself over to Eaton Square once more. There I knocked at every door, and at each asked the same three questions: Did Señor Rodriguez reside there? If he did not, did they know what his address might be? If they did not, had they observed anyone in the area answering to his description? I lost count of the number of doors I called at, and the answers I received, but it was of no consequence, for all the answers were 'no.' I then called in at Scotland Yard, to enquire if anything was known there of Señor Rodriguez. It had occurred to me that as a foreigner resident in London, he might perhaps be known to the authorities."

"Did you make any progress?" asked Holmes.

Michael Elder shook his head. "No. They had never heard of him. I saw a detective inspector named Lestrade, but I wasn't able to give him such a detailed account of the matter as I have given to you, as he was a little impatient for me to finish, and kept interrupting me."

"What was his response?"

"He said that he would make a note of it all, and if anything turned up he would let me know."

Holmes laughed. "I regret to have to disabuse you of any hopes in that regard, Mr. Elder," said he, "but the response you received is something of a stereotype, I am afraid. Translated into everyday English, it means Lestrade will put the paper containing your details into a deep drawer, and forget all about it!"

"So I suspected. He informed me that he was extremely busy, and did not have the time to pursue every trivial matter that was presented to him."

"They are certainly very busy at Scotland Yard; although I sometimes feel they do themselves no service by failing so signally to distinguish the important from the unimportant. Did Inspector Lestrade have any suggestion to make?"

"None whatever. Indeed, he gave me the distinct impression that he thought I was possibly unhinged, and had made the whole thing up myself."

Holmes chuckled. "Do not be discouraged by that response, Mr. Elder! It is the natural tendency of mediocre minds to dismiss as untrue that which they do not understand. Do you have the glove with you?"

"Here it is," responded Elder, pulling a folded glove from his pocket. It was of a dull egg-yolk colour, made of soft, expensive-looking leather, with a little pearl button at the cuff.

"Broad fitting," remarked Holmes as he tried the glove on his hand. "Hum! There is a label on the inside. Let us see: 'Thomas Grove and Son, Gentlemen's Outfitters of Colchester.' Hum! Did Inspector Lestrade see this glove?"

Elder shook his head. "He expressed no interest in it, so I did not show it to him."

"I see," said Holmes. Then, without a further word, he leaned back in his chair, his fingertips pressed together like a church steeple, and his eyes closed. A look of surprise passed over our visitor's features, and he made as if to speak; but I put my finger to my lips, and he remained silent, although his eyebrow was raised in an expression of curiosity at what he no doubt considered my friend's eccentric manner.

For five minutes we remained in complete silence, then Holmes opened his eyes, and reached for his pipe.

"Very well," said he, striking a match, and putting it to his pipe. "You mentioned earlier that Señor Rodriguez had a swarthy complexion and a large moustache. Could you now picture that gentleman once more, and give me a slightly fuller description?"

"Certainly," responded Elder. "He was a touch below medium height," he continued after a moment; "but was powerfully built, with a very broad chest, and large, strong-looking hands. There was something powerful about his features, too, and I seemed to read in them great strength of purpose. His eyes were dark and piercing, he had a sharp, hooked nose, somewhat like a bird of prey, and beneath his left eye was a large, curving scar."

"Thank you," said Holmes in a tone of contemplation. "That information should prove very useful."

"What do you think about it all?" enquired Elder after a moment.

"I think," returned Holmes, "that I should very much like to see the premises of Elder and Kemp for myself. Would that be possible?"

"By all means. We can go along there now, if you wish."

Holmes shook his head. "I should prefer to make my examination when there is no one else there," said he. "I do not wish to be disturbed, nor do I wish to excite any curiosity. Could that be arranged?"

"Certainly. I have a key, and can conduct you round the premises myself."

"That would be ideal. Drop by later, then, when you are certain that everyone at Elder and Kemp has gone home for the day, and we can go along there together. Until then, not a word of this to anyone!"

At a little after six o'clock, we were in a cab with Michael Elder, rattling through the dense traffic towards Southwark. It was a pleasant evening, and as we crossed the river, the low sun emerged from behind a bank of clouds and sparkled like diamonds upon the rippled surface of the water.

"As you will see when we reach Elder and Kemp's," said our companion, "the building has four floors. On the ground floor and the first floor above that are the general offices for the clerks and draughtsmen. On the next floor up are the offices of most of the senior men, including Mr. Wade and Mr. Goreham, and also the main store-rooms. On the top floor is Sir George Elder's private chamber, and that which old Mr. Kemp occupied before his retirement. There are also a couple of smaller, empty rooms, but most of the floor is taken up by the two large rooms I mentioned to you earlier, the conference-room and the boardroom. But you will be able to see it for yourselves in a moment, for we are almost there."

Our cab had turned off the main road into a quieter and narrower street, although even here the pavements were busy with crowds of men hurrying along to the railway station. It was a shadowed, somewhat gloomy street, lined on both sides by tall, flat-fronted buildings. Behind those on our left, as I could see through occasional gaps between them, stood a tall, grimy-looking railway viaduct. A train was passing, sending up an enormous plume of smoke, which drifted lazily over the roofs of the buildings in front. Elder called to the cabbie, and we drew up before one of these gaunt brick buildings.

Our young companion unlocked the door and led us inside and up the narrow, oilcloth-covered staircase, until we reached the top floor. There, a corridor stretched the width of the building, on the right of which were four doors, leading to chambers overlooking the street outside. On the left side, there were just two doorways, each with a pair of double doors. Our guide threw open the first of these, and we followed him into a large room. In the far wall was a broad window, covered with a metal grille, through which the parapet at the top of the viaduct was visible. In the centre of the room was a very large rectangular table, with a dozen or more chairs about it, and against the right-hand wall stood a large mahogany bureau.

"This is the conference-room," said Elder.

"And this, I take it, is where Señora Rodriguez was sitting the other day, when you entered," said Holmes, indicating a chair that stood against the wall behind the open door. "Hum! This door, presumably, leads to the boardroom," he continued, indicating a door at the near end of the right-hand wall. "Let us take a look in there."

The boardroom was an almost exact duplicate of the conference-room. In the centre stood a large oval table, somewhat more ornate and highly polished than that in the conference-room, and about it stood a dozen chairs. The window at the far end was, like that in the conference-room, protected on the inside by a grille of vertical iron bars. Against the side-wall opposite the door by which we had entered was a large, dark green safe, which stood about five feet high and four feet wide.

"It was at this table that Señora Rodriguez was sitting when her husband passed her the glass of water, I take it," said Holmes to Elder.

"That is correct. At this near end."

"And this is the window she wished you to open? Where is the key now?"

"I will get it for you," said Elder. "It is in a box in the bureau in the other room."

We followed him back into the conference-room, where he pulled open the deep bottom drawer of the bureau. From the back of this he took out a wooden cigar-box which he opened on the table. Inside was a miscellaneous assortment of keys, pens and pencils.

"Does the same key open the windows in both these chambers?" asked Holmes.

Elder shook his head. "Every window in the building has a different key." He selected a key from the box, and held it out on the palm of his hand. Attached to it was a small piece of tape, on which the word "boardroom" was written in indelible pencil.

Holmes took the key and examined it closely. "Did you bring the key back here when you had opened the window, or leave it in the lock?" he asked.

"The latter; for I knew that I should shortly have to close up the grille again."

"Has the key been used since then?"

"I do not believe so."

Holmes nodded, then he held the key to his nose and sniffed, like a bloodhound seeking a scent. In an instant, I saw a spark of excitement light up his eye. From his pocket he took a powerful lens, with the aid of which he examined the key very carefully. At length, evidently satisfied, he led us back into the boardroom, where he unlocked the grille which covered the window, then pulled both it and the window open.

"It is a long way down from here," said he, as we leaned out of the window.

"It is a fearsome drop," I concurred, gazing down into the narrow lane which ran behind the building. Although the sun had not yet set – indeed, even as I leaned from the window, its last, yellowed rays were gilding the pinnacles of a church in the distance – the narrow alley below, hemmed in so tightly between the building and the railway viaduct, was already in deep shade. The vertiginous appearance of this awesome, man-made chasm was made the greater by its very narrowness, for the parapet of the railway viaduct was barely a dozen feet from the window, and the characteristic railway smells of soot, tar and oil came distinctly to my nostrils.

"It is to be wondered what Señora Rodriguez thought of the fresh air she had sought, when you had opened this window for her!" remarked Holmes with a chuckle.

At that moment, with a thunderous roar and the sharp hiss of steam, a train passed along the viaduct at high speed, belching great clouds of thick, dark smoke about it. Quickly, we closed the windows.

"Do you not find the frequent passage of trains disturbing to your work?" I asked Elder, as he closed and locked the window-grille.

He shook his head. "You become accustomed to it," said he. "Besides, it is only on the top floor of the building that the noise is as loud as this. On the lower floors, it is scarcely audible. The engineers involved in constructing this railway line through such a crowded area faced immense difficulties, as you will imagine, which is why it is, unfortunately, so close to so many buildings. Per yard, as you are perhaps aware, it is the most expensive length of line ever built, a distinction which is unlikely to be challenged in the foreseeable future. But, with regard to the noise, the design of the viaduct – its height, the shape and size of the parapets, and so on – ensures that most of the noise rises away from the buildings. If noise were visible, like that smoke you see swirling about in the breeze, you would observe it rising upwards in the shape of an inverted cone. Civil engineering has brought knowledge of such matters to a very high degree!"

"Fascinating though it is to hear an expert speak on his own subject," remarked Holmes, "we must return from engineering to the matter in hand. Is there generally much of value kept in this safe?"

"There are some highly confidential papers, and the company's books, of course; but no great amount of cash, if that is what you mean."

"The wages of the staff?"

"The amount is calculated weekly by Mr. Jenkins, under the supervision of Mr. Goreham. It is then ordered every Thursday from the bank, the Southwark branch of the London and Home Counties, and delivered here on Friday."

"Who has a key to the safe?"

"There are four. Sir George Elder, of course, has one. Our secretary, Mr. Wade, has another; and our accountant, Mr. Goreham, a third. The fourth key is spare, and is kept in the little box from which I took the window key."

Holmes's eyebrow went up in surprise. "That does not seem the safest of repositories for such an important key," he observed.

"It is thought unlikely that anyone would come upon it by chance," responded Elder; "or would recognize it for what it was if he did so. It is disguised. If we return to the other room, I will show you."

We followed our companion back into the conference-room, where the wooden cigar-box lay open upon the table. He replaced the window-key in it, and took out another, which he held out for us to see. On the little slip of tape attached to the key I read the words "map cupboard".

"This is, despite its label, the key to the safe," said Elder.

Holmes chuckled. "And the real key to the map-cupboard?"

"There isn't one. The map-cupboard does not have a lock."

"How charmingly eccentric!" exclaimed Holmes in delight, as he took the key in his hand. "How refreshingly *outré!* Henceforth, I shall certainly regard engineers in a new light! Who is aware of this little subterfuge?"

"All the senior men in the company," returned Elder: "Sir George, Mr. Wade, Mr. Goreham, Mr. Troughton and myself."

"And is the key very often used?"

Elder shook his head. "Of course, Mr. Wade and Mr. Goreham have frequent occasion to open the safe in the course of their duties, but as they both have a key of their own, they would not need to use this one."

"I see," said Holmes. He raised the key to his nose, as he had done with the window-key, and sniffed carefully at it, a frown of concentration upon his face. Then he took out his lens once more and examined the key closely for several minutes. Finally, he replaced the key in the box, and turned once more to Elder.

"You stated that during Sir George's present visit to Russia he is to formally hand over the bridge to the authorities, and receive final payment for the work."

"That is correct."

"How is the payment to be made?"

"In gold."

"Through the London branch of the St Petersburg Bank?"

"No, in bullion and specie. This arrangement is not so unusual as people might imagine, for these foreign contracts. Sir

George is travelling with the gold from St Petersburg to London."

Holmes clapped his hand to his head. "And his ship docks on Saturday!" he cried. "The case is complete! I now know everything."

"Everything?" cried Elder in surprise.

"Well, I know the who, the why, the where, the when and the how. If there are any aspects of the matter not comprehended under those headings, my knowledge may not be complete."

"What will you do?" asked Elder in a tone of bewilderment.

"I shall go to see Inspector Lestrade at once, and explain to him why he should have paid somewhat more attention to your account. I confidently predict that when he hears what I have to tell him, the piece of paper on which he wrote your details will come back out of the deep drawer I mentioned earlier. I shall communicate with you later in the week, Mr. Elder. Until then, you must say nothing of this matter to anyone. Do you understand?"

"Certainly."

For a moment, Holmes regarded his young client, a look of doubt upon his face.

"Your story of Señor Rodriguez, his strange, silent wife, the Antofagasta railway, the yellow glove and all the rest of it, is certainly an interesting one," said Holmes at length. "You might feel tempted to speak of it to someone."

"Yes."

"But you must not."

"No."

"Believe me when I tell you, Mr. Elder, that not merely the security and prosperity of this company, but the entire future course of your own life may depend upon your adhering to this instruction. If anyone should ask you about Señor Rodriguez or the proposed railway in South America, speak freely and enthusiastically about it, just as you might have done on the day of his visit to you. But do not, under any circumstances whatever, mention the incident of the glove, nor your visit to me."

"I understand," responded Elder, clearly impressed by the gravity of Holmes's manner.

We drove at once then to Scotland Yard, but my friend was destined to be disappointed that evening, for Lestrade was not on duty. With a sigh of frustration, he made an appointment to see the policeman in the morning, and we returned to our chambers in Baker Street. There, Holmes sat smoking in silence for almost two hours, impatiently brushing aside all the questions I put to him, before retiring early to his bed.

In the morning my friend had taken his breakfast and gone out before I was up, and I did not see him all day. He returned late in the evening, in a state of extreme fatigue. He had evidently spoken to the landlady before coming upstairs, for she appeared a minute or two later with a large glass of milk and a plate of gingerbread. These he consumed in silence, then, begging forgiveness for what he termed his uncivil manner, he retired once more to his bed.

The next day he had again risen and left the house before I was awake, and I was left once more to conjecture as to the direction in which his enquiries were taking him. About four o'clock, however, I had fallen into a brown study with an open book in my hand when I was roused from my reverie by the sound of footsteps upon the stair. I assumed that it was Holmes, and I was considering what questions I would put to him, when all at once the sitting-room door was flung open, and a dirty-looking ruffian, with a greasy, straggling beard, burst into the room without knocking. Above his eyebrow was an ugly gash, encrusted with blood.

"Halloa!" I cried, springing to my feet. "How you gained access to this house I do not know; but unless you have an adequate explanation, you will certainly leave it as swiftly as you entered!"

"My dear fellow!" came a well-known voice. "I must beg a thousand pardons for startling you in this way! I have been in these disreputable-looking garments for so long that I had quite forgotten I had them on, and that my friends would not recognize me!"

"Holmes!" I cried. "Whatever is the purpose of assuming such an appearance?"

"You see before you, Watson, Mr. Jervis Jones, newly arrived in London from Cardiff, seeking work," returned my friend, affecting a soft Welsh accent. "I have been in search of information, and judged that I should be more likely to acquire it in this guise, rather than as myself."

"You have acquired a wound, anyhow!"

He put his hand up to his forehead, and gingerly touched the cut there. "It bled rather freely at first," said he; "but it is not very deep, and probably appears worse to your professionally honed concern than it really is. I was in a pub down Limehouse way when a drunken buffoon took a dislike to me. Unfortunately, considering the guise I had adopted, he declared in unequivocal terms his abiding dislike of the Welsh, and then, suiting the action to the word, as it were, hit me over the head with a beer-bottle. I responded somewhat more classically – if I may be allowed to be judge in my own cause – with a left uppercut to the jaw, and the upshot was that we were both ejected from the premises!"

"You never cease to amaze me!" I cried with a chuckle. "I am glad, at least, that you have returned relatively unharmed, Holmes! Were you able to acquire any of the information you sought?"

"I picked up the scent of a couple of rumours, but nothing of great value. To be frank, I had had only faint hopes of success when first I set out, so I am not especially disappointed." He glanced at the clock. "If you would be so good as to order us some tea, Watson, I shall give you a full account of the Elder case, and of how it came to take me down to Limehouse, once I have completed some very vigorous ablutions! You might also put a match to that fire, for there is a distinct chill in the air this afternoon, and I fear it will be a cold evening." In the doorway he paused. "The nights are drawing in, Watson. Summer is almost over, and giving way to the season of mist and fog. Suitable weather for a little adventure, would you not say? The game is afoot, my friend, and if you are up to the rigours of the chase, I think I can promise you an adventure tomorrow night which you will not quickly forget!"

An hour later, Sherlock Holmes and I were seated on either side of a blazing fire, drinking tea and smoking our pipes. Outside, the daylight was fading into the grey twilight of early evening. Inside, with his old mouse-coloured dressing-gown wrapped about him, my friend explained to me his analysis of the strange events that his young client had described to us so vividly earlier in the week.

"To begin with," said Holmes, "it was difficult to judge whether Señor Fernando Rodriguez was an honest gentleman, who spoke nothing but the truth, or a fraud, whose purpose in calling upon our client earlier in the week was not as he represented it."

"The latter, surely!" I cried, laughing; but my friend held up his hand.

"Do not be too quick to jump to conclusions." said he. "It cannot be denied that the events of the other day had a suspicious quality to them, but I have known men condemned before on account of the suspicious manner of their actions, who were in reality perfectly innocent. It was just possible, I considered, that, despite the odd circumstances, Señor Rodriguez was a sincere and genuine man, who happened to have an unusual wife and a powerful desire to conceal his true address from everyone, even from the man with whom he was proposing to do business. A man in very great fear for his safety – or that of his wife – might well have acted as Señor Rodriguez did."

"I suppose it is possible," I concurred, but without much conviction.

"However, the glove he left behind him rather settled the matter."

"Why so?"

"Because it had been purchased from a shop in Colchester. It seems highly unlikely, to say the least, that a South American gentleman, recently arrived in this country, would travel fifty miles into the Essex countryside to purchase gloves. Nor does it seem likely that a man described by Elder as elegantly dressed, and giving all the appearance of a man of means, would have purchased the gloves second-hand in London. It seems probable, therefore, that Rodriguez was being less than fully honest about his antecedents. But if he were lying to that extent, then he might also be lying about anything else, including the name he had given and his purpose in calling at Elder and Kemp. Now, it is always a sound rule when dealing with liars to ignore completely what they say, and to concentrate instead upon what they do. If we therefore leave aside the discussion of South American railways which took place the other day, what then remains?"

"Señor Rodriguez contrived to get sight of the confidential plans for the Scottish bridge that Elder mentioned to us."

"That is true; and yet it is difficult to believe that that was the real purpose of the charade that was played out earlier in the week. As an explanation it fails to account for the presence of the wife, and her unusual behaviour. You must remember that if the man calling himself Rodriguez had been speaking the truth, then it might just have been the case that he had an odd, nervous wife; but if he were lying, then the whole explanation given for her presence with him at Elder's falls to the ground, and we must presume that, so far from her presence there being an incidental and unimportant matter, the consequence, simply, of her not wishing to be left alone, it was, rather, of central importance to their scheme. In other words, if their purpose was a dishonest one, then she must have accompanied her husband there for a specific reason. What could that reason be?"

"I cannot imagine."

"Well, then, consider the woman's actions. What, precisely, did she do?"

"She complained of a headache, and went to sit in the boardroom by herself. She then asked for a window to be opened, and later requested a glass of water."

"Precisely!"

"I do not follow you. None of these things seems very significant."

"In themselves, perhaps not; but if the purpose of this couple was a dishonest one, then we must assume an ulterior motive for all their actions. The request for a glass of water, for instance, we must suppose was a planned ruse to get Elder out of the way for a few minutes. In fact, by the time the plan was implemented, it may no longer have been necessary, as Elder had already been absent for some time, bringing the plans of the Muchty bridge, but the woman, who had been in the other room, may not have known that. Now, why would they want Elder out of the way? Clearly, so that they could examine something in his absence. What could that something be? The woman's request that the window be opened might have seemed of little significance had the window been an ordinary one. But it is unusual: it is protected by an iron grille, which must be unlocked with a key. Perhaps, then, I conjectured, it was this key that was the focus of their attention."

"I observed that you held the key to your nose when Elder showed it to you," I interjected, "although I could not imagine why."

"I wished to know if there were any lingering scent of soap upon it," returned Holmes. "For if they had wanted to make a copy of the key for some reason, the easiest way would have been to press it into a bar of soap and use the impress later as a mould to make an exact duplicate. I was gratified to discover that my surmise was correct: the key bore a faint but unmistakable odour of soap. A close examination of the key with the aid of a lens confirmed the matter, revealing as it did minute traces of soap adhering to the metal. Clearly, these people wished to gain access to the premises of Elder and Kemp at some later time. It still remained to discover what their purpose might be, but the presence in the boardroom of the company safe suggested a likely motive. When Elder showed us the spare key to the safe, which was also kept in the little wooden box, the question was settled beyond doubt, for my examination of it revealed similar traces of soap to those I had found on the window-key.

"The purpose of the charade played out by these villains was thus laid bare. They wished to provide themselves with duplicate keys so that they could re-enter the premises later, when no one was about, and open the safe. But what was it they sought there? For Elder informed us that there was not usually much of value kept in the safe. It was only when he revealed to us the details of the Russian payment that this aspect of the matter became clear. On Saturday afternoon, Sir George Elder arrives back in London with a quantity of gold. You perceive the significance of the day, no doubt?"

I considered the question for a moment. "Of course!" I cried at last. "On Saturday afternoon, all London banks will be closed, and he will not be able to deposit his gold safely until Monday morning!"

"Precisely, Watson! The gold will thus have to be stored on the firm's premises in Southwark from Saturday afternoon until Monday morning. These villains have got wind of this fact, and have concocted a charmingly complex scheme to obtain access to the premises whilst the gold is being stored there."

"But who are these people?" I asked.

"There, if I am correct," Holmes responded, "my knowledge of the criminal classes gives me an advantage. You recall Elder's description of Señor Rodriguez?"

"He described him as very swarthy, with a large dark moustache, a hooked nose and a curving scar beneath his left eye."

"If we set aside the swarthiness and the moustache, both of which could be assumed for the role being played, we are left with the hooked nose and the large, distinctive scar. Now, as it happens, I know of someone whose appearance precisely matches that description. He is, moreover, just the sort of person who might interest himself in Sir George Elder's Russian gold. Have you ever heard me speak of Albert Foulger or his gang?"

I shook my head.

"He is a highly resourceful criminal, Watson, as cunning as he is ruthless, and has the distinction of being the third most sought-after villain in the country. You do not recollect his name, but you may be familiar with his work. Do you remember the Hatton Garden diamond robbery, of three years ago?"

"Certainly. It was a daring raid, in the middle of the night. The gang got away with a small fortune in diamonds, and was never caught."

"Those, indeed, are the chief facts of the matter. Several senior policemen were assigned to the case, including our old friend, Inspector Lestrade. Their enquiries eventually led them to believe that the Foulger gang was responsible, but conclusive evidence was lacking. Albert Foulger, the head of the gang, could not be questioned, for he had disappeared without trace. There were rumours that he was somewhere on the south coast, in Southampton, or Portsmouth, or Brighton; but if he was, the police could never find him, and after a while the trail went cold. The official view, which I think is probably correct, is that the gang made such a profit from their haul of diamonds that they have since found it unnecessary to engage in their usual nefarious work.

"Now, as you have no doubt surmised, Watson, Albert Foulger is the gentleman I referred to, as having the hooked nose and scar that Mr. Elder described. The scar is a souvenir he carries of the murderous war for superiority which was fought between the Foulgers and the Maynard gang at the end of the 'seventies. This ended in complete victory for the Foulgers, and the death of the rival gang-leader, Tobit Maynard, and one of his sons. All this was known for a fact to the police, but, of course, as is the way with these things, nothing could ever be proved against anyone.

"However, to return to the present: Albert Foulger has two sons, Patrick and Jimmy, and, unless I am much mistaken, tomorrow night will see all three of them making an attempt upon Sir George Elder's gold. It is just such a prize as could tempt Albert Foulger out of retirement, and lead to the reconstituting of his gang. It also represents the best, indeed, perhaps the only opportunity for Lestrade to collar the lot of them, as I succeeded in convincing him yesterday. He has, I trust, been making his preparations today, while I have been touring the pubs of the East End, in the faint hope of picking up a little more information. It was a delicate business, despite what you might think," added my friend with a chuckle; "for it was, of course, vital that I gave no hint to the Foulgers or their associates that we were on their trail."

"I don't know about 'delicate'," I remarked, laughing; "it sounds a simply hopeless task to me! Why, there are thousands of pubs at that end of London! You could probably spend a month going round them, and not see them all!"

"I did have the advantage of knowing some of Albert Foulger's old haunts," my friend responded; "but your estimate of the task as fairly hopeless is probably correct, nevertheless. I learned little which related to the Foulgers or their plans. Still," he added with a dry chuckle, "the day was not entirely devoid of interest, and had at least the merit of novelty!"

"What of the woman?" I asked, as my thoughts returned to young Elder's tale. "Do you have any idea of her true identity?"

My companion paused, in the act of knocking his pipe out on the hearth, and burst out laughing.

"I very much fancy," said he after a moment, "that our Señora Rodriguez is in reality Jimmy Foulger."

"What!"

"He has played a similar part before, in a fraud the gang attempted down in Kent, five years ago."

"Well, I never!" I exclaimed.

"It will no doubt discomfit our young client to learn that he has been taken in by such an imposture; but he should not consider himself too great a fool, for Jimmy Foulger undoubtedly plays the part with great conviction! And now," my friend continued after a moment, "I think, if you have no objection, Watson, that I shall distract myself with a little soothing music, to drive what has been a rather fatiguing day from my mind!"

So saying, he picked up his violin, and after adjusting the strings for a few moments, began to play a series of the most languid and haunting melodies. I lay back in my chair, and closed my eyes to listen, reflecting as I did so on what a singularly assorted fellow I shared chambers with.

The following day, Holmes went out shortly after breakfast, and did not return until late in the afternoon, and then only briefly.

"You have had a successful day, I trust?" I enquired, as he bustled about the room.

"Satisfactory enough," said he in a brisk tone. "I have seen Sir George Elder and his young cousin, and also Inspector Lestrade. Everything is now in place, Watson. If you do wish to accompany me this evening," he added, "you had best make ready, for it would be safest to get there before dark. It is essential that we are in position when our quarry turns up at the water-hole, as it were. Our night's expedition should, I think, be an exhilarating one!"

My experience of camp life in India had made me a quick and ready traveller, and in a few minutes we had left the house and were hurrying up Baker Street. The streets were choked with traffic, so Holmes proposed that we travel by the Metropolitan Railway to the nearest point and proceed from there on foot. Thus it was that, some forty minutes later, we made our way down from Mansion House station to the river, and so across Southwark Bridge. From there, my companion led me into a maze of narrow, shady streets, which passed this way and that between tall, flat-fronted industrial buildings and warehouses, until we at last reached a lane which lay in the shadow of a towering railway viaduct. This we followed a little way, then Holmes turned into a narrow alley which passed through one of the arches beneath the viaduct. This brought us into another shaded lane, over which the viaduct on the one side, and the buildings on the other seemed to loom and glower as if they might meet together high above us, close off the sky, and plunge the lane into total blackness.

"Why!" I cried, as I looked about me. "This is the lane at the back of Elder and Kemp's building!"

Even as I spoke, my companion gave a sharp rat-a-tat-tat with his knuckles on an unmarked brown door. It was opened at once by a uniformed policeman, and we passed inside. A thin, sharp-nosed man in a grey overcoat came forward out of the shadows to meet us, and I recognized our old friend, Inspector Lestrade.

"Good evening, Dr. Watson," said he to me as we shook hands. "It is good to see you out on the hunt with us again!"

"I hope the night will be a successful one," said I.

"So do we all, I'm sure," returned the policeman. "I've waited a long time to get my derbies on old Foulger, I can tell you!"

"Is Sir George here?" asked Holmes.

"Yes; he is upstairs with his cousin."

"Splendid!" said Holmes. "Any further developments to report, Lestrade?"

The policeman nodded his head enthusiastically.

"There are indeed!" said he. "Acting on the information I gave them, as to the shop from which the lost glove had been purchased, my colleagues in Colchester were able to discover the address of everyone who had bought such gloves there in the last year. Enquiries in the district have now eliminated all of those purchasers save one, and that one – a man going under the name of Henshaw, who has been resident in the town about three years – is, they are certain, Albert Foulger. He is away from home at present, but there are men watching his house day and night, ready to seize him the moment he shows his face."

"Excellent!" cried Holmes. "And Troughton's house?"

"That, too, is being watched. Every move he makes is being marked down."

"Troughton?" I interrupted. "What! Mr. Troughton, the chief draughtsman of Elder and Kemp? What has he to do with these criminals?"

"Surely it was apparent," returned Holmes, "that before the Foulgers visited here, in the guise of Señor Rodriguez and his wife, they must already have known that the spare key to the safe was kept somewhere on the top floor of the building, along with the key to the window-grille. We cannot imagine that they lit upon these keys by chance. The obvious conclusion, therefore, is that someone here told them of the keys. Yet, according to Elder's account, of those that do not have a key of their own to the safe, only Troughton knew of the spare key and its whereabouts. The inference that Troughton is in league with these villains is inescapable."

"Why did you not mention this inference to your client?"

"I gave him, if you recall, a general warning against speaking of the matter to anyone. I did not specifically mention Troughton's name, because I feared that, if I did so, Elder's manner towards him might be altered, and he might thus be alerted to our suspicions."

"Is it not possible that someone else at Elder's might know of the keys kept on the top floor?" I queried. "In which case, Troughton might, after all, be innocent."

"It is just possible that one of the senior men may have mentioned to one of the junior clerks that the spare safe-key was kept on the top floor, but it seems unlikely."

"Such speculation is no longer necessary," interrupted Lestrade. "I now have definite information that Troughton is in league with the Foulger gang."

"How did you establish the connection between them?" asked Holmes.

"Ah!" responded the policeman. "You can't beat an old dog, when all is said and done! After you had stumbled on the clue concerning Troughton's possible involvement in the matter, Mr. Holmes, I mentioned Troughton's name to my colleague, Inspector Barker, who has made something of a speciality of the criminal gangs of the East End. He recognized it at once. 'Why!' says he; 'there is a man of that very name who runs a shop in the Mile End Road, selling jewellery and other articles of value. We have often suspected that he is also involved with criminal gangs, and is one of the chief agents in London for the disposal of stolen goods'. Well, I need hardly tell you, Mr. Holmes, that all I need is the scent of such a clue and I am on the trail at once, and don't give up until I find what I am looking for. You can't beat the methods of the official force, you know! To cut a long story short, I have established that the Thomas Troughton that works in this building is the cousin of Ezra Troughton, the shopkeeper of the Mile End Road. Furthermore, Thomas Troughton was yesterday evening followed by one of my smartest men from his house near the Elephant and Castle to his cousin's shop. The two men are thus not merely related, but intimately acquainted."

"That is good work!" cried Holmes, clapping the policeman on the shoulder. "So, our traps are all set, and now we must wait for the game to emerge from the shadows and take the bait! Have you reconsidered the disposition of your men, Lestrade?"

The policeman shook his head. "My mind is made up on the point," said he.

"Very well. The decision is yours. Now we must see how the Elders are faring, Watson. The daylight will begin fading shortly, and Sir George might light a lamp, which would be fatal to our plans."

We left the Scotland Yard man beaming, and ascended the steep stairs.

"'Stumbled on the clue' indeed!" said Holmes to me in an indignant tone. "The cheek of the fellow! Were it not for the information I have given him, he would be as far from apprehending the Foulger gang as he has ever been! As it is, his stubbornness threatens to ruin everything!"

"What do you mean?"

"He insists upon keeping most of his men downstairs. I have told him that it is a waste of time. The copying of the window-key indicates beyond doubt that it is through the window that the criminals intend to enter the building. Within reach of that window, therefore, is where Lestrade's men should be. His argument is that his men must be able to get out of the building at a moment's notice, in order to apprehend the criminals, and thus must remain on the ground floor. I have told him he is making a mistake, but he will not listen. Having accepted my analysis of the matter, he declines to accept the conclusion which that analysis necessitates. That, I suggest, is as good a definition of pig-headedness as one could imagine! I am inclined, Watson, to wash my hands entirely of the affair. After all, I have already fulfilled my own particular commission. I have solved young Elder's little mystery, and have ensured that his eminent cousin's gold will not be stolen. But here is Mr. Elder now; and Sir George, who appears less than entirely happy!"

Holmes's client had emerged from the conference-room as we reached the head of the stairs, followed by a large, stout man, whose expression was one of irritated annoyance. Holmes introduced us, and we all shook hands.

"I shall feel happier when this night is over," said Sir George Elder.

"Have no fear!" returned Holmes in a cheery voice. "Your gold could scarcely be safer were it in the Bank of England! Inspector Lestrade appears to have half the division deployed downstairs!"

"No doubt," said Sir George, a sceptical note in his voice; "but these criminals are desperate men, so I understand."

"Indeed they are; but our trap is laid; now all we have to do is wait for our quarry to put in an appearance! One of these rooms which face the front of the building will probably be best for our vigil."

Sir George Elder opened a door. "This is old Mr. Kemp's private chamber," said he. "We can sit in here. I imagine we shall have a long wait."

"It may not be so long as you suppose," returned Holmes, as we followed Sir George into the office. "They will not, of course, make a move until after dark. But once the daylight has gone, they may not wait very long. It must be remembered that from the criminals' point of view there are two problems which must be overcome. Their first problem is to gain entry to these premises and seize the gold. But their second problem is to transport the gold across the centre of London without attracting attention to themselves. They will probably judge that they are more likely to achieve that successfully in the evening, when there are still plenty of people about, than later in the night, when the streets will be practically deserted."

So the four of us sat in that small chamber and waited. And what a wait it was! Slowly the light faded, until the sky outside was a deep, inky blue and the first stars appeared, by which time my companions were but vague shadows in the gloom. At Holmes's request, Sir George Elder entertained us for a while with an account of his time in Russia; but, in truth, I missed much of it, for my attention wandered constantly, as faint sounds from without set my senses alert.

We had been sitting in the dark for about an hour when there came the sound of a footstep upon the stair, and we heard the voice of Inspector Lestrade. Holmes called softly, to guide him to where we were sitting, for it was by now almost pitch black within the building, and he made his way slowly to the doorway of our room.

"Is all in order up here?" asked he in a low tone.

"Perfectly," returned Holmes. "Both of the doors into the boardroom, from the corridor and from the adjoining conference-room, are slightly ajar, so that we shall be able to see and hear anything that goes on in there."

For a few moments, they discussed the matter further, then Holmes announced that he was going to take a look from the window of the conference-room, and I said I would accompany him. Slowly and with great care, we made our way across the corridor and into the large conference-room. My sense of touch was of necessity my chief guide, for it was now so dark that one could not see one's hand before one's face. Ahead of us, the wide window showed up faintly as a grey blur.

"It should be safe enough to take a look from here," murmured my companion, as we positioned ourselves by the window. "It is almost as dark out there as it is in here. It is a cold night," he continued. "It is clear enough now, but I'll wager the fog will thicken as the evening wears on."

"We may be above the fog at present," I remarked, craning my neck in an effort to see into the dark alley below. "It appears to be thicker down in the lane."

At that moment, with a tremendous throb and roar, a train passed on the viaduct, opposite the window. For an instant, the dark shape of the driver and fireman were visible, lit by the glow from the locomotive firebox, then the engine was past, and was succeeded by a line of swaying, rattling carriages, their compartments illuminated by the yellow glow of oil-lamps. In another instant, the carriages, too, had passed, and the scene before us had returned once more to one of Stygian blackness.

It was some time after the lighted train had passed us before my eyes became accustomed again to the darkness. Then I could once more make out some of the taller features atop the railway viaduct – a telegraph pole or two and a signal mast with a ladder leaning against it at an angle, all wreathed in thin wisps of fog. So close was the viaduct, that when a gang of railway workers passed along it, carrying between them a long plank of some sort, I could hear their voices quite clearly, although I could not make out what they were saying. Then another train approached, making for the centre of London, which slowed down as it passed us, until it drew to a halt exactly opposite to where we were crouching by the window. For a minute, as it stood there, we had a clear view into the compartments, where some of the passengers were standing up, and beginning to gather their belongings together, ready to alight when the train reached the terminus. Presently, with a hiss and a clank, the train began to move slowly forward once more, until, at length, it had passed beyond our view. A few moments later, the gang of workmen returned from wherever they had been. They put down their plank and exchanged a few words. It had just struck me that they appeared to be staring across at our window, when I felt Holmes's hand on my arm, pulling me slowly back from the window.

"Careful!" said he in a whisper. "Don't let them see you! Wait here, and I shall bring the others!"

I lowered my head a little, so that my eyes were just above the window-sill, and watched as the men on the viaduct continued their discussion, several times pointing across to the Elder and Kemp building. Then, as Holmes returned, and Lestrade, Elder and Sir George crouched down beside me, the workmen picked up their plank once more and placed one end of it on top of the viaduct parapet, so that it projected outwards two or three feet. For a moment, it remained there, and I saw the men look about them cautiously, then, slowly and carefully, they pushed it forward, across the gap between the viaduct and our building.

"Magnificent!" murmured Holmes appreciatively, in a soft tone. "What enterprise! What bold imagination!"

"What the devil are they doing?" interrupted Sir George in a sharp whisper.

"It is something in your own line, Sir George," returned Holmes. "They are attempting to throw a bridge across the chasm between the railway viaduct and this building. They will hope to locate this end of the bridge upon the outside window-sill of the boardroom."

"By Jove!" exclaimed Sir George hoarsely. "Whatever next!"

"Once they are confident that their bridge is secure, one of their party will be sent across to attempt to open the window," said Holmes. He paused as a dull thud indicated that the heavy plank had reached the window-sill. For a few moments the men on the viaduct stared along their bridge, no doubt endeavouring to be certain that the far end was securely located on the window-sill. One of them leaned over and thumped the plank several times with his fist, then, a moment later, climbed onto the parapet, and so onto the plank. Crouching down, and proceeding in an infinitely careful manner, he then began to make his way slowly across.

"He will smash the glass in the window," whispered Holmes. "Do not be startled by the noise, Sir George. He will probably use a small hammer. He will then put his hand through the broken pane and between the bars of the grille, and unlock the grille with the duplicate key they have had made. He will then push the grille open, and reach up and unlatch the window."

Holmes paused again, as there came a sharp tap on the boardroom window. After a moment, there came a second tap, slightly louder, accompanied by the tinkling sound of breaking glass. I held my breath. Through the open door that communicated between the boardroom and the conference-room came the sound of furtive activity. A few seconds later, a low metallic creak indicated that the grille was being pushed open, then came a sharp snick as the window-latch was unfastened. By this time, I judged that all my unseen companions were holding their breath, for there was utter silence in the building, so that one might have heard the fall of a pin. A few moments later, I heard soft footfalls in the adjoining room, and the slight creaking of a floorboard. Then came a slight metallic click, and a dull yellow light showed through the open doorway, as the intruder opened a shutter on a small lantern. A second click, and the light vanished as abruptly as it had appeared, then I heard the intruder call softly across to his companions on the viaduct.

"All right, Jimmy! Come on!"

I turned my attention to the viaduct once more. A second man, no more than a dark blurred shape, was climbing onto the parapet and making his way onto the plank. I had the impression that there was a third man behind him on the viaduct, wearing a cap of some sort, but I could not be certain, for the fog was thicker now, and swirled like the sea before one's eyes.

The second man had almost reached the windowsill, in the same crouching posture as the first, when there came a sudden surprising interruption. From somewhere in the building below us, there came a momentary clattering noise, as if someone had lost his footing upon the stair. It was not a loud noise; in normal circumstances it would probably have passed unremarked. But in the still silence of that dark night it captured all one's attention, as a faint and distant gunshot might catch the ear of the night watch at an army camp. It was followed by a moment of utter stillness, as if the whole world had, for an instant, ceased to move, then the man in the next room slid open the shutter of his lantern once more, and it was clear from the movement of the light through the door-crack, and upon our ceiling, that he was making his way towards the far end of the boardroom. The yellow spread of light around the half-open door became gradually brighter. Then, all at once, I saw an arm push the door between the two rooms fully open. The next moment, the intruder had stepped through the doorway and was playing the light of his lantern about the conference-room. In less time than it takes to record it, the light moved from the dark recesses at the far end of the room to where we crouched by the window, and the dazzling light was fully in my eyes.

There was a moment of silence, then rapid footsteps, as the lantern and the man carrying it vanished from the room.

"Get back, Jimmy!" we heard him call out. "It's a trap! Get back!"

Holmes and Lestrade sprang forward, and there came a piercing blast from a police-whistle, close to my ear. I hurried after them as fast as I could. In the boardroom, a violent scuffle was taking place on the floor by the window, but I could not make out clearly who was involved. Then a constable pushed open the door from the corridor behind me, and asked what he should do.

"Over here, Timpson!" called out Lestrade in an urgent tone, and the constable pushed past me to lend his weight to the struggle. A moment later, I saw Holmes's dark silhouette show up before the grey blur of the window, as he stood up.

"Are your men in position on the viaduct, Lestrade?" said he in an urgent tone.

"They are there somewhere," returned Lestrade's voice from the darkness.

I heard Holmes groan with annoyance.

"I told you that this is how they would do the job," cried he. "I said that unless you had more men on the viaduct, you would not land your catch. What is the use of fishing with a net full of holes! Is that you there, Watson? Good! Come on! We must try to stop them!"

In an instant he had climbed onto the window-sill and was making his way along the wooden plank. "Hold it firmly on the sill!" he called back when he was half-way across.

I should never have described my friend as foolhardy or reckless – he was much too thoughtful and intelligent a man to warrant such a description – but there was, in his otherwise severely rational nature, a spark of romance and adventure which could be kindled to a blaze by his own enthusiasm, or by the excitement of the chase. Then the intensity of his desire to bring some matter to a successful conclusion would drive him on, heedless of his own safety. These thoughts flashed through my mind in an instant, as, with some trepidation, I watched as he made his way along the plank to the viaduct.

Reaching the other end, he sprang down from the parapet onto the level of the railway tracks and turned.

"Come on, Watson!" he called. "Quickly! It is not far! The plank is a thick one," he added, evidently perceiving my hesitation; "it bends very little. You need not fear – I'll hold it firmly against the window-sill!"

For a moment longer I hesitated; but I was conscious that any further delay would only make the criminals' escape more likely, and I did not wish to be held responsible for that. So, perhaps foolishly, and certainly with a knotted sensation in my stomach, I put my foot onto the window-sill, and, stepping onto the plank, began to inch my way forwards.

I looked down at my feet, and my gaze was irresistibly drawn further, beyond the wooden plank, to where the dense fog swirled and drifted like a dark sea, far below.

"Don't look down!" came my friend's voice, containing an unmistakable note of concern. "Look forward, to where you are stepping!"

I raised my eyes for a moment, saw Holmes leaning his whole weight against the end of the plank, and made to resume my cautious progress. But in looking up, and through the wraiths of fog that drifted sideways before my eyes, I had somehow lost my sense of the vertical. At one and the same time, I had the conflicting impressions that I was standing upright and that I was slowly slipping sideways. My mind reeled in confusion. I had no idea which way I should lean to prevent myself tumbling from the narrow plank into the abyss. Then, through the mist, came Holmes's firm voice.

"Crouch down on the board," said he.

I leaned forward, bent my knees and touched the plank with my finger-tips. This last action restored some, at least, of my sense of balance, and after a moment in that position, I was able to push myself up with my extended fingers, and move forward once more.

"Here!" called Holmes, holding out his hand to guide me. "If such things are to be done, they are best done quickly," said he, as I reached the end of the plank.

I had my hand on my friend's shoulder, and was about to lower myself down onto the level of the railway tracks, and reply to his observation, when there came a sudden sharp cry from behind me. Almost at the same instant, I felt the board beneath my feet quiver and move. I sprang down at once, and turned.

Lestrade's prisoner had evidently broken free, for he was running pell-mell across the board towards us. But his flight was too vigorous, and was bending and shaking the narrow bridge. In an instant, the far end of it had bounced and slipped from its narrow purchase on the windowsill. I saw it go, and grabbed for the near end, but it was no use; the plank was too heavy for me to hold it in position. At the same instant, I saw the man before me, his eyes wild and staring, stretch out his arms in a vain effort to reach the parapet wall.

I lunged forward and seized his sleeve, then had both hands upon his arm; but the effort had almost pulled me over the parapet, and I knew I could not long hold him unless he could gain some purchase with his other hand. Then, in an instant, as I heard the plank crash to the ground, far below, Holmes was leaning over the wall beside me and had seized the man's other arm, and between us we hauled him up, over the parapet-top, and to safety.

As our prisoner lay by the wall, panting and shaking, Holmes leaned down and snapped a pair of handcuffs onto his wrists.

"Now," said he, "for the others."

At that moment, however, two large police-constables appeared out of the fog a short distance along the tracks. Between them they held a slighter figure, who bore a striking resemblance to the young man who lay at our feet.

"Here is Jimmy, come to join Patrick!" said Holmes. "Have you seen anyone else?" he asked the policemen as they approached.

"No, sir!" one of them returned. "No one, save only a railway official."

"In a peaked cap?"

"Yes, sir; of course! It was he that told us to get along this way."

"Where is he now?"

"Gone to alert the station authorities, he said."

"A short man?" Holmes asked; "with a sharp, hooked nose, like that of an eagle, and a deep scar below his left eye?"

"Why! That is the man exactly!" returned the policeman in a surprised tone. "How can you know?"

"That man was Albert Foulger," said Holmes, "the chief of this daring little gang. I think, Watson," he continued, turning to me, "that unless the authorities manage to take him at his hidey-hole in Colchester, this is the last we shall see of Mr. Foulger for a while!"

My friend's words were to prove prophetic. Troughton and his cousin were arrested and later convicted for their part in the matter, along with Patrick and James Foulger; but of Albert Foulger himself no trace was to be found. Although a watch was kept for some time upon his house in Colchester, and upon his known haunts in London, he was never seen. Once again he had succeeded in disappearing completely.

Two days after the dramatic events I have described above, there was a full account of the affair in the *Standard*, which I read aloud to Holmes as we sat at the breakfast-table. The paper also devoted an editorial to the subject, which concluded with the following words:

> Thanks to the alertness of the police officers concerned, especially Inspector G. Lestrade of Scotland Yard, a daring attempt at robbery was foiled, and most of the gang arrested. In this case, it is certainly no exaggeration to declare that by their prompt actions, the police have earned the gratitude of the whole of London.

"It does not mention your name at all," I observed, as I finished reading.

"For which I am very relieved," returned my companion in a dry tone. "It is not a case with which I should choose to be associated."

"But without your intervention," I protested, "the gold would certainly have been stolen, and the gang would have escaped scot free. It is you, Holmes, who has earned the gratitude of the whole of London, and the newspaper should acknowledge that fact! I have a good mind to write to the editor and apprise him of the true facts of the matter!"

My friend shook his head.

"The point of Saturday night's little exercise was not to save Sir George Elder's gold, Watson," said he. "Had that been our purpose we could have achieved it with considerably less trouble by simply moving the gold elsewhere, or by changing the lock upon the window. The whole point of our efforts was, rather, to trap Albert Foulger. This we did not succeed in doing, and he remains still, regrettably, the third most sought-after villain in England. I therefore consider the exercise a failure, and the fact that Foulger is a very cunning man does not lessen my mortification at being beaten by him. It may be that one day we shall once more have within our grasp this enemy of all honest citizens, but until that time, I should be obliged if you would suppress your letter-writing impulses, my dear fellow. Any further attention drawn to the matter will, I fear, serve only to reveal that it was somewhat less of a success than is supposed, and can only diminish what little reputation I now possess!"

THE THIRTEENTH STEP

I NEED NO RECOURSE to my notebooks to recall that it was a pleasant, balmy day in late spring when Lady Temperley, wife of the former under-secretary at the Foreign Office, called at our chambers in Baker Street to consult Sherlock Holmes. For several weeks the buds on the trees in the park had been slowly swelling. Now, following a period of bright, sunny weather, the trees had burst forth into the most beautiful display of blossom. I remember this particularly, as Lady Temperley herself, although no longer young, had, nevertheless, something of the freshness of the spring about her. A handsome woman of late middle age, she was dressed in a smart blossom-pink walking costume and seemed to bring a welcome breath of the English countryside to the brick-built fastness of London.

She had travelled up from Derbyshire the previous evening, she informed us, and had stayed the night at the Midland Hotel.

"I received the telegram you sent," said Sherlock Holmes. "There is, I understand, some problem or puzzle on which you wish to consult me, but your message gave no indication as to the nature of the problem."

Lady Temperley frowned. "It is difficult to describe," said she at length. "Indeed, you may think me foolish for coming all this way to consult you over such a vague, indeterminate business. But it has been troubling me greatly in recent days, Mr. Holmes, and I have been unable to sleep at night. Last night, at the hotel, I lay awake for several hours."

Sherlock Holmes eyed his visitor keenly. "Have you spoken to anyone else about the matter?" he asked.

"I have mentioned some aspects of it to Ralph – my husband, Lord Temperley – or have tried to, at least, but he believes I am troubling myself unnecessarily. Even he admits, however, that recent events have not been quite as one would have wished, although he describes it as a series of unfortunate coincidences. But it is all so vague, Mr. Holmes, that I scarcely know where to begin."

"It is apparent that you are suffering from great anxiety, Lady Temperley. Do not trouble yourself over getting matters in perfect order before you begin. Simply recount the relevant facts as they occur to you. We can sort out the order of events later."

"Very well," said our visitor. "You should perhaps know first that we live, my husband and I, at Hardshaw Hall in Derbyshire, where his family has resided for many generations. Our life there is, generally speaking, a quiet and uneventful one. Our son, Michael, is no longer at home, being posted to India at present with his regiment. We frequently have visitors, however, sometimes for very extended periods, and it is the great pleasure of our lives to do so. My husband, I know, is very proud of the reputation for hospitality which Hardshaw enjoys throughout the length and breadth of the country, and he is always ready to accommodate anyone who wishes to come.

"Last autumn, for example, at the request of the Prime Minister, we put up Prince Balkovsky and his family from Russia for several weeks, and, more recently, for a similar period of time, Sir John Meacham and his wife. He had, as you may be aware, just returned from several years in the West Indies, where he had been governor of the island of St. Stephen. At the same time, for almost a year now, we have been putting up an old friend of my husband's, Major Thomas Lockhart. He and my husband were comrades-in-arms in their army days, although they had been out of touch for several years until they happened to run across each other in London, one day last summer. When Major Lockhart left the army he had knocked about the world for some time – Australia, India, Africa and so on. I think my husband was rather envious of that: when he left the army, he had had to return immediately to Hardshaw to take up his duties there, as his late father was becoming old and frail. Major Lockhart was under no such constraints, and had set his heart upon a farm in Australia. He had expected to come into a considerable inheritance, which would have made this possible, but there was some delay about it, so he had been kicking his heels in London for some time when my husband ran across him. Ralph was so pleased to see him that he invited him to come and stay with us at Hardshaw until the inheritance business was sorted out. And there, save occasional trips up to London to consult his solicitor, he has been ever since.

"I think that Major Lockhart was very grateful for Ralph's offer of hospitality, but, really, my husband benefits from the arrangement just as much as the major does. I think he had been finding Hardshaw rather dull before, and Major Lockhart's presence has brightened the old place up considerably. He and my husband share a taste for riding, shooting and fishing, and when they are not so engaged, they spend hours on end discussing horse-breeding, farming methods and the like. In the course of his travels, Major Lockhart had stayed with various people, including several connections of my husband's – his cousin, Wilfred Docking, who farms in South Africa; an old Army friend, Maurice Foster, who now lives in New Zealand; and numerous others – and Ralph very much enjoyed hearing the latest news of all these people. I suppose it is inevitable that Major Lockhart will eventually leave us, but when he does so, it will be something of a wrench for u We have become so used to his presence at Hardshaw that I am sure we shall miss him greatly when he goes.

"That, then, is the background to the present events," said Lady Temperley after a moment, "and you will appreciate, then, why I said that our life at Hardshaw has generally been a placid and uneventful one. I come now to more recent events:

"Towards the end of last year, my husband received a letter from a distant cousin of his, the Wilfred Docking I mentioned, who lives in South Africa. The gist of this was that Docking hoped that his son, Edward, who was nineteen years old, would be able to enter All Saints' College of Oxford University this coming autumn. This possibility had first been raised when Major Lockhart had been in South Africa, and his opinion had been sought as to whether Edward should seek a commission in the Army or try for a place at Oxford. The major had favoured the latter course, pointing out that once Edward had completed his studies at Oxford, it would still be possible for him to then apply for a commission should he wish to do so.

"Wilfred Docking had agreed with this view, and they had therefore made a preliminary application to All Saints' College, with which Docking's family had some previous connection. This preliminary application had been favourably received, and now Docking wondered if it might be possible for us to put his son up for a few months beforehand, perhaps help him with any correspondence that was necessary, make sure he was prepared and so on. Of course, we said we should be delighted to do so. There then followed various delays while arrangements were made, during which, I understand, Edward, with the careless irresponsibility of youth, took the opportunity to travel all over South Africa, bidding fond farewells to various cronies of his. He eventually ended up in Cape Town, where he stayed for a few days with an old school-fellow, Andrew Cotter, while he waited for the boat, and at last set sail and arrived in England in the middle of February this year."

Lady Temperley paused. "I mention Edward's friend, Andrew Cotter, particularly," she continued after a moment, "as I shall have cause to refer to him again later. However, to continue my account: Shortly after Edward's arrival, we learned that his application to All Saints' had been finally accepted, subject only to his proving satisfactory in an entrance examination for which he would be required to sit in July.

"This may all sound fairly straightforward," Lady Temperley continued with a shake of the head, "but, although neither my husband nor I are experts on the matriculation requirements of an Oxford college, it soon became apparent to us that Edward was likely to fall short of them. I don't doubt that his heart is in the right place, but he is wild and boisterous, like a gale blowing into a house through an open window and disturbing the order within. He is a very good horseman – in fact he is good at all outdoor sports and any activity requiring physical strength – but his general level of education, although adequate for most purposes, is not, we felt, up to the required level for a scholar at Oxford. We therefore thought it wise to employ a tutor to coach him in all those branches of learning in which he seemed deficient. This tutor – a man by the name of Philip Sowerby – has therefore also been staying with us for several months, although he goes home to Derby at the end of each week and returns to Hardshaw each Monday morning.

"I understand from Mr. Sowerby that Edward is making progress, and he is confident that the young man will perform satisfactorily in the forthcoming examination. I must say I am glad that he has expressed that opinion, as I should not myself have drawn that conclusion from appearances. Sometimes the coaching seems the other way about, with Edward introducing Mr. Sowerby to riding, shooting and other outdoor pursuits, of which, I understand, the tutor had had little previous experience. Neither my husband nor I have raised any objection to this, so long as the schoolwork is not neglected, which Mr. Sowerby insists it has not been. Meanwhile, in his free time, Edward soon struck up a friendship with Stephen James, a boy of about his own age who is the son of a neighbouring farmer. In fact, the two boys already knew each other, by letter at least, for, coincidentally, when my husband happened to hear some years ago from Matthew James, Stephen's father, that his son was looking for a boy of his own age with whom he could correspond, preferably someone from overseas, he had suggested that Stephen write to his cousin's son, Edward, in South Africa. This he did, and the two boys exchanged letters for two or three years in their schooldays, so I understand, although I don't think they had been in touch for the last year or two.

"Edward and Stephen have spent an enormous lot of time riding pell-mell across the countryside. Whenever I have chanced to see them, they always seemed to be leaping recklessly over hedges and stone walls without a thought for safety or caution, and I have been constantly worried that they would break their necks one day. At the same time, Edward has made the acquaintance of the James boy's sister, Agnes, a sweet and delightful girl, a little younger than her brother, and I have been just as anxious about that, fearing constantly that Edward's impetuosity would lead him to do or say something inappropriate or unseemly and cause a breach between the James family and us."

Lady Temperley paused then, and asked if she might have a glass of water. More than ever now, her features appeared to indicate that she was under a great strain, and it was some time before she continued her account. Holmes, meanwhile, passed no remark, but I could see that he was watching her closely.

"I come now," said she at length, "to the most recent events. Sometime after Easter, there was a spring fair in the local village. It is a traditional event, and takes place at the same time every year. My husband and I always contribute something to the festivities, and invariably put in an appearance on the Saturday afternoon. This year we attended with Edward, who had never seen anything quite like it and was enjoying it immensely.

"In one tent was a fortune-teller who called herself 'Rose Spindle, Spinner of Destiny'. I don't really care for such things, and don't usually bother with them, but Edward badgered me to try it, and insisted it would be fun. Eventually I gave in to the lad, much against my better judgment. I very much wish now that I had not. There was an odd smell in the fortune-teller's tent, and the air was thick with some sort of cloying incense. The fortune-teller greeted me cordially enough and examined the lines on my hand, then spread some cards on the table between us. After she had studied these for a few moments in silence, she looked up at me with her dark, penetrating eyes.

"'I almost wish that you had not come,' said she in a deep voice. 'But, still, it is best to know the truth.'

"'Whatever do you mean?' I asked.

"'I see some misfortune,' she replied. 'I see a great loss – perhaps even a death.'

"'Death?' I cried in a state of shock. 'My death?'

"'No, no,' said she quickly with a shake of the head. 'I do not think so, but it might be the death of someone close to you.'

"'A relation of mine?'

"'No, not a relation, but someone very close to you. That is strange,' she added, as she continued to study the cards: 'you will receive a warning of some kind, but for some reason you will do nothing. Perhaps there is nothing you can do.'

"I did not wait to hear any more, but staggered from that dark tent to the bright afternoon outside, desperate to get some fresh air into my lungs. I can scarcely convey to you how I felt; it was as if a great weight had been placed upon my shoulders and I could not shake it off. I know you will think me foolish, but–"

"Did you recognize the woman?" Holmes interrupted. "Was it anyone you had seen about in the village?"

Lady Temperley shook her head. "She was wearing a heavy veil and I could not see her face very clearly. There were some Gipsies camped at the end of the village that week – perhaps it was one of them. I made a few enquiries at the time, but could not learn who it was."

"Did you mention to your husband, or anyone else, what the woman had told you?"

"Not at first. When I was asked about it, I made up some trifling matter on the spur of the moment, and dismissed it as nonsense. Later, I did relate some of it to my husband, but he refused to take it seriously. I have never given anyone a full account of it before today."

"Very well. Pray, continue."

"A couple of weeks later, my husband, Major Lockhart and I were chatting over breakfast one morning. Edward had already finished and gone out somewhere. It was a bright, sunny day, and the French windows to the terrace were standing open.

All at once, our conversation was interrupted by the rapid clatter of Edward's feet on the steps outside, which lead from the lawn up to the terrace. A moment later, he burst into the room like a whirlwind, flopped onto a chair and helped himself to a cup of tea.

"'Do you know how many steps there are supposed to be, up to the terrace, Uncle Ralph?' he asked.

"'There are twelve,' replied my husband. 'Why do you ask?'

"'That's the funny thing,' said Edward in a puzzled tone. 'I always count the steps when I'm running up them, and it usually comes to twelve, but today it came to thirteen.'

"'Oh, you must have made a mistake, Edward,' I said quickly.

"'No, Aunt Felicity, I didn't,' he insisted. 'Or, if I did, it was a very odd one.'

"We let the matter drop then. A few moments later, my husband left the room, and shortly afterwards Major Lockhart and I did the same. The subject was not raised again until late that evening, when my husband and I were alone.

"'What was that young fool playing at this morning, talking about the steps like that?' my husband demanded in an angry voice. I could see that he was terrifically upset.

"'Don't be too hard on the boy,' I responded. 'It's not his fault, Ralph. He doesn't know about it. You know what he's like – he approaches everything like a bull at a gate. It can't be helped.'

"My husband shook his head, snorted loudly and took himself off to bed without another word. It was clear that the matter had been preying on his mind all day. You see, Mr. Holmes, what Edward didn't know, as it is scarcely ever mentioned, is that there is an old tradition at Hardshaw Hall, associated with those very steps he had run up so gaily, an unpleasant and sinister tradition. It goes back nearly two centuries, to when one of Ralph's ancestors, Sir John Temperley, walked up those same steps, counting them off absent-mindedly as he went. On that occasion, too, instead of counting twelve, as usual, he counted to thirteen, which is traditionally regarded, of course, as an unlucky number. Now, Sir John Temperley was not at all superstitious, and simply assumed he had made a mistake. In fact, it amused him so much that he told everyone he knew about it, although some, it seemed, chided him for what they thought inappropriate levity. Less than two weeks later, their caution seemed justified: Sir John's wife was dead, killed in a riding accident.

"Such a terrible misfortune, and the circumstances surrounding it, made a very great impression upon everyone, especially those of a superstitious cast of mind, and, as the years passed, the tragedy became firmly embedded in local folk-lore, and known to everyone in the district. Even so, one might have expected that such an incident would at length pass, forgotten, into the pages of history, but occasional little mishaps at Hardshaw, real or imagined, which could in any way be connected to the steps, served to keep the matter fresh in the general mind. Then, twenty-odd years later, there occurred another serious incident which sealed forever the place in superstitious history of the garden-steps at Hardshaw Hall. A visitor to the house, all unaware of the tradition, commented in amusement on what he described as 'the surprising fact' that there were thirteen steps leading from the lawn up to the terrace. Within a week, this visitor was dead, having fallen from his bedroom window in circumstances which could never be fully explained. Thus, you see, 'the thirteenth step at Hardshaw Hall' is taken, with good reason, as a forewarning of death or disaster. There is even a little verse on the subject, although I don't know when it was written."

Lady Temperley unfastened the small embroidered bag she had been holding, and took from it a folded sheet of paper which she passed to Holmes. He studied it for a moment, then passed it to me and I read the following:

Beware the steps at Hardshaw Hall
If your life you wish to save
Take twelve steps only from lawn to wall
The thirteenth step is to the grave.

Holmes sat in silence for several minutes, his brows drawn down into a frown as he considered the matter. "And has anything untoward occurred yet?" he queried at length in a sceptical tone.

"Indeed," replied his visitor. "Something far worse than you could possibly imagine."

"Surely there has not been a death?" said Holmes sharply, a note of surprise in his voice.

Lady Temperley nodded her head. "It is worse than that," said she. "Not one, but two deaths have occurred, one at Hardshaw, one elsewhere but directly connected to Hardshaw. One is the result of a dreadful, tragic accident, but the other may well be murder."

Holmes frowned again. "The details, please," said he.

"I have described to you how Edward and the neighbours' boy, Stephen James, have spent a great deal of their time in recent months galloping back and forth wildly across the local countryside. On the Monday of the week before last, they were setting off as usual when they decided to make a race of it, a steeplechase, in fact. They began in the field beside the Hardshaw stables, their destination being the church at Boarsley. That is about five miles away, although the church spire can be seen far in the distance as soon as one breasts the first hill on the Hardshaw estate.

"They set off together, but after the first half-mile or so they parted, the two boys each choosing a different route to their destination. Edward eventually reached Boarsley, and as there was no sign of Stephen there, he assumed he had won the race. He waited some considerable time, but Stephen never appeared. At length Edward concluded that his rival must have met with an accident, so he set off back to try and find him.

"He was just approaching Blackwood Copse, which stands in an area of rough heathland, when he saw his tutor, Mr. Sowerby, trotting away from the copse in the direction of the Hall. Edward called out to him, he turned his horse, and the two of them met up by the wood. Mr. Sowerby informed Edward that he had seen Stephen's mount wandering about, but had seen no sign of Stephen himself. The two of them then dismounted and searched the wood on foot. It did not take them long to make a most melancholy discovery – the body of the unfortunate James boy, stone dead. He had suffered a grievous wound to the head, and they could only conclude that his mount had stumbled on the rough, broken ground and flung him off. This was also the official verdict of the inquest which was convened to consider the matter two days later.

"Of course, Edward was devastated. He told me that it had been his suggestion that they should have a race, and he kept blaming himself for what had happened, although I told him he shouldn't. And it was not just Stephen he felt terribly sorry for, but also Stephen's sister, Agnes. As I mentioned earlier, Edward had become very fond of Agnes and he was mortified that he should have been at least partly responsible for causing her such anguish. I don't think he was able to sleep for several days, and he kept muttering over and over to himself that he must try to make it up to her somehow.

"Three days after this terrible misfortune, we received a letter from South Africa, from Edward's father, informing us that it was his intention to come to England in about three weeks' time. I had mentioned to him in a previous letter about Edward's coaching with Mr. Sowerby, and he referred to that and said he was very much looking forward to hearing how Edward was progressing. After this cheering information, however, he mentioned that he had, unfortunately, some bad news for Edward. A close friend and former school-fellow of Edward's, the Andrew Cotter I mentioned before, who had been working away from home in Cape Town and had been out of touch with his family for some considerable time, had been found dead in a wild, uncultivated area, a mile or two outside the town. It was not known how long his body had lain in the place in which it was found, but the surgeon who conducted the examination gave it as his opinion that he had certainly been dead for at least six weeks, and probably longer. Indeed, but for a signet ring he was wearing and some papers in his jacket pocket, it was thought unlikely that the body would ever have been identified. It was all terribly sad, for it seemed from what Mr. Docking said that this boy, Cotter, had fallen in with vicious, criminally-inclined companions in Cape Town and was in fact being sought by the police there in connection with a robbery. Furthermore, from the location of the body and marks visible upon it, the police thought it very likely that Cotter had been murdered.

"I have never seen anyone so completely shocked and distraught by anything as Edward was by this news. All the blood seemed to drain from his face as I read the letter out to him, and I thought that, strong lad though he is, he was going to faint. My husband gave him a tot of brandy, which seemed to steady him a little, but he remained sitting in a dazed stupor for some time. I suppose it was not very surprising, considering that this dreadful news had come so hard on the heels of the death of poor Stephen James. I tried to imagine how I would feel if two of my closest friends had been found dead within a few days of each other, but I couldn't bear to even think about it."

Lady Temperley shook her head. Her gaze had been cast down to the floor as she recounted these disturbing events, but now she raised her eyes to Holmes, a pathetic, pleading expression on her features.

"That is where we are, Mr. Holmes," said she, her voice trembling with emotion, "in a waking nightmare of death and predictions of disaster, made low by what has happened, and with no idea what might happen next. All I know is that there is something wrong – I feel it in my bones – and if there is anything – anything at all – that you can do or say to help me, I shall be eternally in your debt."

Sherlock Holmes did not reply at once, but sat with his eyes closed, his brow furrowed with intense concentration. For myself, I confess I could make no sense of what Lady Temperley had told us, and did not know what to think of it, other than that she and her relations had been the victims of the most atrocious misfortune. I could not really believe that there was any connection between the doom-laden prophecies of a Gipsy fortune-teller and the deaths of two young men, many thousands of miles apart, nor that the old tradition of "the thirteenth step at Hardshaw Hall" could really foretell misfortunes to come. And yet, try as I might to dismiss what must surely be mere superstition, I could not quite shake off the disturbing effect of our visitor's account. Round and round these strange and melancholy facts my thoughts circled, unable to reduce them to something rational, something that was not simply an incomprehensible enigma. Glad I was, then, when Holmes at last spoke. But if I had hoped that a keener intellect than my own might perceive some clear way through the puzzle, my hopes were not entirely satisfied by his opening remarks.

"It is possible," said he in a measured tone, "that some of the incidents you have described to us are, indeed, simply coincidental. One must always allow for that possibility."

"Does that mean that you have no hope of ever bringing light into the darkness?" asked Lady Temperley, a clear note of disappointment in her voice.

"Not at all. You misunderstand me. My remark about coincidences is not a negative one, an admission of defeat, but a positive one, pointing out to you that we may be able to shed light on some of the facts you have mentioned by setting some of the others aside for the moment. It can sometimes be an error to try to explain every single thing that puzzles you by one over-arching theory. All it takes then is one aberrant fact, one fact which your theory cannot justifiably explain, to destroy the theory and leave you with nothing. Do you understand the point?"

"I think so," said Lady Temperley in a doubtful tone. "Is there anything else you wish to know, or anything I have not made clear?"

Holmes nodded his head. "I have two questions for you, Lady Temperley. First, am I correct in believing that you and your family are the owners of the famous Temperley Emeralds, and that these are kept at Hardshaw Hall?"

"Yes, that is so. They have been in my husband's family for generations."

"Second, do you intend to return to Derbyshire this afternoon?"

"Yes. I feel my place is there, at Hardshaw, and I would wish to get back there as soon as possible."

"Very well. If I accept your case, I take it you give me *carte blanche* to make any enquiries I wish, and to take any steps I consider necessary?"

"Certainly, by all means."

"Then I shall meet you at St. Pancras station before your train departs, and accompany you back to Hardshaw this afternoon."

When Lady Temperley had left us, Holmes sat for some minutes in silence, with his eyes closed, evidently going over again in his mind all that our visitor had told us. Then, as if he had reached a decision, he sprang to his feet, opened the top drawer of his desk and took out his revolver.

"Will you come?" he asked me, as he examined the chambers of the gun.

"If I can be of any assistance to you."

"Then I should be obliged if you would bring your own pistol."

"Are you expecting trouble?" I asked in surprise.

"I sense that the matter is coming to a head," said he, "and it is always as well to be prepared for the worst."

Our train had passed St. Albans and was well on the way to Bedford before Holmes alluded once more to the business which was taking us to the North.

"I wish to know a little more about the Temperley Emeralds," said he, addressing Lady Temperley. "Are they in the form of a necklace?"

"Partly. There is indeed a very large and ornate necklace, but also an elaborate matching bracelet and a pair of ear-rings."

"Do you wear these jewels very often?"

Lady Temperley shook her head. "They may be fabulously valuable, as seems to be widely known, but, personally, I do not care for them. The setting of the stones is heavy and old-fashioned, and they are, of course, bright green. I do not think that the colour suits me at all. The last time I wore them was about two years ago, at a grand ball thrown by the Duke of Holdernesse."

"Where are they usually kept?"

"Inside a locked case, in a locked drawer in my bedroom."

"Have you had any reason to take them out of the drawer recently?"

"Only once in the last two months, as far as I can recall. Edward and his tutor, Mr. Sowerby, expressed an interest in the emeralds, so I got them out to show them one day. But why are you asking me all these questions about the Temperley Emeralds, Mr. Holmes?"

"Such valuable gemstones are not infrequently the focus for crime, Lady Temperley. As I am considering all the events which have so disturbed you recently, and all the circumstances surrounding those events, it would, I feel, be remiss of me to omit consideration, too, of so famous a prize as your emeralds. Tell me, Lady Temperley, how did you come to select Mr. Sowerby as tutor for Edward Docking? Was he recommended to you by someone?"

"I do not believe so. I cannot be certain, as my husband dealt with the matter, but I believe he simply advertised the position in the Derby evening newspaper. I understand that Mr. Sowerby had been a schoolteacher of many years' experience, but had recently retired. He is very scholarly and bookish in appearance, and he evidently struck my husband as the most suitable of the candidates. I think that Mr. Sowerby himself was very pleased to get the position, as he is not, I understand, very well off."

Holmes nodded his head at this information, but made no response, and lapsed then into thoughtful silence. Save to reply in the most perfunctory manner to odd remarks of mine or Lady Temperley's, he scarcely spoke another word until our train reached Bakewell, in the Peak District of Derbyshire. Lady Temperley had wired ahead the time of our arrival, and a carriage was waiting for us in the station yard.

As we rattled slowly up the narrow, hilly roads, between the ever-present grey stone walls which divide up the countryside in those parts, I was struck by the wild beauty of the landscape. Flocks of sheep were busily grazing the short, springy turf in the fields, moorland birds wheeled high above us, buffeted by the strong, capricious winds, and, over all, the sun was shining brightly. It was hard to imagine that anything very sinister could occur in such fresh and open countryside.

After about twenty minutes, we turned off the road, passed between two lichen-blotched stone gateposts, and followed a track through a dense stand of trees, emerging at length before the ancient stone manor house which was Hardshaw Hall. It was a solid-looking, square-edged sort of building, early Tudor in origin, I judged, with no pretensions to unnecessary architectural refinement, but built rather, it appeared, to withstand the strong Peak District winds and the annual assault of the elements.

As we drew up before the front of the building, a door opened and a butler descended the steps and opened the door of the carriage. He informed us, in answer to a query from Lady Temperley, that her husband was taking tea in the drawing-room with Major Lockhart and Mr. Sowerby.

"Is Edward not with them?" asked Lady Temperley.

"Mr. Docking went for a ride with Mr. Sowerby shortly after luncheon, milady. Mr. Sowerby has now returned; Mr. Docking has not yet done so."

The three men in the drawing-room rose to their feet as we were announced. The first, a distinguished-looking man with grizzled grey hair and moustache, I recognized, from photographs I had seen in the illustrated press, as Lord Temperley. The second, a large, broad-shouldered man with dark hair and a waxed black moustache, I took, from his military bearing, to be Major Lockhart, and the third, a scholarly-looking man with a bald head and a slight stoop, I knew must be the tutor, Mr. Sowerby.

"My dear," said Lord Temperley to his wife, "It is good to see you safely back home again. I trust that your visit to London was satisfactory."

"Yes," said she. "This is Mr. Sherlock Holmes and his colleague, Dr. Watson," she continued, introducing us, as Holmes had suggested to her earlier, as historians of old tales and traditions, who were going to look into the business of the thirteenth step for her. "I thought," she added, "that we could put them up for a few days while they conduct their researches in the old family papers."

"By all means," said Lord Temperley affably. "Come and take a seat, gentlemen, and we can all have some tea."

As she sat down next to her husband, Lady Temperley enquired after Edward Docking, and it was clear that she was concerned at his absence.

"Mr. Sowerby was just telling us where they got to earlier this afternoon," said Lord Temperley.

"How came you to part company?" Lady Temperley asked the tutor.

"I am ashamed to say I was exhausted, Lady Temperley," he replied, "and could not carry on. But Edward wanted to go further, so I came back alone. I'm sure he will be all right. He is a much better rider than I am."

"I was over in that general direction myself a little later," interjected Major Lockhart, "but I didn't see anything of Edward, so I think he must have gone all the way up to Burnage Edge. If so, that's quite a long ride, so I suppose that's why he's late. I did see Agnes James up that way, out for a trot by herself, and had a little chat with her. She told me that she and Edward had arranged to meet up somewhere in that vicinity, but she hadn't seen anything of him either. No doubt he will be back soon."

"I certainly hope he is," said Lady Temperley. "I don't like him going off by himself. I worry about the boy, Ralph. He's had several bad shocks lately, and the last time I saw him he looked as pale as a ghost."

I was struck by Lady Temperley's concern for Edward Docking. She had made no reference to it during our railway journey, but it had clearly been on her mind all day. I supposed that, in the absence of her own son in India, her maternal concerns had transferred themselves to this son of her husband's cousin. There is certainly something in the recklessness of youth to cause concern in anyone's breast, and that concern must inevitably be intensified when one is placed in a position of responsibility for someone else's son or daughter. And yet, I reflected, most young men succeed in passing through their reckless youth to reach their adulthood more or less unscathed. As we sipped our tea, I observed that the men, Lord Temperley, Major Lockhart and Mr. Sowerby, did their best to assuage Lady Temperley's anxieties, and presently the conversation moved on to other topics. Sherlock Holmes was asked about his interest in the singular old tales and traditions which are to be found in the ancient manor houses of England, and did a first-rate job of making it sound like his consuming passion, citing numerous examples from all parts of the country. For myself, I was glad that I was not questioned too closely on the subject, for I doubted that my replies would have sounded either so convincing or so knowledgeable as those of my friend.

Sometime later, I was in my room, sitting on the side of the bed and staring out of the window, wondering if our presence at Hardshaw Hall would really serve any purpose, when I heard noises from outside. I rose to my feet and looked down into the drive. A man on horseback had just arrived. I watched as he sprang from the saddle, ran up the steps to the front door and thundered on the door-knocker. As he did so, a low farm-cart appeared round the corner of the building behind him and drew to a halt by the steps. In the back of the cart was a bundle of some sort, covered with a tarpaulin. There seemed to be a sense of urgency about these people, whoever they were, and I wondered idly what their business might be. As for our own business, I could not imagine where we would begin, and I lay on the bed to ponder the question.

Ten minutes had passed, and my aimless thoughts had given way to drowsiness, when I was rendered fully awake by a loud knock at my bedroom door. I opened it to find one of the young housemaids there, who informed me in a breathless tone that Sherlock Holmes required my presence downstairs without delay.

I followed the girl downstairs, and ran across Holmes as he crossed the hallway. He took my arm and led me towards the back of the house.

"It's bad news, Watson," said he in a low tone, as he pulled open a door and we passed into a narrow corridor beyond. "It's Edward Docking."

"What has he done?" I asked.

"He is dead, Watson."

I stopped abruptly. "Good God!" I cried. "Surely not!"

"I'm afraid so. He appears to have been flung from his horse, just as Stephen James was. That is what everyone supposes, anyway. He was found in a copse by some of the estate workers. Lady Temperley almost passed out at the news. She is now lying down in her bedroom."

We passed through a doorway, across a small yard and into one of the numerous outbuildings there. Inside, a still figure lay on a stone table, and several men stood around, among whom I recognized the three gentlemen we had been speaking to in the drawing-room just a short time previously.

"My colleague is a medical man," said Holmes to Lord Temperley. "The local doctor has been sent for, Watson," he continued, turning to me, "but if you would care to give us your opinion, it might be helpful."

"Of course," I said, and stepped forward to examine the body. The front of the skull had been smashed in, as if by a severe impact against a large stone. There were no other marks on the body that I could see, and I gave it as my opinion that the blow to the head was undoubtedly the cause of death.

As I finished my examination, Sherlock Holmes stepped forward and began to rummage in the dead youth's pockets.

"What on earth are you doing, Mr. Holmes?" asked Lord Temperley, a note of disapproval in his voice.

"I am just seeing if there is anything of interest in these pockets," returned Holmes without looking up. "Ah! What is this?"

As he spoke he drew forth from an inside pocket what appeared to be a large string of green gems. There were gasps of amazement all around me, and as he held it up and it caught the light, I saw that it was an elaborate necklace, consisting of intertwined gold chains set with a great many green stones.

"The Temperley Emeralds!" cried Lord Temperley in astonishment. "I cannot believe it! Why in Heaven's name did Edward have the emeralds in his possession? And how did he get hold of them?"

Holmes pushed open the door and carried the necklace out to the yard. There, he took a small lens from his pocket and began to examine the necklace closely. "You had better have the jewel-case brought down to the drawing-room," he said after a moment to Lord Temperley, who had followed him out to the yard. "Then we can see if the bracelet and earrings are still there."

"I'll get it myself," returned Lord Temperley. "It's locked in a drawer in my wife's room, to which the servants don't have access. What about the necklace?"

"I'll hold onto that for the moment," replied Holmes. "I'll take it into the drawing-room."

For a fraction of a second, Lord Temperley hesitated and looked at Holmes, but there was something in the latter's manner which inspired confidence and trust, even in those to whom he was a perfect stranger. "Very well," said Lord Temperley, then turned away to return to the house. As he did so, however, three men came round the corner of an outbuilding, into the yard. The first, who was carrying a leather case, looked every inch the country medical practitioner in his tweed suit and gaiters, but the other two were policemen, the first in the braided uniform of an inspector, the second a very large, burly constable.

"Hello, Dr. Horrocks," said Lord Temperley. "Grim business here, I'm afraid. The young man we've been putting up for the last three months has had a bad riding accident. But what brings these policemen here?"

"We happened to be all together when your message reached us," returned the doctor. "Inspector Waltham thought he'd better come along and see what's happened."

"I don't think there's anything here in your line, Inspector," said Temperley with a shake of the head.

"Perhaps not, sir," said Inspector Waltham, "but this is the second such accident in just a few weeks, so I thought I'd better verify the matter for myself. Might I enquire who all these gentlemen are, sir?"

"This is Major Lockhart, whom I think you may know," replied Temperley. "He's been staying with us all year. This is Mr. Sowerby, the unfortunate boy's tutor. And these two gentlemen, who arrived with my wife just a short time ago this afternoon, are Mr. Sherlock Holmes and Dr. Watson."

The policeman turned to Holmes, an expression of recognition on his features at the name he had been given.

"Excuse me, sir," said he, "but might you be Mr. Holmes the London criminal expert?"

"Among other things," returned Holmes in a dismissive tone. "I am here because Lady Temperley asked me to look into some matter for her."

"A crime?" asked Inspector Waltham.

"Not exactly," said Holmes.

"Might it be anything to do with that jewellery you are holding?"

Before Holmes could reply, Lord Temperley stepped forward. "No, it isn't," said he in a testy voice. "Look, Inspector, there's no point our standing out here discussing the matter. When you've finished here, come through to the drawing-room and we can sort it all out then. I'll send someone to show you the way." With that, he turned on his heel and was gone.

Major Lockhart and Mr. Sowerby followed Lord Temperley through the doorway into the house, but as I made to do the same, Holmes tweaked my sleeve and drew me back, out of earshot of the others. "I take it, Watson," said he in a low tone, "that you observed the oddity of Edward Docking's hands."

"I saw nothing unusual about his hands," I responded in surprise.

"Yes," said Homes. "That was the oddity."

A few minutes later, Lord Temperley joined us in the drawing-room. He was carrying in his hand a large flat jewel-case, covered in pale pink velvet.

"The bracelet and earrings are still in the case," said he.

"If you would bring them over to the window," said Holmes, "we can examine all the pieces together."

I watched with interest as they held up the various items of jewellery by the window, examining them carefully. The daylight was beginning to fade now, but the sinking sun cast its vivid beams through the tall window and sparkled on the green stones.

"I am no expert on gemstones," said Holmes after a few moments, "but I am not at all sure that these stones in the necklace are genuine. They seem to me to be distinctly duller and less vivid than the stones in the bracelet and ear-rings."

"But that is impossible," cried Lord Temperley. "Here, let me see." There followed several minutes of silence, then at length he cried out. "You are quite right, Mr. Holmes. I am certain of it. Even in this poor light, you can see that the colour of the stones in the necklace is nowhere near as vivid as the others. And, now I look carefully, I can see that the setting of the stones is not as it should be, either. It is somewhat cruder than I remember. What the devil does it mean?" he cried in a tone of despair. "If these are not the Temperley Emeralds, what are they? Where are the real emeralds, and why did Edward have this imitation in his pocket? Come over here a moment, gentlemen," he said, turning to where I was sitting with Sowerby and Lockhart, "and give us your opinion."

For several minutes we examined the jewellery in silence. At length I ventured the opinion that the stones in the necklace seemed to me a little dull compared to those in the bracelet and ear-rings. Sowerby's opinion concurred with mine; he thought that the emerald necklace did not appear so vivid as on the previous occasion he had been shown it, a month or two previously. Major Lockhart's opinion of the necklace was the same, although his grounds for saying so were slightly different. In demonstration of his view, he held up the necklace to the window and looked through one of the larger stones directly at the setting sun. He then did the same with one of the ear-rings, and declared that whereas the stone in the ear-ring was undoubtedly genuine, the stones in the necklace were not.

"We are all in agreement, then, gentlemen," said Temperley. "The stones in the necklace are false. In fact, I believe the whole necklace is false."

"But how can that be?" cried Sowerby. "And why should Edward have been carrying an imitation of the Temperley Emeralds about with him?"

"Yes, it doesn't make much sense, Temperley," said Major Lockhart. "Unless," he added, "Edward had given the real necklace to someone and received the imitation in return – but what possible reason could he have for doing that? And, in any case, how could he have extracted the real necklace from where it was securely locked up?"

"I think I can get to the bottom of the matter," said Holmes, "but first I need to ask Lady Temperley a question."

"What question?" demanded Temperley.

"I should rather not say until I have asked Lady Temperley herself."

"But she is utterly prostrated by what has happened this afternoon," said Temperley, "and cannot be disturbed,"

"She does not yet know all that has happened," returned Holmes. "She will answer my question – that I can promise you."

"Oh, very well," said Temperley in a tone of resignation, "if you insist. I will call for her maid to show you up there."

A few moments later, the maid entered and she and Holmes left. The discussion in the drawing-room continued in a desultory fashion for a little while, but reached no conclusion, as no one could suggest what had become of the real emeralds, nor why Docking should have been carrying with him a duplicate set. The whole business seemed utterly inexplicable. As the minutes ticked by and Holmes did not return, I began to wonder where he had gone, and what he was doing. At length I could stand the tension no longer and, making some excuse, I left the drawing-room and went up to my bedroom. There, I sat on the bed, but left the door ajar, so that I might hear anyone passing in the corridor outside.

For several minutes, all was silent, then I heard footsteps on the stairs and the sound of voices approaching, which I recognized as those of Lord Temperley and Major Lockhart.

"I'll go and see how Felicity is getting on," said Temperley, "and see what Mr. Holmes is up to. Do you know where Sowerby has gone?"

"No, I've no idea," replied Lockhart. "Anyway, I'll be in my room if you want me."

I heard them move off, and, for a few moments, silence descended again on the upper floor of Hardshaw Hall. My mind had wandered once more to speculation as to what Holmes might be doing, when all at once, I heard a cry of surprise, followed by a cry of anger from the same voice, then the sound of a scuffle. I had not the faintest idea what was happening, but I sprang from my bed, seized my revolver and hurried out into the corridor.

For an instant I paused. Then I heard further cries, among which I thought I recognized Holmes's voice, which seemed to come from a doorway a little further down the corridor. I hurried that way and, finding the door ajar, pushed it wide open. As I did so, I almost cried out in astonishment at the scene which met my eyes. The room was in utter chaos, with drawers pulled out and furniture overturned, and, in the centre of the room, two men grappling fiercely. One was Sherlock Holmes, the other Major Lockhart. At the very moment I pushed the door open, the two of them overbalanced and tumbled to the floor. Lockhart stretched out his hand, picked up a poker from the fireplace and raised it up to strike a blow. I sprang forward at once and clapped the pistol to the side of his head.

"Put that down or I fire," I cried. There was a moment of stillness, then, as I pressed the muzzle into his temple, he threw the poker into the hearth with a clatter. "Now get to your feet and don't try anything."

I took a step back, keeping the pistol pointed at Lockhart, as he and Holmes scrambled to their feet. A voice from behind me made me half turn. In the corridor stood Lord Temperley and Inspector Waltham.

"What the devil is going on here?" demanded Lord Temperley.

"I have been looking for your emeralds," said Holmes. "Here they are," he added, holding up a large ornate necklace, set with vivid green stones. "They were in the bottom of Lockhart's trunk, as I'd suspected they would be."

"It's a lie!" cried Lockhart. "I don't know what your game is, Mr. Holmes – you and that crony of yours – but you'll have to do better than that!"

"How can you possibly justify such a serious accusation, Mr. Holmes?" demanded Temperley in an angry voice.

"Because, Lord Temperley, it is true," replied Holmes. "It has been Major Lockhart's plan all along to steal the emeralds. Everything that has happened has been with that one aim in view, since long before he ever came to stay here."

"I find that very hard to believe," said Temperley in a tone of stupefaction. "Why, Major Lockhart has been staying with us for nearly a year now. If he had really wished to steal the emeralds, I am sure he could have done so long ago. In any case, how, if at all, does this relate to the poor boy lying dead downstairs? Why did he have the duplicate necklace in his pocket, and where did it come from?"

"I fancy Major Lockhart could shed some light on that subject, considering that it was he who had the duplicate necklace made," returned Holmes. As he spoke he dipped his hand into Lockhart's trunk and brought out a folded sheet of paper. "I have here a letter addressed to Lockhart from Holland and Westwood, jewellery manufacturers of Hatton Garden in London, discussing the details of the manufacture of the imitation necklace."

"You devil!" cried Lockhart in a wild, hoarse tone, his eyes bulging with rage. "How dare you make free with my private correspondence!" Abruptly, with no warning, he sprang forward and clamped his large, powerful hands round Holmes's throat, as if he would strangle the life out of him. "You fiend!" he cried. "You damned, interfering fiend! I'll swing for you, so help me!"

I stepped forward quickly and raised my revolver, but as I did so I saw Holmes bring his hands up swiftly, grasp hold of his assailant's fingers and slowly pull them away from his throat. There was a cry of pain from Lockhart, as Holmes pressed his fingers backwards and forced him down to the floor.

"Let's get the bracelets on him and get him downstairs," said Inspector Waltham in a brisk tone, producing a pair of handcuffs from within his jacket.

As Lockhart and the policeman left the room, Temperley turned to Holmes.

"If Lockhart had the duplicate necklace made," said he in a weak, trembling voice, as if he could scarcely believe the words he himself was uttering, "how came it into Edward's pocket, Mr. Holmes? Do you believe that Lockhart somehow managed to slip it in there?"

"I think not," replied Holmes. "I fancy that Lockhart was just as surprised as everyone else when the imitation emeralds turned up where they did – although not for the same reasons."

"Do you believe there is anything suspicious about poor Edward's death?"

"I am certain of it," said Holmes. "There is not a doubt in my mind that he was murdered. But, come. Let us go downstairs, Lord Temperley, and I will explain to you my view of the matter. It is a more complex business than you perhaps realise."

Two hours had passed. Major Lockhart had been taken away in a police van, but Inspector Waltham had at length returned by himself to discuss the case with Sherlock Holmes and Lord Temperley. Holmes, meanwhile, had had a long private discussion with Lady Temperley and seemed to have succeeded in calming and reassuring her, so that she had taken her place at the dinner-table with the rest of us. It had been a strange meal, with very little conversation. The tutor, in particular, had seemed very uncomfortable to be there at all, but, in truth, I think that none of us could concentrate on anything, so keen were we all to hear Holmes's analysis of the surprising and puzzling events which had recently disturbed the historic calm of Hardshaw Hall.

Now, our meal finished, we had repaired to the large drawing-room. A fire had been lit, for the evening had brought a chill with it, and its familiar friendly crackle was as comforting to the mind as its warmth was comforting to the body. Inspector Waltham had joined us as we sat, sipping our coffee, and, at last, in response to a request from the policeman, Sherlock Holmes prepared to begin.

"The first thing that caused me concern," said he, "was Lady Temperley's account of her visit to the fortune-teller at the village fair, and what she was told there."

This remark elicited cries of surprise from all present.

"I have always understood that you were highly sceptical of such superstitions," I interjected, "and your remarks to Lady Temperley this morning gave no indication that you attached any credence to the fortune-teller's predictions."

"Yes, of course that is so. You misunderstand me, Watson. My train of thought was simply this: that such fortune-tellers generally predict good things for those that consult them, or, at the very least, a mixture of good and bad. They do, after all, wish their customers to leave the tent feeling glad that they have paid a visit, so that they will recommend the experience to their friends. But Lady Temperley was given only bad, gloomy predictions, which upset her profoundly. I felt sure there must be some reason for this, and I wondered if the Gipsy fortune-teller had been bribed to say what she did. If so, that certainly threw suspicion in my mind onto Edward Docking, without whose insistence Lady Temperley would probably not have visited the fortune-teller at all.

"We then come to the incident of the thirteenth step. Lady Temperley believed that it was simply Edward's ignorance of the old Hardshaw tradition which had led him to speak so light-heartedly of counting the steps, and, despite his irritation over the matter, I imagine that that was also the view of Lord Temperley. But as I listened to Lady Temperley's account, suspicious as I already was of Docking, I could not help but think that this seemed of the same pattern as the fortune-teller business, and I wondered if he were quite so ignorant of the old tradition as he pretended to be. It seemed to me, rather, that the stage was being deliberately set for some misfortune to befall the family, but what might this be? I at once thought of the famous Temperley Emeralds, which I knew were fabulously valuable.

"As to the purpose of these superstitious warnings of misfortune, I could think of no specific reason for them, and thought it possible that they might be intended simply to confuse the issue, so that when the 'misfortune' occurred, rational consideration of the matter would be hampered. Incidents which appear to fulfil a 'prophecy' tend to strike the mind differently from incidents which occur 'out of the blue,' as it were. This seemed to me the most likely purpose of these warnings of impending doom. But why should a young man who was hoping to enter the University of Oxford in the autumn, and who was being very kindly put up and tutored in the meantime by distant relatives of his father, have been plotting against his generous benefactors in this way? It seemed to me that such deep plotting would only be entered into by someone who had no real intention of taking up a place at Oxford at all, and who did not really care a fig for Lord and Lady Temperley.

"As my thoughts circled round Edward Docking in this fashion, it occurred to me that as he had been brought up in South Africa, and Lord and Lady Temperley had never met him before, they had no way of knowing that he really was who he said he was. It was therefore perfectly possible, as far as I could see, that he was not really Edward Docking at all, but someone else entirely."

There were cries of incredulity from Holmes's audience at this suggestion, but he waved his hand to still their protests.

"I realise that that may strike you as fantastically improbable," he continued, "but it can scarcely be denied that the whole state of affairs was a very singular one, so the explanation for it was always likely to be a singular one, too. Indeed, Lady Temperley herself was convinced that something was very seriously amiss, even if she could not quite put her finger on what it was that troubled her so much."

"That is true," said Lady Temperley, "but I should never have considered such a wild and extraordinary speculation as you are suggesting, Mr. Holmes."

"I imagine not," responded Holmes. "That is perfectly understandable. You had accepted what you had been told by others, and you were in the very midst of all these disturbing events. In such circumstances it is always difficult to free your mind from what you have implicitly taken to be the truth for so long. In my professional life, however, I have generally found it worthwhile to consider all possibilities, however improbable they may seem at first.

"Now," he continued after a moment, "Lady Temperley had mentioned to me that although Edward Docking and the neighbour's boy, Stephen James, had never met, they had corresponded with each other some years ago, in their schooldays. Bearing that in mind, it seemed to me that if the young man staying here were not really Edward Docking, then if anyone was likely to see through the deception, either because of something the supposed Docking said, or something he might have been expected to say but didn't, that person would be Stephen James. Of course, if the James boy did harbour such doubts about his riding companion, and was unwise enough to give any indication that he did, then, if there were any truth to this theory, he would undoubtedly be putting himself in very great peril. When Lady Temperley then described to us how Stephen James had been killed while out riding with the young man taken to be Docking, I very much feared that it was murder, and that what might be termed the 'improbable possibility,' if not entirely confirmed, had at least become somewhat less improbable. So it seemed to me, at least, and I decided to follow this theory as far as it would take me.

"Now, if the young man purporting to be Edward Docking was in reality someone else, who might that someone else be? It could, of course, be someone that nobody had ever heard of, but most likely, I considered, was that it was the Andrew Cotter who had been mentioned to me by Lady

Temperley. He was said to be a former school-friend of Docking's, and Docking had gone to stay with him in Cape Town immediately before sailing for England. He would probably have been familiar enough with Docking's habits to succeed with the imposture, and was probably also sufficiently familiar with Docking's handwriting to imitate it successfully when he was obliged to write to Docking's family from England. But if it were really Andrew Cotter you have been putting up for the last three months, where, then, was the real Edward Docking? On this question, I feared the worst, and thought it very likely that he had been done to death by Cotter, in or around Cape Town.

"When the letter from Docking's father arrived recently, bringing news of the discovery of the body believed to be that of Andrew Cotter, Lady Temperley noted that the young man she took to be Docking appeared terribly shocked and upset at the news. Of course, it was always possible, even if my theory were correct, that Cotter might be shocked and anxious at the discovery of the body of the young man he himself had murdered, but I rather fancied that what really shocked him was the other item of news in the letter, that Edward Docking's father was coming to England in just a few weeks' time, for this would mean that his exposure as both an imposter and a murderer was imminent.

"As I considered the matter in this way, I was aware that there was yet another issue which must be taken into consideration, and that is this: although Lord and Lady Temperley had never met Edward Docking before the young man they believed to be he had arrived in England in February, Major Lockhart certainly had. He had stayed with the Dockings for a while during the time he spent in South Africa. Now, according to my theory, the young man who came to stay here at Hardshaw Hall was an imposter – probably Andrew Cotter – yet when he arrived here, calling himself Edward Docking, Lockhart said nothing. I gave this question a lot of consideration, but could think of no convincing reason why Lockhart should have remained silent on the matter if he were an honest man, and I was obliged to conclude then that he was not, and that his intentions here were dishonourable. If that were so, then what appeared to have been a chance meeting between Lockhart and Lord Temperley last year in London, which led to Lockhart's coming to stay here, might well not have been so accidental as it seemed. It is not too difficult to deliberately contrive a supposedly 'chance encounter' with someone if you really wish to do so, as I am sure countless young men would attest each time they recall how they first struck up a conversation with some young lady or other who happened to be the object of their admiration."

Lord Temperley nodded his head. "Incredible though it seems to be saying this," he remarked, "I am sure now that you must be right. There have been one or two odd little incidents in the last few months which have made me wonder about Lockhart and his supposed plans for the future. No, I didn't mention any of these things to you, Felicity," he added, as his wife made to speak: "they were all very trivial and might have meant nothing, and you had enough to worry about as it was. I'll give you a couple of examples, Mr. Holmes, so you can see what I mean: I chanced to notice one morning that Lockhart had had a letter from those jewellers you mentioned, although I had no idea, of course, what it was about. When curiosity got the better of me and I asked him about it, he said it was to do with an old ring which had belonged to his mother, which he was having reset. I remember I had the distinct impression from his manner as he said this that he was not telling me the truth. I explained this oddity away to myself afterwards by conjecturing that he was perhaps short of funds and was selling the ring to raise a little money but did not want to admit it, so I gave it no further thought. On another occasion, a couple of months ago, Lockhart and I were talking. We had been discussing Edward's impressive horsemanship, and Lockhart referred to him in passing as 'Andrew.' Of course, he corrected himself at once, and I thought it was just an unimportant slip of the tongue, and didn't give it any more thought. Lockhart even made a joke of it, I recall, and deliberately referred to the boy subsequently as 'Benjamin' and 'Bertie,' laughing heartily at his own jest. But now that I recall the incident, it does seem to me that Lockhart appeared inordinately bothered and embarrassed about it, much more so than one might expect if it had really been simply a trivial slip of the tongue."

Holmes nodded. "I believe that Lockhart and Cotter had plotted the whole business together, their ultimate aim being the theft of the Temperley Emeralds, after which, no doubt, they both intended to disappear, probably to Australia or somewhere else far away, where they would hope to avoid all attempts to find them. But if it had been Lockhart's intention all along to steal the emeralds, as I believe, why should he have involved Cotter in his criminal plan? The likeliest explanation, as I see it, is that Lockhart knew that he himself had no talent for opening locks and closing them up again in a way which could not be detected, and he knew that Cotter, with his criminal experience in South Africa, did have this skill. This in turn suggests that the plan was first hatched when the two of them met during Lockhart's time in South Africa. Cotter's ability to pick locks was no doubt his chief contribution to the scheme, Lockhart's being the ordering of the imitation necklace. It must, I imagine, have been during those periodic trips to London which I understand he took that Lockhart arranged to have the duplicate necklace made. When was the last time he went up to London, Lord Temperley?"

"Just last week. He went on the Wednesday and came back on the Friday."

"Then that was probably when he collected the completed duplicate necklace from the jeweller. It must have been their intention to leave the duplicate necklace in place of the genuine one, to prevent – or, at least, delay – the discovery of the theft, but this of course meant that they could do nothing until the duplicate necklace was ready. And now, having at last got the duplicate necklace, they would wish to put their plan into operation at the earliest opportunity, for with Docking's father due to arrive in just a couple of weeks – by which time they must both have hoped to have left Hardshaw completely – the time available to them was rapidly running out.

"As to what happened in the last twenty-four hours, we can only speculate. One thing, however, seems certain, which is that Cotter was murdered. He is supposed to have been flung from his horse, and to have struck his forehead on a stone. That means that he must have fallen forwards, in which case he would naturally use his hands to try to break his fall. And yet, despite the fact that he was not wearing gloves, his hands are completely unmarked. I have never known such an accident in which the victim's hands were not at least dirty and grazed, if not cut and bruised. I therefore think that Cotter had dismounted when he was attacked, and that he was deliberately struck down by someone. That someone must have been Lockhart. They had probably arranged to meet in the copse where Cotter's body was subsequently found, in order for Cotter to hand the necklace over to Lockhart. No doubt Cotter had taken the necklace from Lady Temperley's room this morning. Her absence in London for the day would, of course, have provided him with an ideal opportunity. But if both Lockhart and Cotter were intending to leave Hardshaw very soon, Lockhart, it seems, also had his own separate plan, which was to rid himself of his partner-in-crime forever, by murdering him. We can only speculate as to when Lockhart decided on this course of action. It may have been a recent decision, or it may be that he had intended all along to get rid of Cotter in this way, once the younger man had served his purpose and the robbery had been accomplished. This would, of course, save Lockhart having to share the spoils with him. However that may be, it is clear that things did not go quite as Lockhart had planned.

"The fact that he had gone to the trouble and expense of having the duplicate necklace made can only mean, as I mentioned, that he intended it to be left in the jewel case, in place of the genuine necklace. But when Cotter had taken the genuine necklace from the case, he evidently decided for some reason not to leave the imitation necklace in its place, but to take it with him when he went riding. As this, of course, set at nought the whole point of their careful plan, we must suppose two things: first, that Lockhart was not party to this decision, and had no idea when he murdered Cotter that the duplicate necklace was in his pocket, and, second, that Cotter had some very compelling reason for taking the duplicate necklace with him. What I suspect is this, that having deliberately got rid of Mr. Sowerby this afternoon by riding further than he knew the tutor would wish to go, Cotter then intended, after his rendezvous with Lockhart, to meet Agnes James, as it seems they had arranged. Perhaps, then, his reason for taking the necklace with him was that he intended to offer it to the girl, in an attempt to win her favour."

"If so," interrupted Inspector Waltham, "he must have been a complete fool. She would have recognized at once that it was a part of the famous Temperley Emeralds. It is inconceivable that she would have accepted it."

"I quite agree," said Lady Temperley. "And even if he had explained to her that it was just a copy of the original, it is such a heavy-looking, old-fashioned piece of jewellery that I can't believe that a young girl such as Agnes would find it an attractive thing to wear."

"I am sure you are right," said Holmes, nodding his head. "I think, however, that Andrew Cotter must have been very much smitten with Agnes James, and it is my experience that when a young man is in thrall to a woman in that way, there are no lengths he will not go to, however troublesome, no stratagems he will not attempt, however absurd, in order to win the woman's heart. No man is spared, but passion makes a fool of every one."

"You may be right about the whole business, Mr. Holmes," said the policeman after a moment. "In fact, I don't doubt that you are. But I can see that we're going to have the devil of a job to prove it all against Major Lockhart."

"The murder charge may indeed be difficult to prove in a court of law," agreed Holmes, "even though the circumstantial evidence is compelling. But you should at least be successful with the charge of theft. The genuine necklace was in Lockhart's trunk upstairs, and we know the name of the jewellers in London who made the duplicate necklace for him, so that is a start. It should also not be too difficult to prove, with the aid of photographs from South Africa, that the young man who has been known here as Edward Docking was in reality Andrew Cotter."

Inspector Waltham nodded his head, scribbled a few lines in his note-book, then closed it up. "I'd best be getting back to the station," said he, as he slipped the note-book into his pocket and rose to his feet. "I thank you very much for your help, Mr. Holmes. I'll take the duplicate necklace with me, and the letter from the jewellers, and set enquiries in motion at once."

When the policeman had left us, we sat in silence for some time, each no doubt pondering the dreadful recent events from his own point of view. At length the silence was broken by the tutor, Mr. Sowerby.

"This may be a very trivial point," he remarked in a hesitant tone, "but I am still puzzled about one little thing, Mr. Holmes. When you left the drawing-room earlier this evening, you said that there was one question you wished to ask Lady Temperley, and you implied that her answer would shed light on the matter. I confess I have racked my brains, but I cannot think what on earth that question could have been."

Holmes chuckled. "Nothing very subtle, I'm afraid, Mr. Sowerby," he replied. "When the duplicate necklace turned up, and the genuine article was found to be missing from the jewel-case, I was convinced that my theory was correct and that Major Lockhart had the emeralds, probably hidden somewhere in his bedroom. But the discovery of the imitation emeralds in Cotter's pocket – not to mention Inspector Waltham's inadvertent revelation of my true profession as a criminal investigator –

would also have been the first warning that Lockhart had had that his plans had gone awry, and I thought it likely that he would take the earliest opportunity to move the emeralds to somewhere where they would be much more difficult to find. It was therefore my intention to search his bedroom for the necklace without delay, the only problem being that I had no idea which of the rooms was his. The simplest solution to this difficulty, it seemed to me, was to ask Lady Temperley, which, as she was alone in her room, I could do without anyone else overhearing. That is therefore precisely what I did. It is a singular fact, but sometimes the dullest, most banal little question can yet be the most important!"

Little remains for me to tell of what had been a singularly strange, unpredictable and dreadful case. Subsequent enquiries proved beyond all doubt that the surprising theory which Sherlock Holmes had expounded to us in the drawing-room at Hardshaw Hall was indeed correct in every detail. As Holmes had predicted, Major Lockhart was acquitted of the murder of Andrew Cotter due to a lack of evidence, but was convicted of the theft of the Temperley Emeralds, and of conspiring to conceal the death of the real Edward Docking, for which he received a lengthy prison sentence. As Holmes and I journeyed back to London, the day after the surprising and dramatic events I have described above, an odd and striking thought occurred to me. Although Cotter had cynically tried to use the old tradition of "the thirteenth step of Hardshaw Hall" for his own ends, without, presumably, giving it any real credence, it had, nevertheless, once again correctly predicted a death at Hardshaw. But this was a death which that villain could never have expected, the death being his own.

Also from MX Publishing

MX Publishing is the world's largest specialist Sherlock Holmes publisher, with over a hundred titles and fifty authors creating the latest in Sherlock Holmes fiction and non-fiction.

From traditional short stories and novels to travel guides and quiz books, MX Publishing cater for all Holmes fans.

The collection includes leading titles such as *Benedict Cumberbatch In Transition* and *The Norwood Author* which won the 2011 Howlett Award (Sherlock Holmes Book of the Year).

MX Publishing also has one of the largest communities of Holmes fans on Facebook with regular contributions from dozens of authors.

www.mxpublishing.com

Also from MX Publishing

Our bestselling books are our short story collections;

'Lost Stories of Sherlock Holmes' , 'The Outstanding Mysteries of Sherlock Holmes', The Papers of Sherlock Holmes Volume 1 and 2, 'Untold Adventures of Sherlock Holmes' (and the sequel 'Studies in Legacy) and 'Sherlock Holmes in Pursuit', 'The Cotswold Werewolf and Other Stories of Sherlock Holmes' – and many more……

www.mxpublishing.com

Also from MX Publishing

"Phil Growick's, 'The Secret Journal of Dr Watson', is an adventure which takes place in the latter part of Holmes and Watson's lives. They are entrusted by HM Government (although not officially) and the King no less to undertake a rescue mission to save the Romanovs, Russia's Royal family from a grisly end at the hand of the Bolsheviks. There is a wealth of detail in the story but not so much as would detract us from the enjoyment of the story. Espionage, counter-espionage, the ace of spies himself, double-agents, double-crossers...all these flit across the pages in a realistic and exciting way. All the characters are extremely well-drawn and Mr Growick, most importantly, does not falter with a very good ear for Holmesian dialogue indeed. Highly recommended. A five-star effort."
The Baker Street Society

Also from MX Publishing

The American Literati Series

The Final Page of Baker Street
The Baron of Brede Place
Seventeen Minutes To Baker Street

"The really amazing thing about this book is the author's ability to call up the 'essence' of both the Baker Street 'digs' of Holmes and Watson as well as that of the 'mean streets' of Marlowe's Los Angeles. Although none of the action takes place in either place, Holmes and Watson share a sense of camaraderie and self-confidence in facing threats and problems that also pervades many of the later tales in the Canon. Following their conversations and banter is a return to Edwardian England and its certainties and hope for the future. This is definitely the world before The Great War."
Philip K Jones

www.mxpublishing.com

Also from MX Publishing

The Detective and The Woman Series

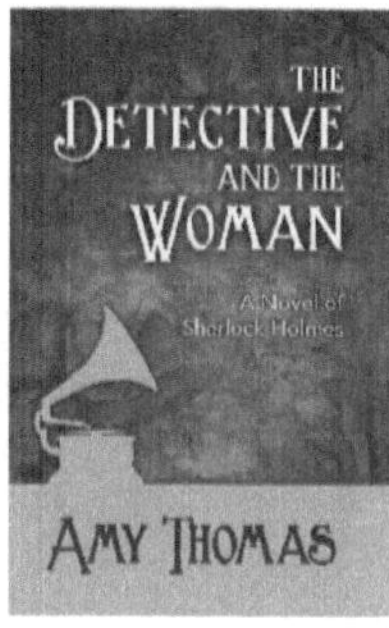

The Detective and The Woman
The Detective, The Woman and The Winking Tree
The Detective, The Woman and The Silent Hive

"The book is entertaining, puzzling and a lot of fun. I believe the author has hit on the only type of long-term relationship possible for Sherlock Holmes and Irene Adler. The details of the narrative only add force to the romantic defects we expect in both of them and their growth and development are truly marvelous to watch. This is not a love story. Instead, it is a coming-of-age tale starring two of our favorite characters."
Philip K Jones

www.mxpublishing.com

Also from MX Publishing

The Sherlock Holmes and Enoch Hale Series

The Amateur Executioner
The Poisoned Penman
The Egyptian Curse

"The Amateur Executioner: Enoch Hale Meets Sherlock Holmes", the first collaboration between Dan Andriacco and Kieran McMullen, concerns the possibility of a Fenian attack in London. Hale, a native Bostonian, is a reporter for London's Central News Syndicate - where, in 1920, Horace Harker is still a familiar figure, though far from revered. "The Amateur Executioner" takes us into an ambiguous and murky world where right and wrong aren't always distinguishable. I look forward to reading more about Enoch Hale."
Sherlock Holmes Society of London

www.mxpublishing.com

www.ingramcontent.com/pod-product-compliance
Lightning Source LLC
Chambersburg PA
CBHW030808310726
48980CB00006B/416/J